DEPARTMENT NINETEEN

Department 19

RAZORBILL

Published by the Penguin Group
Penguin Young Readers Group
345 Hudson Street, New York, New York 10014, U.S.A.
Penguin Group (USA) Inc., 375 Hudson Street, New York, New York 10014, U.S.A.
Penguin Group (Canada), 90 Eglinton Avenue East, Suite 700, Toronto, Ontario, Canada M4P 2Y3 (a division of Pearson Penguin Canada Inc.)
Penguin Books Ltd, 80 Strand, London WC2R 0RL, England
Penguin Ireland, 25 St Stephen's Green, Dublin 2, Ireland (a division of Penguin Books Ltd)
Penguin Group (Australia), 250 Camberwell Road, Camberwell, Victoria 3124, Australia (a division of Pearson Australia Group Pty Ltd)
Penguin Books India Pvt Ltd, 11 Community Centre, Panchsheel Park, New Delhi – 110 017, India
Penguin Group (NZ), 67 Apollo Drive, Mairangi Bay, Auckland 1311, New Zealand (a division of Pearson New Zealand Ltd)
Penguin Books (South Africa) (Pty) Ltd, 24 Sturdee Avenue, Rosebank, Johannesburg 2196, South Africa

Penguin Books Ltd, Registered Offices: 80 Strand, London WC2R 0RL, England

First published in hardcover by Razorbill 2011
Published in this edition 2012

10 9 8 7 6 5 4

ISBN: 978-1-59514-485-0

Library of Congress Cataloging-in-Publication Data is available

Printed in the United States of America

DEPARTMENT NINETEEN

NINETEEN

WILL HILL

razor
bill

AN IMPRINT OF PENGUIN GROUP (USA) Inc.

I have been one acquainted with the night.

I have walked out in rain—and back in rain.

I have outwalked the furthest city light.

—Robert Frost

"We want no proofs. We ask none to believe us!"

—Abraham Van Helsing

MEMORANDUM

From: Office of the Director of the Joint Intelligence Committee

Subject: Revised classifications of the British Governmental departments

Security: TOP SECRET

DEPARTMENT 1 Office of the Prime Minister

DEPARTMENT 2 Cabinet Office

DEPARTMENT 3 Home Office

DEPARTMENT 4 Foreign and Commonwealth Office

DEPARTMENT 5 Ministry of Defense

DEPARTMENT 6 British Army

DEPARTMENT 7 Royal Navy

DEPARTMENT 8 Her Majesty's Diplomatic Service

DEPARTMENT 9 Her Majesty's Treasury

DEPARTMENT 10 Department for Transport

DEPARTMENT 11 Attorney General's Office

DEPARTMENT 12 Ministry of Justice

DEPARTMENT 13 Military Intelligence, Section 5 (MI5)

DEPARTMENT 14 Secret Intelligence Service (SIS)

DEPARTMENT 15 Royal Air Force

DEPARTMENT 16 Northern Ireland Office

DEPARTMENT 17 Scotland Office

DEPARTMENT 18 Wales Office

DEPARTMENT 19 CLASSIFIED

DEPARTMENT 20 Territorial Police Forces

DEPARTMENT 21 Department of Health

DEPARTMENT 22 Government Communication Headquarters (GCHQ)

DEPARTMENT 23 Joint Intelligence Committee (JIC)

PROLOGUE

Brenchley, Kent
November 3, 2007

Jamie Carpenter was watching TV in the living room when he heard the tires of his dad's car crunch across the gravel driveway much, much earlier than usual. Jamie looked at the clock on the wall above the TV and frowned. It was a quarter past six. Julian Carpenter had never, to the best of Jamie's memory, arrived home from work before seven o'clock, and even that was only on special occasions like his mom's birthday or when Arsenal were playing in the Champions League.

He hauled himself off the sofa, a tall, slightly awkward fourteen-year-old with a skinny frame and unruly brown hair, and went to the window. His dad's silver Mercedes was parked where it always was, in front of the garage that stood apart from their house. Jamie could see his father in the glow of the car's brake lights, pulling something out of the trunk.

Maybe he's sick, Jamie thought. But as he looked closely at his dad, he didn't think he looked ill; his eyes were bright and wide in the red light, and he was moving quickly, putting things from the trunk into his pockets. And Jamie noticed something else; he kept looking over his shoulder toward the road, as if he thought—

Something moved in the corner of Jamie's eye, near the oak tree at the bottom of the garden. He turned his head, goose bumps breaking out suddenly along his arms and back, and he realized he was scared. *Something is wrong here,* he thought. *Very wrong.*

The tree looked the same as it always did, its gnarled trunk tilted to the left, its huge roots rippling the lawn and bending the garden wall out toward the road.

Whatever Jamie had seen, his father had seen it, too. He was standing very still behind the car, staring up into the branches of the tree. Jamie looked closely at the tree and the long black shadows the moonlight cast across the grass. Whatever had moved wasn't moving anymore. But as he stared, he realized that there was something different.

There were more shadows than there should be.

The tree's leaves were gone for the winter, and the shadows should have been the straight lines of empty branches. But the dark patterns covering the lawn were thick and bulky, as though the branches were full of—

What? Full of what?

Jamie looked back to his dad. He suddenly wanted him in the house, right now. His father was still staring at the tree, holding something in his hand, something that Jamie couldn't quite make out.

Movement, again, by the tree.

Fear rose into Jamie's throat.

Come inside, Dad. Come inside now. There's something bad out there.

The shadows on the lawn began to move.

Jamie stared, too scared to scream, as the dark patterns began to unfold. He looked up into the tree, and now he could see the branches shifting as whatever was in there began to move, could hear the rustling of the bark as something—*lots of things, it sounds like there's lots of them*—started to move through the boughs of the oak.

He looked desperately at his father who was still staring into the tree, lit by the red lights from the car.

Why are you just standing there? Come inside, please, please.

Jamie turned his head to look at the tree. On the other side of the window, a girl's face, pale, with dark red eyes and lips drawn into a snarl, stared through the glass, and he screamed so loudly he thought he would tear his vocal chords.

The face disappeared into the darkness, and now there was movement as Jamie's father ran up the drive toward the house. The front door slammed open and Julian Carpenter burst into the living room at the same time his wife ran in from the kitchen.

"Get away from the windows, Jamie!" he shouted.

"Dad, what's—"

"Just do what I tell you and don't argue! There isn't time."

"Time for what, Julian?" asked Jamie's mom, her voice tight and high-pitched. "What's going on?"

Julian ignored her, taking out a cell phone that Jamie didn't recognize. He punched numbers into the handset and held it to his ear. "Frank? Yeah, I know. I know. What's the ETA? And that's accurate? OK. Take care of yourself."

He hung up the phone and grabbed Jamie's mom's hand.

"Julian, you're scaring me," she said, softly. "Please tell me what's happening."

He looked into his wife's pale, confused face. "I can't," he replied. "I'm sorry."

Jamie watched in a daze. He didn't understand what was happening here, didn't understand it at all. What was moving through the darkness outside their house? Who was Frank? His dad didn't have any friends called Frank, he was sure of it.

The window behind Jamie exploded as a branch from the oak tree came through it like a missile and smashed their coffee table into splinters. This time his mom screamed as well.

"Get away from the windows!" bellowed Julian again. "Come over here next to me!"

Jamie scrambled up from the floor, grabbed his mom's hand and ran across the room toward his father. They backed up against the wall opposite the window, his dad placing an arm across him and his mother, before putting his right hand into his coat pocket and taking out a black pistol.

His mother squeezed his hand so tightly that he thought the bones would break. "Julian!" she screamed. "What are you doing with that gun?"

"Quiet, Marie," his father said, in a low voice.

In the distance, Jamie heard sirens approaching.

Thankyouthankyouthankyou. We're going to be all right.

Outside in the garden a grotesque high-pitched laugh floated through the night air.

"Hurry," Julian whispered. "Please hurry."

Jamie didn't know who his father was talking to, but it wasn't to him or his mom. Then suddenly the garden was full of light and noise as two black vans, sirens blaring and lights spinning on their roofs, screeched into the driveway. Jamie looked out at the oak tree, now lit bright red and blue. It was empty.

"They've gone!" he shouted. "Dad, they've gone!"

He looked up at his father, and the look on his face scared Jamie more than everything else that had happened so far.

Julian stepped away from his family and stood facing them. "I have to go," he said, his voice cracking. "Remember that I love you both more than anything in the world. Jamie, look after your mother. OK?"

He turned and headed toward the door.

Jamie's mom ran forward and grabbed his arm, spinning him round. "Where are you going?" she cried, tears running down her face. "What do you mean, look after me? What's happening?"

"I can't tell you," he replied, softly. "I have to protect you."

"From what?" his wife screamed.

"From me," he answered, his head lowered. Then he looked up at her and, with a speed Jamie had never seen before, twisted his arm free from her grip and pushed her backward across the living room. She tripped over one of the smashed legs of the coffee table and Jamie ran forward and caught her, lowering her to the ground. She let out a horrible wailing cry and pushed his hands away, and he looked up in time to see his father walk out of the front door.

He shoved himself up off the floor, cutting his hand on the broken table glass, and ran to the window. Eight men wearing black body armor and carrying submachine guns stood in the driveway, the barrels of their weapons pointed at Julian.

"Put your hands above your head!" one of the men shouted. "Do it now!"

Jamie's dad took a few steps and stopped. He looked up into the tree for a long moment before glancing quickly over his shoulder at the window and smiling at his son. Then he walked forward, pulled the pistol from his pocket and pointed it at the nearest man.

The world exploded into deafening noise, and Jamie clamped his hands over his ears and screamed and screamed and screamed as the submachine guns spit fire and metal and shot his father dead.

TWO YEARS LATER

TEENAGE
WASTELAND

Jamie Carpenter tasted blood and dirt and swore into the wet mud of the playing field.

"Get off me!" he gurgled.

A shrieking laugh rang out behind his head, and his left arm was pushed further up his back, sending a fresh thunderclap of pain through his shoulder.

"Break it, Danny," someone shouted. "Snap it off!"

"I just might," replied Danny Mitchell, between gales of laughter. Then his voice was low and right next to Jamie's ear. "I could, you know," he whispered. "Easy."

"Get off me, you fat—"

A huge hand, its fingers like sausages, gripped his hair and pushed his face back into the dirt. Jamie squeezed his eyes shut and flailed around with his right hand, trying to push himself up from the sucking mud.

"Someone grab his arm," Danny shouted. "Hold it down."

A second later, Jamie's right arm was gripped at the wrist and pressed to the ground.

Jamie's head started to ache as his body begged for oxygen. He couldn't breathe, his nostrils full of sticky, foul-smelling mud, and he couldn't move, his arms pinned and 210 pounds of Danny Mitchell sitting astride his back.

"That's enough!"

Jamie recognized the voice of Mr. Jacobs, the English teacher.

My knight in shining armor. A fifty-year-old man with sweat patches and bad breath. Perfect.

"Mitchell, get off him. Don't make me tell you again!" the teacher shouted, and suddenly the pressure on Jamie's arm and the weight on his back were gone. He lifted his face from the mud and took a huge breath, his chest convulsing.

"We were just playing a game, sir," he heard Danny Mitchell say.

Great game. Really fun.

Jamie rolled over onto his back and looked around at the faces of the crowd who had gathered to watch his humiliation. They looked down at him with a mixture of excitement and disgust.

They don't even like Danny Mitchell. They just hate me more than they hate him.

Mr. Jacobs hunkered down next to him.

"Are you all right, Carpenter?"

"I'm fine, sir."

"Mitchell tells me this was some kind of game. Is that true?"

Over the teacher's shoulder, Jamie saw Danny looking at him, the warning clear in his face.

"Yes, sir. I think I lost, sir."

Mr. Jacobs looked down at Jamie's mud-splattered clothes. "It certainly looks like it." The teacher held his hand out, and Jamie took it and pulled himself up out of the mud with a loud sucking noise. A couple of people in the crowd giggled, and Mr. Jacobs whirled round, his face red with anger.

"Get out of here, you vultures!" he shouted. "Get to your next lesson right now or I'll see you all for detention at the end of the day!"

The crowd dispersed, leaving Jamie and Mr. Jacobs standing alone on the field.

"Jamie," the teacher began, "if you ever want to talk about anything, you know where my office is."

"Talk about what, sir?" Jamie asked.

"Well, you know, your father, and . . . well, what happened."

"What did happen, sir?"

Mr. Jacobs looked at him for a long moment, then dropped his eyes. "Let's go," he said. "You need to get cleaned up before the next lesson. You can use the staff bathroom."

When the bell rang for the end of the day, Jamie made his way slowly up the school driveway toward the gate. His instincts were normally sharp, especially where danger was concerned, but somehow Danny Mitchell had crept up behind him during afternoon break. He wasn't going to let that happen again.

He slowed his pace, drifting in and out of groups of children ambling toward buses and waiting cars, his pale blue eyes darting left and right, looking for an ambush.

His chest tightened when he saw Danny Mitchell off to

his left, laughing his ridiculous laugh and waving his arms violently around as he made a point to his adoring gaggle of sycophants.

Jamie slipped between two buses and across the road, waiting for the shouts and running feet that would mean he had been seen, but they didn't come. Then he was into the neat, identical rows of houses that made up the estate he and his mother lived in, and out of sight of the school.

The Carpenters had moved three times in the two years since Jamie's dad had died. Immediately after it happened, the police had come to see them and told them that his father had been involved in a plot to sell intelligence to a British terrorist cell, classified intelligence from his job at the Ministry of Defense. The policemen had been kind, and sympathetic, assuring them there was no evidence that either he or his mother had known anything, but it didn't matter. The letters had started to arrive almost immediately, from patriotic neighbors who didn't want the family of a traitor living in their quiet Daily Mail–reading neighborhood.

They had sold the house in Kent a few months later. Jamie didn't care. His memory of that awful night was hazy, but the tree in the garden scared him, and he couldn't walk across the gravel driveway where his father had died, choosing instead to walk around the edge of the lawn, keeping as much distance between him and the oak as possible and jumping across the gravel onto the doorstep.

The face at the window and the high, terrifying laugh that had drifted through the smashed window of the living room, he didn't remember at all.

After that they had moved in with his aunt and uncle in a village outside Coventry. A new school for Jamie, a job as a receptionist in a GP's surgery for his mother. But the rumors and stories followed them, and a brick was thrown through the kitchen window of his aunt's terraced house the same day Jamie broke the nose of a classmate who had made a joke about his dad.

They moved on the following morning.

From there they caught a train to Leeds and found a house in a suburb that looked like it was made of Legos. When Jamie was expelled from his second school in three months, for persistent truancy, his mother didn't even shout at him. She just handed in their notice to their landlord and started packing their things.

Finally, they had ended up in this quiet estate on the outskirts of Nottingham. It was gray, cold, and miserable. Jamie, an outdoor creature, a country boy at heart, was forced to roam the concrete underpasses and supermarket parking lots, his hood up and pulled tight around his face, his iPod thumping in his ears, keeping to himself and avoiding the gangs that congregated on the shadowy corners of this suburban wasteland. Jamie always avoided the shadows. He didn't know why.

Jamie walked quickly through the estate, along quiet roads full of nondescript houses and secondhand cars. He passed a small group of girls, who stared at him with open hostility. One of them said something he couldn't quite hear, and her friends laughed. He walked on.

He was sixteen years old and miserably, crushingly lonely.

Jamie closed the front door of the small semidetached house he and his mother lived in as quietly as possible, intending to head straight to his room and change out of his muddy clothes. He got halfway up the stairs before his mother called his name.

"What, Mom?" he shouted.

"Can you come in here, please, Jamie?"

Jamie swore under his breath and stomped back down the stairs, across the hall and into the living room. His mother was sitting in the chair under the window, looking at him with such sadness that his throat clenched.

"What's going on, Mom?" he asked.

"I got a call from one of your teachers today," she replied. "Mr. Jacobs."

God, why can't he mind his own business? "Oh yeah? What'd he want?"

"He said you got in a fight this afternoon."

"He's wrong."

Jamie's mother sighed. "I'm worried about you," she said.

"Don't be. I can look after myself."

"That's what you always say."

"Maybe you should start to listen then."

His mother's eyes narrowed.

That hurt, didn't it? Good. Now you can shout at me, and I can go upstairs, and we don't have to say anything else to each other tonight.

"I miss him, too, Jamie," his mother said, and Jamie recoiled as if he'd been stung. "I miss him every day."

Jamie spit his reply around a huge lump in his throat. "Good for you," he said. "I don't. Ever."

His mother looked at him, and tears formed in the corners of her eyes. "You don't mean that."

"Believe me, I do. He was a traitor and a criminal, and he ruined both our lives."

"Our lives aren't ruined. We've still got each other."

Jamie laughed. "Yeah. Look how well that's working out for us both."

The tears spilled from his mother's eyes, and she lowered her head as they ran down her cheeks and fell gently to the floor. Jamie looked at her, helplessly.

Go to her. Go and hug her and tell her it's going to be all right.

Jamie wanted to, wanted nothing more than to kneel beside his mother and bridge the gap that had been growing steadily between them since the night his father had died. But he couldn't. Instead he stood, frozen to the spot, and watched his mother cry.

SINS OF
THE FATHER

2

Jamie woke up late the next morning, showered and dressed, and slipped out of the front door without seeing his mother. He walked his usual route through the estate, but when he reached the turn that led to his school, he carried straight on, through the little retail park with its McDonald's and its DVD rental shop, across the graffiti-covered railway bridge, strewn with broken glass and flattened discs of chewing gum, past the station and the bike racks, down toward the canal. He wasn't going to school today. Not a chance.

Why the hell did she get so upset? Because I don't miss Dad? He was a loser. Can't she see that?

Jamie clenched his fists tightly as he walked down the concrete steps to the towpath. This section of canal was perfectly straight for more than a mile, meaning Jamie could see danger approaching from a safe distance. But although he kept his eyes peeled, the only people he saw were dog walkers and the occasional homeless person, sheltering under the low road bridges that crossed the narrow canal, and he gradually began to let his mind wander.

He could never have articulated to anyone, least of all his mother, the hole his father's death had left in his life. Jamie loved his mother, loved her so much that he hated himself for the way he treated her, for pushing her away when it was obvious that she needed him, when he knew he was all she had left. But he couldn't help it; the anger that churned inside him screamed for release, and his mom was the only target he had.

The person it deserved to be aimed at was gone.

His dad, his cowardly loser of a dad, had taken him to London to watch Arsenal, bought him the Swiss Army knife he could no longer bear to carry in his pocket, let him fire his air rifle in the fields behind their old house, helped him build his tree house, and watched cartoons with him on Saturday mornings. Things his mom would never do, and he would never want her to. Things he missed more than he would ever have admitted.

He was furious with his father for leaving him and his mom, for making them leave the old house he had loved and move to this awful place, leaving his friends behind.

Furious for the glee he saw in the faces of bullies at every school where he was forced to start anew, when the whispers began and they realized they had been presented with the perfect victim: a skinny new kid whose father had tried to help terrorists attack his own country.

Furious with his mom, for her refusal to see the truth about her husband, furious with the teachers who tried to understand him and asked him to talk about his dad and his feelings.

Furious.

Jamie emerged from his thoughts and saw the sun high in the sky, struggling to push its pale light through the gray cloud cover. He pulled his phone out of his pocket and saw that it was nearly midday. Ahead of him, a flattened trail led up the embankment into a small park, surrounded by tall birch trees. The park was always empty; it was one of his favorite places.

He sat down in the middle of the grass, away from the trees and the short shadows they were casting in the early afternoon sun. He hadn't picked up his packed lunch because he would have had to go into the kitchen and deal with his mother, so he had filled his backpack with a can of Coke and some chocolate and sweets. The Coke was warm, and the chocolate was half melted, but Jamie didn't care.

He finished eating, tucked his bag under his head, and lay down and closed his eyes. He was suddenly exhausted, and he didn't want to think anymore.

Fifteen minutes. Just a nap. Half an hour at the most.

"Jamie."

His eyes flew open and he saw black night sky above him. Sitting up, he rubbed his eyes and looked around at the dark park. He trembled in the cold of the evening, and his skin began to crawl as he realized he was sitting at the point where the shadows cast by the trees met one another.

"Jamie."

He whirled around. "Who's there?" he shouted.

A giggle rang through the park.

"Jamie." The voice was lilting, like his name was being sung and allowed to echo through the trees. It was a girl's voice.

"Where are you? This isn't funny!"

The giggle again.

Jamie stood up and did a slow turn. He couldn't see anyone, but beyond the first ring of trees, the park was pitch-black, and the trees themselves were wide and gnarled.

Plenty of room for someone to hide behind.

Something was tapping at the back of his mind, something to do with a girl and a window, but he couldn't remember.

Something crunched underfoot, behind him.

He spun around, heart pounding.

Nothing.

"Jamie."

The voice was closer this time, he knew it was.

"Show yourself!" he yelled.

"OK," said a voice right beside his ear, and he screamed and turned, fists flailing. He felt his right hand connect solidly with something, and adrenaline roared in his veins, then he froze.

On the ground in front of him was a girl, about his own age, holding her nose. A thin stream of blood was running onto her lip, and he saw her tongue flick out and lick it away.

"Oh God," Jamie said. "I'm so, so sorry. Are you OK?"

"You dick," the girl sniffled from behind her hand. "What did you do that for?"

"I'm sorry," he repeated. "Why did you creep up on me?"

"I was just trying to scare you," she said, sulkily.

"Why?"

"For fun. I didn't mean anything by it."

Something else was rattling around Jamie's mind, but he

couldn't put his finger on it.

"Well, you did scare me. So, congratulations, I guess."

"Thanks," snorted the girl. She held out her hand. "Help me up?"

"Oh, sorry, of course," Jamie replied, and reached down and pulled her to her feet. She brushed herself down, wiped her nose with the back of her hand, and stood in front of him.

Jamie looked at her. She was very, very pretty, dark hair tumbling down her shoulders, pale skin and dark brown eyes. She saw him looking and smiled, and he blushed.

"See anything you like?" she asked.

"Sorry, I wasn't staring, I was just, er . . ."

"Yes, you were. It's OK. I'm Larissa."

"I'm . . ."

Tumblers fell into place in Jamie's mind and fear overwhelmed him.

"You used my name," he said, taking a step backward. "How do you know my name?"

"It doesn't matter, Jamie," she said, and then her beautiful brown eyes turned a dark, terrible red. "It doesn't matter anymore."

She moved like liquid, covering the distance between them in an instant. She took his face in her hands, with a grip that felt horribly, immovably strong.

"Nothing matters anymore," she whispered, and he looked into her red eyes and was lost.

ATTACK ON SUBURBIA

3

"I can't do it."

The voice sounded like it was coming from a hundred miles away. Jamie struggled to open his eyes. He was lying on the grass, the girl called Larissa sitting next to him. He tried to crawl away but couldn't move. His limbs ached, and his head was full of cotton wool.

"Damn it, I just can't," she said, apparently to herself. "What's wrong with me?"

He forced his eyes open and looked at her. Her eyes were brown again, and she was looking down at him, a gentle expression on her face.

"Who . . . are . . . you?" he managed. "What did you do to me?"

She lowered her head.

"You were supposed to be mine," she said. "He said so. But I couldn't do it."

"Your . . . what?"

"Mine. In every way."

With a huge effort Jamie forced himself up to a sitting position.

"I don't understand," he said.

"It doesn't matter." She looked up at the sky. "You should go," she said, looking back at him with sadness in her face. "They'll be there by now."

A tidal wave of adrenaline crashed into Jamie's system. "Who? Where?" he demanded.

"My friends. You know where."

Jamie leapt to his feet and looked down at Larissa.

"I've seen you before, haven't I?" he asked, his voice trembling. In his mind's eye he saw a face at a window.

She nodded her head.

Jamie turned and sprinted out of the park, running as though his life depended on it.

Please not my mom. Please don't let them hurt my mom.

When Jamie reached the end of his road, his heart was pounding so loudly in his chest he thought it might explode. His vision was graying, the muscles in his legs screaming, but he pushed through the pain and sprinted the last fifty yards to his house and pulled himself round the gate post and toward the front door.

It was wide open.

He ran into the hallway. "Mom!" he yelled. "Are you here? Mom!"

No answer.

He ran into the living room. Empty. Through into the kitchen. Empty.

No sign of her.

He ran up the stairs and pushed open the door to her bedroom. The window above her bed was open to the dark sky, the curtains fluttering in the evening breeze. Jamie ran across the room and put his head out the window.

"Mom!" he screamed into the inky blackness. His right hand slipped on something on the ledge, and he looked down and pulled it away. Red liquid dripped down his wrist.

He looked at the windowsill. There were two small pools of blood on the white surface and more smeared across the glass of the open window.

Jamie stared in horror at his hand, then something came loose in his head as he realized that his mother was gone, and he put back his head and wailed at the sky.

And miles away, high in the dark clouds, something heard his cry and turned back.

Time passed. Jamie had no idea how long.

He couldn't stay in his mother's room, couldn't look at the blood, horribly bright against the white paint and the clear glass. Somehow he made it downstairs to the living room. He was sitting on the couch, staring blankly at the wall, when he heard something come through the front door and close it softly behind them.

He was beyond fear now. He was numb. So he just watched as the tall, thin man in the gray suit walked into the room and smiled at him with teeth like razorblades, his dark red eyes shining in the gloom.

"Jamie Carpenter," the man said. His voice was like treacle. "It is a supreme pleasure to finally meet you."

The man bared his teeth and took a step toward Jamie, and then the front door exploded into sawdust and an enormous figure, holding what looked like a huge pipe, stepped into the living room doorway.

"Get away from him, Alexandru," the massive newcomer said, in a voice that shook the entire house.

The man in the gray suit hissed and arched its back. "This is not your concern, monster," he spit. "There is unfinished business here."

"It will stay unfinished," the figure replied, then pulled the trigger hanging below the pipe. There was an enormous bang, like a giant balloon being burst, and something sharp exploded out of the weapon and flew across the room so fast it was a blur, trailing a metal cord behind it. Alexandru leapt into the air, impossibly quickly. The projectile smashed a hole in the wall of the living room, before retracting as rapidly as it had been fired, spiraling back into the end of the pipe.

The creature in the gray suit hung in the air, its eyes blazing with anger. It snarled at the figure in the doorway, then smashed through the big window at the front of the house and accelerated into the sky.

Jamie hadn't moved.

The giant darted to the window and craned its enormous neck in the direction the thing called Alexandru had disappeared.

"He's gone," the figure said. "For now."

It turned to Jamie, and in the light of the living room, he got his first look at his savior and cried out.

The huge figure was a man, at least seven and a half feet tall and almost as wide. He had mottled grayish-green skin, a high, wide forehead, and a shock of black hair above it. He was wearing a dark suit and a long gray overcoat. A wire ran up his sleeve from the end of the pipe he was holding and disappeared somewhere over his shoulders.

He walked forward, and as fear and loss started to shut down Jamie's mind, he saw two wide metal bolts sticking out of the sides of his neck. The man extended his hand toward him.

"Jamie Carpenter," he said. "My name is Frankenstein. I'm here to help you."

Jamie's eyes rolled back white, and he fainted into sweet, empty darkness.

SEARCH AND RESCUE

4

Staveley, North Derbyshire
Fifty-six minutes earlier

Matt Browning was sitting at his computer when it happened.

He was working on an essay for his English literature class, a comparison of the speeches by Brutus and Mark Antony in *Julius Caesar*, typing quickly into his aging laptop, when something thundered out of the sky and crashed into the small garden behind the terraced house he shared with his sister and his parents, throwing dirt and brown grass into the evening air.

Downstairs he heard his mother shriek and his father slur at her to shut up. In the bedroom next door, his little sister Laura started to cry, a high wail full of confusion and determination.

Matt saved his work and got up from his desk. He was small for his sixteen years, and skinny, his brown hair flopping across his high forehead and resting against the tops of his glasses. His face was pale and close to feminine, his features fine and soft around the edges, as though he were slightly out of focus. He was wearing his favorite crimson Harvard T-shirt and dark brown cords, and he slid his feet into a pair of navy Vans before walking quickly across the small landing and into his sister's bedroom.

Laura was lying in her crib, her face a deep, outraged red, her eyes squeezed shut, her mouth a perfect circle. Matt reached into the crib and picked her up, resting her against his shoulder and quietly shushing her, bouncing her gently in his arms. There was a glorious moment's silence as she took a deep breath, then the cries began again. Matt crossed the tiny room, pulled the door open, and headed downstairs.

In the kitchen at the back of the house, his mother was frantic. She was wearing her cream dressing gown and a pair of pale blue slippers and flitting back and forth beneath the two windows above the sink, peering into the dark garden and telling her husband over and over to call the police. Greg Browning stood unsteadily in the middle of the room, one hand pressed against his forehead, a can of lager in the other. He looked around as Matt walked into the kitchen.

"Shut your sister up, would you?" he grunted. "She's giving me a headache." Then he turned back to his wife. "Will you stop flapping and take the damn baby?" he said, his voice starting to rise.

Matt's mother quickly took Laura from Matt and sat down with her at the table.

"Get the phone for your mother."

Matt lifted the phone from its cradle on the wall next to the door and passed it to his mom. She took it with a confused look on her face.

"Now you can call the police while me and Matt go and take a look in the garden."

"No, Greg, you shouldn't. . . ."

"Shouldn't?"

Matt's mother swallowed hard.

"I mean, don't go out there. Please?"

"Just shut the hell up, OK, Lynne? Matt, let's go."

Greg Browning opened the door to the back garden and stopped in the doorway, listening. Matt walked over and stood behind him, looking over his father's shoulder into the darkening sky.

The garden was silent; nothing moved in the cool evening air.

Matt's father took a flashlight from the shelf beside the back door, turned it on, and stepped out onto the narrow strip of patio that ran below the kitchen windows. Matt followed, scanning the dark garden for whatever had fallen past his window. Behind him in the kitchen, he could hear his mother trying to explain what had happened to the police.

His dad shone the flashlight in a wide arc across the flowerbeds that bordered the narrow strip of lawn. At the edge of the grass, the beam picked out a flash of white.

"Over there," said Matt. "In the flowerbed."

"Stay here."

Matt stood on the patio as his father walked slowly across the threadbare lawn. He inhaled sharply as he reached the edge of the grass.

"What is it?" Matt asked.

No reply. His father just kept staring down into the dark flowerbed.

"Dad? What is it?"

Finally, his father turned toward him. His eyes were wide.

"It's a girl," he said, eventually. "It's a teenage girl."

"What?"

"Come and look."

Matt walked across the lawn and looked down into the weed-strewn flowerbed.

The girl was lying on her back in the dirt, half buried by the force of her landing. Her pale face was smeared with blood, and her eyes and mouth were grotesquely swollen. Black hair fanned out around her head like a dark halo, matted with mud and clumped together in bloody strands. Her left arm was obviously broken, her forearm joining her elbow at an unnatural right angle. Her light gray shirt was soaked black with blood, and Matt realized with horror that there was a wide hole in her stomach, along the line of her abdomen. He saw glistening red and purple, and looked away.

"It looks like someone tried to gut her," his father said quietly.

"What is it, Greg?" shouted Matt's mother from the kitchen doorway. "What's happening?"

"Shut up, Lynne," Greg Browning replied automatically, but his voice was low, and for once he didn't sound angry.

He sounds scared, thought Matt, and crouched down beside the girl. Despite the damage to her face, she was beautiful, her skin so pale it was almost translucent, her lips a dark, inviting red.

Behind him his father was muttering to himself, looking from the sky to the ground and back again, searching for an explanation for why this girl had fallen into their garden.

Matt placed his hand on the cool skin of her neck, checking for a pulse, knowing he wouldn't find one.

Who did this to you? he wondered.

The girl opened her swollen right eye and looked straight at Matt. He screamed.

"She's alive!" he yelled.

"Don't be stupid," shouted Greg Browning. "She's—"

The girl coughed, a deep spluttering rattle that sent new streams of blood running down her chin. She turned her head toward Matt and said something he couldn't make out.

"My God," said Matt's father.

Matt pushed himself up off the grass and slowly approached his father's side. He looked down at the stricken girl, who was moving her head slowly from side to side, her lips curled back in a grimace of pain.

"We have to do something, Dad," said Matt. "We can't leave her like this."

His father turned on him, his face full of anger.

"What do you want me to do?" he shouted. "The police are on their way; they can deal with it. We shouldn't even touch her."

"But Dad—"

Greg Browning's face twisted with rage, and he raised a fist and took a step toward his son. Matt cried out, covering his face with his forearms and turning away.

"You'll be quiet if you know what's good for you," his dad grunted, lowering the fist.

Matt looked at his father, his cheeks flushed red with shame and impotence, his brain alive with hatred. He opened his mouth to say something, anything, when a deafening roar filled the evening air and a squat black helicopter appeared over the trees that stood at the bottom of their suburban garden.

Matt covered his face and did his best to remain upright as the helicopter's rotors churned the dust and dirt of the garden. He could see his dad shouting but could hear nothing over the thunder of the engines and the shriek of the wind. He craned his neck, his hands shielding his eyes, and watched the helicopter disappear over the roof of their house.

Matt turned and raced toward the house, past his mother who was standing motionless at the back door, through the kitchen and the narrow corridor and toward the front door.

Behind him he could hear his dad shouting his name, but he didn't slow his pace. He flung the front door open in time to see the black helicopter lowering itself on to the gray tarmac of the road, its rotors whirring above the parked cars that lined their street.

Matt's dad appeared behind him in the corridor, grabbed his son's shoulder, and spun him around.

"What the hell do you think you're . . ."

Greg Browning's voice trailed off as he stared out into the street. Matt turned and watched as a door slid open in the side of the helicopter and four figures emerged.

The first two were dressed all in black and looked like riot policemen, their uniforms covered with plates of black body armor, their faces hidden beneath black helmets with purple visors.

Both were carrying submachine guns in their gloved hands.

Behind them followed a man and a woman in white biohazard-containment suits, their faces visible behind the thick plastic of their masks. Between them they were carrying a white stretcher.

They cleared the helicopter and quickly approached Matt and his father. The first of the figures—*soldiers, they look like soldiers*—stopped in front of them.

"Was an emergency call made from this house?" it asked. The voice was male and didn't sound much older than Matt's.

Neither he nor his dad answered.

The soldier took a step forward.

"Was an emergency call made from this house?"

Terrified, Matt nodded his head.

The black figure turned to the others and beckoned them toward the house, then pushed past Matt and Greg Browning, and disappeared into the hallway. The rest of the new arrivals followed, leaving Matt and his father in the doorway. They stood there, staring at the helicopter with no idea what to do, until Matt's mother started to scream, and they turned and ran into the house.

They found her in the kitchen, holding Laura in her arms, the two of them screaming in unison. Greg Browning ran across the room and took his wife in his arms, whispering to her, telling her everything was going to be OK, telling her not to cry. Matt left them by the table and walked out into the garden.

The two soldiers were standing on either side of the girl, their guns lodged against their shoulders and pointing at the sky. On the ground, the man and woman in the biohazard suits were examining her.

Matt walked toward them, but before he was close enough to see what they were doing, the nearest soldier turned toward him and leveled the black submachine gun at his chest. Matt froze on the spot.

"Please stay where you are, sir," the soldier said. "For your own safety."

"What's going on here?" said a small voice from behind Matt. He was too scared to move, but he craned his head over his shoulder and saw his dad standing on the narrow patio. He looked like someone had deflated him.

"Take your son into the house, sir," the soldier said.

"I want to know what's going on," Matt's father repeated. "Who are you people?"

"I'm not going to tell you again, sir," the soldier replied. He sounded as though he was reaching the limit of his patience. "Take your son inside. Now."

Greg Browning looked like he was going to reply but thought better of it.

"Come inside, Matt," he said, eventually.

Matt looked from his father to the soldier pointing the gun at his chest. Behind him he could see the other soldier and the biohazard team watching him. He was about to turn and do as his father said when the girl lifted her head from the flowerbed and sank her teeth into the arm of the man in the white plastic suit.

All hell broke loose.

The man screamed and wrenched his arm out of the girl's mouth. Blood pumped out of the ragged hole in the plastic, and splashed across the lawn.

The second soldier swung his gun. The heavy stock of the weapon crashed across the girl's chin, and she instantly stopped moving, as though she had been turned off.

The soldier who had been facing Matt lowered his gun and turned to his colleagues.

"How bad is it?" he yelled.

The woman in the biohazard suit had knelt down next to her partner and was examining the wound. She looked up at the sound of the soldier's voice.

"It's bad," she replied. "We need to get him out of here."

"Bag the subject," the soldier said. "Do it quickly."

"There isn't time. He needs clean blood, right now."

"He'll get it. Bag the subject."

The woman stared at the soldier for a fraction of second, then let go of her colleague and laid the white stretcher flat on the lawn.

"Help me," she said to the other soldier.

The soldier crouched down and took hold of the girl under her shoulders and pulled her out of the flowerbed. Matt gasped as he saw the damage to the lower half of the girl's body.

Both her legs were snapped mid thigh, the white bones piercing the blood-soaked jeans she was wearing. Her left foot was horribly twisted at the ankle, and the right was missing three toes, the red stumps bright in the fading light.

Matt ran toward her. He didn't know what he was going to do, just that he had to do something. He heard his father shout at him but ignored him. The soldier who had hit the girl with his gun turned, saw him crossing the lawn, and started to move, a shout of warning issuing from his lips. But he wasn't quick enough; Matt slid onto his knees beside the broken girl and looked at the woman in the biohazard suit.

"Can I hel—"

The girl's arm flashed out and slid across his throat. Matt

felt a millisecond of resistance as her fingernails dug into the smooth skin of his neck, then it was gone, and an enormous spray of something red burst into the night air, soaking his chin and his chest.

There was no pain; just surprise and a suddenly overwhelming tiredness. Matt stared at the dark liquid squirting into the air and only realized it was his own blood as he fell gently backward onto the patchy grass of the lawn. It pattered thickly onto his upturned face, and as his eyes closed, he felt hands pressing against his neck and heard one of the soldiers telling his father that this had never happened.

INTO THE DARKNESS

Jamie Carpenter dreamed of his father.

When he was ten, his dad came home from work, holding his hand under his coat, and disappeared upstairs without saying hello to his son. Jamie's mother was visiting her sister in Surrey, and after a moment, he followed his father, treading on the balls of his feet, taking the steps one at a time, slowly.

Through the half-open bathroom door he saw his father standing with his right hand in the sink. There were spots of red on the mirror and the white porcelain.

Jamie crept across the landing. His father was running the hot tap over his hand, grimacing at the temperature. He turned the tap off and reached for a towel, and Jamie saw his hand. There was a long bloody cut running from his wrist to his elbow, and in the middle of the gash, something dark was sticking out, dirty brown against the red.

His father dabbed the blood away from the cut and slowly reached into the wound. He gritted his teeth, then pulled the dark object out of his arm, letting out a sharp grunt as it came free. Jamie stared. It looked like a fingernail, more than an inch long, sharp and curved like a talon. A chunk of ragged meat hung from the thick end of the nail, glistening white in the bright light of the bathroom.

He gasped. He hadn't meant to. His father turned around sharply, and Jamie stood rigid, speechless. His father opened his mouth as if to say something, then kicked the bathroom door shut, leaving Jamie standing on the dark landing.

Jamie drifted awake. He was moving, a loud car engine rumbling somewhere behind him, the sound of rain hammering against glass close to his head. He slowly opened his eyes and found himself looking out of a window at a dark forest, the trees blurring as they passed, water tumbling from the sky in sheets. He turned his head to the driver and cried out. Instinctively he reached for the passenger door handle and turned it, not caring what would happen if he jumped from a moving car, just knowing he had to get out, get away from the horror in the seat next to him.

"Don't bother," said the driver, his voice so loud that it drowned out the engine. "It's locked."

Jamie pressed himself against the door.

In the seat next to him was Frankenstein's monster.

This is a dream. Isn't it? It has to be, this can't be real.

"It's not polite to stare," the monster said, and Jamie thought he heard the faintest hint of a laugh under the booming, granite voice.

"Who are you?" Jamie managed, his mind screaming warnings at him. *Don't talk to it! Are you stupid? Just shut up!*

"My name is Victor Frankenstein. I did introduce myself. I assume you don't remember?"

Jamie shook his head, and Frankenstein grunted.

"I suspected as much. Good thing I locked the doors."

He laughed, a huge sound like a clap of thunder.

"There is only a certain amount I am permitted to tell you," he continued. "I'm taking you to a safe place. My superior will tell you whatever else he decides you need to know."

"Who is your superior?" asked Jamie.

No reply.

"I asked you a question," he repeated, his voice rising. "Did you hear me?"

Frankenstein turned his enormous head and looked at Jamie.

"I heard you," he said. "I chose not to answer."

Jamie recoiled, and then the image of the blood on the bedroom windowsill crashed into his head, and he remembered.

"My mother," he said, his eyes wide. "We have to go back for her."

Frankenstein shot him a look of concern.

"We can't go back," he said. "She's gone. You know that."

Jamie fumbled his cell phone out of his pocket, scrolled through his contacts until he found his mother's number, keyed the green button and held it to his ear.

Nothing happened.

He pulled the phone away from his ear and looked at the glowing screen. The network logo that usually shone in the middle was gone, as was the bar that indicated the strength of his signal.

"Phones don't work around here," said Frankenstein.

Jamie grabbed again at the door handle, wrenching it until the plastic began to bend in his grip.

"Stop that!" roared Frankenstein. "You will be of no help to her if I have to scrape you off the road!"

Jamie turned to the monster, his eyes blazing. "Stop the car!" he yelled. "Stop it right now! I have to help my mom!"

The car didn't slow, but the huge man in the driver's seat looked over at him.

"Your mother is gone," he said, softly. "You may or may not believe me when I tell you I find that fact almost as distressing as you do. But the fact remains: she's gone. And running around in the dark will not bring her back."

Jamie stared angrily at the bolts in the huge man's neck, and not for the first time, his mouth got the better of him.

"I thought Frankenstein was the creator, not the monster," he muttered.

The brakes of the car squealed, the wheels locked, and they slid to a halt. Frankenstein took a deep breath.

"Victor Frankenstein made me," he said, his voice like ice. "And for a time I was a monster. But after Frankenstein died, I took his name. To honor him. Now, do you have any more impertinent questions, or should I get us to safety?"

Jamie nodded. "I'm sorry," he said, quietly.

Frankenstein didn't respond.

"I said I'm sorry."

"I heard you," grunted the monster. "I accept your apology, as I accept the fact that you're worried about your mother, and worry can make people say unwise things. I need you to accept that I share your concern about Marie, and that I'm taking you to the only people in the country who may be able to bring her back to you. And most of all, I need you to shut up and let me drive."

Jamie turned away and watched the road they were traveling on snake through the quiet forest. The trees were thick on all sides, blurred by the pounding rain, and the headlights of the car illuminated little more than the road itself, a single lane of concrete that looked oddly well-maintained in this deep countryside.

Every few minutes, he looked over at the man in the driver's seat. Frankenstein's eyes were glued to the road, and he didn't so much as glance in Jamie's direction.

Around the car, the woods seemed to be thickening. Jamie leaned forward and craned his neck upward. He could no longer see the night sky; the trees had arched over the road from both sides and fused into an impenetrable ceiling of wood and leaves.

This didn't just happen. This is a tunnel. Someone made this.

The car rounded a sharp corner, and Jamie gasped.

In front of them was a huge dark green gate. It stretched across the width of the road and disappeared into the canopy above them, leaving no edges in sight. In the middle of the gate hung a large white sign, illuminated by a strip light above it. Rain lashed against the bulb, sending running shadows across the sign, on which four lines of bright red text had been printed.

MINISTRY OF DEFENSE
THIS IS A RESTRICTED AREA
UNDER THE PROVISIONS OF THE OFFICIAL SECRETS ACT
NO TRESPASSING

Smoothly and utterly silently, the enormous gate slid open. Beyond it was absolute darkness. There was a pause, then an artificial voice sounded through the rain.

"This is a restricted area. Please move your vehicle into authorization."

Frankenstein eased the car forward, and for a brief moment, panic gripped Jamie.

Don't go in there. Take me home. I want to go home.

The gate slid shut behind the car, cutting off the faint light from the woods.

"Place your vehicle in neutral," the voice ordered, and Frankenstein did so.

Machinery whirred into life underneath their car, and they began to move. They stopped after an unknowable distance, and then the car was enveloped by a pressurized cloud of white gas that billowed from beneath them, the noise of its release deafening in the enclosed space.

Jamie instinctively reached out and grabbed Frankenstein's arm.

"What's that?" he cried.

"It's a spectroscope," Frankenstein replied. "It detects the vapors released by explosives. It's making sure we aren't booby-trapped."

He gently lifted Jamie's hand from the sleeve of his coat and placed it back in the boy's lap. The artificial voice spoke again.

"Please state the names and designations of all passengers."

Frankenstein rolled down the driver's window and spoke loudly and clearly into the darkness.

"Frankenstein, Victor. NS302-45D. Carpenter, Jamie. No designation."

Two halogen spotlights exploded into life, enveloping the car in a circle of blinding white light.

"Non-designated personnel are not permitted access to this facility," the artificial voice said.

This time Frankenstein roared through the window.

"Non-designated personnel present on the authority of Seward, Henry, NS303-27A."

There was a long, pregnant pause.

"Clearance granted," the voice said. "Proceed."

The spotlights disappeared, replaced with warm electric light, and Jamie's eyes widened in amazement. They were in a tunnel at least a hundred feet long and thirty feet wide. Covering most of the floor was a dark gray treadmill, in the middle of which sat their car. A white concrete path ran the length of the tunnel on either side. The walls were immaculate white, stretching up to a ceiling that had to be at least twenty feet high. Where the walls and ceilings met, lights of numerous shapes and sizes pointed down at the treadmill. Jamie could see the wide circles of spotlights, and rows of thick rectangular boxes with purple lenses.

Frankenstein breathed out heavily, filling the car with warm air, and drove forward along the treadmill. As they neared the end of the tunnel, another gate, as silent as the first, slid open. They drove through the gate, and Jamie got his first look at a world very few people knew existed.

Light bathed the car, purple and yellow, creating an atmosphere that was both cold and warm. Ahead of the car, at the end of a strip of tarmac lit by lights that stood at fifteen-feet intervals, a wide, low gray dome rose out of the ground, like the visible part of a ball buried in the earth. To the left of the car, and far to the right, a pair of enormous red and white radar dishes revolved slowly atop squat gray buildings. Beyond the dishes lay a long runway, lights flashing at intervals along its length, two huge beacons shining at one end. Sitting on this runway, partially hidden by the low dome, was a white airliner with a red stripe running the length of its fuselage. As Jamie watched, a steady stream of men and women, dressed in civilian clothes, appeared from behind the dome and walked up a ladder truck to the plane's door. He could hear voices and laughter carrying on the night air.

Frankenstein pressed the accelerator, and the car moved slowly forward. As it did, Jamie craned his neck, looking for the tunnel they had emerged from. He saw it, a wide black semicircle disappearing as the gate they had passed through slid back into place, but what lay to the sides of the tunnel caused him to gasp audibly. A road, branching off the one they were slowly traveling along, curved back and ran parallel to the tunnel, the exterior of which was a flat, nondescript gray. Fifty feet before the tunnel disappeared into the tree line, it curved again, this time into a long, shallow arc that ran parallel to a huge metal fence. Jamie's eyes widened.

"Wait," he said. "Stop the car. I want to see."

Frankenstein grunted and shot him a look of annoyance, but he drew the car to a halt. Jamie threw open the door and stepped out. His head was spinning as he tried to take in what he was looking at.

The inner fence was at least fifty feet high, made of thick metal mesh and topped with vicious snarls of razor wire. Set into the fence at a hundred-yard intervals were guard towers, cubes of metal on top of sturdy-looking pylons. There were no lights in them, but Jamie's eyes caught movement in the one nearest to him. He turned to look at the next tower, a hundred yards further away, and the next, and the next. The fence ran for as far as he could see, in what appeared to be a vast circle. It passed the end of the runway before it disappeared from view beyond a series of low rectangular buildings on the far side of the landing strip. He turned slowly, taking everything in.

Past the low buildings his view was obscured by the dome. Further to the right, a large building sat flush against the runway, its huge metal doors closed. Beyond it Jamie again picked up the path of the fence, the towers evenly distributed along its incredible length. He continued his turn, ignoring Frankenstein, who was looking at him with a certain amount of gentle bemusement. The road running along the inside of the fence continued until it met the tunnel again, then curved back to join the central road no more than twenty feet from where he was standing.

Beyond the inner fence was a wide strip of dirt, crisscrossed with hundreds of thousands of red laser beams; the complexity of the patterns would have made the world's greatest jewel thief weep. This strip of no-man's-land was bordered on the other side by a second fence, almost as high as the one by the road. Beyond it lay the woods, a wall of twisted branches and leaves, running a perfectly even distance from the outer fence.

Every square inch of the space between them, a dirt run about fifteen feet wide, was illuminated by bright purple ultraviolet light, shining down from black boxes set at ten-feet intervals along the outer fence.

Excitement surged through Jamie as his eyes drank in the sheer strangeness of what he was seeing.

What is this place? Why are there so many fences and lights and towers? What are they keeping out?

As his eyes adjusted to the brilliant red and purple illumination before him, he saw that set in between the flickering laser grid was a series of giant spotlights, the wide round lenses pointing into the sky. He looked up, and his mouth fell open.

"Oh my God," he whispered.

There were no visible beams rising from the spotlights, but their purpose was clear as soon as he tilted back his head. Above him, shimmering gently in the night air, an enormous canopy of trees hung in the sky, extending seamlessly from the edges of the woods and covering the whole of whatever this place was. From underneath the image was flat and faintly translucent, like a film of oil on a puddle of water, but he could see erratic shapes and uneven rises bristling the upper side. The effect was disorientating.

"What *is* it?" he asked, his voice full of wonder.

"It's a hologram," Frankenstein answered. "It keeps away prying eyes."

He fought off the urge to ask who those eyes might belong to and instead asked how it worked.

"There's a suspended field of reflective particles that lies over the whole base. The spotlights project a moving image on to it from underneath."

"Like a big movie screen?"

Frankenstein laughed, a strange barking noise that did not sound as though it came naturally to him.

"Something like that," he replied. "From above, all anyone sees is the forest. Have you seen enough?"

Jamie hadn't—nowhere near enough—but he told his companion that he had, knowing it was what the giant man wanted to hear.

"Good," Frankenstein said, not unkindly, and got back into the car. Jamie did the same, and they moved forward, toward the low gray dome.

In front of the building were several military vehicles, a heavy-looking truck with an open rear, a row of jeeps, and a surprising number of civilian cars. Between one of the jeeps and a 3-series BMW that had seen better days, a parking bay was stenciled on the tarmac in white paint. Frankenstein guided their car into it and pulled it to a halt. The giant man and Jamie stepped out of the car and walked back around to a flat indentation where the dome faced the road they had just driven along. Set into the gray material of the building was a door. It stood open, waiting for them.

Frankenstein motioned for Jamie to enter, then followed him in when he did so. They were standing in a white corridor, featureless except for a sculpted crest that looked down at them from high on the wall opposite them.

"What now?" asked Jamie.

"We wait," replied Frankenstein.

Jamie studied the crest as he did so. A crown and portcullis sat above a wide circle, in which had been carved six flaming torches encircling a plain crucifix. Beneath the circle three words of Latin were etched into the wall.

LUX E TENEBRIS

"What does that mean?" asked Jamie, pointing up at the crest.

"*Light out of darkness*," translated Frankenstein. "It was the favorite phrase of a great man."

"Who?"

The door closed behind them, sliding silently until it met the opposite wall, where it thudded into place with a loud clunk. There was a sound like spinning gears moving heavy machinery, then a quieter, yet somehow ominous second clunk. Instantly, the wall at the far end of the corridor slid aside to reveal a silver metal elevator.

"Not now," said Frankenstein, and walked down the corridor. After a moment's hesitation, Jamie followed him.

The elevator had no buttons, and as soon as they stepped inside, the door closed and they began to descend. It was such a familiar, mundane feeling, the shift in his stomach, the vibrations in his legs, that the mild hysteria Jamie realized he had been feeling ever since the thing in the gray coat had walked through the door of the house he shared with his mother threatened to pitch him into a fit of laughter. He steadied himself and waited for the door to reopen. As they settled to a halt and it began to slide open, his mind raced with the possibilities of what he might see next.

It was a dormitory.

A long, wide room, lined on both sides with thin beds

covered in olive-green sheets and blankets. The beds were pristine, as though they had never been slept in, and the metal lockers that stood between them shone like new.

"What is this place?" he asked Frankenstein.

The monster opened his mouth to reply, but a deafening siren drowned out the words. Jamie pressed his hands to his ears, and when the siren paused, Frankenstein looked at him with a worried expression.

"You're about to find out," he said.

THE LYCEUM
INCIDENT, PART I

The Strand, London
June 3, 1892

The carriage clattered to a halt on Wellington Street, in front of the tall pillars of the Lyceum Theatre. A fine rain was falling, and the driver pulled his cloak tight around his shoulders as he waited for his passenger to disembark.

"Bring my bags, boy, both of them," said the old man, impatiently. He stood in the cobbled road, the brim of his wide hat low over his face as he watched the sun descending toward Trafalgar Square.

"Yes, sir," replied his valet, lifting a black leather surgeon's bag and a tan briefcase down from the back of the carriage.

The aging black horse that had pulled them through London shifted as the weight was removed and took a step backward into the valet, sending the man down to one knee on the wet cobblestones and the tan briefcase to the ground. A sharpened wooden stake rolled out and settled at the feet of an overweight man in evening dress, who stooped down, grunting at the effort, and picked it up.

"You, boy," he said, in a superior, goose-fed voice. "Have a care, would you? A man could go full-length with blasted logs rolling around his ankles."

The valet picked the briefcase out of the road and stood up.

"I'm sorry, sir," he said.

"See that you are," said the man, and handed the stake back to the valet while his equally large wife giggled at her husband's wit.

The valet watched them totter away toward the Strand, then handed the bags to his master, who had watched the exchange with an expression of impatience on his face. He took them without a word, turned, and strode up the steps. The valet waited a respectful second, then followed.

Inside the rich red lobby of the theater the old man waited for the night manager to greet them. Looking around, he took in the wide staircases that led up to the left and the right, the posters for previous productions that lined the walls, the majority of which showed the face of the man who had called him here: the actor Henry Irving.

The handsome, pointed face of the great Shakespearean was as well-known as any in London, and his rich baritone voice equally so. The old man had seen his *Othello*, two seasons previous, and deemed it entirely satisfactory.

"Professor Van Helsing?"

The old man awoke from his musings and regarded the stout, red-faced fellow who was standing before him.

"That is correct," he replied. "Mr. Stoker, I presume?"

"Yes, sir," the man replied. "I'm the night manager here at the Lyceum. Am I right in thinking that Mr. Irving explained why your presence was requested?"

"His message told me that a showgirl was missing, that he suspected foul play, and that I may have some expertise on the type of foul play in question."

"Quite," said Stoker. "But this isn't just any showgirl. There's . . ." He trailed off.

Van Helsing regarded the night manager more closely. His face was a deep beetroot red, his eyes watery, and his head enveloped in a gentle cloud of alcoholic vapor. He had clearly sought the courage for this night's work at the bottom of a bottle.

"Mr. Stoker," Van Helsing said, sharply. "I have traveled from Kensington at the request of your employer, and I wish to be about this business before the sun is long beyond the horizon. Tell me everything that I do not already know."

Stoker looked up as though stung. "I apologize, sir," he began. "You see, the girl who has vanished, a chorus girl by the name of Jenny Pembry, is a favorite of Prime Minister Gladstone himself, who has been kind enough to visit us no less than four times this year already. Her absence was mentioned by the prime minister after he attended our production of *The Tempest*, two days past, and Mr. Irving promised to find out what had become of her. When he reported back to the prime minister that he had been unable to do so, he was told that a telegram to the famous Professor Van Helsing of Kensington might prove useful."

"And so here we are," boomed Van Helsing, drawing himself up to his full bearing, his voice suddenly loud and deep. "Standing in an empty theater, with no reason to believe that this missing girl has done anything more mysterious than tire of the stage and choose a more dignified line of work for herself, and certainly nothing to suggest that this affair merits my attention. I fail to see what you expect me to do here, Mr. Stoker."

The night manager had taken a step backward. He took a handkerchief from his pocket and furiously dabbed his forehead with it.

"Sir, if you would spare the time to examine the dressing rooms," he said, his voice catching in his throat. "Mr. Irving informs me that the prime minister is most upset by this business, and I do not wish to tell him I have not exhausted all avenues of inquiry. Ten minutes, sir, I beseech you."

Van Helsing looked at the small red-faced man before him and felt his anger subside, replaced with a deep frustration. Nine months had passed since he and his friends had returned from the mountains of Transylvania, and although none of them had spoken publicly about what had happened, rumor of what had taken place beneath the stone peaks of Castle Dracula had spread, and he had found himself deluged with requests for help, with everything from creaking floorboards to ghostly apparitions and, it now appeared, missing chorus girls.

He longed for the quiet of his surgery, where his research into what he had seen in the East could continue. But there were worrying stories emerging from the Baltic, tales of blood and shadow. Thankfully though, nothing yet suggested that the evil condition that had caused the deaths of two of his friends had found its way back to London, and God was to be praised for that, if for little else.

"I apologize to you, Mr. Stoker," he said. "If you will lead the way, I will examine the dressing rooms, as you suggest." He turned and spoke to his valet. "You may return to the carriage, boy. There is nothing here that will require your assistance."

"Nonetheless, sir, I will accompany you so long as it does not offend."

Van Helsing waved a hand at him, dismissively. "Do as you wish."

Stoker led them through the theater, past the long rows of red velvet seats and the orchestra pit, through a door, and into the backstage area. The narrow passages were piled high with props and set furniture from old productions—a wooden tower from Verona, a broken fairy throne, ermine cloaks, rusting helmets and crowns, row upon row of daggers and swords, silver paint peeling from the wood and collecting in small drifts on the floorboards. As the night manager led Van Helsing and the valet through the dusty corridors, he talked nonstop, his confidence refueled by the professor's apology and the contents of the small hip flask from which he was now openly taking regular sips.

". . . Of course Mr. Irving is a great man, a truly great man, as fine an employer and as gracious a companion as he is skilled an actor. He has always encouraged the players to excel, to . . . *improve*, has given his time to tutor those with promise and to always gently, most gently, discourage those without. My own small ambitions have always found a sympathetic ear with him, although of course he has so many more important claims upon his time, a great man, truly. He has promised me, one man to another, that he will read my play, should I ever complete the cursed thing. What kindness! What generosity!

Although I fear I may never be able to accept his kind offer. The confines of the play confound me endlessly, and I am close to accepting that it may not be the medium to which I am best suited. Perhaps the novel holds the answer? I think it may do. Perhaps I should write of a theater, from which people keep disappearing without a trace? That may entertain, if only for a short while. I may even presume to base the hero on Mr. Irving, such a great man, such a—"

"'*Keep* disappearing'?" Van Helsing interrupted, his voice low.

They had reached a stop. The door in front of them led to a nondescript dressing room, barely larger than a pantry, in which stood three small desks, each facing a dusty mirror, and three hard wooden chairs. In the corners were piled costumes and pages of lyrics and dialogue.

"Sir?"

"'*Keep* disappearing,' you said. Are you telling me that this girl Pembry is not the first to vanish from the Lyceum without explanation?"

Stoker mopped his brow, the confusion clear in his face. "Well, yes, sir. There have been others. But as you yourself said, the theatrical life is not for everyone. Many choose to pursue their fortune elsewhere."

"How many others?"

"In total, sir, I do not know. In recent months, four others, to the best of my knowledge. A trumpet player, an understudy to Titania, and two chorus girls whose names I must confess I do not remember."

"Four others!" bellowed Van Helsing, making Stoker cower back against the open door frame. "You are the manager of this theater, five of your employees disappear in quick succession without an explanation between them, and you do not consider this unusual? And not worthy of mentioning to me, even after I was summoned here to investigate the most recent of them, even now not by you, but rather to satisfy the whim of a politician! Are you an imbecile, sir?"

Stoker stared back at him, his mouth hanging open. He closed his mouth and muttered something too quietly to hear.

"What's that, man? Speak up if you have something to say," demanded Van Helsing.

"I'm only the night manager," replied Stoker, in a small voice.

"That is no kind of excuse, no kind at all, and well you know it. Attend to me now: Has anything notable occurred in recent months that coincides with these disappearances? Think now."

Stoker turned away from Van Helsing, who looked over at his valet standing several feet away, his face expressionless. They waited for the night manager.

Eventually he turned back to them. His eyes were redder than ever, and a gasp in his breathing suggested he was close to weeping.

"I cannot recall anything of significance, other than the sad business of our conductor Harold Norris."

"What business?"

"Mr. Norris suffered from a nervous disposition, sir. Six months ago, Mr. Irving granted him a leave of convalescence, in the hopes that an absence from the bustle of London would help with his condition. As I said, sir, Mr. Irving's generosity knows no—"

Van Helsing cut him off impatiently. "What happened?"

"Sadly, Mr. Norris died. He returned no better for his absence, complaining of fever and hunger, and then no more than two weeks after his return, we received word from his brother that he had passed away. We have only just found a permanent replacement this past month."

"Where did this Norris take his convalescence?"

"In Romania."

The valet drew in a breath. Van Helsing spoke in a voice full of menace. "Where did this conductor live?"

Stoker looked at him with open confusion.

"Sir, Harry Norris was a kind, gentle man of more than sixty years and was with the Lyceum for at least twenty of them. He would not have hurt a fly, sir, I assure you. And even if I am wrong, the poor man is dead and cannot possibly be involved with the disappearance that occupies us tonight."

Van Helsing's hand shot out from the folds of his cloak and gripped the night manager around his upper arm. Stoker cried out.

"Where did he live?" the old man said.

"I don't know!" the night manager pleaded. "Truly I don't. He was always the last to leave the theater, and he lived alone. Now, please, sir, release my arm, I beg you!"

Van Helsing let go of Stoker, who immediately grabbed his arm with his hand and looked at the old doctor with a look of pure terror.

"What is underneath this building?" Van Helsing asked.

"I do not know," whispered the night manager, still clutching his arm.

"Perhaps it is time you found out. Take us to the orchestra pit, quickly now."

"It's this way," Stoker said, his voice still low and full of fear and pain, and led them into the bowels of the theater.

Their second journey through the backstage of the Lyceum was silent.

The night manager led them through corridors of dressing rooms, past a large door separate from the others upon which was written MR. H. IRVING in elegant script, past doors marked MAKEUP, ATELIER, BRASS, WIND, PERCUSSION, and PRIVATE, down a narrow staircase, and finally through a door that opened into the rear of the orchestra pit. Van Helsing placed a hand on Stoker's shoulder and entered the pit first, walking quickly through the neat arrangement of chairs and stands, up two shallow wooden steps to the entrance to the conductor's box. He stayed on the top step, not entering. The valet and the night manager stood behind him on the floor of the pit.

In the box was a circular red rug that covered the floor, an ornate music stand holding the score for *The Tempest*, and nothing else. Van Helsing ordered Stoker and the valet to stand back. He reached in and gripped the edge of the red rug and then pulled it violently out of the box.

"Sir, I must protest!" cried Stoker. "This is most—"

"Come up here," interrupted Van Helsing. "And see if your objection still holds."

Stoker and the valet stepped up into the conductor's box. In the middle of the floor was a heavy wooden trapdoor.

Van Helsing turned to the night manager and the valet.

"Be very, very careful from here on," he said.

IT'S HARD TO BREATHE WITH A HAND AROUND YOUR THROAT

The lighting in the dormitory switched to a purple ultraviolet as the alarm hammered into Jamie's skull. Frankenstein pulled a radio from his belt and keyed in three numbers. He held the radio to one ear, placed a giant hand over the other, and listened.

"What's going on?" Jamie yelled. Frankenstein held a hand out toward him and turned away, his ear hunched into his shoulder, trying to hear what was being said on the radio.

Jamie looked around. There was a door in the wall to his left, and he ran toward it, desperate to get away from the noise that was making his head swim and his stomach churn, desperate to get away from this place and find his mother. Frankenstein reached out and grabbed for him, but Jamie saw it coming, slipped around the outstretched fingers, shoved the door open, and ran through it.

He had just enough time to register that he was in a long

gray corridor before something crashed into him and he sprawled across the smooth floor. His head cracked hard on the ground, and he saw stars as a voice shouted at him and he sat up.

"What the hell are you playing at?" A short, overweight man in a white doctor's coat was standing over him with a look of extreme annoyance on his face. "Who are you? What are you doing here?"

"I'm Jamie Carpenter," he shouted. "Can you tell me where I am? Please?"

"What did you say your name was?" the doctor yelled, his eyes wide.

Jamie repeated it.

"Christ. Oh Christ." The doctor looked around, as if he hoped there would be someone to tell him what to do. "You'd better come with me," he eventually yelled, extending a hand toward Jamie. "Seward'll skin me alive if anything happens to you. Come on, on your feet."

Jamie hauled himself upright.

"Where are we going?" he yelled.

"Arrivals," the doctor yelled back. "Something's inbound, so it's the safest place for you to be."

"Why?"

"Because it's where the guns are."

Jamie ran down endless corridors, his head ringing with the relentless wail of the alarm and the thumping strobe of the purple lights. The doctor was short and round, but he ran with a grim determination, his jaw clenched, his eyes staring into the middle distance, and Jamie found himself sprinting just to keep up.

The doctor finally stopped running in front of a wide elevator platform, little more than a steel frame striped black and yellow. Jamie stepped onto it, the doctor pushed a button set into one of the metal columns, machinery far above them ground into life, and the platform began to ascend. Its passengers doubled over, hands on their knees, trying to catch their breath.

Jamie pulled air into his lungs and stood up straight. As he did so, they passed a cavernous open floor, in the middle of which hulked a vast angular shape, purple track lighting on the walls and floor illuminating tantalizing details: three huge sets of wheels, a dark triangular fuselage, and two wide wings that stretched almost to the walls. Jamie crouched down as they rose toward the ceiling, but the shape disappeared below him as the elevator continued its ascent.

"What was that?" Jamie asked.

"Don't you worry about that," wheezed the doctor in reply. "You keep your eyes in this elevator."

Jamie looked at him, then shrugged and turned away.

Fat idiot. Don't tell me where I can't look.

Gears crunched above his head, and the elevator started to slow. They were rising through a dull gray shaft, which suddenly opened out into a wide room, full of movement and noise.

One whole side of the vast semicircular room was open onto a wide tarmac area that led out to the middle of the long, brightly lit runway. Inside, two lines of black-clad figures, eight wide, stood facing the huge open doors, submachine guns set against their shoulder, pointing out into the darkness. A chill ran up Jamie's spine when he saw them.

I've seen people like this before. They look like soldiers; they look like the men who—

He couldn't let himself finish the thought. He looked away from the dark figures and saw the round crest he had seen in the white corridor, stenciled high on the huge hangar wall. The same three Latin words were stamped below it, running almost the entire length of the vast surface.

LUX E TENEBRIS

Behind the rows of soldiers, dozens of white-coated men and women bustled across the vast concrete floor of the room—*hangar, it's a hangar, they don't make rooms this big*—shuttling gurneys and IV drips back and forth, shouting instructions and questions to one another. A steel shutter door slid upward to Jamie's right, and four figures in full biochemical-hazard suits pushed a pair of metal gurneys covered in plastic oxygen tents into the hangar.

In the distance, Jamie heard the heavy thud-thud-thud of an engine.

"Incoming!" yelled one of the soldiers.

"How much time?" asked a tall, skeletally thin man who stood behind a portable computer array on a heavy steel trolley.

"Ninety seconds!"

The activity in the hangar accelerated, doctors and scientists and soldiers running in every direction, the heels of their shoes and boots drumming on the concrete floor.

A huge crash boomed out to Jamie's left, and he jumped. A

heavy metal door had thumped open, slamming against the wall with a deafening clang. Frankenstein thundered through the door, his huge head surveying the room. His eyes locked on Jamie's; he smiled a smile with absolutely no humor in it and came toward him.

Jamie stood frozen to the spot as Frankenstein crossed the hangar in a dozen of his giant strides, grabbed him by the neck of his T-shirt and lowered his enormous head down so they were face-to-face. His mouth was set in a straight line, his jaw clenched, deep breaths blasting out of cavernous nostrils and blowing the hair from Jamie's forehead.

It's trying hard not to kill me. Really, really hard.

Frankenstein's wide misshapen eyes, the pupils slate gray, stared into Jamie's. Eventually, the monster spoke. "That will be the last time you run away from me," it said. "Do you understand?"

"I—"

"Say nothing," Frankenstein roared. "Not a word. Nod if you understand. I don't want to hear your excuses. *Do you understand?*"

Jamie nodded, then turned his head away, tears of shame and humiliation coming to the corners of his eyes. Several of the troops and doctors had stopped what they were doing and were watching the confrontation, even as the blinding lights of a helicopter illuminated the wide landing zone beyond the hangar doors; Jamie could no more meet their stares than he could that of the giant in front of him.

Movement in the corner of the hangar caught his eye. A section of the blank concrete wall slid aside, and four black-clad figures emerged. They wore large black machine pistols on their right hips, short black tubes on their left, from which wires ran to shallow square tanks on their backs. Jamie recognized the tubes immediately—they were a smaller version of the weapon he had seen Frankenstein fire in the living room of his mother's house.

My God, this is all really happening. I'm not going to wake up.

My mother is really gone.

The four soldiers emerging from the hidden corridor took up positions, two on either side of the door, and a figure strode quickly out of the darkness, through their guard, and headed toward the giant open side of the hangar. The newcomer was dressed in the same sleek black gear as the others, but without the deep purple visor. Jamie saw a flash of gray hair, swept back from the man's forehead. As he strode across the concrete floor he cast his eyes quickly around the hangar, and they met Jamie's. Surprise rippled across the man's face. He turned to one of the soldiers, said something, then marched across the hangar toward Jamie.

"Victor!" the old man shouted, crossing the distance rapidly. Frankenstein turned around, saw him coming, and swore under his breath. Then he looked back down at Jamie, his eyes clearing, as though he had forgotten he was holding a teenage boy by the neck of his T-shirt, and swore again, loudly this time.

He's not really angry with me. It's something else. He looks scared.

Frankenstein released Jamie and told him to stand up straight. Jamie did so, grudgingly, as the old man arrived before them.

"Victor," he said again. "Can you explain to me why there is a civilian teenage boy inside the most classified building in the country? I hope you can, for your sake."

Frankenstein stood straight as a board, towering over both Jamie and the old man.

"Admiral Seward," he said, from above their heads. "This is Jamie Carpenter. I pulled him out of his house as Alexandru Rusmanov was about to tear out his throat, sir. His mother is missing, sir. And I didn't know where else to take him, sir."

Seward did not appear to have heard anything after Jamie's name. He had recoiled, visibly, when he heard it, and now he was looking at the boy with a look of complete surprise.

"Jamie Carpenter?" he said. "Your name is Jamie *Carpenter*?"

"Yes," replied Jamie. He was beyond confusion now, and when Frankenstein barked at him to say sir, he added "Yes, sir" without objection.

Admiral Seward was rallying, his composure returning.

"Ordinarily, I would tell you it is a pleasure to meet you," he said to Jamie. "But this is not an ordinary night, nor has it been an ordinary day by the sounds of it. And you . . ." He trailed off, then regrouped. "I would like to see you in my quarters, Mr. Carpenter, when this matter is resolved. Victor, will you escort him?"

Frankenstein agreed that he would, and then the helicopter landed outside the hangar doors, and everything started to happen very quickly.

As its rotors began to wind down, a door slid open in the sleek metal side of the chopper, and a black-clad figure jumped down onto the concrete and waved an arm, beckoning the scientists and doctors forward. As white coats rushed across the landing area, the soldier reached up into the belly of the helicopter and helped a man in a biohazard suit down to the ground. The hood of the suit had been removed, and the arm was torn open. Blood, sickeningly bright under the yellow-white lights of the helicopter, shone through the hole. The soldier threw the man's other arm around his shoulders and half walked, half dragged him toward the hangar.

Admiral Seward strode out to meet them, his voice loud above the rapidly declining helicopter.

"Report," he demanded.

"Sir, his pulse is weak, his leukocyte count is through the floor. Sir."

As the soldier gave his summary, the scientists in their biohazard suits arrived beside him, pushing a stretcher. They unwound the injured man's arm from the soldier's shoulder and lifted him onto it.

Admiral Seward turned and watched as the scientists, almost running, wheeled the stretcher back across the hangar and through a heavy metal door marked with yellow warning triangles, then turned his attention back to the helicopter, from which more figures were emerging.

A second soldier and a woman in a biohazard suit leapt down from the chopper and pulled a plastic-covered stretcher out after them, extending its wheels and rolling it toward the hangar door. Even from his vantage point at the back of the hangar, Jamie could see that this stretcher wasn't empty. There was a dark shape lying under the plastic, spotted with red.

"Stand aside," Seward yelled as the stretcher approached the crowd of gawking men and women. "Clear a path, for God's sake."

He strode around in front of the stretcher and led it toward a pair of double doors, directly past Jamie. He stepped forward to take a look and felt his heart lurch. Lying beneath the plastic sheeting was a teenage boy, his skin pale, his breathing so shallow, it was almost nonexistent, a huge wad of bandages pushed gruesomely deep into a wide hole in his throat.

Jesus, he's my age. What happened to him?

Then the boy was gone, rushed toward the hangar exit by running doctors. Jamie stared after the stretcher, fear crawling up his spine as reality crashed into him.

That could have been me.

There was a commotion out by the helicopter. A second stretcher was being unloaded from the chopper's belly, and this one was also occupied.

Jamie pushed forward through the crowd of soldiers and scientists, meeting the stretcher as it arrived at the vast open hangar doors. He looked down, then took a stumbling step backward, his heart in his mouth.

Staring straight up at the distant ceiling of the hangar, her face set in a grimace of pain, was the girl from the park, the girl who had attacked him only hours earlier.

The girl whose face he had seen in the window the night his father had died.

He gasped with shock, and she turned and saw him. She smiled. "Jamie . . . Carpenter," she said, her voice cracking, but sounding oddly as though she were trying to smile through the pain. The stretcher lurched to a halt, and the scientist pushing it stared at Jamie.

"How does she know you?" he asked, his voice dripping with suspicion and more than a little fear. "Who the hell are you?"

Jamie looked blankly at him, trying to think of how to answer such a question, but then the girl spoke again, in a voice too low for Jamie to hear.

He leaned down toward the plastic tent.

"What did you say?" he asked. Behind him he heard Seward's voice asking what was happening, and then Frankenstein saying his name, his voice loud and urgent. He didn't care. There was something beautiful about the girl's brown eyes, even through the heavy plastic sheeting, and he leaned even closer and repeated his question.

"Your . . . fault," the girl said, then broke into a wide smile, all traces of pain suddenly gone from her face.

A hand gripped his shoulder, and he knew without looking that it belonged to Frankenstein. But before he had time to move, the girl sat upright, dizzyingly fast, with the plastic tent still covering her, and threw herself at Jamie.

She crashed into him, chest high, and he was knocked flat on his back. His head thudded against the concrete floor, sending a bright pillar of pain shooting into his brain. The girl landed on him, straddling his waist, the awful smile still on her face. Jamie saw Frankenstein grab for her neck with his gloved hands, but she swung a plastic-coated arm and sent the huge man sprawling backward. The backs of his legs collided with the fallen stretcher that had been occupied by the girl, and he went over to it, his head smacking hard on to the ground.

Jamie saw this happen through a thick fog of pain, his eyes trying to close, a deafening high-pitched sound ringing through his head. The girl lunged forward, still covered in the plastic sheet, opened her mouth, then buried her face in his neck.

Jamie felt the sharp points of her fangs through the plastic sheet, felt her mouth squirming for purchase, and opened his own mouth and screamed, until the girl sat up and placed her hands around his throat, cutting off the air supply to his lungs.

I can't breathe. She's going to strangle me.

He looked up dimly at the hideous plastic-coated apparition that was killing him. The girl was bleeding again, dark red spots pattering the inside of the sheet, and she was howling and screaming and tightening her grip on his neck with every passing second. He could hear voices yelling from a long way away, and he saw two more figures—he couldn't make out whether they were soldiers, scientists, or something else—grab the girl and try to pull her off him. Both were sent sprawling by casual flicks of the girl's left arm, which left his throat for a millisecond before returning to exert its deadly pressure.

"Shoot her," he heard someone shout in a voice that sounded like it was coming from underwater, and there were a series of loud cracks, like fireworks. The girl bucked and jolted, and blood soaked the inside of the plastic sheet, some of it spraying through the holes the bullets had torn and landing on Jamie's face in a fine mist. But still she did not release her grip.

Jamie's head was pounding, his vision darkening, his chest burning. He needed air now, or it would be too late.

As he felt his eyes beginning to close, something huge flew across his narrowing field of vision. There was a loud crunching sound, and suddenly, blissfully, the pressure on his throat was gone. He opened his mouth and took a giant, terrified breath, his chest screaming, his pounding head thrown back as oxygen flooded into his desperate lungs.

There was an incredible commotion in the hangar above and around him, but he barely registered it as he realized with savage, victorious elation that he wasn't going to die.

Not now, at least.

His vision was clearing, the thumping noise in his head starting to recede, when a dark shadow appeared above him and knelt down. Jamie looked up at the shape crouching over him; the image came into focus, and he stared into the face of Frankenstein.

"Can you sit up?" he asked, his voice surprisingly gentle, and Jamie nodded.

He pushed himself up with his elbows and looked around the vast hangar. Scientists and doctors were clustered around the fallen soldiers, but almost everyone else was staring at him, concern and fear mingled on their faces. A rush of panic shot through him, and he looked for the girl that had attacked him.

"Don't worry about her," Frankenstein said, as though he could read Jamie's mind. "They've got her."

He pointed to the left, toward the open doors. Jamie turned his head to look, and smiled weakly at what he saw.

Two soldiers were holding up the girl. The whole left side of her face was swollen, her arms and legs dangling limply above the ground. As Jamie watched, a scientist slid a hypodermic needle into her neck and depressed the plunger, sending a bright blue liquid into her jugular vein.

Two doctors picked the stretcher up from the ground, righted it, and wheeled it over to the soldiers, who lowered the girl on to it. The doctors zipped the plastic sheet back into place, as Jamie stared at the figure beneath it. The girl's chest was slowly rising and falling.

"She's not dead," he said, softly. "But they shot her. I saw the bullets hit her."

"She's not dead," confirmed Frankenstein. "She's something else."

THE LYCEUM
INCIDENT, PART II

Beneath the Lyceum Theatre, London
June 3, 1892

The valet descended first, hand over hand down a rope, a lamp hanging from his belt. The hole was pitch-black, but the flickering gas light was strong enough to pierce the edges of the darkness, and he touched down gently.

"Twelve feet, no more," he shouted up to his master. He heard the old man instruct Stoker to find fifteen feet of ladder, smiled, then surveyed the area with his lamp.

He was standing in a round chamber, built of large white stones that had been turned a speckled gray by years of dust and darkness. Four arches were set into the walls of the chamber, the stone crumbling in places but holding steady. The same could not be said for the passages that led away from three of the arches; the roofs had long since given way, collapsing into piles of broken masonry that blocked the way completely. The fourth passage was clear, and its stone floor was scuffed with footprints.

The wooden feet of a ladder thudded to the ground behind him, then Van Helsing and Stoker made their way down, one after the other, holding lamps of their own.

"What is this place?" asked Stoker, his eyes widening as they adjusted to the gloom.

"Catacombs, or cellars, or possibly something else entirely," replied Van Helsing, peering at the stone walls, and the valet felt a shiver dance up his spine. He had never heard his master sound uncertain, not at any point in the two years he had served him.

The old professor approached the arch of the one passable corridor and looked down at the footprints in the dust.

"This way," he said, as he stepped into the passage.

The space between the stone walls only allowed for single file, so Stoker followed Van Helsing, and the valet followed them both, his hand buried in his jacket pocket, gripping something tightly.

Van Helsing led them through the stone corridors, pausing at junctions and tipping small pools of flaming oil on to the dusty floor, markers that would hopefully lead them back to the ladder.

The passages were pitch-black, lit only by the flickering orange of the lamps. At the edges of the light, rats scurried into cracks in the ancient stone, their pink tails leaving thin lines in the thick dust. Heavy, intricate webs hung between the walls, ropy strands of silk that caught in the men's hair and brushed their faces. The dark brown spiders that had woven them squatted in the highest spirals, thick-bodied creatures that Van Helsing didn't recognize, although he kept this information to himself. The stone floor was uneven, cracked and subsiding, and the going was slow. Twice the valet had to reach out and grab Stoker's shoulder when a slab moved under his feet, preventing the night manager from turning an ankle, or worse.

This was no place to be carrying an injured man.

It was difficult to gauge the passage of time in the darkness, but after a period that could have been as much as an hour or as little as ten minutes, the glow of light became visible in the distance, beyond the arc of their lamps. The three men headed toward it.

The light grew brighter and brighter, illuminating more details on the stone walls as they approached. At head height, carved into the wide slabs of the narrow passages, were the grotesque faces of gargoyles, their mouths open wide, forked tongues protruding between triangular teeth, their eyes staring out from wrinkled, finely worked skin. Stoker muttered to himself as they passed them, his hip flask now almost permanently attached to his lips. The valet watched with mixed emotions. He did not want to have to rely on a drunken man if, as seemed increasingly likely, they found trouble at the end of this labyrinth. But nor did he have any desire to answer the night manager's questions, or placate his fears. If the brandy was keeping him quiet and putting one foot in front of the other, the valet supposed that was sufficient.

As they neared the source of the light, it became clear that it was shining through an ornate arch, much larger than the passage they were traveling along. Indeed, as he looked, the valet could see that the walls and ceiling were now tapering gently outward, widening the corridor in a way that was extremely disorientating. Stoker stumbled, yet again, and the valet gripped the man's shoulder and righted him. The night manager murmured thanks, and they pressed on, until they walked under the towering arch and entered hell.

The arch opened into a square cavern, lit on each side by a pair of flaming torches. The lower walls were covered in carvings: gargoyle faces, humanoid figures, and long rows of text, chipped out of the stone in a language the valet had never seen before. On a stone slab in the middle, her arms and legs bound with rope, her skin so pale it was almost translucent, was a girl.

"That's her," whispered Stoker. "Jenny Pembry."

Van Helsing quickly crossed the room and began examining the girl, while Stoker and the valet stood frozen under the arch, taking in the horror that surrounded them.

In the four corners of the room were the missing employees of the Lyceum Theatre.

To their left was the trumpet player, the fraying remains of his dinner suit hanging from his decaying corpse, which had been propped against the stone corner. His legs and arms were missing, and the skin that remained on his face was a green so dark, it was closer to black. Stoker turned back into the passage and retched, his hands on his knees, while the valet approached the body. As he neared it, he saw pages of sheet music had been crammed into the dead man's mouth.

In the next corner was the understudy, clad in what remained of her Queen Titania costume. Her tiara, rough metal painted gold, shone horribly above the decomposing flesh of her face. Her legs had also been removed, and her ballet shoes placed on the floor before the ragged stumps, a practical joke of vicious cruelty. Her eyes were gone, although the valet could not tell whether this had been deliberate or the inevitable consequence of her final resting place.

In the final two corners were the missing chorus girls, arranged so they faced each other. They were less decayed than the others, and their death agonies were still visible on their faces, their teeth bared, their eyes wide. Both girls were naked, their torsos grotesque patchworks of cuts and stitches, done with what the valet realized to his horror were lengths of horse hair from a pair of violin bows that lay between them. They were horribly, unnaturally pale, their veins invisible.

All four of the bodies, the valet realized, had a pair of ragged puncture wounds on their necks.

"She's still alive," said Van Helsing.

At his master's voice the valet turned away from the horrible fates that had befallen the chorus girls and approached the altar. Stoker followed, unsteady on his feet.

On the slab, Jenny Pembry was barely conscious, moaning and turning gently against the ropes that held her fast. The valet pulled his knife from his belt and sliced through the ropes. Van Helsing gently lifted the girl down and passed her to Stoker, who held her at arm's length, his face blank with terror.

"Hold her, damn you!" barked Van Helsing. Stoker flinched and drew the chorus girl tight against him.

"She's been bled almost dry," Van Helsing told the valet. "Recently, too. The jugular blood is still warm."

"Where's the conductor?" asked the valet, his voice low.

"I don't know," replied Van Helsing. "If he's in one of other tunnels, we will need more light, and many more men. If he's—"

A drop of blood landed on the valet's shoulder.

The valet examined the dark material of his jacket, then slowly both men looked up into the roof of the cavern.

Harold Norris hung upside down from the stone roof of the chamber, twenty feet or more above them, his arms folded across his chest, his eyes closed, like a grotesquely swollen bat. His mouth and chin were dark with Jenny Pembry's blood, and as the three men stared upward, drops of crimson fell softly onto the dusty floor between them.

"Be absolutely quiet," whispered Van Helsing. "We must not wake him."

"What. . . what has happened to him?" asked Stoker, his whisper slurred by alcohol.

"There is not sufficient time to explain it to you now. We must leave here at once and return better prepared. We are no match for him if he wakes."

The valet was still looking up at the conductor. The face that hung above him was gentle, kind even, lined with wrinkles and topped with a mane of gray hair. Norris was wearing his evening suit, the jacket spreading out around him like wings, the white collars of his shirt stained brown with blood.

"*Boy*!" hissed Van Helsing.

The valet looked around, shaken from his thoughts. His master and the night manager were standing under the great arch that led into the chamber, waiting for him. He crossed the cavern slowly, anxious not to make any sound that might awake the sleeping monster swaying gently above his head.

He had almost reached his companions when Stoker, his eyes wide with fear and incomprehension, turned and ran down the passage.

He made it only two steps before a stone slab shifted beneath him, and he pitched sideways. Van Helsing made a futile grab for his jacket but gripped only air. The night manager thumped into the wall of the corridor, which collapsed around him in a shower of rubble and a great cloud of choking dust. And in the roof of the cavern, Harold Norris opened his crimson eyes and let out a deep, animal growl.

The conductor was upon them before any of the men had chance to react. He fell like a dead weight into the middle of the cavern, pivoting impossibly barely inches from the ground to land in a deep crouch. He burst forward from this position with dizzying speed, crossing the distance to the arch in the blink of an eye, barreling into them like a snarling hurricane. He gripped Van Helsing around the throat and threw the old man into the middle of the chamber. Van Helsing crashed to the floor, skidded into the side of the altar, and lay still. The valet made to pull his hand from his pocket, but was much, much too slow. The conductor descended on him, a dark thing from hell, his eyes a deep red flecked with black and silver, his face splashed with Jenny Pembry's blood, two long fangs standing out from his mouth.

The valet felt himself lifted from his feet, and then he was in motion, soaring through the air into the cavern. He saw his master lying below him, blood pooling beneath his head, and had time to regard the onrushing stone wall with something approaching dispassion.

I'm going to hit that, he had time to think.

And then he did.

Stoker lay among the crumbled stone of the wall. His back was in agony where he had fallen across the section of the wall that had remained standing, and his nose and mouth were thick with foul-tasting dust. He felt hands reach through the hole in the wall and grasp the lapels of his tunic and breathed a sigh of relief as he was pulled forward into the passage. Then the dust cleared, and he found himself looking into the smiling, inhuman face of Harold Norris, and he threw back his head and screamed.

"Quiet your screeching, you drunken wretch," hissed the conductor. Stoker was horrified to hear that this monster spoke in the same gentle voice that Norris had used night after night to conduct his players. "If I tear the tongue from your head, you will wish you had done as I say."

Stoker forced himself to stop screaming, clenching his teeth together, even though the face inches from his own made him feel as though he were teetering on the edge of madness. He forced himself to speak, to say something, *anything* that might see him escape the same fate that had befallen the others who had found themselves in this old place of dust and death.

"Harold . . . it's me, Bram. Don't hurt me, please. Please."

The conductor laughed and opened his mouth to reply when his eyes suddenly snapped wide and a sharp wooden point emerged through the fabric of his dress shirt. Norris looked down for a fraction of a second before he exploded in a fountain of blood, spraying the night manager from head to toe and covering the cloak and hat of the valet who was standing where the conductor had been, his arm thrust forward, the hand at the end of it clutching a pointed wooden stake.

"What should be done with him?"

"I don't know, exactly. It is possible he will not remember any of this."

"Is that a chance we can afford to take?"

Van Helsing and the valet sat in a dark booth in the corner of the Lyceum Tavern, deep glasses of brandy on the table before them. The valet had supported Stoker and dragged him back through the tunnels and out into the orchestra pit, while Van Helsing did the same with Jenny Pembry. The valet had collapsed the passage before climbing the ladder out of the ground for the final time.

It had been slow going. Van Helsing had received a deep cut to his head when he collided with the altar stone, and he needed to stop twice to rest on the journey back to the surface. Thankfully, the chorus girl was mercifully light, and although she seemed almost catatonic, she had been capable of putting one foot in front of the other.

They had put her in a carriage and instructed the driver to deliver her to the house of a physician friend of the professor's, with a note Van Helsing had scrawled on the back of a discarded program for the evening's performance of *The Tempest*.

The night manager had mumbled and muttered to himself as they hauled him back through the stone corridors and was now sitting between them on a red leather bench, his eyes closed, his chest rising and falling steadily as he slept.

"You realize what this means, boy?" asked Van Helsing.

"Yes, master. I do."

"It means that Transylvania was not the end of this business."

The valet said nothing.

"You played your part extremely well tonight," Van Helsing continued. "Without you, this matter may have ended very differently."

The valet watched as his master's lined, weathered face broke into a rare smile.

"It is possible," he continued, "that we may make more of you than just a valet, Carpenter."

A HARD DAY'S NIGHT

Frankenstein walked Jamie down a long gray corridor until they reached a white door with INFIRMARY stenciled on it in red letters. There was a rush of cold air as the giant man pushed it open and led Jamie inside.

Rows of empty beds ran down one side of the spotlessly clean room. Lying unconscious on one of them was the man who had been carried from the helicopter. The wound in his arm gaped horribly wide, and his face was ghostly pale. A steady stream of blood ran down a plastic tube from a hanging bag and disappeared into his uninjured arm.

At the far end, three frosted-glass doors were set into the wall, marked X-RAY, CT SCANNING, and THEATER. Through the one marked THEATER Jamie could see a frenzy of movement and hear raised voices and a steady mechanical beeping. There was a figure lying on a table, surrounded by white shapes and blocky rectangles of machinery. As he watched, a spray of blood, bright, garish red, splashed against the glass of the door, and Jamie's stomach turned.

Then the door marked X-RAY was flung open, and a middle-aged man in a white coat hurried toward them, his face red and flustered. When he reached them, he stopped, took a PDA from his pocket and poised the stylus over it.

"Name?" he asked.

Jamie looked up at Frankenstein, who nodded.

"Jamie Carpenter," he replied.

Surprise flashed across the doctor's face, and Jamie wondered absently why his name seemed to provoke a startled reaction in everyone who heard it.

But it was a question for another time. He was so tired he could hardly see straight, his legs felt like they were made of wet clay, and it had taken an enormous effort to simply say his own name correctly.

"What are your symptoms?"

Jamie opened his mouth but could shape no further words. He looked helplessly up at Frankenstein, who took over.

"He is suffering from post-traumatic shock, his throat is severely bruised from attempted strangulation, and he is physically and mentally exhausted. He needs to rest. Immediately."

The doctor nodded at this and, with surprising gentleness, took Jamie's arm and led him to the nearest bed. Jamie sat on the starched white sheet, staring up at Frankenstein, dimly aware that he was complying with the doctor's requests to open his eyes for examination, to follow a finger from left to right, to breathe in, hold it, and breathe out as the cold metal of the stethoscope was placed on his chest. The doctor examined his neck, where purple bruising was starting to rise in ugly, violent ridges, then placed a needle in his arm, attached a saline drip, and asked Frankenstein for a word in private. The two men walked quickly over to the door and began to converse in rapid whispers, Frankenstein casting his eyes over at Jamie every few seconds.

Jamie stared at him, his sluggish mind trying to frame the questions he wanted to ask the huge man. He found he was unable to do so; the words ran away from him like sand through his fingers. When the two men finished their conversation and made their way back toward him, he was only able to manage two.

"What happened?"

Frankenstein sat down on the bed next to him. Jamie heard the steel of the frame creak and felt himself slide an inch toward the monster as his huge weight tilted the bed. The doctor was attaching a second bag to the IV drip as Frankenstein spoke to him.

"Now is not the time for explanations," he said. "You need to rest, and there are things I need to do. I will tell you as much as I can tomorrow."

The doctor turned the valve on the second bag, and Jamie felt a glorious calm settle over him, like a warm blanket.

"You . . . promise?" he whispered, his eyes already closing, and as he drifted into gentle oblivion, he heard Frankenstein say that he did.

Frankenstein stood, silently watching the teenager. Jamie's chest rose and fell in the slow rhythm of deep sleep, and his face was peaceful. The doctor had told him that the boy would be out for at least twelve hours, but Frankenstein had ignored him. He found himself unable to look at the swollen purple of Jamie's neck; it ignited a familiar rage inside him, a rage that, were he to give in to it, could only be satisfied by violence.

He pushed it down and continued to watch the boy. He had been doing so for a long time when there was a tap on the glass of the door behind him.

He turned to see Henry Seward looking in at him. The admiral beckoned him with a pale finger, and Frankenstein pushed open the infirmary door and stepped into the corridor.

"Walk with me to my quarters, Victor," Seward said. His tone made it clear that it was not a request.

The two men walked down a series of gray corridors until they reached a plain metallic door. Seward placed his hand on a black panel set into the wall and lowered his face to the level of a red bulb just above it. A scarlet laser beam moved across the admiral's retina, and the door opened with a complicated series of unlocking noises.

Henry Seward's quarters could not have been more incongruous with their gray, military surroundings. As the metal door opened, the scent of hardwood drifted out into the corridor, mingled with the aromas of Darjeeling tea and rich Arabica coffee. The two men stepped inside.

This was only the third time that Frankenstein had visited the admiral's private rooms since Seward had taken up residence. He had spent many afternoons and evenings in them when they had been occupied by Stephen Holmwood, and occasions too numerous to mention when the great Quincey Harker had been in charge. But Seward was different from those open, gregarious men; he kept his own counsel and guarded his privacy.

The door opened onto a wood-paneled drawing room, furnished in a style that was elegant and yet unmistakably official; worn leather armchairs flanked a fireplace that was no longer in use, separated from a mahogany desk by a beautiful Indian rug, now fraying slightly at the edges, that depicted a meditating Shiva, his vast form swathed in clouds. Two doors led from the rear of the room into what Frankenstein knew were a small kitchen and a modest bedroom.

Admiral Seward lowered himself into one of the armchairs and motioned for Frankenstein to do likewise. Frankenstein squeezed himself into the seat, the leather creaking as he did so. He declined when Seward offered him an open wooden box of Montecristo cigars, and waited for the director to light his cigar with a wooden match. Seward drew hard until the tapered end was glowing cherry red and exhaled a cloud of smoke into the air. Finally, he looked at Frankenstein.

"How did you know where the Carpenters were?"

Frankenstein bristled. "The boy is fine, sir, if that's what you meant to ask."

"I'm glad to hear it. But, no, it's damn well not what I meant to ask. I meant to ask how you knew where the Carpenters were."

"Sir—"

Seward cut him off. "*I* didn't know where they were, Victor. Nor did anyone else on this base. Do you know why?"

"I think—"

"Because not knowing where they were was the best possible way of keeping them safe!" Seward roared. "If one person knows, then very quickly two people will know, then four, and so on, and so on. If no one knows, nothing can happen to them. That's how it works, Victor."

"With all due respect, sir, it didn't work tonight," Frankenstein replied evenly.

He was looking directly at the director, refusing to defer to him by looking away, and as he watched, he saw the anger in Seward's eyes fade. He suddenly looked very tired. "Marie is really gone?" he asked.

"Yes, sir."

"Alexandru has her?"

"It's safe to assume so at this point, sir. Although I would still recommend we attempt to get confirmation."

And find out if she's still alive.

Seward nodded. "It may be difficult," he said, slowly. "There will be a great reluctance to assist Julian's family, in any way. It won't matter that Marie and Jamie played no part in what happened."

Anger flashed through Frankenstein. "It should matter, sir," he said. "You know it should."

"Perhaps it should. But it won't."

The two men sat in silence for several minutes, the admiral smoking his cigar, the monster wrestling with his anger, a task to which he devoted many of his waking hours. Eventually, Seward spoke again.

"What have you told him?" he asked.

"Nothing," Frankenstein replied. "Yet."

"What are you going to tell him?"

"I'm going to tell him what I think he needs to know. Hopefully that will be enough."

"And if it isn't? If he asks to be told everything? If he asks about his father? What will you do then?"

Frankenstein looked at the admiral. "You know where my loyalties lie," he replied. "If he asks me, I will tell him whatever he wants to know. Including about his father."

Seward stared at the huge man for a long moment, then abruptly stubbed out his half-smoked cigar and stood up.

"I have a report to write for the prime minister," he said, his voice clipped and angry. "If you'll excuse me?"

Frankenstein levered himself out of the armchair, which groaned with relief. He walked toward the door and was about to hit the button that released it when Seward called to him from next to his desk. He turned back.

"How did you know where they were, Victor?" Seward asked. He was obviously still angry, but there was the ghost of a smile at the corners of his mouth. "It will go no further than this room. I just need you to tell me."

Frankenstein smiled. He had a huge amount of respect for Henry Seward, had fought back-to-back with him in any number of dark corners of the globe. And though he would not compromise the oath he had sworn, as snow fell from the New York sky and 1928 turned into 1929, he could allow the director this one mystery solved.

"Julian chipped the boy when he was five, sir," he said. "No one knew he'd done it, and I was the only person he gave the frequency to. I've known where he was every day for the last two years."

Seward grinned, a wide smile full of nostalgia, which abruptly turned into a look of immense sorrow. "I suppose I should have expected nothing less," the admiral replied. "From you, or from him. Good night, Victor."

THE LYCEUM INCIDENT, PART III

Eaton Square, London
June 4, 1892

Jonathan Harker, Dr. John Seward, and Professor Abraham Van Helsing sat with their host in the drawing room of Arthur Holmwood's town house on Eaton Square, waiting for Arthur's serving girl to dispense coffee from a silver tray. She was dressed all in black; Arthur's father, Lord Godalming, had passed away several months earlier, and the house was still in mourning.

In the middle of the table lay the letter that had been delivered to Van Helsing early that morning, summoning him to an emergency meeting with the prime minister at Horse Guards.

"Thank you, Sally," said Holmwood, when the coffee was served. The girl curtsied quickly, then backed out of the drawing room, closing the doors behind her.

The men poured cream into their cups, took biscuits from the plate, sipped their coffees, and sat back in their chairs. For a contented moment, no one spoke, then Jonathan Harker asked Van Helsing about the previous night's business.

The old professor set his cup back on the table and looked around at his three friends. They had been through so much together, these four men: had stared into the face of pure evil and refused to yield, chasing Count Dracula across the wilds of Eastern Europe to the mountains of Transylvania, where they had made their stand at the foot of the ancient castle that bore their quarry's name.

One of their number had not made it home, murdered on the Borgo Pass by the gypsies who had served the count.

Ah, Quincey, thought Van Helsing. *You were the bravest of us all.*

"Professor?" It was Harker who spoke, and Van Helsing realized that he had been asked a question.

"Yes, Jonathan," he replied. "I'm sorry, last night's exertions have left me tired. Forgive me."

Harker gave him a gentle look that told him clearly that requesting forgiveness was unnecessary, and Van Helsing continued.

He told them of his adventure beneath the Lyceum, the orator in him taking satisfaction as their eyes widened at his telling of the tale. When he was finished, silence descended on the drawing room as the men digested the professor's story. Eventually, Harker spoke.

"So it's as we feared," he said, his face displaying a calm that his voice was not quite capable of matching. "The evil did not die with the count."

"It would appear not," replied Van Helsing. "As to how, I confess the answer escapes me. I can only presume that poor Lucy was not the first to have been transformed by the count's vile fluids."

Seward and Holmwood flinched. The mere mention of Lucy Westenra's name was still a source of great pain to both men.

"Why now, though?" asked Harker. "Why is the evil spreading only now, after the creature itself is dead?"

"I don't know, Jonathan," replied Van Helsing, truthfully. "Perhaps the count guarded his dark power, hoarded it, if you will. Perhaps such restrictions have been lifted with his death. But I merely speculate." He looked at his friends. "And I must ask the same of you all," he continued. "I ask each of you to tell me whether you think the poor business of Harold Norris was an aberration, or a harbinger of things to come. I shall depart for Whitehall shortly, a summons I am compelled to obey, and I will be expected to provide the prime minister with answers."

Silence settled uncomfortably over the drawing room.

Tell me it was an isolated incident, thought Van Helsing. *One of you tell me that. The alternative is too horrible.*

"I fear this is only the beginning." It was Arthur Holmwood who spoke, his voice even and firm. "I believe that the situation is only likely to worsen. I wish I could honestly say otherwise, but I cannot. Can any of you?"

His face did not betray the fear that the old professor knew he must be feeling, nor the great sorrow with which the death of his father had filled him. Van Helsing felt an immense warmth for his friend, who had been dragged unwillingly into the terrible events of the previous year for no greater a crime than proposing marriage to the girl he loved, but had conducted himself with enormous courage and dignity as the matter had taken its course.

"I cannot," said Dr. Seward.

"Neither can I," said Jonathan Harker.

The professor nodded, curtly, trying not to show the dread that had settled in the pit of his stomach. "So we are in agreement," he said, gripping the arms of his chair and pushing himself to his feet. "It is my sincere hope that we are wrong, but I feel it in my heart that we are not. I will convey our conclusion to the prime minister. Let us hope that he surprises us with wisdom enough to heed our warning."

The valet brought the carriage to a halt outside the grand Horse Guards building, dismounted and helped Van Helsing down onto the pavement. Two soldiers of the Household Cavalry, resplendent in their blue tunics and gold ropes, immediately approached and asked them their business. The valet produced the letter from inside his top coat and passed it to the soldiers, who examined it carefully before standing aside.

Inside the arched entrance to the building an elderly butler, clad in immaculate morning dress, informed them that the prime minister would receive them in the study of the commander in chief of the British Army on the first floor. He hovered respectfully as Van Helsing removed his coat and handed it to his valet.

"Wait here, boy," the old man said. "I doubt I shall be long."

The valet nodded and took a seat in a high-backed wooden chair by the entrance, folding his master's coat across his knees.

Van Helsing followed the butler up a wide staircase, his footsteps muffled by a deep red carpet, the oil-painted eyes of the greatest heroes of the British Empire staring silently down at him from the walls.

He was led along a wide corridor on the first floor, turning left and right and left again, until they reached a large oak door, which the butler pushed open. He stepped inside and the professor followed.

"Professor Abraham Van Helsing," the butler announced, then backed silently out of the study. The old man watched the servant close the door, then turned and looked at the six men gathered at the far end of the room.

Seated at an enormous mahogany desk was William Gladstone, the prime minister, looking expectantly at Van Helsing. Flanking him to the left and right were five of the most powerful men in the Empire; Earl Spencer, first lord of the Admiralty; Sir Henry Campbell-Bannerman, secretary of state for war; George Robinson, secretary of state for the Colonies and first marquess of Ripon; Herbert Asquith, home secretary; and Archibald Primrose, foreign secretary and fifth earl of Rosebery.

What a rogues' gallery this is, thought Van Helsing.

He walked across the study. The wall to his left was dominated by a tall row of windows, through which could be seen the green expanse of St. James's Park. To his right, an open fire roared in an ornamental marble fireplace. Lying on the floor between him and the desk was an immaculate tiger skin, the head, paws, and tail still attached and forming a six-pointed star on the dark floorboards. Beyond the rug was a wooden chair, positioned directly in front of the one in which the prime minister was sitting.

Van Helsing stepped around the tiger skin with a look of distaste on his face and stood next to the chair.

"Won't you sit, Professor?" asked Gladstone, his voice higher and more feminine than Van Helsing had expected.

"No thank you, Prime Minister," he replied curtly. "I prefer to stand." *Even though the pain in my hip feels like there is a branding iron being pressed against it. Let it hold up for as long as this takes, grant me that much.*

Gladstone continued. "I saw you admiring the tiger. Isn't he beautiful?"

"*She*," said Van Helsing pointedly, "would be more beautiful were she still alive in the forests of Siberia, in my opinion. Sir."

Secretary Robinson uttered a short laugh. "Professor, you are mistaken," he said, his voice booming from a mouth partially concealed behind a vast beard that reached below his bow tie. "Not about the sex of the beast, as female she surely is, but about her provenance. She's a Bengal, sir. I shot her myself outside of Yangon, two summers ago."

Van Helsing turned and looked down at the animal skin, taking in the size of the head and the length of the tail, both still intact. "I think not, sir," he replied. "*Panthera tigris altaica.* The Siberian, or Amur, tiger."

Robinson's face darkened red. "Are you calling me a liar, sir?" he asked, his voice low.

He bought it, realized Van Helsing, with cruel enjoyment. *Probably in Singapore or Rangoon. Bought it and brought it home as a hunting trophy. How wonderful.*

"I am not suggesting that," he replied, relish creeping into his voice. "I am, however, suggesting that it is you who is mistaken. The thickness of the coat, the pale orange of the fur, the lighter concentration of the stripes, all are unmistakable characteristics of the Amur, as is the fact that she must have stood more than eight feet in length. Perhaps you have been hunting on the Siberian plains in recent years, as well as in Bengal, and merely forgotten from which trip you brought her home? Because, if that is not the case, there is only one conclusion I am able to draw."

He left the accusation unspoken, hanging pregnantly in the air of the drawing room, and after favoring him with a look of pure murder, Secretary Robinson admitted that his son had taken camp in Siberia two summers previously and had brought home a number of fine wild specimens, and it was likely that he had mixed up his Bengal trophy with one of these.

Still you lie, to the faces of your peers. Gilded fools. Preening bookkeepers. Let us be about this business.

The prime minister cleared his throat and took a sip of water from the half-full glass on the desk.

"Professor Van Helsing," he said, his tone warm and rich now, the oily voice of a born politician. "I wish to thank you personally for your endeavors last night and to pass on to you the gratitude of Jenny Pembry's mother and father. The girl is now recuperating with them in Whitechapel and appears to be doing well."

"Thank you, sir."

"However, the incident, although blessed with a satisfactory ending, raises some unusual questions, does it not?"

Van Helsing allowed that it did, and Gladstone nodded.

"Could you, therefore, Professor, explain to us the nature of the creature you encountered last night, and your experience in such matters? We are not beyond the reach of gossip in Whitehall, and I'm sure we have all heard rumors of the business with Carfax Abbey and its Transylvanian occupant, but I would like to hear the truth—from you."

The old man looked steadily at the prime minister, then up at the ministers who were gathered around him. *Like a gaggle of vultures. Looking for a way to turn blood and death to their advantage.* "Very well, sir," he said, and began to talk.

He spoke for no more than ten minutes, but as he finished, it was obvious that his tale had divided the men in the room into two camps. Primrose, Robinson, and Campbell-Bannerman were looking at him as though he were utterly mad, their faces contorted with obvious outrage that they had been forced to listen to such foolishness. Asquith, Spencer, and Gladstone were ashen-faced, their eyes wide with horror, and Van Helsing knew that these three men believed what he had told them.

"Are there any questions?" he asked, looking squarely at the prime minister.

Gladstone opened his mouth to respond but was interrupted by Secretary Robinson. The prime minister gave him a look that suggested he was going to regret having done so at some point in the near future but allowed the marquess to speak.

"This is preposterous," Robinson said, his voice trembling with indignation. "You're asking me to believe in men who can fly, have superhuman strength, drink blood, and live forever, and moreover you're suggesting that there is going to be some form of epidemic of these behaviors? Behaviors that can only be destroyed by exsanguination or the obliteration of the heart?"

"Exactly, sir," Van Helsing replied.

Robinson turned to Gladstone. "Prime Minister, this has

surely gone beyond a joke. I fail to see what—"

"Shut up, George," Gladstone said, evenly.

The colonial secretary looked as though he might burst. Primrose opened his mouth to protest, but the prime minister waved a derisory hand at him.

"Not another word, from any of you," he said. "I appreciate that what Professor Van Helsing has just told us is unsettling, horrifying, even. And I can also appreciate why some of you, perhaps all of you, might have trouble believing his tale. But I have it on good authority that events beneath the Lyceum took place exactly as he describes, and we've all heard the stories about the journey he and his companions made to Transylvania last year. So I confess my inclination to believe him."

It is possible I had this man wrong, Van Helsing thought. *There is an intelligence at work here that I had not given credit for.*

"And as prime minister," Gladstone continued. "It is my responsibility to do what I believe to be in the best interests of the Empire, especially where potential threats to its security are concerned. And that is what I will do. Unless anyone wishes to object?"

He got up from behind the desk and looked closely at each of the men standing behind him, daring them to speak against him. Van Helsing watched, fascinated, as Robinson, literally shaking with righteous indignation, made as if to do so, until Campbell-Bannerman placed a restraining hand on his arm and the colonial secretary looked away.

"Very well," said the prime minister, stepping out from behind the desk and approaching Van Helsing. "Professor," he said. "Popular opinion would suggest that you are our finest authority on the matters you have just outlined. Would you agree?"

The old man allowed that there was some truth in that particular rumor, and Gladstone nodded.

"In which case," he continued, "I am prepared to make your expertise an official position in Her Majesty's Government. Clandestinely, of course. Are you interested?"

"What would the position entail?"

"The investigation and elimination of the condition that you have just explained to us so compellingly. With authority recognized by every appropriate governmental department, annually budgeted expenses, and cooperation guaranteed by all agencies of the Empire. That's what it would entail."

The prime minister looked at Professor Van Helsing and smiled. "So," he said. "Does that interest you?"

Dr. Seward extinguished a Turkish cigarette that smelled to Van Helsing as if it had been lightly laced with opium.

"And?" he asked. "What did you tell him?"

The men were sitting in the red leather armchairs that dominated the comfortable wood-paneled study of Arthur Holmwood's father. Van Helsing's valet had driven his master back to the town house on Eaton Square as soon as the meeting at Horse Guards had ended, and Arthur had led them upstairs to the room in which his father, Lord Godalming, had spent much of the later years of his life. The men had lit cigarettes and pipes, and the old man had just finished telling them about his meeting with the prime minister when John Seward asked his question.

"I told him I needed time to think it over," Van Helsing replied. "I asked for twenty-four hours, which he granted me. I am to deliver my reply by noon tomorrow, in writing."

"What do you intend your answer to be?" asked Harker. The deep bell pipe in his hand had gone out. He was holding it absently, as though he had forgotten about it.

"In truth, I do not know," Van Helsing confessed. "I think in all likelihood, I will accept his proposal, but my happiness at doing so will rather depend on the question I am about to ask you all."

The professor set a wide tumbler of cognac on a shelf beside his seat. He had returned from Whitehall with his mind racing at the possibilities Gladstone's offer might afford him but also shaken deeply by the responsibilities it would bring, and he had gratefully accepted Arthur's offer to open his father's drinks cabinet a little earlier than was usual.

"Gentlemen," he began. "We have all witnessed with our own eyes more of the darkness that inhabits this world than most—and more than any sane man would care to have seen. I flatter myself we did a fine thing in the Transylvanian mountains, something we can all be proud to have played a part in, and if any of you wishes to let your involvement in these matters end there, let me promise you that neither I, nor anyone else, will think even the slightest bit less of you for it. Each of us has more than paid our dues, and a peaceful life, untainted by blood and screams, is not something to give up lightly."

He paused and looked around the study.

"Part of me believes that to ask more of you is a cruelty on my part, one that none of you deserves. But that is what I am going to do. Because I believe a plague is coming to this nation, to all nations, and that Harold Norris was only the prototype. This morning you all claimed to believe this as well, but I ask you to consider how firmly you believe it, for a very simple reason. If we are right, then we are the only men in the Empire with any experience of what is to come. And I cannot stand by and see innocent blood spilled, innocent souls polluted for eternity, knowing that I could have saved even one of them. We swore that we would be vigilant, that were the count ever to return, we would deal with him once more. He has not, and I don't believe he ever will. But the evil that inhabited him has survived and is abroad."

Van Helsing reached for his tumbler with a shaking hand, and drained the glass.

"I will accept the prime minister's offer tomorrow. But when I asked for a period of time to consider it, I also informed him that were certain people to agree to be involved, they would be allowed to do so. I informed him that this was not negotiable. So I am asking for your help, as you once asked for mine. I wish I could offer you longer to think it through, but I can only—"

"I accept," interrupted Jonathan Harker. His face was pale, but a determined smile played across his lips. "I don't need time to consider."

"Nor do I," said Dr. Seward. He had lit another cigarette, and his handsome face was wreathed in smoke.

"And neither do I," said Arthur Holmwood, firmly. He had set his cigar and his glass aside and was looking directly at Van Helsing. "Not a single minute."

Thank you. Oh, thank you.

"Please take one anyway, Arthur," he replied. "All of you. Because there can be no going back if we embark on this journey. You will never be able to tell anyone beyond this room of the existence of our organization. Not even Mina, Jonathan. Are you prepared for that?"

Harker flinched but nodded his head.

"Are you all?" Van Helsing asked.

Seward and Holmwood both agreed that they were.

"In which case," Van Helsing said, "I see no reason to make the prime minister wait. I will dispatch our answer immediately."

THE MORNING
AFTER

Jamie woke shortly before dawn.

He raised his groggy head from the pillow and saw an IV drip running down to a needle that had been placed in his forearm. He didn't remember its insertion; didn't remember much of how the previous day had ended, after the girl had attacked him in the hangar.

He pushed back the sheets and blankets and swung his legs off the bed. He was wearing a white medical robe and was scanning the room for his clothes when a wave of nausea rolled through him, and he thought for a horrible second that he was going to vomit. His throat hurt and it was painful to breathe. He raised a hand to his neck, felt a swollen ridge of flesh tender to the touch, and winced. He closed his eyes and lowered his head between his knees, and after a minute or two, the sick feeling passed. He was about to get down from the bed when the door at the end of the room opened and a doctor walked briskly into the infirmary.

"Mr. Carpenter," the doctor said. "Please lie back down."

The man's voice was familiar and full of authority, and Jamie did as he was told. The doctor examined his bruised throat, pricked his finger and drew blood, shone a small flashlight in his eyes, then slid the needle out of his arm and pronounced him much improved.

"How do you feel?" he asked Jamie.

"I feel OK," he replied, rubbing the neat circular hole left by the needle. "I don't really remember how I got here. Did Frankenstein bring me?"

The doctor nodded.

"Brought you in, then stayed with you most of the night. He only left a couple of hours ago. He asked me to remind you when you woke up that you are to go and see him before you talk to anybody else. He asked me to make sure you understood that. Do you?"

"I suppose so."

The doctor drew a PDA from his pocket and tapped a number of keys with the plastic pen.

"I want you to come back and see me this afternoon," he said. "The bruising is down, and you're no longer dehydrated. You may still be suffering from a degree of post-traumatic stress, but under the circumstances, I'm going to discharge you. Is that what you wish?"

Jamie nodded.

"OK then. Rest here as long as you like, and when you're ready you can get dressed and go and find your friend. He asked me to give you this." The doctor reached into his pockets again, withdrew a piece of paper, and handed it to Jamie. On it, written in a beautiful cursive handwriting, were two short lines of text.

*Level E
Room 19*

Jamie took it from the doctor's hand without a word. The man hovered for a moment, as if slightly unsure of what to do next, then favored Jamie with a smile and a brief nod of his head, and walked back out of the infirmary.

Jamie lay still for a few minutes, then sat back up, grunting at the pain in his neck and arm, and pushed himself off the bed. He wobbled, his legs unsteady beneath him, and reached out and gripped the top of the white cabinet. As his equilibrium returned, he saw his clothes, neatly folded on a low shelf on the other side of the infirmary. He walked gingerly over to them and dressed himself, slowly, searching for the memories of the previous night. Then he looked around the infirmary and gasped as his faltering memory was jolted into life.

A man was lying in one of the beds on the other side of the room, his eyes closed, his chest rising and falling slowly. Jamie walked over and stood beside him, watching the man breathe. His skin was brighter than it had been the previous night, but it was still pale. His right arm was swathed in bandages, and blood ran steadily from an IV hung above his bed. Jamie watched, fascinated, as the crimson liquid crawled down the plastic tube and slid into the man's vein.

There was someone else. There was a boy.

The memory hit him hard, and he looked over at the door marked Theater. A dark shape lay beyond the frosted glass, and he walked toward it. He hesitated, standing in front of the door, then pushed it slowly open.

The teenager lay in a single bed in the middle of the room. Beside him, a tall array of equipment beeped and flashed steadily, and a green line spiked slowly, over and over. Wires ran from the machines and were attached to the boy's chest and arms. His eyes were closed, and his skin was ghostly white. Jamie stood by the door, frozen, staring at him.

He's my age. He's just a kid.

Slowly, he crossed the room and stood beside the starched white bed. "What happened to you?" he whispered.

"He was bitten," replied a voice from behind him, and Jamie's heart leapt in his chest. He spun around and saw the doctor who had examined him standing in the open doorway. "What are you doing in here?" the man asked.

"I remembered seeing him in the hangar," replied Jamie. "Is he going to be all right?"

"Did you touch anything?" asked the doctor, ignoring Jamie's question.

He shook his head. "Is he going to be all right?" he repeated, his voice rising ever so slightly.

The doctor walked to the end of the bed, pulled a metal chart from a clip, scanned it quickly, and replaced it. Then he rubbed his eyes, and looked at Jamie.

"It's too early to say," he said, softly. "He lost an enormous amount of blood, and his heart stopped as we were transfusing. We resuscitated him, but his brain may have been damaged by the lack of oxygen. We induced a coma, to give him the best chance. Now we just have to wait."

Jamie stared blankly at the doctor.

His heart stopped. We induced a coma. His heart stopped.

"How long?" he managed. "How long until you know if he's all right?"

The doctor shrugged.

"A few days, maybe longer. Once the swelling on his brain has gone down, we'll wake him up. And then we'll see."

The man shook his head quickly, and when he looked at Jamie again he was all business.

"Go on, get out of here," he said. "Go and find Colonel Frankenstein. And don't come in here again without permission. This boy is in a very delicate condition, and the next twenty-four hours are vital."

Jamie backed toward the door, unable to tear his gaze from the teenager's blank, pale face. There were no lines on his skin, no wrinkles or blemishes; he looked like a mannequin.

"What's his name?" he asked, as he reached the open door.

"Matt," said the doctor, who was consulting the chart for a second time. He didn't look up as he answered. "Matt Browning."

Jamie walked down the corridor outside the infirmary, keeping his eyes on the gray walls, looking for an elevator. Just before the corridor ended in a flat black screen that stretched from floor to ceiling, he saw a button marked CALL outlined on the wall to his right. He pressed his thumb to the button and waited.

Seconds later the wall in front of him slid open, revealing a metal elevator. He stepped inside and examined the fluorescent yellow buttons set into a black panel at waist height; they were marked 0, A, B, C, D, E, F, G, and H. The C button was glowing red.

Well, at least I know where I am. That's a start. He looked at the piece of paper the doctor had given him. *Level E. Two more floors down.*

He was suddenly overcome with the desire for sunlight and fresh air. He didn't want to go further into the depths of this strange place.

He pressed the 0 button. The door slid closed silently behind him, and the elevator started to rise with a soft whirring noise and a gentle rattling of metal. When the doors opened again, Jamie found himself looking down yet another gray corridor. However, at the end of this new passage were a pair of double doors striped with yellow and black, and he had a feeling that these led back into the hangar where he had been attacked.

He walked toward the doors, noticing as he did so a thin digital ticker set into the wall above them, yellow-green capital letters scrolling right to left, over and over.

0652 / 10.22.09 / SHIFT PATTERN: NORMAL / THREAT LEVEL: 3

Ten to seven. My alarm wouldn't even go off for another fifty-five minutes if I were at home.

He crept up to the double doors and inched one of them open. The huge sliding doors that opened onto the runway were now shut, and the hangar was deserted. Jamie walked out into the middle of the huge room, painfully aware of the quiet slapping noise his trainers made on the concrete floor.

He walked across to a door at the right-hand edge of the giant double doors and tried its handle. It turned, and he stepped through it into the cool bright morning air.

Jamie Carpenter jogged across the wide concrete landing area in front of the hangar, then cut onto the grass, heading toward the long runway that sliced through the center of the vast circular base. He sprinted across it, his feet pounding the tarmac, his arms pumping, his mother's face looming large in his mind, his heart heavy with worry.

He bore right and darted between two of the long metal huts that lined this side of the runway, hit open grass and accelerated, running toward the high wire fence in the distance and the bright red laser net beyond it, the giant projection rippling above him, hanging in the clear sky like a painted cloud.

But as he approached the fence, he saw something that seemed totally out of place. About fifty yards inside the high wire wall, a circular section of the grass, perhaps twenty feet in diameter, had been dug up and replaced by a rose garden.

A waist-high red brick wall ran around the edge, with an opening facing away from the fence and back toward the base. Inside a thin path of wooden boards widened into a semicircular area against the back wall, flanked on both sides by roses of every conceivable color: red, white, pink, yellow, even a purple so dark it was almost black.

Jamie slowed his pace and walked through the gap in the wall. He was immediately overcome by the scent of the flowers, the subtly different aromas of the many varieties mingling into a heady, pungent smell so rich and luxurious that it took his breath away. He wandered down the narrow wooden path, intoxicated by the garden's incongruous beauty. At the back of the garden, Jamie could see a small bronze plaque set into the brick wall. He crouched down in front of it and read the words that had been engraved on it, in simple, elegant lettering.

IN REMEMBRANCE OF
JOHN AND GEORGE HARKER
WHO DIED AS THEY LIVED:
TOGETHER

Jamie sat down next to the plaque, his back to the wall, and closed his eyes. He sat there for a long time, the scent of roses in the air, feeling more alone than he had ever felt in his life, wondering where his mother was, wondering whether she was even still alive.

Some time later, he could not have said how long, he heard the soft crunch of footsteps coming across the grass. From his low vantage point he couldn't see beyond the walls of the garden, and so he waited for whoever was approaching to present themselves.

The head that appeared above the low brick wall was grayish green, with a shock of black hair combed comically neatly into a side parting and two thick metal bolts emerging from the neck below. Frankenstein stepped through the entrance to the garden, turning his enormous frame sideways so he would fit through the gap, and walked along the wooden path, the thump of his feet against the boards deafeningly loud, an ominous sound at odds with the gentle smile that regarded Jamie as the monster approached.

Frankenstein wore a dark gray suit, the white shirt open

at the collar, the huge metal tube that he had fired in Jamie's living room again hanging from his right hip. He sat down next to Jamie without a word, seemingly perfectly content to enjoy the garden and the morning sun that was bathing it in warm yellow light.

"How did you find me?" Jamie asked quietly, his gaze focused on the roses in front of him, rather than on the man beside him.

"Infrared sensors in the ground," Frankenstein replied, his voice irritatingly cheerful. "You left a nice red heat trail on the monitors. Wasn't hard to follow."

Jamie grunted.

"So you found me. What do you want?"

"I want to talk to you, Jamie. There are things you need to know. Things that are going to be hard for you to accept."

"Like what?"

The monster looked away, and when he spoke, it was in a soft voice. "A long time ago, I made a promise to protect the Carpenter family. One of your ancestors saved me, and in his memory I've kept my word for more than half a century."

"Saved your life?"

"Yes," Frankenstein replied, then looked at Jamie. "But that's not the story I want to tell you now. That one's for another time."

"But—"

"Don't ask me. I'm not going to tell you, so let's not waste our time."

Jamie looked at the monster. Frankenstein was regarding the teenager with something that seemed close to love, and he wondered what had happened to provoke such loyalty.

Suddenly, Frankenstein's fury in the hangar made sense; he had let Jamie get away from him, in a place where anything could have happened to him.

"OK," he said. "So is that it? I'm guessing it isn't."

"I've concluded that the best way for me to continue to honor that promise is to tell you what I think you need to know. I think it's too late for your life to ever go back to being normal, if it ever was. Would you agree?"

"Yes," said Jamie, simply.

Frankenstein nodded and began to talk. "My suspicion would be that your father never really told you very much about your family. Am I correct?"

"He told me I had an uncle who died when he was very young. And that my granddad was a pilot in World War II. That's about it."

"Both those things are true. Your uncle Christopher died at birth, when your father was six years old. And John, your grandfather, was a highly decorated pilot. He flew a Hurricane during the Battle of Britain. Did you know that?"

Jamie shook his head.

"He was a fine man. By 1939 he'd been out of the RAF for nine years. But he reenlisted the day Britain declared war on Hitler's Germany, against the wishes of your great-grandfather, who is the man with whom this story really begins."

"I don't know anything about him," said Jamie. "I don't even know his name."

"His name was Henry Carpenter. He was a good man as well, at least the equal of his son. And everything that has happened to your family for the last one hundred and twenty years, everything that happened to you and your mother yesterday, can be traced back to the fact that he worked for a truly great man, a legend whose name I suspect you will know. Professor Abraham Van Helsing."

Jamie laughed; a short, derisory noise, like a dog's bark. He didn't mean to, and the monster swung him a look of deep annoyance, but he couldn't help it.

Come on. Seriously.

"Van Helsing wasn't real," he said, smiling at the monster. "I've read *Dracula.*"

Frankenstein returned Jamie's smile.

"Believe it or not," he said, "that will make this considerably easier."

"I've read Frankenstein, too," said Jamie quickly, before he lost his nerve.

"Good for you," said the monster. "Might I be allowed to continue?"

"OK," said Jamie, disappointed. It had taken all his courage to mention Mary Shelley's novel.

"Thank you. Now, there are certain truths that you are simply going to have to come to terms with, and the quicker the better. Professor Van Helsing was real. The Dracula story, and all the people in it, is real; it happened almost exactly as that lazy drunk Stoker wrote it down. The vampire seductresses who distract Harker from his escape plans are fictional; the wishful thinking of their author. As is the count's ability to turn into a bat, or a wolf, or anything else for that matter. But the rest is close enough. All of which means, in case you need it spelled out for you, that vampires are real. Although that shouldn't be too hard for you to believe; you met two yesterday."

Jamie felt like he had been punched in the stomach. "The girl who attacked me. . . ."

". . . was a vampire, that's correct. As was the man I fired at in your living room. His name is Alexandru. And he is the main reason we're sitting here now, having this conversation."

"Who is he? What will he . . . what will he do to my mother?"

"I'll get to him. The business with Dracula occurred in 1891, two years after your great-grandfather took work in Professor Van Helsing's house. The men who survived the journey to Transylvania, whose names you no doubt know . . ."

"Harker," said Jamie, distantly. "One of them was called Harker."

He turned and looked at the bronze plaque on the garden wall, saw the names engraved on it, and felt things start to click into place in his mind.

You believe him. Or are starting to at least. My God.

"Jonathan Harker," Frankenstein replied. "That's right. He, along with Professor Van Helsing, John Seward, and Arthur Holmwood, swore an oath when they returned home, a promise they would remain vigilant and deal with Dracula again if it was ever required."

There was a sharp intake of breath from the teenager.

"It wasn't," Frankenstein continued, quickly. "Trust me, he's dead. Unfortunately, he was not the only vampire in the world; merely the first—and the most powerful. He was a man once, the prince of a country called Wallachia, named Vlad Tepes. A terrible man, who butchered and murdered thousands of people. In 1476, his army lost its final battle, and he disappeared along with most of his supporters, until he appeared a year later in Transylvania, calling himself Count Dracula. With him were his three most loyal generals from the Wallachian Army. The three brothers Rusmanov: Valeri; Alexandru, who you met yesterday; and Valentin. As a reward for their loyalty, Dracula made them like him, along with their wives. And for four hundred years, they were the only vampires in the world, their power and their immortality jealously guarded by Dracula, who forbade them from turning anyone else. But when Dracula was killed, the rules died with him, and the brothers began to convert a new army of their own. In the last years of the nineteenth century, the condition began to spread. And it's still spreading."

Frankenstein paused, then cleared his throat, a deep sound like a bulldozer's engine starting up. "This organization, the base you are in now, the people you met yesterday, it all grew from the promise those men made to be vigilant. They grew exponentially throughout the twentieth century, founding equivalent organizations in Russia, America, India, Germany, and Egypt, becoming what you see around you."

Frankenstein gave Jamie a sly grin. "Which, to all intents and purposes, doesn't exist. The only people outside the organization who know about us are the prime minister and the chief of the general staff. No one can ever acknowledge its existence or tell anyone they are a member. As your grandfather was. And your father. And as you would have been offered the chance to be in about five years' time."

Frankenstein stopped talking. Jamie waited to see if he had merely paused and, once it became clear that he was finished, tried to think of a way to respond to what he had just been told. "So . . ." he began, "what you're telling me is that my dad was a secret agent who fought vampires for a living. Real vampires, who actually exist, in the real world. Is that right? Is that what you're asking me to believe?"

"I'm telling you the truth," Frankenstein replied. "I can't make you believe it."

"You have to realize how crazy this sounds, though. Surely?"

"I know it is a lot to take in. And I'm sorry you had to hear it like this. But it is the truth."

"But . . . vampires?"

"Not just vampires," answered the monster. "Werewolves, zombies, any number of other monsters."

"Werewolves? Come on."

"Yes, Jamie, werewolves."

"Full moon, silver bullets, all that stuff?"

"Silver bullets are unnecessary," said Frankenstein. "Normal bullets will work just fine. But the moon controls them, as it always has."

Jamie's interest was piqued, despite his skepticism. "What are they like?" he asked. "Have you ever seen one?"

Frankenstein nodded. "They are terrible, tormented creatures," he said. "Savage and instinctive. I hope you never encounter one."

Jamie paused. "And where do you fit into all this?" he asked, cautiously.

"You're a well-read boy," Frankenstein replied dryly. "You work it out."

"But that was just a novel," Jamie replied.

"Like *Dracula*?"

"Well . . . yes."

Frankenstein looked away. "That miserable little girl," he said quietly, almost to himself. "She gave my pain to the world as entertainment."

Jamie tried another angle. "So what happened the night my father died? I mean, what really happened?"

For a moment, he didn't think the monster was going to respond. Frankenstein was staring into the distance, lost in his memories. But then he shook his head, as if trying to clear it, and answered. "I don't think you're ready to hear about that yet."

The cruelty of this statement almost broke Jamie's heart. He composed himself, though not so quickly that the watching Frankenstein failed to notice, and continued. "What about yesterday?" he asked.

"Alexandru has been looking for you and your mother ever since your father died. Yesterday he found you." Frankenstein replied. He saw the look on Jamie's face and anticipated the question that was coming. "We don't yet know how. But he did."

"Why am I still alive?"

"The girl, Larissa her name is, was supposed to kill you. She didn't do it."

"Why?"

"We don't know that either. She says she won't talk to anyone except you."

"Me?" Jamie asked, his eyes suddenly wide. "Why me?"

"Don't worry about that now."

"What about my mother? Is she . . . is she dead?"

"Our assumption is that your mother is being ransomed by Alexandru."

"Ransomed for what?"

Frankenstein looked at the boy with great sadness. "For

you, Jamie."

The monster and the boy sat in silence for a long time, letting those three terrible words sink in, until eventually Frankenstein stood up. His shadow engulfed Jamie entirely, and he reached a hand down to the boy, who took it and let himself be pulled to his feet.

Frankenstein led him along the wooden path and out of the rose garden. They walked in silence across the vast field toward the low dome until they crossed the empty runway and Jamie finally spoke again.

"What do they call all this?" he asked, his voice thick with emotion.

My mother. Oh God, my mother. The thing in the gray coat has my mother.

"This?" Frankenstein replied, sweeping an arm to indicate the huge circular base. "This is Classified Military Installation 303-F. But everyone calls it the Loop, for reasons I'm sure you're clever enough to work out."

Jamie glanced around at the enormous circular base and smiled. "Not the base," he said. "The organization. What's the organization called?"

Frankenstein smiled. "I'll let Admiral Seward tell you that," he answered. "I'm to take you to him now."

"He's going to have to wait."

"And why is that?"

"Because I want to see the girl who tried to kill me yesterday. Right now."

A CRIMSON KINDNESS

Frankenstein pressed H on the panel in the elevator, and they began to descend. The huge man looked straight ahead, his mouth set in a thin line, and Jamie knew that he was angry.

The elevator doors opened onto a round chamber. In front of Jamie were a thick airlock door and an intercom panel. Apart from that, the walls were bare. The elevator doors began to hiss shut behind him, and he whirled around. Frankenstein was still standing in the elevator, looking at him. He lunged forward and stuck his hand in the narrowing gap.

"What are you doing?" he shouted. "You can't leave me down here on my own!"

Frankenstein replied in a tight voice full of edges.

"You wanted to come down here. I didn't tell you to. Instead I have to go and tell Admiral Seward that you'll deign to come and see him when it suits you."

Jamie stared at the huge man. When the doors began to close again, he shoved a hand between them, but he said nothing. He just stared at Frankenstein, who returned his gaze.

When the doors hissed for the third time, Jamie let them close. As Frankenstein's face disappeared behind the sliding metal he thought he saw the monster's face soften and the wide lips part, as if he were going to say something. But then the doors clicked together, and he was gone.

Jamie turned away from the elevator and examined the intercom panel. There was a small button at the bottom of the metal rectangle, and he pressed it and waited. He was about to press it again when a voice suddenly emanated from the intercom, making him jump.

"Code in."

Jamie leaned toward the intercom and spoke into the metal grid.

"I don't know what that means," he said, and was embarrassed by the tremor in his voice.

"State your name."

"Jamie Carpenter."

There was a long pause.

"Proceed," the voice said, eventually, and the huge airlock door unlocked with a rush of air.

Jamie took the handle in his hand, braced himself for the weight of the huge structure and pulled. The door slid open smoothly, and he stumbled backward, gripping the handle to stop himself from falling. The door was as light as a feather.

There must be some sort of counterbalance. I bet you couldn't open it with dynamite if it was still locked.

He stepped through the door and into a white room not

much bigger than a decent-sized cupboard. There was a second door opposite the one he had just come through, which he pulled shut behind him, and waited for the second set of locks to disengage.

Nothing happened.

Panic jumped from nowhere and settled in Jamie's throat. He was locked in, trapped in this tiny space, an unknowable distance beneath the ground. Sweat broke out on his forehead, and suddenly it seemed that the walls were closer than they had been when he walked in. He put his hands out and touched the walls with his fingertips, waiting for the sensation of movement, but there was none.

Then the lights went out, and he clamped his teeth together so he wouldn't scream.

A second later, he was bathed in purple ultraviolet light, as small hatches in the walls opened and flooded the tiny chamber with a rushing white gas.

Then it was over, as quickly as it had begun. The lights came back on, and the second door clunked open. Jamie threw himself against it, pushing it open with his shoulder, spilling out of the—*coffin, it was like being in a coffin*—room.

He gripped his knees with his hands, doubled over, breathing hard. When the panic had subsided, he stood up and looked around. He was in a long, narrow corridor, brightly lit by square fluorescent lights set flush into the ceiling. To his right was a flat white wall; to his left, a small office behind thick transparent plastic. Thirty feet down the corridor, he could see square floor-to-ceiling holes that had to be the cells, running in parallel down the length of the cellblock. A white line was painted onto the floor on each side, about three feet in front of the cells.

He turned to the office. Behind the plastic, a soldier, wearing the now-familiar all-black uniform, sat at a metal desk. He was looking at Jamie with a strange expression on his face, an uncomfortable mix of anger and pity. Jamie supposed the latter was as a result of what had happened to his dad; he did not know what he had done to elicit the former. But when the man spoke, his voice carried no hint of conflict, just the clipped vowels and tight consonants of anger.

"You here to see the new one?" he asked.

Jamie nodded.

"She's at the end on the left."

Jamie thanked the man and turned toward the cells, but the guard spoke again.

"I'm not finished," he said. "There are rules down here, no matter what your name is. Understand?"

Jamie turned back to the office, his face flushing red with anger. The guard saw this, and smirked.

"Oh, you've heard of rules, have you?" he said. "Bet you learned about them from your dad. That right?"

"What's your problem?" snapped Jamie, and the guard flushed a deep crimson. He lifted himself halfway out of his seat, his eyes fixed on Jamie's, then appeared to think better of it, and sat back into the chair.

"Don't pass them anything, don't tell them anything about yourself, don't step across the white line," he said. "Press the alarm next to her cell if there's trouble. If you're lucky, someone might come." With that, he looked away.

Jamie walked past the office and between the first two cells. They were empty, but a surge of panic shot through him when he examined the one to his left. The entire front wall of the cell was open; no bars, no glass, nothing. He looked down the corridor and saw that all the cells appeared to be the same. He stepped back to the plastic-fronted office and the guard spoke immediately, without looking up.

"It's ultraviolet light," he said, his voice utterly disinterested. "We can pass through it, they can't."

"Why not?" Jamie asked.

The guard raised his head and looked at Jamie.

"Because they'll burn into a little pile of ash if they do. Their bodies are vulnerable to UV light. It's why they can't go out in the sun."

He lowered his head again and waved a hand dismissively. Jamie clenched his fists, bit his tongue, and walked back down the corridor.

The first two cells on either side were empty, but the third on the right was occupied. A middle-aged man, neatly dressed in a dark brown suit, sat in a plastic chair at the rear of the cell, reading a thick paperback book. He looked up as Jamie passed but said nothing.

As Jamie made his way down the cellblock, he became aware of a distant noise. It sounded like the howls mating foxes made in the fields behind the house he had grown up in, an ungodly shriek, high-pitched and ugly. As Jamie walked past empty cell after empty cell, he realized it was getting louder, and by the time he stepped in front of the last cell on the left, it was almost deafening.

The girl who had attacked him in the park, and then

again in the hangar, was crawling back and forth across the ceiling of her cell, like a horribly bloated fly. She was almost unrecognizable from the girl he had met the previous day; her eyes gleamed a terrible red, her clothes were torn, and she was caked in blood that had dried to an even brown crust. Her head was thrown back, the muscles in her neck standing out like thick strands of rope, and the guttural howling that was issuing from her snarling mouth made his head swim.

He breathed in sharply. He couldn't help it; the terrible thing crawling across the ceiling was so revolting, so utterly unnatural. She heard the intake of air, and her head snapped round, the red eyes fixing on his. Even through the shrieks, a flash of recognition flickered across her face, and she screamed anew, louder than ever, staring directly at him.

Suddenly, the shrieking stopped and she fell from the ceiling, landing on her knees on the floor. She looked at him for a long silent moment, then began to howl again, her eyes never leaving his.

In the wall next to her cell was a round red button that Jamie assumed was the alarm. Above it was an intercom panel with a small silver button beneath it. He pressed it and waited.

With a crackle, the guard's voice, clearly annoyed at being disturbed, came on the line and asked him what the problem was.

"What's wrong with her?" Jamie asked.

The guard swore heartily down the line. "Don't you know anything?" he asked, sharply. "The hunger is on her."

"What's the hunger?"

"For Christ's sake. She's hungry. Is that clear enough for you? She wants blood. It drives them mad if they go without it for too long."

"Then give her some blood," Jamie said.

The guard laughed. "Why would I want to do that?"

"What use is she like this?" Jamie said, fighting to keep his temper. "If you let this hunger make her crazy, she won't be able to tell me anything useful. Just give her some blood."

"Those aren't my orders," replied the guard.

Jamie looked back into the cell and stifled a scream. The girl had silently crossed the concrete floor and was staring at him from the other side of the ultraviolet barrier, her inhuman face only inches from his. She was twitching and trembling uncontrollably, her whole body vibrating, her red eyes dancing with madness. She opened her mouth and tried to speak to him.

"Pleeeeeaaarrrrrrssssssssssse," she slurred, her mouth slack, her jaw working fiercely trying to form the words. "Teeerrrrllllllll yooooo eveeerrrrythhhhiiinnnnnnnng. Dooooooooo annnnnnythhhiiiiinnnng."

"If you don't give her some blood," Jamie shouted into the intercom, "I'm going to put my arm through the barrier. And then you can explain to Admiral Seward what happened."

This girl might know where my mother is. I don't care if you have to throw a bucket of blood into the cell from across the corridor, I need to know what she knows.

Silence.

Jamie could picture the guard in his office, weighing the decision, not wanting to have to explain anything to Admiral Seward, especially not how someone had been eviscerated in one of the cells on his watch.

"I've called my superior," the guard said eventually. "It's his decision. He's coming down now."

"OK," replied Jamie. There was a pause, and then the guard spoke again.

"You know, what I said to you before, I was just—"

"I don't care," interrupted Jamie, and the intercom fell silent.

Jamie stood in front of the girl's cell and watched her. She had crawled across the room and curled herself into a tight ball on the narrow bed that ran along one wall. She was moaning rather than howling now, a deep sound that Jamie could feel through the soles of his feet, and every few seconds, she lifted slightly into the air, before flopping back down on to the white sheets.

"So you're Julian Carpenter's son," said a voice beside him, and he jumped.

For God's sake, stop being so easy to creep up on.

He turned toward the source of the voice and looked into the handsome face of a man in his forties, dressed in the same black armor as all the soldiers he had met since arriving at the base. The man was carrying a small metal case and regarding him with open curiosity.

"That's right," Jamie replied. "My name's—"

"Jamie. I know. Mine is Major Paul Turner. I'm the Level H duty officer. I understand you want to give this prisoner blood?"

"Yes, sir," said Jamie. The "sir" came naturally; something about this man made him nervous.

"Tell me why I should let you do that. Bearing in mind that she almost killed one of my colleagues last night. And tried to kill you."

"That doesn't matter now," Jamie said. "I need to know what

she knows. All that matters is my mother."

Major Turner regarded him with the merest hint of a smile on his face.

"I knew Marie," he said, and Jamie gasped. "Met her several times. She was a good woman."

"What do you mean *was*?" demanded Jamie, color rising in his face.

"Sorry. Poor choice of words," replied Turner. "I knew your father as well. We were friends. Did you know that?"

"No," said Jamie. "I didn't know that."

The two looked at each other, the space between them thick with a tension that Jamie didn't understand. Eventually Major Turner unclipped the latches on the metal case, reached inside, and withdrew two pouches of dark red blood. He tossed them lightly to Jamie, who caught them, never taking his eyes off the man.

Turner returned his gaze, then said something beneath his breath that Jamie couldn't quite make out, turned smartly on his heels, and walked rapidly back along the cellblock toward the exit.

"Prove me wrong," it sounded like he said. *"Prove me wrong."*

He turned back to the cell. Larissa was still on the bed, but now she was sitting upright on the edge of it, her eyes fixed on the plastic pouches in his hands. Jamie looked down at them and felt a sudden terrible disgust. He threw them through the barrier. They never made it to the concrete floor; Larissa moved like mercury across the cell, plucking them out of the air and dropping to her knees. She tore the top off the first one with her gleaming, pointed teeth, and Jamie turned away as she tipped it up and squeezed the contents into her mouth.

"Thank you," said a girl's voice from behind him. He turned back and looked into the cell. Larissa was standing a yard away, smiling at him. Her face was streaked with blood, but it was a human face once again, and for the second time, Jamie shoved away a thought that rose in his mind, unbidden.

She's beautiful.

She had stopped shaking and was standing with easy grace, one foot crossed behind the other, looking at him with eyes that were once more a beautiful dark brown.

"Do you feel better?" Jamie asked.

"I feel wonderful," she replied, her smile widening. "Thanks to you."

Jamie felt heat rise in his cheeks.

"Good," he replied. "Because there are some questions I need you to answer."

"About your mother?"

Ice spilled down Jamie's spine.

"What do you know about my mother?"

Larissa smiled at him, her blood-stained fangs gleaming under the fluorescent lights.

FIRST DATE

13

"Are you going to let me out?"

Larissa's question was delivered in a sweet, childish tone of voice, like a little girl asking her mother for a kitten. Jamie laughed, incredulous.

"Why would I do that?" he asked.

"Because I spared you," she replied, smiling sweetly at him, the tips of her fangs no longer visible beneath lips that were stained with blood.

"You spared me?"

"I spared you. And you saw what I got for my trouble."

Jamie looked at her. Her gray shirt was torn in places, stained almost black with blood, but she wore it with nonchalant confidence. Her faded blue jeans were also torn, and the scuffed toes of brown boots protruded from beneath the denim.

Her dark hair was long, swept carelessly away from her

forehead. Her face was—*beautiful, she's so beautiful*—a slim oval, her eyes wide, the dark brown irises sparkling under the fluorescent lighting of her cell. Her nose was small, too pointed to be classically perfect, but in keeping with the slender aspect of her features. Blood coated the bottom half of her face, garish against the milky white skin, obscuring the shape of her lips. Streaks of crimson caressed her neck.

She coughed, pointedly, and he shook his head, trying to focus on what he needed to do.

"Why did you spare me?" he asked.

She smiled again. "I didn't feel like killing you," she replied.

"That's not really sparing me, is it? That's just not feeling like it."

"Semantics."

"Not to me."

She looked away from him, inspecting her bloody fingernails, shifting her weight from one leg to the other. When she looked back at him, her smile was more dazzling than ever, and Jamie felt something flutter through his stomach.

"So you're not going to let me out?" she asked.

"I can't let you out, even if I wanted to. I don't have any authority here."

Stupid, stupid, stupid.

"Even with your famous surname? Oh, well. That's a shame."

They eyed each other through the shimmering UV field, and Jamie asked her the first of the two questions he really wanted her to answer. "Why were you trying to kill me?"

Larissa narrowed her eyes. "I wasn't trying to kill you. If I'd wanted to kill you, you'd be dead."

"So you weren't trying to kill Matt either?"

"Who's Matt?"

"The boy whose garden you landed in. The one whose throat you pulled out with your fingernails. He's in a coma upstairs."

"Good for him. Maybe he'll pull through."

"Hopefully. So why did you attack me? What did I ever do?"

"Orders."

"From who?"

"From my master."

A chill danced up Jamie's spine, and he remembered the thing in the gray coat that had let itself into the house he had shared with his mother. He remembered the pale madness on its face, the way it had leapt into the air when Frankenstein fired his huge weapon, before it disappeared into the sky like a missile.

"Alexandru," he said, softly, and Larissa flinched.

"You know his name?" she asked. Her voice had lost a touch of its easy confidence.

"I was told it," he replied.

"By the monster?"

"By Frankenstein, if that's who you mean. Who is he? Alexandru."

The smile returned to her face. "They didn't tell you?" she asked.

"Just his name," he replied.

"He's the second oldest vampire in the world," she said, with obvious relish. "His brothers are the first and third. He's more powerful than you can imagine."

"Like how powerful?"

"Like a God. Like that powerful."

"I don't believe in God."

She smiled at him again, and this time Jamie saw the white triangles below her upper lip, and he shivered.

"You should," she said. "You really should."

For several minutes neither of them spoke. Jamie lowered himself to the ground and crossed his legs, looking directly at her. After a few seconds, she mirrored him, and they sat like this for a while. They did not smile at each other, not exactly, but they did not scowl or frown either. Jamie was concentrating on projecting calm, but inside he was a maelstrom of anger and frustration.

She's not your friend, you idiot. Why are you talking to her like she is, you stupid, stupid idiot? She might have killed you twice yesterday, and she might know where your mother is. Snap out of it, for God's sake. Make her tell you what you need to know.

When he finally spoke, he did so bluntly.

"Is my mother alive?" he asked, taking care not to let his voice tremble at the thought. Larissa sat forward and brushed strands of dark hair away from her face.

"I would think so," she replied.

Calm, calm.

"You don't know?"

"She was alive when I met up with them after it was over. But then Alexandru got a tiny bit angry with me for not killing you, so I got torn to pieces and dropped out of the clouds into some family's garden. So after that, no, I don't know." She smiled at him, and her tongue darted out and licked blood off her lower lip. He tried to ignore it.

"Where would he have taken her?" he asked.

"I don't know."

"I don't believe you."

Larissa shrugged. "That's your prerogative. But it's the truth. Only Alexandru and Anderson knew where we were going next."

"Who's Anderson?"

"Alexandru's right-hand man. Simple—but vicious. Like a guard dog."

"So you don't know anything that can help me?"

"I know where they were until yesterday. And I know how to find out where they are now."

"How?"

"By asking someone nicely."

"Asking who?"

"That would be telling."

"Yes. It would. So tell me."

"I can't," she replied.

Anger surged through Jamie. "Why not?" he asked, his voice rising. He couldn't help it.

"Because then you won't come back and see me."

"This isn't a game!" Jamie exploded. "This isn't funny! My mother's life is in danger!"

Larissa's eyes flashed red, then settled back to their dark brown.

"That's right," she said, in a voice like ice. "Her life. Not my life. Just a single, anonymous human life. What difference will it really make if she lives or dies?"

"All the difference in the world to me!" Jamie bellowed. "Tell me where she is! Right now!"

She sighed and rolled her eyes. "Such bravery," she said, softly. "From behind an impenetrable barrier."

"I'd open this cell right now if I could," Jamie spit. "I'd kill you with my bare hands."

"No," Larissa said, looking at him with terrible sadness. "You wouldn't. And you know it. You're not a killer. Not like me. If you arrange for my release, I will take you to the person who can tell us where your mother is. If you won't, or can't, then I'm afraid you're on your own."

Tears rose in the corners of Jamie's eyes, and he stumbled to his feet. He walked quickly, almost running, down the corridor away from her, determined that she would not see him cry.

Her voice floated down the cellblock after him.

"Come back soon," she cried, her tone warm and friendly. "I'll be waiting."

SPLINTER CELL

By the time he stepped out of the elevator on Level 0, Jamie had more or less pulled himself together. His eyes were red, but that was as much a result of rubbing them dry as it was the tears that had spilled from them. A soldier in black armor walked down the corridor toward him, and Jamie asked if he knew where he could find Admiral Seward. The soldier looked surprised by the request, but he told him where the Head's quarters could be found. Jamie thanked him, then made his way down a gray corridor that looked like all the others.

In front of the door to Admiral Seward's quarters was another soldier, his black uniform covered in armor plates and webbing, the purple visor of his helmet lowered over his face. He saw Jamie as soon as he turned the corner.

"Identify yourself," the soldier said. He did not raise his gun, but his right index finger rested steadily on the outside of the trigger guard.

"I'm Jamie Carpenter," he replied.

The soldier distanced his finger from the trigger, reached up, and flipped open the purple visor.

My God. He's only a few years older than me.

"Say again," the guard said, a strange look on his face, a look that Jamie didn't like at all.

"I'm Jamie Carpenter," he repeated.

Disgust curdled on the guard's face. He strode down the corridor toward him, and Jamie took a step backward, his hands rising involuntarily in front of him in a placatory gesture. The soldier backed him against the wall, and leaned in until his face was inches from Jamie's own.

"Carpenter?" the guard hissed. "Is that what you said? Carpenter?"

Terrified, and incredibly aware of the heavy black gun hanging inches from his body, Jamie nodded.

"And you have the nerve to be standing here? In this building?"

Jamie didn't reply; he was too scared to speak. He stared straight into the cold, hard face of the guard, then a voice he recognized called down the corridor.

"Stand down, soldier."

The guard and Jamie looked in the direction of the voice, their heads turning in unison. Admiral Seward stood in the open door to his quarters. Behind him, looming above the director, was the enormous shape of Frankenstein.

The soldier stood up straight but did not back away.

"Sir, I must protest," he began. "This is the son of—"

"I know perfectly well who he is, Private," interrupted

Seward. "Now stand down, son. That is a direct order."

The guard stepped back into the middle of the corridor and stood to attention, facing the admiral. His face wore a look of blazing anger, but he said nothing more.

Seward stepped out into the corridor, holding the door open. "Come in, Mr. Carpenter," he said. "We have much to discuss."

Admiral Seward sat behind the long desk on one side of the room, while Jamie and Frankenstein occupied the two armchairs next to the fireplace. Jamie glanced at the huge man next to him, who favored him with a thin smile.

"Jamie Carpenter," said Seward. "I would like to welcome you to the headquarters of Department 19. Or Blacklight, as it has always been called by those who are aware of its existence."

Blacklight. I feel like I've heard that word before, a long time ago. Blacklight.

Then a strange thought arrived, unbidden, in Jamie's mind. *It feels like home.*

There was a long silence, then Admiral Seward continued. "I haven't seen you since you were a baby. You look like your father, has anyone ever told you that?"

"My mother," replied Jamie.

"Of course," said the admiral. "I'm sorry to hear what has happened to her. She was a fine woman."

"She still is," said Jamie, staring at the director of Department 19.

Seward moved a pile of papers from one side of the desk to the other, nervously. He seemed unwilling to meet Jamie's gaze, and this infuriated the teenager.

Look at me, old man. It's the least you can do. Look at me.

Frankenstein, as if able to read Jamie's thoughts, reached out and placed an enormous hand on his arm. The message was clear: Stay calm.

"Sir," Jamie said, as politely as he could manage, and when Seward looked up, he continued. "Why did the guard outside in the corridor have a go at me? I haven't done anything."

The admiral looked at him, opened his mouth, closed it, then opened it again and said, "Don't worry about that. It's not important. We need to focus on what we are going to do with you now."

"Let me look for my mother," Jamie said, instantly.

"Out of the question," Seward replied. "We have no idea where she is, or even if she . . ." he trailed off, and straightened a line of pencils that lay in the middle of his desk.

"If you won't help me," said Jamie, his voice low, "I'll do it on my own. Let me out of here, and I'll find her myself."

"I can't do that," replied Seward. "We're taking you off the grid."

"What does that mean?"

"It means that in a little over forty-eight hours there will be no record that you ever existed. It's for your own safety, and the safety of anyone you've ever been in contact with."

Jamie's head swam.

"You're *erasing* me?" he asked, incredulous. "Is that what you're saying?"

Seward nodded. "It's standard procedure in a case like this. Alexandru may try to get to you through people you have known. And his existence, and that of others like him, must remain secret. It's our top priority."

Anger flashed across Jamie's face. "My mother is my top priority," he growled. "I don't give a damn about yours."

"You see?" said Seward, looking helplessly at Frankenstein. "How am I supposed to . . ." He hesitated, then returned his gaze to Jamie. "Your father was one of my closest friends," he said. "Did you know that? No, of course you didn't. But he was. When I joined the Department he was already a legend. He was one of our finest operators. For it to end the way it did . . ."

Jamie waited for the admiral to say more, feeling the heat beneath his skin, pushing his anger as deep as he was able, but the old man appeared to have finished. The glaze had returned to his eyes, and he seemed to be lost in his memories, remembering better days. When Jamie could take the silence no longer, he tried a new approach.

"What about my mother?" he asked in a low voice. "Why didn't she tell me the truth about what Dad really did? After he died, I mean."

Frankenstein spoke in a low rumbling voice, like a landslide. "She never knew anything about Department 19. It's forbidden to tell anyone that it exists."

"So he lied to her his whole life?"

"Yes," said Frankenstein. His vast face was expressionless, but his eyes never left Jamie's.

"It's not so unusual," said Seward, and the teenager and the monster turned their attention back to the wide desk. "All the Security Services require it: MI5, SIS. And Blacklight is classified far beyond either of them."

"So how come I would have been asked to join?" Jamie asked. "Don't you have to be selected, like for the SAS?"

A flicker of admiration passed across the admiral's face, and he nodded. "You're very sharp, Jamie," he replied, "just like your father was. The document that founded Department 19 entrusted the protection of the Empire to the five founder members and their descendants, in perpetuity. It was later amended to include your family. Over the years, we've needed to expand way beyond just the members of six families, and those men and women we draw from the armed forces, the police, the Security Services, just as you suggested. But descendants of the six families listed in the original document are always asked to join, automatically. A tradition that has served us well; a descendant of the founders has headed Blacklight during every year of her history, from Professor Van Helsing's founding reign until now, when the honor has fallen to me."

Curiosity temporarily pushed concern for his mother from Jamie's mind.

"Were any of my family ever in charge?" he asked.

Admiral Seward sighed. "No," he said, and his voice, which had swelled with passion as he talked about the history of Department 19, now sounded deflated. "That was part of the problem."

"What problem?"

Admiral Seward's gaze flicked toward Frankenstein, and Jamie followed it. The huge man's jaw was clenched tight, the veins in his neck standing out, but he nodded.

"All right," the admiral said, a resigned look on his face. "I suppose it's better you hear this from me than from one of the soldiers."

"Hear what?" Jamie asked, knowing as he did so that he

didn't really want Seward to answer.

"Two years ago, the day before he died, your father betrayed us. There was an attack, here at the Loop, and a number of men were killed. The attack was carried out by Alexandru, the same vampire who took your mother last night, who ordered Larissa to kill you. Your father gave him the information that allowed it to happen."

A terrible icy cold crawled up Jamie's spine and into the back of his head.

Impossible. There's no way Dad would have done that. Impossible.

"I don't believe you," he said, his voice little more than a growl.

"I know it must be hard for you to hear this—"

"No. It's not," interrupted Jamie. "It's easy. You're wrong."

Seward looked at Frankenstein. "You see? He's too young to understand this."

"I'm not too young," said Jamie. "I just don't believe you." He looked at Frankenstein and continued. "There were things in our garden the night Dad died. I saw Larissa through our front-room window. There were vampires there just before he was shot. If he sold you out to them, why were they there?"

"There were no reports of any supernatural activity in the area around your house that night," said Frankenstein, softly. "There were—"

"I don't want to hear this!" cried Jamie, his voice suddenly loud in the small room. "I don't want to hear any more. Why are you saying this to me?" He turned to Admiral Seward. "You told me he was your friend. Why are you saying this about him?"

"I was his friend," replied Seward, but he dropped his eyes to his desk, unable to meet Jamie's furious gaze.

"I was his closest friend, Jamie," said Frankenstein. "I knew him for almost twenty years. What he did broke my heart. But it's the truth."

"But why? Why would he do it? You said he was a legend. Why would he have done it?"

"A year before he died, he led a mission into Hungary," Frankenstein replied. "He was following a lead on Alexandru. When your father's team arrived at an estate outside Budapest, Alexandru was gone, but his wife, Ilyana, was still there. Julian destroyed her and brought the team home. But he knew Alexandru would stop at nothing to have his revenge—on Julian and on you and your mother. So he made a deal; he sacrificed us so you would be safe."

Frankenstein looked down at Jamie, and the teenager was shocked to see tears pooling in the corners of the monster's eyes.

"I don't feel very safe," he replied. "I really don't. If he made a deal with Alexandru, what happened yesterday?"

Admiral Seward answered him. "I think we can assume that Alexandru is no longer honoring it."

"But in the tree. The night he died, there were—"

Seward slammed his hand down on the desktop, and everyone jumped.

"Enough!" shouted the director. "That's enough. Documents were found, documents in which Julian very eloquently—and at great length—described his hatred for the founders, for the way he believed his family, *your* family, had been treated over the years. He betrayed us, and good men died, men who deserved better. So you can see why not everyone in this base is pleased to see you and why finding your mother is not a high priority."

A thick red fog descended over Jamie's vision, and he was up and out of his chair so quickly that Frankenstein didn't have time to react. He flew across the room and lunged over the wide desk. The director shoved his chair backward, and Jamie's fingers gripped empty air where Seward's neck had been. Then he was pressed flat to the desktop as Frankenstein tackled him from behind, wrapping his arms tight against his sides. He was hauled upright and stared with blazing hatred into the beetroot face of Admiral Seward, who returned his gaze with one of utter fury.

"How dare you?" roared the director. "You little brat, how dare you?"

"My mother did nothing!" yelled Jamie. "She didn't even know who my father really was, you said so yourself. And you would just let her die? Then let me die, too, trying to help her!"

"I can't do that!" Seward shouted. "Much as I might like to at this moment."

"Why not?"

"Because, you angry little child, you are a Carpenter, and no matter how much your father may have done to blacken that name, you are still a descendant, and it is still my duty to keep you safe, even from yourself!"

Jamie slumped in Frankenstein's bear hug. His head was spinning.

It can't be true. I won't believe it. I won't. He was my dad. I can't believe it.

"What would you do?" continued Admiral Seward. "How

would you get your mother back? You have no weapons, no training, and no plan. Did the vampire tell you where they have taken her?"

Jamie shook his lowered head. Frankenstein cautiously loosened his grip on the boy, and he stood unsteadily in front of the desk.

"No," he said. "She says she doesn't know."

The admiral snorted. "Of course she knows," he replied. "She's just not telling you. Well, we can make her. Ten minutes, at the most."

"I don't think so. She doesn't know where they were going. I believe her. I don't see why she would be loyal to Alexandru after what he did to her."

"So she's useless then?"

"She says she can take us to someone who will know where they've gone."

Seward laughed. "What a surprise. Well, she can forget about that. There's not a chance in hell I'm letting her leave this base."

"We could restrict her, sir," said Frankenstein. "Put a limiter belt on her."

"Out of the question," snapped Seward. "I will not devote the resources of this organizsation to a wild-goose chase. I have not even given you permission to look for Marie yet."

"I'm going to find my mother," said Jamie, in a voice edged with steel. "With or without your help."

Admiral Seward looked at him. "You will find it very difficult to find anyone if I decide to have you confined to the base." He smiled at Jamie, a thin line with no humor in it. "For your own safety of course. One of the oldest and most powerful vampires in the world is looking for you. It wouldn't even be a lie."

"I will look after him," said Frankenstein, softly.

"You are a member of this organization, and you will do as you are ordered," said Admiral Seward, sharply.

"In which case," replied Frankenstein. "I resign."

Jamie gasped, and Seward's eyes bulged in his head. "You what?" the director asked.

"I resign. I swore an oath that I would protect the Carpenter family. If Blacklight prevents me from doing that, then I can no longer be a part of it."

Admiral Seward fell silent. He laced his fingers together and lowered his head. Jamie and Frankenstein stood in front of his desk, waiting. Eventually, he looked up at them. The anger on his face was plain to see, but when he spoke, his voice was level. Jamie suspected it was taking him a great deal of self-control.

"Very well," he said. "You, both of you, may search for Marie Carpenter, under Department 19 jurisdiction. Mr. Carpenter, you will be temporarily seconded to the Department. You are not a Blacklight operator. Do I need to say that again?"

"No," replied Jamie.

"Good. You may not prevail upon this organization for resources beyond the minimum, and the vampire does not leave this base. I will not have her destroyed, in case she decides to become more cooperative, but that is the absolute limit of my generosity on the matter. Is that clear?"

"Yes, sir."

"Men?" asked Frankenstein.

"You may requisition a driver, you may apply for air

transport as the circumstances require, and you may enlist two men at any one time. Only if they are not required for other duties, and only if they agree to assist you once in full possession of the facts. I will not order anyone to help you, for reasons I hope are obvious."

"Thank you, sir," said Jamie.

"All right," said Seward. "Victor, take Mr. Carpenter to the Playground and put him through twenty-four hours of basic training."

Jamie opened his mouth to protest, but Seward cut him off.

"Nonnegotiable. God knows it will probably do you little good, but it may help me sleep a little easier if the first vampire you come across pulls your throat out."

"Thank you, sir," said Frankenstein. He placed an arm around Jamie and turned him gently away from the desk. As they swung open the heavy metal door, Admiral Seward spoke again.

"Find her," he said. "Your family has enough blood on its hands. It doesn't need any more."

Jamie turned back to face the director. "I will, sir," he said, and the resolve in his own voice surprised him. "I will."

THE SCHOOL OF HARD KNOCKS

Jamie Carpenter stared down at the blue mat beneath him. Blood was dripping in a steady stream from his torn bottom lip and pooling on the shiny fabric, mingling with the sweat that was streaming from his head in a soft, salty rain.

"Get up."

The voice had kindness in it but absolutely no pity, so Jamie raised his head and forced himself up onto trembling legs. In front of him stood a man in a gray tracksuit who was almost as wide as he was tall, peering down at him with small eyes set into a head the size and shape of a bowling ball. Half-moons of sweat were visible under the man's arms, but he was breathing easily and looking at Jamie in the playful way a lion looks at a wounded wildebeest.

The man lunged, covering the gap between them in a fraction of a second. Jamie was expecting it, but he was tired, so tired, and all he was able to do was throw his arms up in an exhausted attempt at self-defense. The man slammed his fists down on Jamie's forearms, sending excruciating pain arrowing up Jamie's limbs, reached forward with his big, scarred hands, twisted his head sharply to the left, and lunged toward Jamie's neck.

The man stopped an inch away from the exposed skin of his throat. Jamie stared blankly up at the ceiling of the huge circular room he had spent the last eighteen hours in. He was aware of the man in the tracksuit releasing his head, stepping back and saying something, but it seemed to be happening a long way away.

A hand shot out, quick as a snake, and crashed into the side of his head. He snapped out of his daze and gripped the place he had been struck, from where a dull red pain was spreading rapidly.

"Are you listening now?" the man asked.

Jamie stared at him with a look of utter hatred and told him that he was.

"Good. Be glad you still can. Because if I were a vamp you'd be dead." The man sighed. "Take a minute, then come through and get some breakfast," he said, and walked across the room. When he reached one of the doors that lined the curved wall, he turned back to Jamie and spoke again. "You need to concentrate," he said. "Think about your mother."

Frankenstein had led him straight from Admiral Seward's quarters to one of the nondescript metal elevators. The huge man had said nothing as they had walked, but Jamie didn't think he was angry with him, not exactly. Even after Jamie had lunged for the director, he had still threatened to abandon his career with Department 19 if Seward had refused to permit a search for Jamie's mother. And he was sure that even just making the threat had been a much bigger deal than Frankenstein had shown. Seward's love of this place, his pride in its accomplishments and history, were clear for all to see, but Jamie believed that beneath the glacial gray-green surface of the monster's face, the same feelings burned just as strongly. Jamie was glad that the admiral had not called Frankenstein's bluff; he would not have wanted to be responsible for his guardian making good on his threat.

They had traveled down to Level G and through a series of corridors until they reached an office with a glass door. On it was stenciled PROFESSOR A. E. HARRIS, and Frankenstein had knocked loudly on the letters. The door had been opened by a graying man in his late forties. His hair was swept back from his temples in silver-streaked waves, and he wore a prodigious moustache, an unkempt hedge of gray and black above a dark suit, a blue shirt and a lemon-yellow tie; he looked like the slightly eccentric vice president of a brokerage house.

He nodded familiarly at Frankenstein, then looked Jamie up and down, mild disdain on his face. Jamie, whose temper was not yet wholly under control after the things Admiral Seward had said about his dad, was about to say something to the professor when Frankenstein spoke first.

"Admiral Seward—"

"Just spoke to me," interrupted Professor Harris. "He told me I am to oversee forty-eight hours of training for this boy. I told him what I'll tell you now; I fail to see what I am expected to do in such a short amount of time."

"As much as you can," Frankenstein replied sharply, and the

professor twitched, ever so slightly.

He's scared of him. Good. Let's see if you call me boy again.

Professor Harris looked as though he wanted to say something, but he cast a quick look at Frankenstein and clearly thought better of it. Instead he sighed extravagantly, pushed his office door wide open, and motioned Jamie inside.

The office was small, and looked as if it had been transplanted from a university history department. Every available surface was covered in books, journals, and handwritten notebooks. A battered wooden desk stood in one corner, disappearing under sheaves of papers and teetering skyscrapers of books. *A New History of the Salem Witch Trials* was at the summit; beneath it were volumes about the Dark Ages, the Renaissance, World War I, and dozens of other topics.

"Don't touch anything," warned Professor Harris. "Just follow me."

He walked carefully between the piles of books and papers, pushed open a door that Jamie hadn't even noticed, and beckoned to him. Jamie followed the professor's path, taking moderate care not to knock anything over, part of him hoping he would just to see the man's reaction, and stepped through the door.

Beyond it lay a small classroom. Three rows of plastic and metal chairs stood in front of a pull-down white screen and a blond-wood lectern. A projector hung from the ceiling, and a low shelf at the rear of the room was covered in neat piles of notebooks, pencils, and pens. Professor Harris walked briskly to the front of the room and took a remote control from the top of the lectern.

"Get some paper and a pen and sit down," he said, as he adjusted the screen. Jamie did as he was told while Harris walked back to the door. The professor flicked off the lights, plunging the classroom into darkness, then pointed the remote at the projector and clicked a button.

"Watch, concentrate, try to understand," said Harris, then he stepped out of the room, slamming the door behind him. The screen flickered into life, and Jamie settled into one of the chairs.

An hour later the screen returned to white, and Jamie flopped back in his seat. He could not remember ever having felt so excited; his stomach was churning as if he had just ridden a roller coaster, his arms and spine were tingling, and his heart was pounding at what felt like double its normal rate.

The first film that had played had been called *The Foundation and History of Department 19*. It looked to Jamie like every dull Channel 4 documentary his mother had made him watch on Sunday evenings when he was growing up, made even worse by the fact that the voice narrating the film was clearly that of Professor Harris. So when the professor began the film by speaking about Dracula, Jamie found his concentration wandering.

The idea of Dracula was just too ingrained in his consciousness, too deeply linked to Christopher Lee and tuxedos and red-lined capes. And so, as Professor Harris retold the familiar story, he found himself doodling in one of the notebooks. But when the story shifted back to London and Harris began to describe something called the Lyceum Incident, Jamie glanced up at the screen and froze. Flickering on the wide canvas was a sepia photo from the turn of the century, a photo of a man he recognized instantly, even though he had never seen him before. When the professor's voice confirmed that this was his great-grandfather, Henry Carpenter, he pushed the notebook aside and gave the screen his undivided attention.

For the next twenty minutes, he was rapt, and by the time the credits rolled on the film, it was abundantly clear to him why Admiral Seward spoke about Blacklight with such obvious pride. Jamie was astonished by the things that the men and women of Department 19 had done over the last hundred years, by their bravery and resourcefulness, by the horrors and dangers they had faced.

He listened, barely breathing, as Professor Harris described Quincey Harker's mission into the village of Passchendaele, had felt like cheering when the courageous captain had returned from the front in 1918 and taken over as director of the Department. A lump had risen in his throat when Stephen Holmwood, perhaps the finest Blacklight operator of them all, was taken long before his time, and he had found his chest inadvertently swelling with pride every time one of his ancestors played a role in the event that was being described, most notably a mission his grandfather John had undertaken at the very end of 1928. The description of the mission was frustratingly light on detail, as the film attempted to cover more than a century of Blacklight history in just less than half an hour, but it appeared to have been significant, and Jamie resolved to ask Frankenstein if he knew anything about it.

The second film, again narrated in Professor Harris's dry, slightly pompous tones, was called *The History and Biology of the Vampire*. Medical diagrams filled the screen as the professor theorized that the vampiric condition was passed from one person to another via saliva, usually in the act of biting, how the available evidence suggested that the condition accelerated the infected person's metabolism and heart rate to incredible levels, stimulated a dormant area of the brain the professor referred to as the V gland, which caused the incredible strength and agility that most vampires demonstrated, and how a constant supply of fresh blood was required to maintain this elevated state. The film stated in blunt terms that vampires were neither dead, nor undead, nor demonic, but a form of mutation: They were, in the truest sense of the phrase, "supernatural."

Jamie, remembering the hopeless, pitiless terror of falling, utterly lost, into Larissa's crimson eyes, remembering the way Alexandru had thundered into the night sky after Frankenstein had confronted him, was not entirely convinced; he believed he had encountered evil, had been exposed to something that was far from human.

The screen cut to white as the second film reached its end, and Jamie heard the classroom door open. Professor Harris flicked on the lights, strode to the lectern at the front of the room, and looked impatiently at Jamie.

"Any questions?" he asked. "No? Good, then let's get on. I'm sure Terry is itching to get his hands on you."

For almost an hour the professor quizzed Jamie on what he had just been shown, on the strengths and weaknesses of vampires, on the various ways in which they might be killed. He laughed when Jamie slyly suggested garlic and holy water, and struggled to keep his temper when asked in all seriousness whether a crucifix would work. With the final question answered to the professor's grudging satisfaction, Harris raised the screen, revealing a door that he pushed open. He instructed Jamie to follow the corridor and go through the door at the end.

Jamie walked into a huge circular room, lit from all sides by strips of fluorescent light. A series of long wooden benches split the room in half; the floor in front of him was covered by a large blue mat. At the other end of the room was a raised platform facing a curved screen. He was wondering what it was for when a voice spoke from behind him, and he turned.

The source of the voice was a squat, wide man, his arms and shoulders rippling with muscles beneath a gray tracksuit top. His head was closely shaven, and his face wore a calm, inquisitive expression.

"Mr. Carpenter?" he asked, and Jamie nodded. "My name is Terry. Welcome to the Playground."

He crossed the space between them so quickly that Jamie had no time to prepare himself. The instructor grabbed his head and lunged his mouth toward the teenager's neck. Jamie dangled in the man's grip, taken completely by surprise, and when the pressure was released, he fell to the floor, hard.

"You're dead," said the man. "Or worse. Get up."

And so it began.

Jamie adopted the stance that Terry showed him and tried to defend himself from the man's attacks. The instructor wove in toward him, knees bent, hands moving gently from side to side, then he struck. Without making a sound, Terry danced inside Jamie's defenses and slammed a fist into his stomach. Jamie doubled over, the air rushing out of him with a sound like a bursting balloon, and folded to the floor. Terry backed away, waited for him to catch his breath, then ordered him back to his feet. Jamie hauled himself upright, trembling, then was floored again by a clipped right cross to his chin, a punch that the instructor mercifully pulled at the last second. He spun on his heels and sank back to the floor, his eyes rolling up into his head. He heard Terry order him to get up again, and somehow managed to do so, his eyes struggling to focus, his limbs as heavy as lead. When Terry came for him the third time, he made no attempt whatsoever to resist, and the instructor placed a foot behind his legs and casually swept him over it.

And so it went, for a length of time that Jamie could not have begun to guess at. He was knocked down, hauled himself up, and was flattened again. Some time later, he was sent through one of the doors into a small dormitory and told to get some sleep. He lay down gratefully on the cool sheets of one of the beds and sank into deep, dreamless oblivion. Forty-five minutes later, Terry shook him awake, and it took the last of Jamie's strength not to cry.

Down he went, again and again.

Blood was running freely from a cut above his eyebrow, his stomach was bruised black and blue, and he was permanently winded, his lungs screaming as they tried to drag enough oxygen in through his battered, swollen mouth.

They carried on this way through the night, Terry displaying not even the slightest hint of tiredness, and by the time they reached morning, Jamie was a zombie, operating on a combination of instinct and the most basic of motor functions. When Terry told him to come through and get some breakfast, he slumped to the floor and stared at the ceiling, his chest heaving, every section of his body in pain. Only one coherent thought pulsed in his mind, over and over, the one thought that kept him going.

Mom.

EVERY BOY'S DREAM

16

Jamie slowly pushed open the door that Terry had walked through. His ribs hurt and his arms were heavy. A loud hum of noise, voices mingled in conversation, greeted him as the door opened.

It was a cafeteria. Down one wall ran a long counter from behind which a number of men and women were serving piled helpings of breakfast; yogurt, cereals, eggs, bacon, sausage, towers of brown, and white toast. The rest of the room was full of long plastic tables, around which sat groups of black-clad soldiers, doctors and scientists in white coats, and men in suits. A few of them looked up as he entered, but the stares and whispers he was expecting didn't come. Instead the people turned back to their food, and Jamie joined the end of the line.

He piled a plate as full of eggs, bacon, and toast as was physically possible and stood self-consciously by a cart of empty trays, looking for Terry. A hand shot up in the far corner of the cafeteria, and Jamie headed gratefully toward it. He slid into a plastic seat opposite the instructor and dug hungrily into his breakfast. Terry watched him silently, chewing his way steadily through a bowl of oatmeal, and after a few minutes, he spoke.

"So you're Julian Carpenter's son? That must be tough."

Jamie sighed around a piece of toast. "Looks like it," he replied.

"Awful thing your dad did," said Terry.

The teenager was tired, more tired than he had ever been in his life, and his temper was short. He slammed his cutlery down on the table, hard enough that a number of people at the surrounding tables jumped.

"So you have a problem with me as well?" he growled. "Is that what all that crap in there was about? Punishing me for what my dad did?"

Terry stared at him. "All that crap in there," he replied coolly, "was about trying to keep you alive when they let you out of here. Consider yourself lucky we only have time for the basics. What your dad did, I don't blame you for. I'll judge you on your actions, not his." The instructor took a sip from a cup of coffee. "I can't promise you everyone here will see it the same way though. Just so you know."

Jamie looked at the instructor for a long moment, then picked up his knife and fork, and carried on with his breakfast. Terry sat back silently in his chair and watched the boy eat.

Stepping back into the Playground, Jamie was unnerved to see that a dozen or so people now stood around the edges of the circular room, silently watching him. In the middle of the line was a man in his fifties, wearing a dark suit on which were pinned row after row of brightly colored medals.

"Who's that?" whispered Jamie as he and Terry walked toward the benches in the middle of the room.

"That's Major Harker," replied Terry. "I would stay away from him if I were you."

For an hour they worked through the standard Blacklight field equipment. Jamie pulled on one of the black suits, clipping the battle armor into place, and placing one of the helmets with the purple visors onto his head. He flicked the visor down and was astonished to see the room light up into a series of color patterns. The walls and floor were a pale blue that was almost white, the fluorescent lights were rectangles of bright red, and Terry was a stunning mix of every color in the spectrum, from deep red knots at his chest and head to light green at the ends of his limbs. He raised the visor and looked at the instructor.

"This is amazing," he said. "Does it respond to heat?"

Terry nodded. "The helmet has a cryo-cooled infrared detector built into it. The visor shows heat variance. Vampires show up on it like roman candles, bright red. Useful when you're in the field, believe me."

They moved on to weapons, Terry wheeling out a steel table and taking Jamie through the contents. The push of a button raised a thick concrete wall out of the floor and lowered a series of targets from the ceiling.

Under Terry's supervision, Jamie worked through the weapons on the table. He dry-fired the Glock 17 pistol that every operator carried, loaded and reloaded, then took a stance and fired three clips of bullets into the targets in front of the wall. He shouldered a Heckler & Koch MP5 and moved through the selector switch, firing single rounds, three shot bursts, and finally a thrilling, rattling magazine's worth of full auto. The targets shredded under the impact of the bullets, and a fine dust of concrete floated in the air.

Jamie's arms were numb from the recoil and the vibration of the guns, but he felt exhilarated. He had sent a good number of the rounds thudding into the heads and chests of the targets, and he had heard Terry grunt his approval. But he was most excited because the next item on the table was the metal tube he saw hanging from the belt of every Blacklight soldier, the smaller version of the huge weapon Frankenstein had fired at Alexandru.

Terry lifted the tube from the table and told Jamie to come and stand in front of him. He clipped a flat rectangular gas tank to the teenager's back and strapped a thick black belt around his waist. The tube sat in a plastic ring that hung from the right side of the belt; it felt heavy and dangerous.

"This is the T-18 pneumatic launcher," said Terry, his voice solemn. "You can call it the T-Bone—everyone else does. It's just about the most important thing you will ever own."

"Why T-Bone?" asked Jamie.

"Because it's like a stake—but bigger."

Terry grinned at him, and Jamie grinned right back.

He lifted the T-Bone out of its holster. On the underside of the tube, a thick plastic rubber grip sat snugly in his hand, and his index finger rested lightly against a metal trigger. The weapon was heavy, and he braced the barrel with his left hand, casting a glance at Terry who nodded his approval.

"There's a button on the top of the tank, behind your neck," said Terry. "Turn it on. Gently."

Jamie reached over his shoulder and flicked a metal switch. There was a brief rumble through his back and a low hissing noise. The instructor keyed a series of buttons on the remote control in his hand, and a thick spongy-looking target lowered in front of the concrete wall. It looked like a mattress with concentric circles printed on one side of it. Terry guided him gently to the opposite side of the room, directly in front of it.

"Widen your stance," he said.

Jamie shuffled his feet an extra couple of inches apart, resisting the urge to look over his shoulder at the line of spectators. He could feel their eyes on him, and he would not give them the satisfaction of a nervous glance.

"Brace it against your shoulder."

Jamie did so, feeling his arms settle into a comfortable position and the T-Bone lock into place against the ball of his shoulder.

"Aim."

He looked down the barrel, lining up the two sights along the top of the weapon with the center of the target.

"When you're ready, squeeze the trigger."

Jamie waited. For a long moment, he stood motionless, letting his heart rate settle into long, shallow beats, focusing entirely on the target in his sights. He took a deep breath, held it, and then pulled the trigger smoothly toward him.

There was a deafening noise, and the T-Bone jerked hard against his shoulder. The metal stake exploded out of the end of the tube, so fast it was only a blur, and thumped into the middle of the target with a flat bang. There was a millisecond of calm, then the thin wire that had trailed the stake across the room began to whir back into the barrel. There was a moment of resistance as the wire pulled taut, but Jamie braced himself and the stake sucked out of the target, whirring back across the room and thudding into the tube, rocking Jamie back on his heels. He let the weapon drop to his side, and breathed out heavily, looking across the room at the hole the stake had made in the target.

The hole was perfectly round and sat dead center in the middle of the target. Terry walked past him, clapping him lightly on the shoulder and leading him across the room. Behind him there was a murmur from the spectators. Up close the hole was ragged around the edges, but there was no doubt about the accuracy of the shot. It had completely obliterated the dot in the middle of the target. Terry pushed his hand into the hole and whistled softly.

"That's a hell of a shot," he said. "A hell of a shot."

Jamie flushed with pride. He wanted to explain to Terry how easy, how natural it had felt, standing there with the T-Bone against his shoulder, the only things in his mind the target in front of him and the weapon in his hands. He settled for saying "Thank you" in a low voice.

The instructor and the teenager walked back across the room and stopped next to the steel table. Still lying on the metal surface was a small cylinder that looked like a torch with a handle and a trigger, two rows of black spheres, and a large gun that looked to Jamie a lot like the grenade launchers he had used in a dozen computer games. He reached for the table, but Terry stopped him.

"You don't need to worry about them for now," he said.

Then the instructor lunged for him, and Jamie, caught

totally off guard, failed to even get his hands up in front of him. The flat of one of Terry's palms crunched into his solar plexus and drove him back to the mat, gasping for breath.

"Get up," said Terry.

Jamie defended himself better than he had during the night, deflecting some of the instructor's blows and reading his feints, but he still found himself on the ground again and again. The cut on his forehead reopened almost at once, and Terry exploited it, dancing around at the edge of Jamie's vision, where sticky blood ran into the corner of his left eye. A roundhouse kick appeared from nowhere, and he went down hard. As he pulled himself to his feet, he looked over at the spectators and saw Major Harker smiling. He redoubled his efforts and blocked punches and kicks, twisting his body out of the instructor's range and launching several counterattacks of his own, clumsy, easily telegraphed blows for the most part, but a couple of punches slipped through Terry's guard, and one landed flush on the end of the instructor's nose, snapping his head back and sending a thin trickle of blood running down his upper lip. Terry grinned, smearing crimson across his teeth, and came toward Jamie again.

Jamie stood in the shower, watching tendrils of dark red diffuse in the water that was running down the drain. Every inch of him ached, and his torso was a rapidly darkening rainbow of purple and yellow bruises. He gently washed the blood and sweat from himself, then rested his head against the hard tiles beneath the showerhead and closed his eyes.

His mind was racing. He had been trying to slow it, to shift himself into neutral; Terry had warned him as he dismissed him that he was not done yet, and he was trying to squeeze every possible second of rest out of the break. But his mind was not obeying.

How did I get here? How did I get here? How did I get here?

He was trying not to think about his mother, or his father, or the life it was now becoming clear to him that he had left behind, but he couldn't help it. The difference between the world of skipping school, avoiding bullies, the gray streets of the estate, and fights with his mom, and the world in which he now found himself was almost incomprehensible. He had no friends to speak of, not anymore, but if he had, they would not have believed him even for a minute if he had told them the events of the last three days. And he had no one to tell him that his mom was going to be OK, that he was going to find her and bring her home.

He climbed out of the shower and dressed himself, wincing in pain. When he pushed open the door that led back into the Playground, he gasped; the large circular room was now crowded with people, lining every inch of the curved walls. There were scores of soldiers in their black uniforms, doctors, scientists, and several older, extremely serious-looking men with at least as many, if not more, medals than Major Harker was wearing. Terry was standing at the end of the room next to the raised platform, his arms folded, his eyes fixed on Jamie, and Jamie walked toward him, trying not to look at anyone apart from the instructor.

He stopped next to Terry, who mouthed, "Don't be scared" at him as he approached. The instructor helped him into a set of the black armor, then presented him with a series of items; weird plastic versions of the Glock and the MP5 he had fired earlier, a plastic stake with a rubber handle, and a plastic T-Bone that was just an empty tube with a handle beneath it. At Terry's urging, he stepped up onto the platform and walked out into the middle. It was a large circle of black rubber, at least fifteen feet in diameter, which seemed to be a treadmill that moved in every direction; Jamie took a step forward, and the rubber moved underneath him, returning him to the middle of the circle. He took two quick sidesteps to the right, and the surface moved faster, keeping him again in the middle. He turned back and looked at Terry, who motioned him down toward him. Jamie crouched next to the instructor, who handed him a helmet with a matte-black visor and then spoke to him in a low voice.

"This simulation is extremely advanced," Terry said. "It's the final part of a training program that normally lasts nine months. No one has ever attempted it with as little training as you've had—in eleven years, no one has ever finished it on their first run—so no one is expecting anything. So just try not to panic and do your best, all right?"

Jamie nodded, and as he stood up and put the helmet on, he realized he wasn't scared. He wasn't even nervous; he was excited. The helmet shut out the Playground entirely; he could no longer see the platform or the screen, or hear the excited whispering of the watching crowd. Then Terry's voice spoke directly into his ear, telling him that they were starting the simulation, and a second later, he was standing in the cavernous hallway of a stately home. He looked around him, then moved his gloved hands around in front of his face, and voiced a silent "Wow" as they moved in front of his eyes in photo-real high definition, the smallest detail intact. He took a step forward, and he moved a step into the hallway. He turned in a quick circle, and the room rotated smoothly around him. Reaching down, he pulled the T-Bone from his belt and looked at it. The weapon he could see in his hands was identical to the one he had fired earlier; he could see the metal projectile nestled inside the barrel. He placed it back in its holster and drew the Glock from his hip; it also appeared to be fully functional inside the simulation, the barrel clear, the clip full.

"OK, whenever you're ready," said Terry, his voice loud in Jamie's ear.

"What am I supposed to do?" he asked.

"Just explore the house. It'll all become clear."

Jamie took a deep breath and started forward. He crossed the grand hallway quickly, heading toward a wide staircase that took up most of one end of the room. As he approached the first step, he heard a snarl above him and jerked his head up. A vampire in an elegant dinner suit had appeared at the top of the staircase and crouched, as though readying itself to leap down on him.

Jamie slid the T-Bone smoothly out of its holster, brought it to his shoulder in one fluid motion, and pulled the trigger. The stake shot out of the tube and crunched into the vampire's chest, punching a circular hole through the flesh and bone, before retracting on its pneumatic wire. Before it thudded back into the barrel, the vampire exploded in a gaudy shower of blood and gristle that pattered softly onto the thick carpet of the staircase. Jamie kept the weapon in his hand and crept toward the first stair.

Movement caught his eye, and two more vampires dropped

from the high, shadowy ceiling onto the staircase. Jamie's mind, clear and cold as ice, did the math quickly.

One stake in the T-Bone. Two vampires. No time to fire it twice.

With his left hand, he drew the MP5 from his belt, slid the selector switch to full auto, and sprayed the staircase from left to right with bullets. The rounds tore through the knees of the vampires, dropping them writhing to the ground. He replaced the submachine gun in its holster, transferred the T-Bone to his left hand, drew the stake with the rubber grip with his right, and sprinted up the stairs. The three movements took less than two seconds, and out in the Playground one of the watching soldiers drew in a sharp intake of breath. Jamie reached the vampires, who were screeching and howling on the rapidly reddening carpet, and plunged the stake into their chests, one after the other. He stepped back quickly, and when they exploded, only a light mist of blood sprayed against the body armor on his chest. He turned on the staircase, checking behind him, and saw a fourth vampire, this one a woman in a beautiful flowing ball gown, speeding silently across the hallway toward him. He dropped the stake, drew the T-Bone to his shoulder, led the running vampire by a few feet, and fired.

The stake slammed through her heart, obliterating it.

This time the explosion was smaller, almost petite, and she was gone before the metal cable was fully rewound. Jamie reached down and picked up the stake, placed it back in the loop on his belt, and made his way up the stairs.

Terry allowed himself a small smile. Standing against the wall, watching the teenager's progress on a bank of monitors that had been raised from the floor of the circular room, a soldier whistled softly through his teeth.

"He's good," he said, shaking his head admiringly.

"He's better than that," said the soldier next to him. "He's a natural."

A sharp laugh, like the bark of a dog, echoed through the room. The two soldiers turned and looked at Major Harker, who was watching one of the monitors with his fists clenched tightly by his sides.

"The hallway is child's play," said the major, his eyes never leaving the screen. "Let's see how he does in the garden."

But Jamie passed through the garden, an overgrown labyrinth of ivy and oak trees, without any trouble. He used his weapons in perfect combinations, never allowing a vampire within ten feet of him, staking and moving, disabling them from long distance with the pistol and the MP5, identifying the primary threat in each situation and dealing with it first. He moved along the narrow stone paths cautiously but not slowly, never presenting a stationary target that the vampires could surround. When the garden was clear, he kicked open the door of the crumbling stone shed that stood next to the garden's gate and went inside.

It was dark, so he pulled a thin black torch from his belt and swept it quickly across the room. Against the back wall, no more than eight feet away from him, the beam picked out the pale face of a girl, her fangs clearly visible as triangular points of white, and he drew the MP5 and fired a volley of bullets ten inches below where he had seen the face. Something screamed in the darkness, and he brought the torch back up and shone it against the rear wall. The girl's face was still where it had been, although now it hung limp against her chest, blood coursing from its mouth. He stepped forward, widened the beam, and was surprised at what he saw.

The girl was in her late teens, and she was fixed to the wall by heavy handcuffs around her wrists and ankles, in a deeply uncomfortable-looking spread eagle. The bullets from his gun had turned her chest to dark red jelly, but she was still alive, and as he approached, she raised her head and howled at him. Jamie took a half step back, despite himself, then pressed forward as the girl's head slumped back down.

He shone the torch along each of her limbs to the handcuffs. She was chained at full stretch; there was no way she could apply any leverage to the bolts and free herself. Even so, Jamie drew the stake from his belt, raised it above his shoulder, and stopped. The wounds in the girl's torso were already starting to heal, and Jamie decided he would leave her. She was no threat to him secured to the wall, and killing something that was immobilized, even a vampire, felt like murder. Instead he left the shed and walked through the wrought-iron gate that led out of the garden.

He worked his way through the rest of the grounds of the mansion, luring two vampires down a narrow alley between two garages and spearing them both with a single T-Bone shot, a kill so audacious that a spontaneous round of applause broke out in the Playground until it was silenced by a ferocious look from Major Harker. Jamie stepped lightly over the fans of blood the vampires left on the walls, made his way across a courtyard toward the estate's main driveway, and only at this late stage, did he feel the cold fingers of fear grab at him.

The driveway was wide enough, but it was flanked by two

towering rows of trees, the branches of which met high above, forming a dark green tunnel. As Jamie began to walk down it, he was reminded of the approach he and Frankenstein had made to the Loop, but when the branches began to move and rustle, he was plunged back into the night his father died, and terror threatened briefly to overcome him.

But this was a different situation. He had been powerless to do anything about the things that had crawled through the branches of the oak tree; here, that was not the case. He ripped the MP5 from its holster and sprayed the branches of the overhanging trees with bullets, fire spitting from the end of the gun's barrel. He fired it empty, reloaded, and fired it empty again. Five vampires fell from the branches, hitting the ground bone-breakingly hard, their bodies peppered with holes and spewing blood. Jamie walked methodically across the driveway, staking each vampire in turn. He walked down the driveway toward an ornate metal gate marked EXIT, and was about to grasp the handle when a searing pain tore into the left side of his neck. He looked down at his chest and saw with amazement that blood was coursing down it in rivers. Jamie turned slowly around and stared into the face of the girl from the shed. She was looking at him with blazing red eyes, full of triumph, and as he reached for his T-Bone, she blurred, then disappeared, along with the rest of the simulated world.

Suddenly, everything was dark, and Jamie fought back panic. One of his hands flew to his neck and felt only slick, sweaty skin and the bottom of the helmet he had forgotten he was wearing. He shoved it from his head and squinted under the bright lights of the Playground. He looked down and saw Terry staring up at him, his face full of open admiration. He turned and saw the crowds of watching Blacklight soldiers and staff staring up at him, and as he looked blankly at them, one soldier began to clap. The applause was taken up throughout the line of spectators, and soon it had become a deafening roar, punctuated by cheers and congratulations. Jamie allowed a smile to creep over his face, allowed it to widen when he saw Major Harker, his face as dark and ominous as a thundercloud, striding away from the crowd and toward the nearest exit.

Jamie climbed down from the platform and was nearly flattened by a thumping pat on the back from Terry. The instructor's face was full of pride, and Jamie looked away, embarrassed. Terry helped him remove the armor and the simulated weapons, then stepped in and gave him a quick rib-crushing hug that lifted him off his feet.

"Did I do all right?" Jamie asked. "I thought I failed."

"Everyone fails the first time," replied Terry. "Everyone. Most don't make it out of the house, never mind the garden. And you only failed because you showed compassion. It was misplaced, but it was admirable."

"Thanks," said Jamie, grinning widely now.

Behind him, the crowd was beginning to disperse. The men and women of Blacklight made their way around the walls of the Playground toward the various doors, many shaking their heads at what they had seen, several smiling in his direction, offering thumbs-ups and silent claps. None of them approached him, and Jamie thought he knew why; down here, Terry was the boss, not Admiral Seward, and they would not interrupt the student and the instructor.

Jamie watched them leave, then felt a sickening burst of pain in his kidneys as a fist slammed into his side. He crumpled to the ground, rolling over as he did so, and found himself looking up into Terry's smiling face.

"Get up," the instructor said.

THE BLACK SHEEP

Jamie turned off the shower and stepped out from under the water. Terry had dismissed him a little over half an hour ago, and the teenager had fled gratefully for the soothing drumming of the hot water on his stretched, beaten skin. He was covered in cuts and bruises, and his limbs felt as heavy as concrete. But despite the pain, or perhaps because of it, he felt invigorated; his mind was racing even as his body begged for rest.

Jamie dried himself with a towel, then walked out of the shower block and into the changing room. His clothes were piled on one of the benches, but there was something hanging above them, something that hadn't been there when he had run for the shower thirty minutes earlier. He looked around and saw that there were also two metal cases on the bench to his left. Stepping forward, he examined the dark object hanging above the damp ball of training clothes and then took a sharp breath.

It was a Blacklight uniform.

The jumpsuit was jet black in the fluorescent light of the changing room, the lightweight matte material reflecting nothing. Taped to the front of it was a handwritten note.

Put this on.

Jamie did so, stepping into the legs of the suit, sliding his arms down the sleeves, pulling the zip up to his throat, then fastening a flap over it. The uniform was incredibly light and cool; the material conformed to the contours of his body, and as he moved his arms and bent and dipped his shoulders, there was not a whisper of noise of fabric folding or rubbing against itself. He walked excitedly across the room and stood in front of one of the long mirrors.

He barely recognized himself. Even with his gray socks poking out beneath the legs of the suit, he looked like a different person; a young man, rather than a teenage boy. His arms hung easily at his sides, his stance casual and well-balanced. The awkward, jittery boy he had been, a boy who was always looking over his shoulder, was gone.

Good.

He turned away from the mirror and walked over to the metal cases sitting on the bench. One was the size of a laptop case, the other a lot bigger. He opened the smaller one first, and his eyes lit up when he saw its contents.

Lying in hollows of molded black foam were a Glock 17 and a Heckler & Koch MP5, the same guns he had fired out in the

Playground. He lifted the weapons out of their slots and held them in his hands. A calm chill spread down his spine, and a voice in the back of his head whispered to him.

They feel like they belong to you, don't they? If you put them on, they do. Once you put them on, you never take them off. Not really.

Jamie knew this was a pivotal moment, the point at which the door to a life that did not involve guns and vampires might shut forever, at which the course of the rest of his life hung in the balance. And there was a part of him that wanted to put the guns down, wanted to walk out of this room in his own clothes. But he knew in his heart it was not an option; if he left his mother would die, he was sure of it, and he would gladly turn the rest of his life over to violence and darkness if it meant he could save her. So he lifted two clips from the foam slots that sat at the edge of the case, loaded the guns, and slipped them into the holsters on either side of his uniform.

No going back.

He lifted the layer of foam that had held the guns out of the case, sure he knew what was going to be lying beneath it. He was right. A metal stake with a black rubber handle lay next to a gleaming T-Bone and a black gas tank. He lifted them from the foam, slid the stake into the loop on his belt, but he did not attach the T-Bone; instead he opened the second case.

Springs pushed four metal wire grids up into a set of shelves half the width of the case, in which lay the components of the Blacklight body armor. Beside the shelves sat a jet-black helmet with a purple visor. Jamie looked at it but did not reach out and touch it. The helmet seemed to radiate danger and power, and for a moment, he was scared of it.

Too late. Too late for that.

He knew that was true.

It was too late.

Jamie reached out and slid his hand over the smooth metal of the helmet, as if to prove he was not afraid of it, then closed both the cases, picked them up over the protests of his aching arms, and walked out of the changing room.

Terry was waiting for him in the Playground. The instructor looked Jamie up and down as he entered, a faint smile creeping into the corners of his mouth, then he extended his hand toward Jamie, who took it immediately. They shook.

"You did well," Terry said. "Better than anyone could have expected, even me, and I've been doing this for a long time. Keep your eyes open, be aware of your surroundings, and remember what happened in the shed. You'll be all right out there."

Jamie thanked him. He stood where he was, waiting to see if there was more to be said, but Terry nodded toward the exit and said, "Dismissed." Jamie nodded, picked up the case, turned sharply on his heels, and headed for the door. He was about to leave when Terry spoke again.

"Don't listen to what anyone says about your dad. You can't change what he did, you can't change what people think of him. But you can change what they think about you. So go and do it."

Jamie turned back to reply, but Terry was already striding away down the Playground, his back to the boy. The door marked EXIT slid open and Jamie walked through it.

Frankenstein was waiting on the other side. "There are some people who want to meet you," he said. "Come with me."

Frankenstein led Jamie up one level and through a winding series of corridors before stopping in front of a pair of double doors. Engraved on a brass plaque on the wall next to them were the words OFFICER'S MESS. Jamie read them and frowned.

"I can't go in there," he said.

"You are my guest," replied Frankenstein. "So, yes, you can." He pushed open one of the doors and stepped through it. Jamie followed him after a second or two, looking around nervously.

A chorus of greetings filled the air as the door closed behind him. The source of the noise was a cluster of armchairs arranged in a loose arc around a vast flat-screen television. Frankenstein raised a hand in greeting, and the occupants of the chairs all rose and made toward them. Jamie had a moment to cast his eyes around the room before he was surrounded.

The mess was large and almost square. Along one wall ran a beautiful wooden bar, behind which stood two immaculately dressed barmen, their faces masks of professional serenity, even as the room exploded into noise and movement around them. The middle of the room was given over to a number of low wooden tables, some round, some rectangular, around which more armchairs were gathered. Not many of the chairs were occupied, but the men and women in the ones that were had all turned around to see what the fuss was about. The tables were covered in backgammon sets, chessboards, unfinished card games, and glasses and bottles of every shape and size. At the far end of the mess was a long wooden dining table with at least twelve chairs down either side of it. In the wall beyond the table were two dark wooden doors, on which DINING 1 and DINING 2 were stenciled in flamboyant gold script. Jamie had never been in a gentlemen's club, but he had an idea that he was looking at something very close to one now. The air was thick with cigarette and pipe smoke, and the heady scents of wine, port, and brandy. Then Jamie was surrounded by noise and extended hands, and he focused on the men around him.

"Don't smother the boy," said Frankenstein, but he was smiling as he did so. "Jamie, let me introduce you to some of my colleagues. Thomas Morris."

A man in his late twenties stepped forward and offered a hand, which Jamie accepted. Morris wore a Blacklight uniform, with an ancient-looking bowie knife hanging loosely from his belt. He grinned at Jamie, then clapped him hard on the back.

"Thought you were going to do it," he said, excitedly. "I really did. No one ever has, not the first time, but I thought you were. Can't believe the girl from the shed got you."

His smile widened, and Jamie felt one of his own spread across his face. The man's excitement was contagious.

"Christian Gonzalez."

Morris stepped aside, and an extremely handsome Latino man replaced him. Jamie guessed that he was in his forties, but he could have been much younger; black hair fell casually across the dark skin of his forehead, and his eyes shone with vitality. They shook hands.

"It's a pleasure to meet you," Gonzalez said. "My father

wanted very much to be here, but he was called away to Germany. He asked me to pass on his congratulations on your performance, to which I add my own."

"Thank you," said Jamie. "Please thank your father as well."

The man said that he would and stepped aside.

Jamie's head was spinning. The warmth of these greetings—the happiness in the faces of these men—was so different from the majority of the treatment he had received since Frankenstein had rescued him, that it brought a thick lump into his throat.

"Cal Holmwood."

The name was instantly familiar to Jamie, and he looked at the man who approached him with great curiosity.

A descendant of the founders. Like me.

This member of the legendary Holmwood family was a small, neat man in his thirties. He wore clear, rimless glasses, and he had the face of an academic rather than a soldier, but when Jamie took his outstretched hand, the grip was strong.

"Mr. Carpenter," Holmwood said. His voice was the very definition of politeness, but there was warmth there as well. "It's a shame we are not being introduced five years from now, but circumstances are what they are. Welcome to Blacklight."

Jamie thanked him, and Holmwood moved aside.

"Jacob Scott," said Frankenstein.

"Let's have a look at him then," said a loud voice, shot through with a streak of Australian accent. The man it belonged to stepped out from behind Frankenstein and grinned at Jamie. Scott was in his sixties at least, his tanned skin weathered and creased, but his eyes were bright, and the grin on his face was wide and welcoming. He grasped Jamie's hand and held it tight, squeezing until the bones creaked and Jamie pulled his hand free.

"Not bad for an old boy," said Scott, cheerfully. "Eh?"

Jamie smiled, massaging his throbbing hand, and the old man playfully punched him on the upper arm. Jamie rocked slightly and forced his smile to remain where it was. Scott peered at him, then looked up at Frankenstein.

"I like him, Frankie," he said. "Got a bit of grit in him. Respects his elders too."

"You can tell him yourself, Jacob," smiled Frankenstein. "He's right there."

Scott returned his gaze to Jamie. "You need anything, boy, you just let me know. Don't be shy."

"I won't," said Jamie. "Thank you."

The man walked stiffly away toward the armchairs, and Jamie watched him go, overwhelmed. Had these men all known his father? He supposed they must have, yet they were obviously pleased to see him. Jamie suspected that the word Carpenter was working for him rather than against him for the first time since he had arrived at the Loop; he believed these men were proud to see another member of one of the founding families joining Department 19.

"Paul Turner."

Jamie started. In front of him, standing motionless and exuding the same sense of menace that he had felt last time they had met, was the major from the cellblock. Jamie gulped, hoped that it hadn't been visible, then extended his hand. For a moment, it hung there, pale even in the warm lighting of the mess, then Turner shook it briskly and smiled at Jamie.

"Nice to see you again," he said, and Frankenstein glanced at the major.

"You, too," replied Jamie.

"You did well," said Turner. "I haven't seen a debut like that in a long time. Reminded me of my own."

Jamie examined the man's face for an insult, but didn't see one. Instead the major was still smiling, and he smiled back.

"Thanks," he replied. "I still screwed it up at the end though."

"Everyone fails the first time. Better to do it in here than out there. No second chances in the field."

"I'll be careful," said Jamie.

"Do that," replied Turner, and stepped away.

Then everyone was talking at once, and Jamie was about to ask Frankenstein whether he could go to bed when suddenly the room fell silent.

The men were looking past Jamie, toward the door. He turned around, and found Major Harker standing in front of him. The old man walked deliberately up to Jamie, stared into his eyes for a long, precarious second, then slowly, ever so slowly, raised his right hand and held it out. Jamie took it, cautiously, and the major leaned in and spoke four words.

"Don't let us down."

Then, as suddenly as he had arrived, he released Jamie's hand, spun stiffly on his heels, and walked out of the mess.

Behind Jamie there was an audible exhalation of relief, and the group of men began to disperse, chatting among themselves, some heading toward the chairs in front of the TV, some making their way toward the bar. Only Frankenstein and Thomas Morris stayed where they were, and Jamie took a step toward them.

"It's been a long day," he said. "I think I might go to bed."

Frankenstein told him that was fine, but Morris looked

slightly agitated, casting glances between Jamie and the monster.

"What is it, Tom?" asked Frankenstein. His tone was impatient, and Morris flinched slightly.

"There was something I wanted to show Jamie," he replied. "It won't take long."

Frankenstein shrugged and looked at the teenager. "It's up to you, Jamie," he said.

Jamie looked at Morris's earnest, excited face. "OK," he replied. "As long as it won't take long. I really am tired."

"Great!" replied Morris. "Fifteen minutes, I promise you no longer than that. Let's go!"

He threw an arm around Jamie's shoulder and led him toward the door. Jamie cast a look over his shoulder at Frankenstein, then they were through the doors and out of the mess.

Jamie was led down gray corridors to one of the elevators. While they waited for it to arrive, Morris talked incessantly, telling Jamie facts and figures about Department 19 that he knew he had absolutely no chance of remembering. Eventually, as his companion took a microscopic pause for breath, he interjected.

"Mr. Morris," he said. "Where are we going?"

"Tom, please," replied Morris. "I'm sorry, of course I should have told you already, I'm just a little excited. I hope it doesn't show. We're going to see our ancestors."

"Our ancestors?"

"That's right."

The elevator doors opened, and Morris stepped inside. Jamie followed him, and they descended in silence, the excitement seeming to have either worn the Blacklight officer out or taken him over so completely that he could no longer speak at all.

They emerged on Level F, into a corridor as gray as all the rest, but mercifully Morris stopped at the first pair of doors on the left, tall smoked glass with the word ARCHIVES printed across them in black type.

There was a rush of air as the doors were pushed open, and Jamie's arms broke out into goose bumps as the temperature dropped appreciably. The room was long and extremely wide, and looked like a cross between a library and a meat locker. Tendrils of cold air snaked around his ankles as he walked forward between two long metal sets of shelving. Racks of studded metal and clear plastic extended away on both sides to the distant walls. There were at least forty of them, and each one was loaded with books, folders and manuscripts, hidden behind clear plastic doors that each featured a small nine-digit keypad next to them.

At the other end of the room, the end that Morris was leading him toward, a glass partition separated the climate-controlled racks from a comfortable-looking study area; blond-wood tables and padded chairs, rows of computer terminals, and a wall of black filing cabinets. Morris slid open a glass door, and as they entered this area, Jamie felt warmth creep back into his skin. In the middle of the wall at the back of this second area was a large stone arch, beneath which was a heavy-looking wooden door. There was no keypad here, just an ornate brass handle, which Morris turned and, with an audible grunt, pushed the door open.

The atmosphere inside this final room was like that of a

church. It was almost silent; the only noises that could be heard were their breathing and the clatter of their boots on the hardwood floor beneath them. The room was a narrow gallery, with dark red walls and ceiling. It was at least a hundred feet long, and the walls on both sides were covered in painted portraits. Jamie looked at the first one on his right and saw a young man looking down at him, his body at a quarter turn, his uniform identical to the one Jamie was now wearing, a small smile of what looked like pride creeping into the corners of his mouth. He looked at the gold plaque below the portrait and read what was engraved there.

GEORGE HARKER, JR.

1981–2007

"What is this place?" he whispered.

"It's the Fallen Gallery," Morris replied, also lowering his voice as he did so.

"These are all the Blacklight operators who've died?"

Morris laughed, then put a hand over his mouth for a second, as if afraid he was about to be chastised for such levity. He withdrew it and replied.

"Not quite. You would need a bigger room than this to hang a portrait of every member of Blacklight who has been lost. An awful lot bigger. No, this is for the elite of Department 19, the best and the brightest, or those who died before their time. This is where our ancestors live on, Jamie. Every member of both of our families is in this room."

Jamie was awestruck by Morris's words and by the sights around him.

He walked slowly forward, looking at the men and women who stared down at him from the red walls, reading the plaques, seeing the same names over and over again as he made his way down the gallery: Benjamin Seward, Stephen Holmwood, Albert Harker, David Harker, Quincey Morris II, Peter Seward, Arthur Holmwood II, John Carpenter, David Morris, Albert Holmwood.

Three-quarters of the way down the gallery, a single bust of a man's head stood atop a marble pillar in the middle of the wooden floor. It was carved from dark gray stone and stared down the gallery toward the door, as if challenging anyone who might enter. The face was rugged, had probably been handsome in its youth, and wore a thick mustache above a thin mouth and angular jaw. Jamie stopped to read the inscription on the marble, and Morris, who had been walking quietly six feet behind the teenager, did likewise.

QUINCEY HARKER

ALL THAT WE ARE, WE OWE TO HIM

1894–1982

"Jonathan Harker's son," breathed Jamie, and Morris nodded.

Jamie walked around the bust, and continued through the gallery. The portraits were getting older now, the paint fading in some, cracked in others, the frames duller and more beaten down by the years. He reached the end of the gallery and looked up at the six paintings that faced him from the wall, their eyes full of pride, the men who had sat for the portraits all long dead.

ABRAHAM VAN HELSING
1827–1904

JONATHAN HARKER
1861–1917

QUINCEY MORRIS
1860–1891

JOHN SEWARD
1861–1924

HON. ARTHUR HOLMWOOD
1858–1940

HENRY CARPENTER
1870–1922

On a low shelf beneath the portraits, a number of small items had been placed; a stethoscope, a small gold pin with an ornate family crest engraved on it, a battered cowboy hat, and a kukri knife in a leather scabbard.

"My God," breathed Jamie. "They were real. I don't think I realized until now. They really lived."

"Lived—and died," said Morris. "Some before their time."

He turned to Jamie, tears in the corners of his eyes, and when he spoke again, his voice was charged with passion. "You and I are very similar," he said, his eyes bright. "Descendants of founders. Members of the six great families of Blacklight.

But we're both black sheep. Both weighed down by the actions of our ancestors."

"How so?" asked Jamie.

"The trouble your father has caused for you must be obvious by now. Mine began over a century ago."

"Why?"

Morris looked at him for a long moment, as if weighing a decision in his mind.

"I'm not going to tell you it all now," he said, eventually. "It's late, and it's a tale that deserves telling well. But it boils down to one essential truth; you or I could save the world a hundred times over, but we'll never be a Harker, a Holmwood, a Seward, or a Van Helsing. The inner circle will always be closed to our families."

"What do you mean?" asked Jamie.

"Follow me," Morris replied, gesturing down the gallery. They walked most of the way back to the arched doorway and then stopped in front of a portrait. Jamie looked at the plaque below the frame.

DANIEL MORRIS
1953–2004

"Is that? . . ."

"My father? Yes. He was the director of Department 19."

Jamie frowned. "No Carpenter has ever been director. Admiral Seward told me."

"My father barely was," replied Morris. "He was re-moved from office almost before he got started. Too aggressive, too reckless, or so they told him. Yet Quincey

Harker, whose bust stands in the middle of this gallery, who was named after my great-great-grandfather, turned the Department into an army and was deified for doing so."

Fire had risen briefly in Tom's eyes as he spoke, but now it faded again. His hand fluttered to the bowie knife on his belt and touched the handle.

"Was that his?" asked Jamie softly, gesturing toward the weapon.

Morris looked down at his belt, then back at Jamie, surprise on his face.

He didn't know he was touching it.

"It was my great-great-grandfather's," Morris replied. "It's the knife that he pierced Dracula's heart with, the last thing he ever did. It was given to my grandfather when he joined Blacklight. He passed it on to my father, and it was left to me when he died."

Jamie was speechless.

The knife that killed Dracula. My God.

He forced himself to speak. "What happened to him?" he asked.

Morris laughed bitterly. "My father? I think he just had the wrong name. Our name. Not one of the four that matter around here."

"Why are you telling me this, Tom?"

Morris sighed. "Because I like you, Jamie. And I want you to understand what you've got yourself into. You can believe in this place too much, buy into it too completely. It'll take everything from you that you're prepared to give—and more. But you'll only ever be the descendant of a valet and the son of a traitor, just like I'll always be the son of the only director to be removed from office. I'm telling you this because you need to stay focused on the two things that matter: finding your mother and bringing her home."

IN THE MOUTH OF MADNESS

"Wake up."

The voice was low and smooth, but there was kindness in it, as well as the hint of an eastern European accent, and Marie Carpenter rose slowly from unconsciousness.

She opened her eyes a fraction, and screamed.

In front of her was a face she had seen before, a thin, pale face topped by dark waves of shoulder-length hair, with sharp features and sunken eye sockets, from which blazed two dreadful crimson orbs. The thing's mouth was twisted into a wide snarl, and two razor-sharp white fangs were pointing directly at her.

It screamed right back at her, its foul breath blowing the hair away from her face. She screamed again, and it matched her, an awful high-pitched howl that hurt her ears. Then the thing smiled at her, and terror overwhelmed her. She had time to see that they were in a long, low room, with stone walls and a concrete floor, had time to think it looked like a cellar or a basement, then her vision turned white, and she slipped back into darkness.

Some time later, she drifted awake into a world of pain.

The cuts on her face and arms were lines of throbbing heat, and her stomach churned with nausea. She opened her eyes and looked around her.

She was lying on a cold concrete floor in a low, bare room. The walls were exposed brick, and the only concessions to domesticity in the room were a pair of armchairs facing an incongruously ornate fireplace. The chairs were empty; she was alone.

At the far end of the room, a rough wooden staircase rose to a trapdoor in the low ceiling. She knew with absolute certainty that the trapdoor would be locked from above, knew that there was no point in even checking, but she got to her feet nonetheless. She could not just lie on the ground and wait for something to happen; she was a proactive woman, as she had been an energetic and stubborn girl, and it was not in her nature. Not while her son was out there; not while Jamie needed her. She would not even entertain the idea that he could be dead. But he might be hurt, he was almost certainly scared and confused and lost, and the thought broke her heart. She took a deep breath and started across the room, treading as softly as she was able on the balls of her feet.

The bottom step was barely six feet away when she heard a bolt slide back and saw the trapdoor at the top of the staircase elevator open. Marie stared in horror as a pair of scuffed black boots descended onto the top step and realized that she was caught. She watched helplessly, frozen to the spot with fear, as the hemline of a gray coat flapped gently through the trapdoor, a pale white hand gently slid down the rough banister, and the man who had dragged her from her home dropped into view. There was a gentle smile on his face, a smile that widened into a grin of pure joy when he stepped off the bottom stair, looked around the room, and saw Marie standing in front of him.

He stepped forward so quickly she didn't even see him move, and gripped a handful of her hair. She screamed in pain, grabbing his wrist with both her hands, but it was immovable. The thing in the gray coat hauled her back across the room without any apparent effort, and she howled as her heels tore across the concrete. She twisted and thrashed in the thing's grip, she yelled and screamed for it to let her go, but it was useless; she slid relentlessly across the floor, away from the staircase.

The man deposited her in a heap in the corner. She shoved herself back against the cold exposed brick of the wall, looked up at the smiling face peering down at her, and burst into tears. It made her furious with herself, but she couldn't help it. The helplessness of her situation sank into her; she thought of her son, her brave, fragile son, somewhere out in the darkness without her.

Eventually, the thing squatted down next to her and spoke in a gentle, friendly voice. "I'd stop that if I were you," he said. "You're exciting my friend."

She forced herself to stop sobbing and looked over the man's shoulder. Standing behind him, ten feet away for her, was a second man, this one a huge, hulking creature, lumpy and misshapen like a sack of coal. He had a tiny round head atop his enormous shoulders, and the wide, open face of a child. His red eyes were staring at her, unblinking, and his child's face wore an expression of open lust. Marie shuddered and wiped her eyes and nose on the backs of her hands.

"That's better," said the thing in the gray coat, then flopped down against the wall next to her as though they were old friends, drawing his knees up and wrapping his long arms around them.

"We haven't been introduced," it said, favoring her with a dazzling smile of sharp white teeth. "My name is Alexandru Rusmanov. And you, of course, are Marie Carpenter, wife of Julian and mother of Jamie. Now we know each other. Now we can talk as friends."

At the mention of her son's name, Marie's eyes, which had been half-lidded by tears and downcast with fear, flew open. "Where's my son?" she asked. "What have you done with him?"

"Your son," replied Alexandru, with obvious relish, "your precious son. Tell me, does he look like his father?"

Marie didn't respond. She was disorientated by the smooth, velvety voice issuing from the hateful thing's mouth.

Alexandru's eyes flared red, and his arm unwrapped from his knees with the speed of a striking cobra. The long, pale hand at the end of it grabbed her by the forehead, pulled her forward, then sent her crashing back into the wall. Her head hit the bricks with a meaty thump, and she saw stars. She felt something warm and wet slide down the back of her head and onto her neck, and she stared blankly at Alexandru, lost in a nightmare she could not wake up from.

"I asked you a question!" he roared, and slammed her head

into the wall a second time. "Does he look like his father?"

The back of her head collided with the wall a third time and panic overcame her terror.

He's going to beat my brains out against this wall unless I answer him. Oh God, what is this creature?

"Yes, yes, he does! Please stop hurting me!" she shrieked.

Alexandru let go of her forehead, his eyes reverting back to their usual dark green, and he sighed, as though mildly inconvenienced.

"I know he does," he said. "I should have killed him myself. It might have been satisfying."

A great vacuum opened in the middle of Marie's chest, a hole where her heart should be.

"He's dead?"

Alexandru stared at her with great solemnity, then burst into peals of giddy, childlike laughter. Above them, the second man broke into a slow, plodding laugh of his own, a sound like a braying donkey.

"No, he's alive," Alexandru replied. "He shouldn't be, but he is. But that's what you get for delegating. It's like I've always said—if you want someone murdered right, do it yourself. Haven't I always said that, Anderson?"

He looked up, pointedly. Hesitation flashed across the small round face of the man standing above them, who was still laughing his metronomic laugh. He stopped, and appeared to disappear deep into thought.

"Yes," he eventually said, carefully.

"Yes what?"

"Yes, that's what you always say," replied Anderson, a small smile of satisfaction playing across the childish features.

"What do I always say?"

This time the look on the swollen figure's face was pure panic. "I don't know," he said.

Alexandru gave Marie an embarrassed roll of his eyes, the kind of look one gives when their child has misbehaved, or their pet has soiled a carpet. Then he was on his feet, so quickly that Marie gasped out loud. He crossed the distance between himself and Anderson in a couple of milliseconds, and then his fingers were dancing across the terrified, infantile face. Marie squeezed her eyes shut as Anderson let out a scream, a high-pitched howl that vibrated through her teeth, a scream that was suddenly cut off by a wet tearing noise that caused her stomach to lurch.

With a thud, Alexandru flopped back down next to her, and she opened her eyes. She didn't want to, but she wanted to provoke this monstrous creature even less. He was smiling at her, then he flicked his left hand and something red flew away into the shadows.

His tongue, she thought. *He pulled out his tongue. My God.*

She looked up at Anderson. Blood was pouring out of the man's mouth, and running freely down the front of the black jacket he was wearing. His eyes were wide, and his whole body was visibly trembling, in pain, or fear, or both, but he was standing where he had been before the attack, looking straight ahead, at the wall above her.

He didn't run. Or try to defend himself. He didn't do anything.

For a moment, she felt pity for this pathetic, downtrodden creature, but then the image of his expression as he watched her cry appeared in her head, and she shoved it quickly away.

"Don't worry," said Alexandru. "It'll grow back."

Marie's gut twisted with disgust.

"What do you want from me?" she snarled, and Alexandru jerked his head back, an expression of admiration on his pale, feminine face. "What do you want with my family?"

The vampire threw back his head and laughed, the wavering howl of a wolf, deafeningly loud in the basement.

"You don't know, do you?" he said. "You really don't. Oh, how wonderful. I have so much to tell you."

He sprang to his feet, dusted himself down, and looked at her with immense enjoyment. "There are many things that require my attention," he said, gravely. "But I will make sure that you and I speak again soon. I will be genuinely looking forward to it."

Then he turned and strode away from her. He barked at Anderson to follow him as he passed the huge man, who tore his gaze away from Marie with obvious difficulty, and did as his master ordered. They clattered up the wooden staircase and threw open the trapdoor, letting in a brief square of tantalisingly warm light, then the wooden hatch slammed shut, she heard the blot slide into place, and she was alone in the basement again.

I'm sorry, Jamie, she thought, as she slipped back into unconsciousness.

I love you.

I'm sorry.

BLOOD AND LETTERS

Jamie didn't think he had ever felt so low. Every inch of him was in pain, from his throat to his feet, and his head was heavy with tiredness and sickly remorse. His mother was still missing, and it was up to him to find her and rescue her. He had demanded to look for her, had threatened to defy Admiral Seward and anyone else who tried to stop him; now he was free to begin the search, and he was terrified.

What if I can't do this? What if I never see her again? What happens to me?

Jamie limped into the shower block at the end of the dormitory, washed himself as carefully as he was able, gasping when his fingers touched a particularly sensitive area of bruising, toweled himself dry, then dressed in the Blacklight uniform he had been given by the instructor. It no longer looked as enticing as it had the previous day; in the cool of the morning, it looked violent and ugly, and he shuddered slightly as he slid it over his body.

There was a knock on the door at the other end of the dormitory. Jamie didn't answer, and after a couple of seconds, the door swung open. Frankenstein stepped through, ducking his head slightly, and walked toward Jamie. He stopped in front of him, the thick thatch of black hair atop his huge misshapen head brushing lightly against the whitewashed ceiling, and looked down at him.

"You need to see something," said Frankenstein. "Are you ready?"

Jamie shrugged.

"Since you can't be bothered to answer me, I'll assume you are," continued the monster, and he strode back across the dormitory. Jamie watched him until he was almost at the door, then let out a long petulant sigh, stood up, and followed him.

Frankenstein walked quickly through the corridors, and Jamie struggled to keep up, realizing how much the huge man usually slowed down to accommodate him. He followed him into an elevator, down two levels, along a wide central corridor, and into the infirmary where he had spent the night he arrived at the Loop. His stomach clenched as he stepped through the swinging doors, the memory of Larissa's attack leaping into his mind, the feeling of terrible powerlessness as her fingers cut his air supply, the warm patter of her blood on his face.

In the middle of the infirmary was a metal gurney and clustered around it were three men he recognized: Paul Turner, Thomas Morris, and the doctor who had treated him. They looked around as Frankenstein and Jamie approached and moved aside so they could join them. A small metal table covered in medical implements stood next to the gurney, on which lay a large shape covered in a white sheet.

Mom?

His legs were suddenly made of lead. He couldn't move them, couldn't even begin to try. Acid rolled into his stomach, and he thought he was going to be sick.

"It's not your mother," said Frankenstein in a low voice. Jamie looked up at him, his face sick with fear, and Frankenstein repeated himself. "It's not your mother. I promise."

The bile in his throat retreated, and he forced his legs back to life, one after the other, and made it to the gurney.

If it's not Mom, then who is it? There's someone under there.

His skin broke out in goose bumps as Morris clapped him on the back and said, "Good morning."

"Morning," he replied, his voice shaking.

Morris flashed an inquiring look at Frankenstein, who shook his head. Paul Turner watched the exchange, his gray eyes cold and calm.

"Shall we get on with it?" he suggested.

"We should," agreed the doctor. "Jamie, this might be upsetting for you to see, but Colonel Frankenstein believes it is necessary. Do you need a glass of water?"

He shook his head.

"Very well," said the doctor, and pulled back the sheet.

Jamie looked down at the figure on the gurney, then turned away and retched. His hands went to his knees and he swayed, his head lowered, his eyes squeezed shut, saliva flooding his mouth. Above and behind him he heard the doctor apologize, and Morris let out a low whistle. Frankenstein and Turner didn't appear to respond at all.

On the gurney was the naked body of a man in his mid-forties. His skin was pale, his eyes were closed, and he might have looked peaceful were it not for the terrible damage that had been inflicted to his chest and stomach.

The man's torso looked like it had been through an abattoir; it was covered in dark, glistening blood, rivers of which had run down his abdomen to his groin and over his ribcage toward his back. Cut into the flesh were five words.

TELL

THE BOY

TO

COME

Jamie felt a hand placed cautiously on his shoulder and shrugged it off.

"I'm all right," he croaked. "Just give me a minute, OK?"

He had only seen the corpse for a split second before he turned away, but the sheer violence of the man's injuries had taken his breath away.

How could you do that to someone? How could you take a knife and do something like that to another human being? My God, what am I up against here?

Steadying himself, he took a deep breath and stood upright. His head swam for a moment, but it passed, and he turned slowly back to the gurney. It was worse than he had first thought, much worse, but with the element of surprise gone, he was able to step forward and take his place next to his colleagues. He was gratified to see that both Morris and the doctor were taking ragged, shallow breaths, their eyes wide, their faces tinged with gray. Frankenstein and Paul Turner looked perfectly composed, and Jamie wondered at the things the two men must have seen.

"This is a good thing," Frankenstein said, eventually. "Very good."

Jamie flinched. "How can this possibly be good?"

Frankenstein looked at him, and some of the usual kindness had returned to the monster's eyes. "Because it means Alexandru wants you," he replied, carefully. "It shows that you're important to him."

"And why is that good?"

Paul Turner answered in his smooth, empty voice. "Because he won't hurt your mother until he gets what he wants. He knows she's the only thing that can make you come to him, and he knows that if he kills her, we'll make sure he never gets within fifty miles of you."

"How do we know she isn't dead already?"

The doctor stepped forward with something in his hand. "Because this was in his mouth," he said softly, and held a crumpled ball of paper out to Jamie. He took it from the doctor's fingers, unfolded it, took one look at it, and then his world seemed to fall out from beneath him.

He couldn't breathe. He couldn't think. All he could do was stare.

In his hand was a bloody Polaroid photograph of his mother, clearly terrified but equally clearly alive, lying on a concrete floor with a brick wall behind her, staring up at the camera with a look of hopeless misery on her face.

Fury exploded through him, burning everything in its path, flooding him to the tips of his fingertips. He grabbed the metal table, let loose a primal scream of pure anger, and flung it against the wall with all his strength.

Morris yelled and covered his eyes as wickedly sharp instruments flew in every direction. The doctor leapt away from the impact, turning his back and dropping into a crouch with his hands laced behind his head. Frankenstein lunged forward and wrapped the bellowing teenager up, pinning his arms to his sides and lifting him off the ground. Paul Turner didn't even flinch; he just watched, the ghost of a smile playing across his lips as the table hit the wall.

"Where is she?" Jamie yelled, the cords in his neck straining as he struggled in the monster's grip. "Where is my mother?"

"We don't know," Frankenstein answered, his mouth close to the boy's ear. "We don't know, I'm sorry. Calm down, Jamie, we'll find her. I promise we'll find her."

His voice had lowered to a whisper and he was rocking Jamie from side to side, holding him like an infant. Gently, he set him down on the tiled floor and slowly released his grip. Jamie pushed himself free immediately and spun around to face Frankenstein, his face red, his eyes blazing. But there was no second explosion.

"The lab is analyzing a copy of the photo now," said Morris. "But the preliminary results are that there are no clues to a location. I'm sorry."

"She's my mother," said Jamie, his eyes fixed on Frankenstein. "Do you understand?"

"No," said Frankenstein, simply. "I don't. I can't. I never had one. But there was a man who I have come to think of as my father. So I can imagine."

"I don't know if you can," said Jamie. He regretted it

instantly, although the giant man showed no offense; he just looked down at Jamie with his huge, asymmetrical gray eyes, his face expressionless.

Morris broke the tension.

"Where was he found?" he asked, nodding toward the man on the gurney.

"On the road," answered Turner. "About three miles from the gate, hung in one of the trees. A patrol found him at 0600. Says he wasn't there at 0550."

A shiver ran through Jamie.

Three miles. There were vampires three miles from here, maybe the ones who did that to his chest. While I was asleep. He pushed the thought aside. "We need to find my mother," he said, as calmly as he was able. "This won't happen to anyone else if we do."

He looked up at Frankenstein. "Where do we start?"

THE CITY THAT NEVER SLEEPS, PART 1

New York, USA
December 30, 1928

John Carpenter stood on the prow of the *RMS Majestic* as the great liner steamed slowly into Upper New York Bay. It was just after nine o'clock and dark; a pale covering of cloud hung low in the night sky, from which heavy flakes of snow were steadily falling.

To the starboard, the high walls of Fort Hamilton were lined with soldiers, who clapped and cheered and waved their caps in the air as the *Majestic* passed. She was the largest ship in the world, more than nine football fields long with eight stories of blazing light above her enormous hull, and her arrival was an occasion, even in a city as used to the spectacular as New York.

Carpenter pulled his overcoat tight around his shoulders and lit one of the Turkish cigarettes his wife had packed for him, curling his hand over it to protect it from the snow. It was settling on the damp deck and in his hair, and it was getting cold, the night air crisp and still, punctuated by snatches of music and laughter from below decks. Dinner was being served in the ballroom below the funnels, but Carpenter wasn't hungry. He was impatient to leave the ship, and he would eat once he had done so.

He had wanted for nothing on the crossing from Southampton; his state room was almost obscenely opulent, the stewards and staff as attentive as anyone could ask for, the days brimming with agreeable diversions and pastimes. Despite this, he had spent most of his time in the small library at the rear of the quarterdeck, studying the man he was pursuing.

He's not a man. Not anymore. Remember that.

Carpenter breathed perfumed smoke into the night. High above him, the ship's horn sounded, deafeningly loud in the still winter air. He looked to the northeast, where the towering lights of Manhattan shone a watery yellow through the falling snow. Checking the watch Olivia had given him before he departed, he saw that the *Majestic* was going to arrive more than two hours early.

A good start.

He pitched the half-smoked cigarette over the rail and walked back along the promenade deck, quickening his pace as the skyscrapers of New York loomed behind him.

Carpenter was first to leave the ship, having packed his trunk long before the *Majestic* sighted land. He walked down the gangplank, which had been covered in a rapidly dampening red carpet, nodded curtly to the tuxedo-clad steward, and stepped onto American soil.

The heels of his boots crunched the settling snow as he walked along Pier 59 toward the White Star terminal. His passport and papers safely stamped, he pushed through the murmuring throng of waiting relatives and photographers and out onto the West Side Highway.

"John Carpenter?"

The voice hailed him from the corner of West Thirty-Fourth Street. Through the falling snow, he could make out the shape of a man in a dark overcoat and hat, shifting his weight rapidly from one foot to the other, perhaps impatiently, perhaps in an attempt to stave off the rapidly plummeting temperature.

"Who inquires?" Carpenter replied. As he spoke, he slipped his right hand into his coat pocket and gripped the wooden stake he had placed there before he disembarked.

The man who stepped from the shadows was a short, rotund fellow in his mid-forties, wearing a brown tweed suit and a red-and-white polka-dot bow tie. Above this garish neckwear was an alcohol-rouged face that beamed with benevolence, eyes twinkling beneath wildly bushy eyebrows, flanking a squat tomato nose that, in turn, nestled above an impressively wide moustache. The man wore a dark brown trilby, and he smiled broadly as Carpenter approached.

"It is you," he said, sounding relieved. "John Carpenter. You look exactly like your photograph."

"I say again," Carpenter replied, his voice flat and even, "who inquires?"

"Why, I'm Willis, Mr. Carpenter. Bertrand Willis. I was given to believe you were expecting me, so I must confess I find myself—"

"Credentials," said Carpenter. "Slowly," he added, as the

man moved his hands to his pockets.

Willis drew a leather billfold from the inside pocket of his suit jacket and held it out to Carpenter, who lifted it carefully from the man's fingers and flipped it open.

Inside were three documents; the first was a passport in the name of Bertrand Willis of Saddle River, New Jersey; the second was a telegram containing Carpenter's travel itinerary and likeness; the third was a memorandum from the attorney general of the State of New York, authorizing Willis to take whatever measures he deemed appropriate to assist a Mr. John Carpenter of London, England, in the resolution of his duties, without fear of legal recourse.

He closed the wallet and passed it back to Willis.

"Everything appears to be in order," he said. "Apologies for my caution, but one can never . . ."

Willis waved a hand that suggested that if any offense had been taken, it was already forgotten. "I understand perfectly, sir," he said. "Especially in such trying times. In fact, I would venture that such caution is what led the founders to entrust you with such a valuable task as your first solo assignment, no?"

Carpenter looked at Willis for signs of mockery, saw none, and smiled instead.

There is steel in this fellow, beneath the smiles and good cheer.

He stepped forward and extended his hand. "John Carpenter," he said. "At your service."

"Bertrand Willis," the man repeated, accepting the hand. "At yours. It is very fine to meet you, John, very fine indeed. Are you hungry? Shall we repair for supper?"

Carpenter's stomach rumbled. "That sounds like an

excellent idea," he replied.

Willis beamed from ear to ear. "I know a fine place, not five blocks from here. The chef does a pork belly that will simply melt in your mouth. This way!"

Willis turned and headed off along West Thirty-Fourth Street at a pace that was surprising for a fellow of his stature.

The two men walked briskly across the junctions of Eleventh and Tenth Avenues. Willis talked incessantly, about everything and nothing: the snow, the architecture, the baseball results, the relentless rise of the Wall Street banks. Carpenter's head spun as he attempted to keep up with the endlessly diverging topics of conversation, but he found the man engaging company; his enthusiasm and boundless good cheer were infectious.

At the corner of Eighth Avenue, Willis made a right turn, and halfway down the block between Thirty-Fourth and Thirty-Third, he ducked under a red-and-white awning stenciled with the words CHELSEA BAR AND GRILL.

The room beyond the door was dark, lit only by tall red candles that were placed on the clustered tables, with the heady scents of garlic and rosemary filling the air. Nearly all the tables were occupied; well-heeled men and women, dressed for the theater, sat alongside dockworkers in battered oilskins fresh from the yards and jazz girls in feather boas and veils, fueling themselves for the late-night exertions of the city's dance halls.

Willis weaved past the waiters to a small table at the rear of the room. A disarmingly handsome olive-skinned waiter appeared next to their table, flicking a long curl of black hair away from his forehead, and Willis ordered tea and bread. They sat in companionable silence until the young man returned with a basket of focaccia, a large teapot, and two china cups, and asked if they were ready to order. Carpenter ordered the pork belly, noting a small nod of approval from Willis as he did so, with roast potatoes and green beans. Willis ordered the same, then lifted the teapot and poured dark red wine into the cups.

"I'm sorry that we cannot drink from glasses like civilized men," said Willis. "Prohibition has reduced us to this. However, the quality of the wine should not be impaired by the vessel."

Carpenter raised his cup, took a long sip, then told Willis that he would like to hear everything that he knew about the man he had pursued across the Atlantic. The American took a long pull from his own cup, settled himself comfortably into his chair, and began to talk.

"Jeremiah Haslett. Born 1871 in Marlborough, England, to a schoolteacher and a civil servant. Educated at Charterhouse and Cambridge. Made his fortune during the war, selling munitions to the Kaiser." He took another sip. "Invested in property after the war, in London and New York. Unmarried, with no children. Ran with a fast London set and started to pursue somewhat—let's call them *unusual*—interests. Satanism, black magic, demonology. Although I'm given to understand this doesn't make him particularly unique in postwar Britain, at least as far as the upper classes are concerned?"

"Far from it," replied Carpenter.

"Indeed. He spent time with Aleister Crowley at the Abbey of Thelema in Sicily, and stayed in Italy after Crowley and the rest of his followers were expelled in 1923. I assume his connections to the Fascists spared him the indignity that befell his companions. Then around the same time, Haslett became obsessed with the legend of Dracula, and in 1925 he made a pilgrimage to the ruins of the castle in Transylvania. When he returned to London, he was no longer human."

"We don't know exactly what happened to him in the East," said Carpenter. "I have come to believe that his conversion was arranged in advance—and paid for—although who carried it out is unknown."

"That would seem to fit," agreed Willis. "I'm sure his money is capable of turning heads in any circle. It certainly allowed him to return to London and indulge his appetites without sanction."

"So it appears."

"His town house in Knightsbridge became notorious. Apparently, God-fearing men and women would cross the road to avoid it. There were stories of terrible gatherings, of torture and sacrifice, of rituals in the basement and garden. Then six months ago, the daughter of a prominent member of parliament was found running naked and bloody through the woods near his country estate, on the morning after the winter solstice. Haslett fled the country the following day, as the authorities finally opened their eyes to the monster in their midst. Once abroad he spent time in Paris and Bucharest, then arrived here in New York two weeks ago. He has taken rooms at the Waldorf-Astoria, on Fifth Avenue."

Willis refilled his cup and took a deep slug of the crimson liquid.

"Did I miss anything?" he asked, smiling at Carpenter.

"No."

"Good," said Willis. "I should have been disappointed to have failed the test."

Carpenter studied the man's round face for insult, but again saw nothing.

"Have you seen him? In the flesh, so to speak?"

"Mr. Carpenter, it should not surprise you to know that I have followed him every night since he arrived. And before you ask, no, he has done nothing that could be classed as suspicious. He has taken dinner with a number of ladies, he has gone dancing on several occasions, and he has spent a great deal of time in his rooms." Haslett paused as the waiter reappeared, placing two plates on the table.

The pork belly glistened in dark gravy, nestled between crisp golden mountains of roast potatoes.

"Please," Willis said, motioning to the plates.

Carpenter dug into his food as Willis continued to talk.

"I saw a note," he said. "I have an arrangement with one of the chambermaids at Haslett's hotel, and it was handed to me yesterday. It was from someone who signed themselves only with a V, and was apparently accompanied by invitations to a New Year's Eve event. I thought that it would perhaps provide our best opportunity to apprehend Haslett—a private gathering with many people around, where his defenses may be lowered. There were no details on the note however—location, time, and such."

Carpenter swallowed a sliver of meat that was every bit as good as Willis had promised. "Can we not just follow him on the night in question?"

"We can, and I would certainly suggest that we do. However, if the event is invitation only, we may have difficulty in gaining entrance. I had a journalist friend look into the notable New Year's Eve balls, and he found none hosted by anyone whose name began with V. Which means that uninvited guests are unlikely to be welcome."

John considered this as he and Willis finished their food. He had spent long hours on the crossing considering how best to gain access to Haslett, and he believed the American was right; a social situation was the most likely place to find him with his guard down. And after all, Carpenter's orders would not take more than a moment to carry out, especially if he were able to surprise his quarry.

The waiter reappeared beside their table and inquired whether they wanted coffee. Willis told him they didn't.

"I hope that's all right," he said. "I thought we might take a nightcap elsewhere, if that's agreeable? Your hotel is on the way, so you can leave your luggage at the reception."

Carpenter told him that sounded fine.

His luggage safely deposited with the receptionist at the hotel on West Twenty-Third Street, Carpenter followed Willis at a brisk pace down Eighth Avenue and onto Hudson Street. They turned left on Grove Street, then right onto Bedford, and came to a halt in front of a plain brown door. Willis rapped on it and stood back. After several moments, a panel slid aside, and a pair of eyes peered out at the two men.

"Good evening, Jack," said Willis.

"Bert," replied a voice from behind the door. There was a series of creaks and thuds as a number of locks were withdrawn, then the door opened. Smoke, laughter, and jazz music spilled out onto the cold street, and Willis led Carpenter inside.

A girl in a cocktail dress and a feather boa took their coats and led them through a pair of double wooden doors into a large room crammed with tables and booths. A man in a tuxedo was hammering out a jazz standard on a piano in one corner, and waitresses glided between the tables, carrying trays of drinks. Smoke hung thickly in the air, and the room was alive with conversation and laughter.

"What is this place?" asked Carpenter.

"It's called Chumley's," replied Willis. "It's a little oasis in the dry desert of temperance. What'll you have?"

"I'm happy to be led by you," Carpenter replied.

The American led them to the long bar that ran the length of one wall of the speakeasy, where they squeezed into a narrow space, Willis's elbow striking a neat man in a scarf and coat waiting to be served. The man turned at once and regarded Willis with red, alcohol-soaked eyes.

"I'm terribly sorry, sir," he said, his upper-class accent mildly slurred. "Allow me to furnish you and your companion with a libation."

"No need, sir, but thank you," replied Willis.

"Sadly, I must insist," said the man. "Will you tell me your preference, or must I guess?"

"Guesswork won't be necessary. Two scotches on the rocks will be most appreciated."

"Educated palates," exclaimed the man. "How delightful."

The barman, a thick red-faced fellow wearing a white apron and drying his hands on a black towel, appeared in front of the man.

"Two scotches on the rocks, a gin and bitters and a vodka tonic, if you would be so kind."

As the barman set about preparing the drinks, the man turned to Carpenter and Willis. He was perhaps in his mid-thirties, with his hair neatly parted on the right-hand side and a dark red tie beneath the white scarf he had draped around his shoulders.

"Scott Fitzgerald," he said, offering a hand toward them. "A pleasure to make your acquaintance."

The two men took his hand in turn and introduced themselves. The barman delivered their drinks to the wooden counter, and Fitzgerald withdrew a small sheaf of bills from a tan leather wallet. As he did so, he looked over at his new acquaintances. "Would you care to join me and my companion at our table?" he asked, depositing a handful of notes on the bar.

After a moment's hesitation, in which a glance that was mostly bemusement passed between them, Carpenter and Willis agreed and followed Fitzgerald toward the corner of the tavern.

The three men weaved through the thick fog of smoke and men and women in various states of inebriation. In the corner of the speakeasy was a small round table, at which was sat a huge figure. The man was awkwardly perched on a three-legged wooden stool, and such was his size that the seat looked as though it had been procured from a doll's house. He looked up as the three men approached and grunted.

"Took your time."

"Sorry, Henry," replied Fitzgerald. "The line was quite significant. I hope you haven't become too thirsty in my absence?"

"Thirsty enough."

Fitzgerald laughed, as though this was the most delicious witticism he had ever heard, and turned to Carpenter and Willis, who were standing by the table, looking down at the huge man.

"Do sit down, gentlemen," Fitzgerald said. "John Carpenter, Bertrand Willis, this is Henry Victor."

"Pleased to make your acquaintance, Mr. Victor," said Willis, extending a hand. It hung pregnantly above the wooden table for a long second, until the giant slowly reached out and took it. Carpenter followed suit, then sat back, his mind racing.

Can it be him? The file is so vague, but the description is supposedly reliable.

A chill raced up his spine.

Henry Victor was dressed in dark clothes, a heavy overcoat with high collars on top of a thick wool jumper with a turtle neck that reached to his jaw and a flat leather cap that cast a deep shadow over his face. As Carpenter looked closely, he saw two bulges in the thick material at the sides of the man's neck.

"Something wrong?" asked Victor.

"My apologies," said Carpenter, as smoothly as he was able. "The crossing was tiring, and I must confess I was in a world of my own there for a moment."

Henry Victor took a long look at Carpenter, then turned his attention to Fitzgerald, who had enthusiastically engaged Willis in liquor-fuelled conversation.

". . . It went without saying that the reviews would be poor," he was saying, his face a swollen picture of drunken unhappiness. "If you write a novel about the superficialities of the rich and shallow, then you do not expect them to reward your efforts in the literary supplements. I must confess, I thought some of the notices unnecessarily unkind, but such is the literary game. I met with my editor today and found the conversation largely fruitless, as he wants what I do not have to offer him: a new novel."

He looked around at his companions, suddenly aware that he had become the center of attention. He beamed an unconvincing smile. "But the trip from Wilmington, long though it was, has also brought me to this table and into the company of you gentlemen. So it cannot be considered anything other than a success. And besides . . ." Fitzgerald reached out and drained his gin and bitters. He lit a highly perfumed cigarette and inhaled deeply. "She laughs at nothing," he said in a small voice. "My wife. She sits surrounded by giant furniture and laughs at nothing." He looked up. His eyes were red and tears stood in their corners. "But let's have no more talk of such gloomy matters," he said. "Tell us of London, Mr. Carpenter. I am almost ashamed to say I have never been there."

Carpenter did as he was asked, and the conversation resumed. After a time, Willis fought his way to the long bar and refilled their drinks, and the remainder of the night passed agreeably.

THE WRONG SIDE OF THE TRACKS

21

From the outside, the vehicle was unassuming; a black Ford Transit identical to the thousands that rolled along Britain's roads every day. But this particular van was different. The engine that was propelling it at a steady ninety miles an hour had been taken from a prototype Piranha VI, a top-secret Swiss armored personnel carrier that weighed almost twenty tons, and the reactive armor that lay inconspicuously beneath the metal paneling of the van's body belonged on a Challenger 2 battle tank. The van had been lowered, its chassis strengthened, its suspension stiffened and fitted with computer-controlled roll bars; a titanium safety cage had been threaded through the vehicle; a thick explosive-proof ceramic plate had been attached to the underside; the wheels had been equipped with run-flat tires; and the glass windows had been replaced by bulletproof thermoplastic.

Inside, the driver was in control of a vast array of

communication and geographic positioning technology, encrypted satellite relays that could place the vehicle to within a couple of millimeters anywhere on the planet. The back of the van was both a mobile briefing room and a tactical command center. Swung down on a bracket across the rear doors was a high-definition touch screen, wirelessly connected to the Blacklight mainframe. Two lines of padded seats faced each other; above each an alcove was set into the wall that would hold a Blacklight helmet securely, and on the floor in front was a black slot from which a smaller touch screen could be raised at the flick of a switch. A narrow wall locker at the right of each seat was divided into compartments that would hold the standard-issue Blacklight weapons. All but two of them were standing empty.

Jamie and Frankenstein sat facing each other in the two seats nearest the rear doors. They had made their way to the Blacklight motor pool after leaving the infirmary, collecting their driver, a young private named Hollis, from the open mess on the way. Thomas Morris had asked to come with them, asked more than once, with increasing desperation in his voice, but Frankenstein had told him it would not be necessary. Morris eventually accepted this decision, sulkily, and had promised Jamie he would wait in the lab for the final results of the photo analysis, in case the technicians found something that could help. Jamie didn't believe they would but thanked him anyway.

Private Hollis had seemed slightly in awe of Frankenstein and had immediately, enthusiastically agreed to drive them. The young operator was visually cut off from them by a dividing wall behind the van's cab, but his nervous, excited voice came through an intercom every few minutes, updating their progress.

Frankenstein said something, and Jamie tore himself away from thoughts of his mother and looked at the huge man. "Sorry?" he said.

"I asked if you were ready for this. I think I just got my answer."

Jamie felt a warm blush rise in his cheeks. "I am ready," he said. "I am. Tell me what I need to know."

Frankenstein gave him a long look, then began to talk.

"Most vampires in the world are not like Alexandru, or Dracula, or any of the others you may have seen on TV. The idea of an elegant, mysterious race of civilized monsters makes for good drama, but it's not the reality. The reality is that there is a vampire society out there that mirrors human society, with every type of lifestyle represented. There really are vampires who live in stately homes and wear suits and dinner jackets and drink from crystal glasses, just as there are humans who live that way. But there are also vampires who live in cul de sacs and on council estates, who live in family units and avoid attention at all cost, who live the same anonymous lives that millions of humans do. There are vampires who live on the edges of society, on the borders, the same dark places that many humans find themselves. There are vampires who have sworn never to take a human life, or taste human blood, just as there are vampires who will feed on nothing else, who will kill and torture for the sheer pleasure of it. Some have been driven mad by the hunger, others hate themselves for what the hunger compels them to do but aren't strong enough to stop themselves."

On the screen, the English countryside flew past, but Jamie didn't notice; he was focused on the man in front of him.

"The point I'm trying to make to you is that every vampire is different, and every single one needs to be approached with extreme caution. Do you understand me?"

"I think so," replied Jamie.

"Make sure you do. The vast majority of them will kill you without a second thought. They are still monsters, no matter how harmless or pathetic they might appear."

"You hate them, don't you?" said Jamie quietly. "The vampires."

"Most of them," Frankenstein replied. "They are an aberration, a violent, dangerous aberration. They don't belong in the world."

Jamie eyes widened, involuntarily, and the monster saw them. He leaned nearer to Jamie's face. "Do you want to say something to me?" he asked.

Jamie shook his head, and Frankenstein sat back in his seat. "I know what you were thinking," he said. "But I was created with free will. The things I've done—some of them terrible, unforgivable things—I did because I chose to. Vampires have a compulsion to feed that makes violence and suffering inevitable, and most of them are not strong enough to resist it. Many of them don't even try."

Jamie said nothing. He looked at the molded locker standing beside Frankenstein's seat and saw that it contained the weapons he had been forbidden to touch in the Playground, the small black cylinder and the black metal spheres.

"What are those things?" he asked, pointing. "Terry wouldn't tell me."

Frankenstein followed his finger. "Why wouldn't he tell you?"

"He said I didn't need to know."

The monster laughed, shortly. "He's right. You don't."

Jamie stared at Frankenstein, without expression, until the monster rolled his eyes and lifted the cylinder and one of the spheres out of their housings.

"All right then, if you must know absolutely everything. This is an ultraviolet beam gun. It fires a concentrated beam of UV light, like a powerful torch. It will ignite any vampire skin it touches. This is a UV grenade. It fires a high-powered UV beam in every direction at once, for five seconds. Happy now?"

"Why wouldn't Terry just tell me that?"

"Because he probably thought it was more important to teach you about the things that might actually keep you alive. Neither of these weapons is lethal, all they do is buy you time. Stick to your guns and your T-Bone, and try to remember what he did teach you, instead of focusing on what he didn't. Now, no more questions. We'll be there soon."

"Where are we actually going?" asked Jamie.

"We're going to see a vampire called the Chemist. He produces something called Bliss," replied Frankenstein.

"Bliss?"

"A drug for vampires—very addictive, very powerful. The Chemist has a supply network that covers the entire country. If he hasn't heard anything about Alexandru, it's because there has been nothing to hear."

"So you know where he lives?" asked Jamie.

"That's right."

"So why don't you stop him?"

Frankenstein looked at him.

"Because Bliss is useful," he replied. "It keeps a large section of the vampire population docile. When they're worrying about where their next fix is coming from, they're not thinking about hurting people. But of course, from an official standpoint, Blacklight is unaware of where Bliss comes from, or who makes it. Do you understand?"

"It sounds like you're saying you look the other way," said Jamie.

"Good. Now be quiet."

An hour later, the van drew to a halt outside a farmhouse on the edge of an expanse of moorland. The rear doors slid open, and the smell of wood smoke drifted in from the clear night sky.

Jamie stepped down from the vehicle. They were on a narrow country road, lined on one side by a row of trees, on the other by the open expanse of Dartmoor. The farmhouse, a rambling two-story building made of pale stone, sat behind a rock wall, the forest quickly thickening into a solid mass of black beyond it.

Frankenstein was waiting for him at the side of the road. When Jamie reached him, he pushed open a wooden gate. They walked up the neat path together, a pair of mismatched silhouettes in the dark. Before they reached the red front door to the farmhouse, it opened, and a tall man, with the gray hair and lined face of late middle age, smiled at them.

"Please," he said, "follow the path to the back garden. I'll meet you there."

Jamie smiled a bemused smile as they made their way around to the garden: The warm, friendly welcome was not what he would have expected from either a vampire or a manufacturer of illegal drugs—and certainly not from a creature that was both. The scent of fallen blossom filled the air as they stepped carefully along a narrow path that ran along the side of house, and when they emerged into a wide, beautiful night garden, the gray-haired vampire was waiting for them beneath an apple tree.

A wooden path ran down the center of the garden to a sturdy-looking gate at the far end, splitting halfway along to pass round the wide trunk of the tree, then joining back together. Two wide semicircles of lawn stood on either side of the path, and the rest of the garden was filled with a series of overwhelmingly beautiful flowerbeds.

Great sprays of angel's trumpets and moonflowers bloomed in the darkness, as the scents of lavenders and hyacinths mingled in the air. Creeping clusters of Jacob's ladder and Adam's needle shone in the pale moonlight, the white lines standing out brightly, the gray leaves shimmering silver. Jamie looked around, overcome, as Frankenstein watched him, a smile threatening to emerge on his lips.

"Do you like the garden?" asked the Chemist, as Frankenstein steered the gawking teenager toward the tree.

"It's . . . magnificent," Jamie said. "I've never seen anything like it."

"That's because you sleep through the most beautiful part of the day," said the Chemist, a smile of pride on his face. "The darkness hides flaws and sins; the moon illuminates only the delicate and the elegant."

"Who said that?" asked Jamie.

"I did," the Chemist said with a grin. "Colonel Frankenstein, always a pleasure. Follow me, please, we'll talk in the lab."

The vampire floated down the garden, and the two men followed. They walked through the gate, which the Chemist opened using a small touchpad concealed behind a curtain of ivy, and stepped onto a concrete path as smooth as a bowling lane. Orange lamps hung in the lower branches of trees, illuminating their destination.

At the end of the path was a long metal building, with flat ends and a rounded canopy that emerged from the ground on both sides. It looked as though someone had buried an incredibly long tin can in the ground. Electric light shone through narrow windows cut into the walls, bathing the surrounding trees in pale white. The vampire turned a handle on a door at the front of the building, held it open, and the two visitors entered the lab.

It was much louder than Jamie had been expecting. The laboratories he was used to were quiet places, with oddly shaped glass beakers bubbling above Bunsen burners.

This room was more like a small factory.

Large extractor fans ran the length of the building on both sides, humming loudly. The Chemist passed pairs of plastic goggles to Jamie and Frankenstein, and led them to the end of the room.

Next to a large, vibrating extraction unit stood a bench covered in rectangular blocks of yellow-white powder.

"What's that?" Jamie asked, inquisitiveness getting the better of him.

The Chemist appeared at his shoulder. "That's recrystallized heroin base," the vampire replied. "It's what my shipments arrive as. I treat them with—"

"He doesn't need to know the details," said Frankenstein from behind them, his voice tinged with warning.

Jamie shot him a look full of wounded independence. "I want to know," he said.

Frankenstein shrugged, turned away, and examined the wall of the lab, where a map of the UK had been hung. It was covered in yellow circles, some of them overlapping each other, that covered almost every inch of the country.

The Chemist smiled at Jamie. "It's heartening to see a boy who wants to learn about the world," he said, then guided Jamie to a second bench on which sat six shallow plastic bowls. Two were half full of a clear liquid; the other four contained a thick white solution.

"This is sulfuric acid," he continued, motioning at the clear liquid. "The heroin is dissolved into it, then we add methyl alcohol, then ether, and that leaves us with this." He gestured to the tanks with the white liquid in them. "The mixture stands until it begins to crystallize, then I add more ether, as well as . . . the final ingredient . . . and then leave it until it becomes solid. What you're left with is Bliss, about seventy-five percent pure."

"The final ingredient?" asked Jamie.

The vampire smiled and guided Jamie to a third bench, which held seven large plastic containers filled with a dark red liquid. "This is what makes Bliss into Bliss," said the Chemist, with obvious pride.

"Blood?" said Jamie.

"Of course," smiled the Chemist. "Human blood, mixed into the heroin before it solidifies. Seven different types, for seven different drugs. A, AB, B, and O: the basics, the cheap stuff. O negative, A1 negative, and OB positive for my premium customers."

"What's so special about them?" asked Jamie.

"They're rare," said Frankenstein, his voice booming in the enclosed space. "They're not so easy to acquire."

"Easier than you might imagine," said the vampire, smiling oddly at the monster, before returning his gaze to Jamie. "The last batch of the day needs to go into the acid," he said. "Would you care to do the honors?"

Jamie could feel the disapproving heat of Frankenstein's gaze on the back of his neck and knew the monster was watching him, waiting to see what he would do next.

"Cool," he said. "Let's do it."

The vampire supervised as Jamie lit the burners under the two bowls of acid, then carefully spooned the yellow-white powder into them, being careful not to drop it from a height that might cause the liquid to splash, putting each spoonful into a new bowl so none was overfilled. Once the bowls were bubbling away gently, the question that had been nagging at Jamie for several minutes burst to the surface.

"Where do you get all this stuff? If it's just you out here on your own, where does it all come from?"

The Chemist smiled at him. "An excellent question, young man," he replied. "The heroin base comes from Myanmar, and the blood comes from the National Health Service of this fine country of ours. As to how it all arrives here, unmolested, so to speak, I suggest you ask you partner."

Jamie turned to Frankenstein, who flinched, ever so slightly. "Not now," he said, sharply. "There are more important things to discuss."

The Chemist raised his hands, deferentially. "By all means," he said. "I so enjoyed seeing someone take an interest in my work that I forgot to even ask you why you were here. I presume you are looking for information of some kind?"

Frankenstein nodded. "Alexandru," he replied. "We need to know where he is. I thought you might have heard something, from one of your dealers, or your customers." He almost spit the final word, his face drawn into a grimace of distaste, and the Chemist's mouth narrowed.

"I'm afraid I haven't heard anything," the Chemist replied, and it felt to Jamie as though the temperature in the lab had lowered by several degrees.

On the bench next to Jamie, one of the bowls of sulfuric acid began to bubble violently. The Chemist moved toward it, and Frankenstein's hand slipped to the handle of the T-Bone on his belt. The vampire stopped and stared at him.

"I don't believe you," said the monster, evenly. "I wonder why that is?"

"Perhaps it's because of your suspicious nature," replied the Chemist. "Or perhaps it's because you're not stupid, and you know full well that anyone who knows anything about the three brothers is going to lie to you."

He took another step toward Jamie, and Frankenstein pulled the T-Bone from its holster, letting the weapon hang by his side. "I'd appreciate it if you stayed still," he said, his voice rumbling.

Jamie looked back and forth between the monster and the

vampire. Then the bowl of sulfuric acid convulsed in a huge bubble, spraying boiling liquid into the air of the lab, and sizzling onto the exposed skin of Jamie's neck and jaw.

He screamed in pain, and both Frankenstein and the Chemist ran to him. Jamie clamped his gloved hand over the wounds, and the fabric began to smoke. The pain was beyond anything he had ever felt before; it was as though a million tiny knives were cutting into his flesh. He screamed again, as his skin began to melt.

The Chemist flew to the corner of the lab, opened a small metal fridge, and returned to Jamie's side with a bottle of purified water. Frankenstein had picked him up and carried him out of reach of the bowls and was holding him still with one hand while trying to pry Jamie's hand away from his wounds so he could inspect the damage. The Chemist's pale hand shot between them, gripping Jamie's wrist and pulling his hand clear of the burns. Jamie's head was thrown back, the cords in his neck standing out like ropes, his teeth clenched together in a grimace of agony.

The vampire flicked the top off the bottle and tipped water over the burns, irrigating the wounds. They gushed smoke as the liquid flushed them clean, and Jamie bellowed. Then the wounds, a bright red patch of at least ten individual burns, stretching from the collar of his uniform to just below his right ear, began to bleed.

The Chemist's eyes turned red.

Frankenstein saw it happen and fumbled for the T-Bone, which had fallen to the laboratory floor. But before he could reach it, the vampire threw himself backward into the air, away from the fallen teenager and the crouching monster, and hovered by the door that led back to the garden.

"Bring him into the house once the bleeding has stopped," he said, his voice guttural and full of lust. "There is a first-aid kit above the fridge."

And with that he was gone, opening the door and swooping through it and into the night.

Frankenstein left Jamie, who was staring at the ceiling, his face white, his eyes wide, and pulled a green box down from a shelf above the fridge. He made his way back across the lab, turning off the gas rings beneath the bowls of acid as he did so, and crouched down next to the teenager, who looked at him with eyes that were starting to regain their focus.

"Are you all right?" asked Frankenstein.

Jamie was shocked to hear the monster's voice so full of worry. "Fine," he croaked in reply. "I've . . . I've never felt anything like it. I couldn't breathe, it hurt so much."

"Does it still hurt?"

Jamie nodded. "But not like it did," he said. "It feels like a normal burn now."

Frankenstein wiped the blood from the boy's skin, then pulled a gauze pad from the first-aid kit and gently placed it over the burns. Jamie winced but did not protest. The monster unrolled a strip of white bandage, laid it over the gauze, and fixed it in place with surgical tape. Jamie pushed himself up into a sitting position as Frankenstein closed the kit, took it back across the lab, and replaced it on the shelf it had come from. When he turned back, Jamie was looking at him.

"He was going to turn the gas off," the teenager said, slowly. "He knew what was going to happen."

"I couldn't have known that," replied Frankenstein, walking

back to the boy.

"I'm not blaming you," said Jamie, his face full of pain. "I was just saying."

"All right," said Frankenstein.

"Help me up?" asked the teenager, and the huge man reached down a misshapen hand. Jamie gripped it and pulled himself to his feet, wincing as he did so.

He hesitantly touched the bandage on his neck, then looked up at Frankenstein. "I want you to let me do the talking," he said. "In the house. OK?"

The monster looked down at him. "Fine," he said, after a pause. "Do whatever you think is best."

The back door was open when they reached it, and they stepped through into a warm, ramshackle kitchen. A kettle was boiling on a huge Aga, and the Chemist was sitting at a wooden table in the middle of the room, looking uneasily at the two men.

"I'm sorry," he said. "I haven't tasted human blood in more than a decade, but I can't control my reaction to it."

"It's all right," said Jamie. He looked down at an empty chair opposite the vampire's, and the Chemist quickly invited him to sit down, then told Frankenstein to do the same.

"I'll stand," rumbled the monster.

"As you wish," replied the Chemist.

Jamie carefully took his seat and looked at the Chemist, who was eyeing the teenager nervously. "I know you were going to turn the gas off," said Jamie, and the vampire breathed out a long sigh of relief.

"I was," he said, eagerly. "I could see it was going to boil over, but then your partner told me to stay still, and I didn't want to provoke the situation, and . . ." He trailed off.

Frankenstein rolled his eyes but said nothing.

"I know," said Jamie. The Chemist seemed to him to be genuinely shaken up by what had happened in the lab, and he pressed forward. "How did you end up here, doing this work?" he asked.

The vampire looked at him and then laughed. "You want to hear how I was reduced to this, is that it?" he replied. "I'm sorry to disappoint you, Mr. Carpenter, but it really isn't much of a story. I was a biochemist for a pharmaceutical firm, I was turned, and I carried on with my job. I just make a different product now."

Jamie's face fell. He had thought that taking an interest in the Chemist might open him up a little and make him more willing to talk about Alexandru.

"However," continued the Chemist, casting a pointed look in Frankenstein's direction. "It is refreshing to be asked a polite question. Especially when said question isn't posed behind the point of stake. You have manners, young man. Your mother must be proud."

Jamie saw his opening, and leapt for it. "I think she is, yes," he replied. "I can't ask her though, because Alexandru has her. That's why we're looking for him."

The Chemist looked at the teenager with naked sympathy. "I'm sorry to hear that," said the vampire. "Truly I am. You must be going through hell."

Jamie nodded.

"But I don't know where he is," said the Chemist. "You can choose to believe me, or not to. I can't make that decision for you. But I will tell you one thing that I do know, which is less than prudent on my part."

"Anything," said Jamie. "Anything that might help."

"He is still in the country. How I know that, I will not tell you. But he is still here. Which makes it extremely likely your mother is, too."

Frankenstein snorted. "That's it?" the monster asked. "He's still in the country? So that means we only have to search about 160,000 square miles to find him."

The Chemist stared at Frankenstein, his face twisted with open loathing. "You leave my house knowing more than you did when you arrived," he said. "I doubt that will be the case anywhere else you choose to conduct your search. The brothers have eyes and ears everywhere, and no one else will be willing to tell you anything."

Jamie stood up from the table, clenching his teeth so he wouldn't cry out as the muscles below his burns moved. He shot Frankenstein a look of pure anger, warning him to say nothing more. "Thank you for your help," he said to the Chemist, who nodded politely. "We'll leave you to your work."

They followed the path back to the road in silence. Private Hollis was leaning against the door of the van.

"Where to next?" he asked, as they stopped beside the vehicle.

Jamie kicked the metal side of the van as hard as he could, the clang echoing through the silent night air. He kicked it again, and again, then rounded on Frankenstein, his face red with rage.

"You're so stupid!" he yelled, spittle flying from his lips. "He obviously knew more than he told us, much more! And he would have told me if you hadn't been such a dick to him! Why did you do that? Don't you want to find my mom? What the hell are you doing here?"

Frankenstein was too shocked to reply. The boy's anger was steaming off him in waves.

"Stupid! Stupid! Stupid!" Jamie bellowed, punctuating each word with a thunderous kick to the van's side. Then as quickly as it had come, the anger was gone, and he slumped to his knees on the bumpy road.

There was silence.

Tentatively, the driver reached toward him, but Jamie shoved his hand away.

"Don't touch me!" he yelled, rising back to his feet. "Just leave me alone!"

He ran, stumbling into the forest, leaving the two men by the van.

Jamie sat at the base of a wide oak tree. He could see the van's headlights through the black maze of the forest and could hear the driver's and the monster's low voices.

Let them look for me. They won't find me in here. Let them think they've lost me.

His head rushed with frustration, anger, and guilt. The chemist would have told him more about Alexandru, he was sure of it, if the stupid monster hadn't opened his big, stupid mouth. They could be on their way to rescue her right now, could be hot on her heels, but instead they were no further along the path that led to her than they had been before they arrived. It had never even occurred to him that Alexandru would have taken his mother out of the country, not after the message that had been carved into the man's chest and left for him to find, so that information was useless—Frankenstein had been right about that. But it was what was going to come next, what he was *sure* the Chemist was going to go on to say that might have helped them. Because Jamie was convinced one thing the vampire had said was true: No one else would be willing to risk Alexandru's wrath to help them.

Then he realized that was wrong. There was one person.

He pushed himself up from the ground, ignoring the howl of pain from his injured neck and crashed blindly back through the trees toward the headlights. He emerged to find the driver and Frankenstein leaning against the van. The look on the monster's face suggested he had not been overly concerned.

"Got that out of your system, did you?" asked Frankenstein, his voice containing a hint of laughter, and Jamie scowled at him.

"Take me back to the Loop," he said. "I want to talk to her again."

Frankenstein's mouth narrowed.

"Talk to whom?" he asked.

"You know who," said Jamie, and smiled.

THE CITY THAT NEVER SLEEPS, PART II

New York, USA
December 31, 1928

John Carpenter was roused from sleep by a loud knocking on the door of his room. He awoke instantly, his hand reaching for the wooden stake he had placed on his bedside table. He slipped from beneath his bedding and padded softly across the carpeted floor to the door.

"Who is it?" he asked.

"Henry Victor," a low voice boomed from the other side of the wooden panels.

Carpenter put the hand containing the stake behind his back and opened the door six inches, the length of the sturdy chain he had left fastened. Henry Victor stood in the hallway, his vast frame reaching to within an inch or two of the ceiling. He looked down at Carpenter with a look of anger on his face.

"You know who I am," he said. It was a statement rather than a question.

"I believe I do," answered Carpenter.

"Who did you tell?"

"I told nobody."

"Your partner. Willis. Not even him?"

"Not even him."

Victor reached into the pocket of his overcoat and withdrew a thick white envelope.

"Then perhaps you will be able to explain this to me," he said, handing the envelope to Carpenter.

Carpenter took it, noting as he did so the enormous size of the man's hand, and slipped the chain off its latch. He opened the door wide.

"Come in," he said, walking over to the small desk beneath his window and placing the envelope on the wooden top. Victor did so, shutting the door behind him. Carpenter pulled three sheets of stiff card from the envelope. The first two were invitations, gold-edged rectangles of board with three lines of ornate printing on them.

CENTRAL PARK WEST AND WEST EIGHTY-FIFTH STREET
DECEMBER 31, 1928
11 P.M.

He set these aside and looked at the third card. It was a note, handwritten in beautiful copperplate script.

Dear Mr. Frankenstein:
Please do me the honor of gracing me with your presence this evening. And do bring your new British friend—he has taken

a room at the Hotel Chelsea on West Twenty-Third Street, in case you need to find him. Masks are mandatory, black tie is preferred.

Yours,

V

"I haven't used that name since I arrived in America," Frankenstein's voice said from above Carpenter's head. "More than a year ago."

"Do you know anyone whose name starts with a V?" Carpenter asked.

"No."

V for Valentin, thought Carpenter and a shiver ran up his spine. *The youngest of the three brothers turned by Dracula himself. Could it be him?*

"What about Haslett? Jeremiah Haslett?" he asked.

"No."

"Are you sure?"

Frankenstein took a deep breath that sounded very much to Carpenter like an attempt at keeping his temper. "Mr. Carpenter, I keep myself to myself. Especially where vampires are concerned."

Carpenter snapped his head round. "What did you say?"

Frankenstein laughed. "I'm sorry. Did you assume that you and your friends were the only ones who knew?" He laughed again, this time at the look of surprise on John's face. "I am a creature of the night, Mr. Carpenter, for reasons that should be obvious to you. I have traveled widely and seen and heard a great many things. I knew the sorry tale of Dracula before the Irishman wrote it down. I heard the rumors about

Crowley and others like him. I have heard about your little organization. I have even heard of you, Mr. Carpenter. Or your father, at least."

Carpenter stared at the monster, stunned. "Then you know why I am here," he said, trying to regain his composure.

"I presume you are here to make sure that Mr. Haslett does not return to England's green and pleasant land?"

Carpenter nodded.

"And I would imagine that this evening's gathering strikes you as your best opportunity to carry out your task?"

"I am certainly hoping so. Will you let me have both invitations?"

Frankenstein laughed and shook his head. "I'm afraid not, Mr. Carpenter. I want to ask this V certain questions of my own. But I will accompany you, and if the opportunity to assist you in your mission presents itself, then I will certainly consider doing so. How does that sound?"

"That sounds fine." Carpenter hesitated for a moment. "One of the oldest vampires in the world is believed to live in this city. His name is Valentin Rusmanov. Have you heard of him?"

"The youngest of the three brothers."

"Indeed. I wonder if he could be the V who sent the invitations."

"If that turns out to be the case," said Frankenstein, "we will be well-advised to be extremely careful."

Carpenter showered and dressed quickly after Frankenstein had left but was still ten minutes late meeting Willis in the diner on Broadway that the American had selected as they said their farewells the previous evening. He slid into a red leather booth opposite Willis, ordered coffee and eggs, and quickly filled his partner in on the morning's developments. Willis listened intently, then asked the question Carpenter had been waiting for.

"Surely you realize that this invitation is a trap of some kind?"

"Of course I do," replied Carpenter. "But it still represents the best opportunity for me to carry out my mission. Surely *you* realize that?"

Willis sipped his coffee.

"I do, John," he said. "I just felt it necessary to draw your attention to the fact that this V's motives for inviting you and the monster are unlikely to be honorable. I meant no offense."

Carpenter felt his anger dissipate.

Control yourself. This man is not your enemy.

"Needless to say, I will take up position outside the building and will be ready to assist in any way that is required," Willis continued. "Unless that does not sit well with you?"

"That sits fine," replied Carpenter. "I will be grateful for your presence."

"That settles it then," said Willis, and he forced a smile. "Now, let us turn our attention to breakfast. It promises to be a long day."

John Carpenter stood at the corner of Central Park West and West Eighty-Third Street, waiting for Frankenstein. The sun had long since disappeared below the horizon, and the night was cold and dark.

He had left Willis in the diner and caught a carriage uptown to take care of some errands. He purchased a dinner suit from a tailor that Willis had recommended on Madison Avenue, continued north into Harlem to pay a short visit to a builder's merchant before returning to his hotel to prepare himself for the ball, eating a light dinner in a restaurant on Sixth Avenue and making his way toward the wide expanse of Central Park.

"Cold night," said a deep voice from behind him.

Carpenter started and spun around. Frankenstein towered above him, a beautiful dinner suit covering his huge frame. He was looking down at Carpenter with a faint smile on his face.

"Sorry if I startled you," he said, and the smile widened a fraction.

"Apology accepted," Carpenter managed in reply.

You bloody fool. Concentrate on the matter in hand, for God's sake. To be so easily surprised is unacceptable.

Frankenstein nodded. "Glad to hear it," he said. "Shall we?" He gestured along Central Park West, to the corner of the Upper West Side that was their destination.

The two men walked quickly to the address the invitations had specified. On the corner before them was a vast Gothic town house, dominated by a tall circular tower that rose high above the slanted roof. The many windows of the building blazed with light, and even from their position across the road, the sounds of laughter and music could be heard. Standing by the large wooden door was an equally large figure in a dark gray overcoat and an expressionless Venetian mask, and it was to this apparition that the two men presented their invitations.

The figure studied them carefully. "Masks," it said, in a flat voice.

Carpenter pulled a black eye mask from his pocket and

set it in place. Frankenstein carefully looped the ribbons of a white mask with a long, narrow nose over his ears, and the doorman stood aside.

The hallway was wide and grandly appointed, mirrors and paintings hanging at intervals along the walls, vases of fresh flowers on every flat surface. A black-and-white tiled marble floor gleamed beneath their feet. An elderly waiter clad in immaculate white tie appeared beside them, proffering a tray of delicate crystal champagne flutes. The two men accepted and walked down the corridor toward a pair of double doors, from behind which came the sounds of a ball in full swing.

Carpenter opened one of the doors, and they walked inside. There were at least two hundred people in the cavernous ballroom, some on the wide marble dance floor, others standing in groups around the edges of the room, or sitting at round tables, laughing and conversing. At the back of the room, a low stage held a jazz quartet who were thumping out a furious rhythm of bass and drums, over which the pianist was rattling out a ragtime melody. The air was full of cigarette smoke, the pungent scents of opium and incense, shrill peals of laughter, and the hum of a great many voices mingled together.

"Look how big you are!" shrieked a voice to their left, and the two men turned.

A young woman with a feathered mask hiding her face and her figure wrapped in a dark red ball gown that brushed the floor was staring openly at Frankenstein, a look of wonder on her face as she swayed ever so slightly on towering stiletto heels.

"It's considered rude to stare," said Carpenter.

"Don't be so silly," the woman replied, turning her face toward him. Through the holes in the mask Carpenter could see that the woman's eyes were struggling to focus, and he relaxed.

"I believe you may have had too much to drink," he said to her. "Perhaps a little fresh air would do you good. I'm sure you don't wish to embarrass yourself."

He stepped back and opened the door to the corridor, holding it for her. She looked at him for a moment, as if she were trying to construct a riposte, then lifted her nose high into the air and strode unsteadily into the hallway without giving them a second look.

"Thank you," Frankenstein said as soon as the door was again closed. "I would have surely lost my temper had you not removed her."

"You're welcome," Carpenter replied. "I suggest we part company and search for our respective targets."

Frankenstein agreed, turned away, and disappeared into the crowd. Carpenter went in the other direction, skirting the edge of the dance floor, looking for Jeremiah Haslett.

He passed a table full of sleek young men, their dinner suits gleaming black, the pleats razor sharp, and he found himself unable to look away. There was something intoxicating about them, the cigarettes dangling casually from their pale fingers, the easy manner of their conversation, the—

"Watch where you're going, for heaven's sake," said a loud voice.

Carpenter pulled his gaze from the table, sought the source of the reprimand, and felt his heart lurch. In front of him stood a large, stocky man wearing a carved vulture mask, from the eyeholes of which flashed a dark red glow. The man leaned forward, peering at Carpenter. He seemed about to speak when a young woman in a black dress danced into him, and he spun around and berated her for her clumsiness. When he turned back toward Carpenter, the glow from the mask was gone, and the man shoved roughly past him and disappeared.

I saw them, though. I saw his eyes. What is this place?

He worked his way to the long bar and was about to place an order when he saw a skeletally thin shape in the corner of his eye and turned toward it.

Jeremiah Haslett was standing fifteen feet away from him, leaning on the corner of the wooden bar, talking to a beautiful blonde woman who could barely have been more than a teenager. He was wearing a red velvet eye mask and a triangular hat, but Carpenter recognized the sharp nose and the thin, cruel mouth from the photographs that had belatedly filled the London newspapers.

Carpenter reached into his pocket, withdrew a narrow wooden stake, and let his arm drop to his side, concealing the weapon in his hand. He stepped forward, slowly, not wishing to announce his presence before it was necessary, then suddenly found the path to his target blocked by a group of laughing men and women, as they carried a tray of drinks and cigars away from the bar and back to the tables. He pushed one of the women gently out of the way, trying not to lose sight of his quarry, and she rounded on him, hissing loudly, the same dark red glow emanating from the holes in her delicate feathered mask. His heart leapt, but he stepped past her.

Haslett was gone.

Carpenter cursed and ran to where his quarry had stood,

attracting looks of disapproval from the throng of drinking, dancing men and women. He looked around in every direction, but there was no sign of the Englishman.

Behind him the band struck up a new number, and the activity on the dance floor intensified. A grandfather clock set between two long mirrors behind the bar tolled once, and Carpenter looked at it; the hands on the ornate face told him that it was a quarter to midnight.

He no longer wanted another drink. He pushed on into the crowd, looking for Haslett, or for Frankenstein, but could see neither man. He passed a heavy locked door that he presumed led into the rest of the house, then found himself caught among a large group of guests and was carried out onto the dance floor, his feet barely touching the ground.

He pulled free of the good-natured hands that grabbed at his arms and spun, disorientated. He tried to make his way toward the band, but a pretty redheaded woman blocked his path, smiling seductively at him, the tips of her incisors sharp and gleaming beneath the fractured light of the enormous crystal chandelier that hung above them. He turned about and struck out in the opposite direction but had no more success. A ring of men and women rotated in a frenzied circle of kicking feet and flailing arms, their momentum spinning him like a top. As a young man swung past him, his long blond hair flying out behind him, Carpenter saw the red glow beneath the material of his feline mask, and his skin ran cold. He turned and almost ran into the wide chest of an elderly man, who was dancing with great enthusiasm with a girl young enough to be his granddaughter. The man turned and snarled at him, his white mask glowing red, two pointed teeth appearing beneath his upper lip.

Oh God, there are hundreds of them. What have I done?

He reached into his pocket and pulled the stake free, but a girl wearing a diamond tiara above a Japanese kabuki mask thumped into him, and the weapon clattered to the floor. He swore beneath his breath and stooped to look for it, but a dozen feet kicked it beyond his reach. Carpenter stood up and a wave of terror so strong it was almost physical flooded through him.

Standing before him was a luminously elegant man. He wore no mask, and his face, the features hinting at an eastern European ancestry, was so pale it was almost transparent, the veins tracing a faint pattern of blue across the milky flesh. Around them the dancing seemed to have intensified, if that were possible, yet no one collided with the man, or even appeared to come close to doing so. It was as though he were surrounded by a magnetic field that repelled the revelers.

It is him. Dear God, it really is. The youngest of the three.

Valentin Rusmanov regarded Carpenter with a look that made him feel like a specimen in a laboratory. The man's eyes were the same pale blue as the veins beneath his skin and had a hypnotic quality; he felt himself sinking into them and struggled to pull his gaze away. He was about to say something, although he had no idea what it was going to be, when thundering peals of bells began to count the chimes of midnight.

Everything stopped. The chimes rang on, three, four, five, but they were now the only sound in the room. The dancing had ceased, as had all conversation. Carpenter looked around, sure what he would see, but fear still flooded his system when he saw that he was right.

Everyone in the room was staring silently at him.

The final chime rang out, echoing in the quiet air, and from the back of the room a voice shouted, "Unmask!" There was a second of hesitation, then Valentin nodded, and there was a frenzy of movement as the guests removed their masks, a red glow filling the room as they did so. Carpenter looked around helplessly as the hundreds of men and women turned back to face him.

He was surrounded by vampires.

They regarded him with smiles on their faces, their fangs now fully extended, their eyes gleaming terrible crimson.

This is how it ends. Torn to pieces on my first mission. My father would be ashamed.

23

ROUND TWO

Jamie marched along the cellblock corridor, Frankenstein following a couple of steps behind. Jamie had refused to go to the infirmary and have his neck properly dressed, had not even changed his acrid-smelling uniform. Several Blacklight operators had stared at the white wad of bandages as he stormed through the hangar, the huge colonel following in his wake.

Jamie stopped in front of Larissa's cell, the UV wall shimmering in front of him. She was lying on her bed, her eyes already fixed on him, as though she had been expecting him to arrive. Then Jamie realized that she had probably heard him from the first moment he entered the block; he found it strangely easy to forget that she was a vampire.

She smiled at him, and then the smile died on her lips as Frankenstein stepped into her field of vision and stood next to Jamie. She had a book splayed over her lap, and she immediately brought it up to her face, obscuring it from their view.

"I need to talk to you," said Jamie.

The book didn't move.

"Did you hear me?" he asked, anger rising in his voice. "I said I need to talk to you."

"I heard you," said Larissa, from behind the book. "And there's nothing I'd like more in the world than to talk to you back. But I don't do threesomes."

Frankenstein muttered something under his breath.

"Nothing personal," said Larissa.

Jamie looked at the monster, ready to plead with him to leave them alone, but Frankenstein was already turning away from him.

"Thank you," he shouted, as the huge man's footsteps thumped away along the corridor. When the door at the end of the block clanged shut, Larissa put the book down, jumped off the bed, and walked over to him, a wide smile on her face.

"I knew you would be back," she said.

"This isn't a social visit," Jamie said, sharply.

Her eyes dropped from his as he spoke, and then widened as she observed the bandage over the right side of his neck. "What happened to you?" she asked. "Don't tell me someone bit you?"

The concern in her voice made Jamie's heart flutter. "Nothing like that," he replied. "I got burned. On a mission."

"A mission!" she exclaimed. "Was it a super secret one? I bet it was. Ooh, tell me all about it!"

Jamie blushed a deep scarlet, and Larissa laughed.

"I'm sorry," she said. "You just looked so serious with your bandaged neck and your dirty uniform. Did you come down here to tell me off?"

"I came down here to ask you about Alexandru," he said. "I came down here because I thought you might be the one person willing to help me."

Larissa tilted her head to one side and fluttered her eyelashes.

"That's so sweet," she said, choking back fake emotion. "Am I your only hope?"

Jamie turned away from her and strode up the corridor, forcing himself to slow his pace, determined that he would not run away.

"Wait," she called, and he stopped. "Please. Come back. I was only playing."

He stood in the corridor, between two empty cells, breathing hard. It was embarrassment that had caused him to run, embarrassment that she was not taking him seriously. And although he couldn't have explained why, it was imperative to him that she do so. He composed himself and walked slowly back to her cell.

She smiled as he reappeared, but he saw the last flicker of genuine concern on her face, and he was glad.

"I'm sorry," she said. "I haven't spoken to anyone for two days. The guards don't even look at me."

Then they're idiots, Jamie thought, and blushed.

Larissa sat down cross-legged on the floor of her cell, and waited for him to do the same. He folded himself crouching to the ground, carefully, moving his neck as little as was possible, and then they were facing each other, no more than three feet apart, the UV field flickering between them.

"Will you tell me where Alexandru is?" he asked.

She shook her head.

"Why not?"

"Because I don't know. Honestly."

"Will you tell me where the last place you saw him was?"

She shook her head again, causing a lock of dark hair to fall across her forehead. Jamie tried not to look at it; the urge to brush it away was overwhelming.

"Why not?"

"Because if I tell you, I'll never leave this cell again."

"I can talk to them—"

"It won't work. I'll take you there, but I won't tell you. I hope you can understand the difference."

Jamie lowered his head. He knew she was right. If she admitted to not knowing anything, Seward would have her destroyed; if she told him what she did know, Seward would have her destroyed. Her only chance was to admit she had information, refuse to reveal it, and hope they became desperate enough to play the game on her terms.

He looked up. "So, you're useless then?" he said, as spitefully as he was able.

She flinched, and a tremor of hurt rippled momentarily across her face.

Good. Good.

"I didn't say I wouldn't help you," she said, sounding for the first time like the teenager she had been before she was turned. "I just won't tell you where I last saw Alexandru. Ask me something else."

"There's nothing else I want to know."

"Really?"

"Really. All that matters is him—and my mother."

"You're really worried about her, aren't you?"

Jamie looked at her. "Of course I am," he said.

"You should be. You have no idea what Alexandru is capable of."

A shiver ran up Jamie's spine.

I don't want to hear this. I know I need to, but I don't want to.

"What's he like?" he asked, cautiously.

"He's the second oldest vampire in the world," Larissa replied. "He does whatever he wants, whenever he wants. He kills humans for food, he kills vampires and humans for fun. There's nothing you can do to stop him."

"I don't believe that."

"You need to. You'll get hurt if you don't. And I don't want to see that happen." She smiled at him, and he felt his stomach revolve. "A year ago, a girl who was running with him killed a farmer in Cornwall," she continued. "She came back to the place we were staying covered in his blood, absolutely dripping with it. Anderson asked her if anyone had seen her, and she confessed that the man's family might have seen her leaving the barn where she found him."

"What happened?" asked Jamie.

"Alexandru tore her to pieces. In front of everyone, he pulled this poor, stupid girl limb from limb and laughed at her as she screamed. There were probably twenty vampires in the room, some of them old, all of them powerful, and no one said a word. Or looked away. Even when he ate her heart."

Jamie felt bile rise in his stomach.

"He sent Anderson out to the farm the girl had come from," she continued. "Anderson killed the farmer's family—his wife—and three children. He cut their throats and let them bleed out on the kitchen floor, staring at each other as they died." Larissa looked at him, a gentle expression on her face. "*That's* what Alexandru is like," she said, softly. "He's an animal. A clever, cunning animal, who delights in violence and mayhem. He's stronger and faster than anyone on the planet, human or vampire, and he can sense danger before it appears. You can't trick him, or sneak up on him, and you certainly can't fight him."

Jamie stared at her, hopelessness filling his chest. "Then what am I supposed to do?" he asked.

"That's easy. You're supposed to make sure you never cross his path. But that's not an option for you, is it?"

"Not really."

"In that case I don't know what you're supposed to do. I don't see any way you pursuing Alexandru ends with anything apart from him killing you." Larissa looked at the disconsolate expression on Jamie's face, and sympathy overwhelmed her. "I'm not the authority on Alexandru," she said, gently. "Talk to people. Maybe someone knows something I don't."

Jamie looked at her, and his pale blue eyes were heavy with despair. "No one will tell me anything," he said, his voice cracking. "They're all terrified of him. No one will risk him finding out they talked to me."

"Talk to the monster."

"Why?"

"Because all this started with your dad. And my understanding is they were close."

"Frankenstein said the same thing."

"Ask him about Ilyana. Ask him about Hungary. Ask him

why he hasn't told you about it already. And if you're feeling brave, ask him whose side he's really on."

Jamie felt a wave of nausea shoot through him. "Thank you," he said, stiffly.

She flashed him a dazzling smile and reclined on the floor of her cell. Her gray shirt rode up, exposing a band of pale midriff, and Jamie fought the urge to stare at it.

"Always glad to be of service," she said.

He knocked on the door to Frankenstein's quarters, and waited. It was late, well past midnight, but he doubted the monster would be asleep. He had been standing in the corridor for almost fifteen minutes, preparing himself, thinking about his father, *really* thinking about his father for the first time since his life had been turned upside down.

He had rejected the things Seward had told him, out of hand. The thought that his dad could have betrayed his friends and allied himself with someone like Alexandru was impossible for him to accept.

But then he had thought about his mother, asking her husband every evening, year after year, how his day had been, and thought about his father smiling and lying to her face, inventing people who didn't exist and stories that hadn't happened, and his faith in the man he had loved more than any other had been shaken.

Larissa was right: He needed to know more about Julian Carpenter, about the real man his father had been.

There was a shuffling noise from behind the door, then it opened, and a huge face loomed out of the darkened room.

"Is something wrong?" the monster grunted.

Jamie shook his head.

"So why are you here?"

"I want to ask you some questions."

"About what?"

"About my dad."

Frankenstein looked at the teenager for a long moment, then sighed deeply. "Give me five minutes," he said, and closed the door.

THE CITY THAT NEVER SLEEPS, PART III

New York, USA
January 1, 1929

"Happy New Year, Mr. Carpenter," said Valentin, in a smooth, gentle voice. "I wonder if it will be your last?"

Carpenter turned slowly to face him. The man's eyes now shone red, a red that was somehow simultaneously both dark and bright against the pale perfection of his skin.

"Do you know me?" Valentin continued.

Carpenter nodded.

"Good. We are well met, and I welcome you to my home. Although why you are here is a question that interests me a great deal."

Valentin glanced over at someone in the crowd and nodded. There was a commotion as the guests parted, creating a path to where Carpenter and Valentin stood. Through this gap two large men in white tie appeared, dragging a barely conscious Frankenstein between them and depositing him heavily onto the floor. The monster's eyes rolled in his head, his mouth hanging stupidly open.

Carpenter made to kneel next to the fallen man, but Valentin told him sharply to stay where he was, and he forced himself to comply.

"Your friend has an impressive appetite for opium," said Valentin. "It isn't easy to incapacitate a man of his size, but we persevered." He smiled at Carpenter, but when he spoke again, his voice contained not a trace of humor. "Tell me, Mr. Carpenter, are you here to kill me?"

Carpenter was surprised to find his equilibrium returning; the likely inevitability of his death had sunk into him, and he was determined that he would not show this creature fear if he could help it.

"No," he replied. "That is not my mission. But I would certainly consider it a bonus."

Valentin took half a step toward him, his teeth bared, an awful, serpentine hiss rising in his throat, then quickly regained his composure and laughed—a high, feminine sound that echoed around the cavernous ballroom.

"I admire your honesty," he said. "Most refreshing. So, if you are not here for me, who are you here for? Given what I know of your father and his friends, I am disinclined to believe you are in New York for a holiday. Am I correct?"

"You are. I came here for one of your guests."

"Anyone in particular?"

"Jeremiah Haslett."

A low murmur of interest rolled through the crowd.

"And what has Mr. Haslett done to warrant transatlantic pursuit?"

"His crimes are too numerous to list. But they are also

largely irrelevant; he is a vampire, and that alone is enough to warrant his extermination."

The crowd around him pulsed and hissed, but he felt no fear; it was already clear to him that Valentin alone was going to decide his fate, that the crowd of snarling vampires would do nothing without his permission.

Their host regarded him for a long moment, then spoke. "Bring Mr. Haslett before me."

There was a cry of outrage from within the crowd, and then a commotion as the skeletal figure of Jeremiah Haslett was gripped by four vampire men and dragged through the revelers. He was thrown to his knees before Valentin, spluttering and protesting. He rose to his feet, brushing down his dinner jacket, and in an act that must have required superhuman will, Frankenstein did the same, his eyes focusing more clearly on Carpenter, a look of terrible shame on his huge face.

The four figures stood in a circle, eyeing each other.

"What to do?" mused Valentin.

"What on earth do you mean?" cried Haslett. "There is no decision to be made here, surely? Kill him, and this abomination as well, and let us return to our celebration."

"Be quiet, Mr. Haslett," said Valentin.

Haslett blustered, his face reddening, but did as he was told.

"Mr. Carpenter," Valentin continued, almost cheerfully. "What do you think we should do about this unfortunate situation?"

"Let us leave," replied Carpenter, instantly. "We will go without a fuss, and you will not see us again."

Around him, the vampires howled with derisory laughter. Valentin didn't even smile. "Why should I do that?" he asked.

Carpenter took a deep breath.

Please. Please let this work.

He slipped his dinner jacket off and pushed his cummerbund down to his waist. Beneath it was a leather belt, wrapped tightly with three rows of light brown sticks. Inserted into the one nearest the belt buckle was a brass fuse, wired to a trigger that was now resting lightly in John Carpenter's hand. "Because of this," he replied. "This is gelignite. And it will bring this entire house down on all our heads unless you do as I say."

There were gasps and shouts from the assembled vampires. Valentin made no sound but regarded him with a look of genuine admiration.

"Bravo, Mr. Carpenter," he said. "It is rare to be confronted with a man who is genuinely prepared to die for what he believes in. Bravo." He looked at Haslett, whose narrow face was white with fear, then at his guests, then back to John Carpenter. "You may go," he said.

There was a communal howl of anger from the crowd, and a bellow of objection from Haslett. Valentin's eyes flared crimson, and he stepped into the air, hovering a foot above the ground, so that everyone in the room could see his pale, beautiful face.

"Silence," he roared. "You will do as I say, or none of you will see another night sky." The room fell silent, and he looked down at Carpenter. "You are free to go," he said. "I am sure we will see each other again, and I'm capable of patience."

"What?" screamed Haslett. "He's free to go? He came here tonight to kill me."

"That's right," replied Valentin. "He did. It's because of you that he is here." He looked at the crowd. "Take him," he said.

Haslett opened his mouth to say something, but the words died in his throat as the first vampire landed on him. A second leapt from the crowd, then a third, and he screamed as he was borne to the ground, disappearing under a blur of dinner jackets and ball gowns. Tearing sounds, horribly loud, came from within the squirming pile of bodies, and Haslett's screams reached an earsplitting pitch as dark red liquid began to seep out across the marble floor.

Carpenter turned away, nausea rising in his stomach.

"Look!" shouted Valentin. "This is why you are here, so look!"

Carpenter turned back and watched.

Eventually the screams stopped, and the vampires began to stand up, their clothes and faces drenched in crimson blood. They stared at him with frenzied hunger in their eyes.

"I suggest you leave now, Mr. Carpenter," Valentin said.

"I will not leave without him," Carpenter replied, gesturing at Frankenstein, who stared at him with an uncomprehending look on his face.

"Fine," Valentin replied. "Take him with you. In truth, I cannot imagine anything worse than the taste of his warmed-over blood."

Carpenter stepped forward, gripping the trigger tightly in his hand, and put his other hand on Frankenstein's shoulder. "Can you walk?" he asked, in a low voice.

Frankenstein nodded.

"All right," said Carpenter. "Follow me. Slowly." He turned around and walked carefully toward the crowd of vampires, who stepped out of his way, reluctance painted openly on their faces.

The two men walked between the silent, red-eyed guests, to the wide double door that they had come through, less than an hour earlier. Carpenter took the carved wooden handle in his hand and was about to turn it when Valentin's voice echoed across the ballroom, and he turned to face the pale vampire.

"Our paths will cross again, Mr. Carpenter," he said, happily. "Of that, I have no doubt. Happy New Year."

Carpenter almost replied but forced himself not to. Instead he opened the door, walked down the hallway, and led Frankenstein out into the night.

The two men staggered down the steps of the town house. They had gone no more than ten yards from the building when a familiar voice hailed them, and the sound of running footsteps echoed in the still night air.

"Good God, John," said Willis, skidding to a halt in front of them, his eyes taking in the gelignite belt around Carpenter's waist and the dazed look on Frankenstein's face. "Are you injured? Do you need me to call the uniforms? Are you—"

Carpenter cut him off. "I'm fine," he said. "We're fine. The mission was a success."

"Well, that's splendid," exclaimed Willis, but his face still wore a mask of concern. "I shall need to speak to you before I prepare my report, but perhaps tomorrow would be more agreeable?"

Carpenter told him that he was sure it would be and thanked the American. Willis took a final look at the two men in their now disheveled dinner suits, and then turned and disappeared along West Eighty-Fifth Street.

Carpenter and Frankenstein walked slowly down

Central Park West, looking for a carriage. After two blocks, Frankenstein stumbled to his knees and vomited into the icy gutter, but when he stood up, his eyes were clearer, and he looked at John Carpenter.

"I let you down," he said. "I'm sorry."

"We both still live," Carpenter replied. "That is all that matters."

"Thanks entirely to you."

Carpenter regarded the huge man. His voice was low and trembling, but his face twitched with anger; he was obviously deeply ashamed.

"You saved my life," Frankenstein said. "When you could have left me, you didn't. Why didn't you?"

Carpenter shrugged. "The thought never occurred to me," he answered.

Frankenstein studied him carefully, looking into the Englishman's open, honest face. He saw nothing but the truth, and in the sluggish opium-addled depths of the monster's mind, a decision was made.

"I owe you my life," Frankenstein said, slowly. "I don't say that lightly." Carpenter opened his mouth to protest, but Frankenstein waved a hand at him, and continued. "If there's anything I can do to help you, you only have to ask. Whatever it is, wherever you are."

"I appreciate the offer," Carpenter replied. "But I don't need a bodyguard."

"Given the last thing Valentin said to you," Frankenstein replied, "I'm not sure that's entirely true."

HE WAS MY FRIEND, AND I LOVED HIM

Jamie and Frankenstein sat in one of the offices on Level 0. The base was quiet; soldiers made their way through the halls, heading for patrol duties as their comrades slept on the lower levels. Frankenstein was nursing an enormous mug of black coffee that he had stopped to collect from the officers' mess as they made their way up through the base. Jamie had poured a plastic cup of water from the dispenser in the corner of the office and was looking expectantly at the monster.

Frankenstein tipped the coffee to his lips, eyeing the teenager over the rim of the mug. Eventually, he spoke.

"Stop looking at me like that," he said. "I don't know what you want me to tell you, so if you've got questions just ask them."

"OK," replied Jamie, settling himself into his chair. "When did you first meet my dad?"

Frankenstein tilted his head, stared at the ceiling, and cast his mind back.

"I met him the day he joined us," he said, eventually, "1979, that was. We knew he was coming—the birthdays of descendants always get around. It's a big moment. You've seen how seriously Blacklight takes its history; a new descendant is that history, in the flesh. And Julian was something special, we knew that before he even arrived."

"What was special about him?" asked Jamie. He had leaned forward onto his elbows as the monster talked.

"He was famous, inside the military and out. When he passed his Admiralty Interview Board—"

"What's that?" interrupted Jamie.

"It's what you have to pass if you're going to be an officer in the Marines."

"Hold on. The Marines? As in, the Royal Marines?"

Frankenstein sighed. "Yes, Jamie, the Royal Marines. Your father scored off the scale at the Interview Board, and word got around the military about it. Then he broke three Commando-course records, and people started to really pay attention to him. And by then, he was playing rugby for England, so he was already—"

"He was doing *what*?" exclaimed Jamie.

"This will be much easier," said Frankenstein, leveling his eyes with the teenager's, "if you don't interrupt me every thirty seconds."

"Sorry," said Jamie.

"It's all right. Julian was a top-class rugby player. He played for England schools, for the under-eighteens, then broke through into the full national team when he was nineteen, his first full year in the Marines. He was capped seven or eight times."

"Why only seven or eight?"

"He stopped playing when he joined Blacklight. But when he turned up here on his twenty-first birthday, he was already well-known. There was no Internet in those days, but his name had been in the papers, and everyone was excited to meet him. He arrived with your grandfather John, and he was met by Peter Seward, who was the director at the time. I've never seen those old men so proud, so excited about a new recruit."

Frankenstein looked at Jamie, a pained smile on his face.

"Tell me," said Jamie, quietly. "Don't stop now."

"It was an incredible time," Frankenstein said after a pause and a deep gulp of coffee. "Quincey Harker had stepped down as director a decade earlier, and Peter Seward had taken over. He didn't really want the job, but he was Quincey's closest friend, and when Harker retired to look after his wife, Seward saw it as his duty to carry on his friend's work. And he did a good job of it, a damn good job, even though he would never believe it. He oversaw the changing of the guard, from the generation that dragged Blacklight up after World War II, to the new generation who would take it forward again." He smiled, a genuine smile full of nostalgia.

"Legends walked these corridors: Albert and Arthur Holmwood; David Harker, who was Quincey's oldest son; Ben Seward, who was the director's son; Leandro Gonzalez; David Morris, your friend Tom's grandfather; and your own grandfather, of course. John Carpenter was Peter Seward's closest friend in the Department after Quincey left; they retired at the same time, in 1982, convinced that Blacklight was in safe hands."

"Was it?" asked Jamie. His eyes were wide as he listened to the monster's story.

"For a while," said Frankenstein. "When your father joined, a new generation were starting to come into their own, centered around Stephen Holmwood, who was Arthur Holmwood's son. He was a truly brilliant man, a once-in-a-generation intellect: He spoke six languages by the time he was fifteen, he played cricket and hockey for England schoolboys, and was a Cambridge blue. He didn't join Blacklight when he was twenty-one, which caused an enormous scandal. His father begged him, but he was determined to finish at the university, which he did. Then he won a Rhodes scholarship to Harvard and went to America for a year. He came home in 1965 and joined Department 19 when he was twenty-three."

Frankenstein looked at Jamie. "Stephen could have done anything he wanted. He could have been prime minister. But he chose Blacklight."

Jamie's head was pounding; he felt as though he had been holding his breath since the monster had started talking. He breathed out, took new air into his lungs, sipped his water, and trained his attention back on Frankenstein.

"So there was Stephen and his brother Jeremy and their cousin Jacob Scott, whom you met yesterday. Ben Seward was still around, and his son Henry, who's the director now, joined a few years after your father. George Harker was there, and Paul Turner, who married Henry Seward's sister, and Daniel Morris, Tom's father. And Julian, of course. These men were the future of Blacklight, with Stephen Holmwood in the middle. They rose quickly through the ranks, transforming the Department as they did so. When Peter Seward stepped down in 1982, Stephen was the unanimous choice to replace him as director. And then things really started to happen."

Frankenstein drained the last of his coffee and set the mug down on the table. "Everything you see around you, this base and everything in it, is the result of Stephen Holmwood's tenure as director. He petitioned the government to increase Blacklight's budget, and he sank the new funds into this place. He sent your father on a fact-finding mission to America in 1984 to visit NS9, which is their equivalent of Department 19. He was gone for ten weeks, and he returned home with a report that was the blueprint for the Loop. We expanded, taking the best men from all three branches of the military, widening our sphere of operations, hunting across Europe and beyond, running missions in Africa and Asia for the first time since the war. Stephen worked with the Departments of other countries, sharing data and resources, sending men on exchanges to every corner of the world, organizing and establishing areas of responsibility, so the entire globe came under the jurisdiction of the various organizations." He grinned, wickedly.

"The vampires were decimated," he continued. "They had come to believe that if they kept their heads down, they would be safe. But that was no longer true. We pursued them, chasing them from town to town, from country to country even, and we destroyed them, one after the other. There was nowhere for them to hide." He stopped talking and looked down at the surface of the table.

"What happened?" asked Jamie.

Frankenstein raised his head and looked at him, and Jamie was alarmed to see that the monster's misshapen eyes were damp with tears. "Stephen died," he said, simply. "He had a heart attack in 1989. No warning. He just died, at his desk in his quarters."

"That's horrible," said Jamie, in a low voice.

"It was," said Frankenstein. "It devastated the Department. No one knew what to do; Stephen had been the heart of everything, and suddenly he was gone. There was no director, and the people who were best able to step up and keep us going were the people who were most shattered by his death. So when Daniel Morris put himself forward, everyone was so grateful that they said yes before they'd even really thought about it."

"Tom told me his father was director," said Jamie, remembering the conversation in the Fallen Gallery. "He said it wasn't for very long though."

"Too long," spit Frankenstein, and Jamie recoiled. "Dan Morris wasn't a bad man," he continued, after a pause. "Far from it, really. He was impulsive, and he was aggressive, and that made him a great operator, but a terrible director. It was difficult for him, to take over in the circumstances he did. It would have been difficult for anyone; Stephen cast such a long shadow. But that doesn't excuse the risks he took, and the people who got hurt."

Frankenstein got up from the table and poured himself water from the dispenser. He sat back down heavily in front of Jamie. "We should have seen it coming; I should have seen it coming. But it took a long time for Blacklight to recover after Stephen died, and so for at least a year, no one was paying much attention to what Dan was doing. A night mission here, an overseas operation without proper clearance there. Small things, at least to start with. But some people did notice them and began to keep a closer eye. Your father was one of them, Henry Seward was another. And so was I."

The monster sipped his water. "In March of 1993, Dan ordered an operation into Romania—modern-day Transylvania—where all this started in 1891. That part of the world is under the jurisdiction of the SPC, the Russian Supernatural Protection Commissariat, and they have never taken kindly to foreign Departments operating in their sphere of influence. Under the Soviets, it was almost impossible even to enter their territory, and the penalties for doing so were severe. But then the USSR collapsed and the SPC started slowly to extend its hand toward the other Departments. Your father led a delegation to Moscow in late 1992, the first of its kind in almost fifty years, and he came home excited about having Russia back in the fold. Then Dan ordered Operation Nightingale, and we nearly lost them forever."

"What was Operation Nightingale?" asked Jamie.

"It was a mission to destroy a blood factory near Craiova. A vampire gang was kidnapping people, mostly drug addicts and the homeless, from all across central Europe, and bleeding them in an old slaughterhouse. Hundreds of men and women a year for God knows how long, then selling the blood on the black market. We'd known about it for a couple of years and had reported it to the SPC on a number of occasions. We got nothing back, not even an acknowledgment that the message had arrived. That's what it was like when the Iron Curtain still stood; information disappeared into a black hole. Then when the Curtain came down, we reported it again, and this time we got a reply, saying that the factory was a priority SPC target.

Six months later, still nothing had happened, so Dan sent a team in."

Frankenstein looked at Jamie. "When I think back to that day—"

"You were there?" interrupted Jamie. "You went on the mission?"

"Of course," replied Frankenstein. "Me, your father, Paul Turner, and seventeen other Blacklight men. We flew in on the 18th of March 1993, and we reached the factory in the late morning of the following day."

"What happened?"

"They were waiting for us. More than seventy vampires, all well fed and rested, wide awake and waiting when we went through the door. I noticed that the black paint covering the windows was still wet, and I told your father, who ordered everyone to retreat. But it was too late. They came down from the rafters. We never stood a chance."

"But you made it out. And so did my dad and Major Turner."

"We were lucky. That's all there is to it. Maybe we were a little more experienced; some of the team were just boys, no more than a year or two under their belts. When we saw them coming, we turned and ran. I was the last one to make it out of the building."

"How many of you made it?" asked Jamie, his voice taut with horror.

"Six of us," replied Frankenstein. "Six of us made it into the sunlight, and fourteen men died in a dark building full of blood and death."

Frankenstein reached for his mug, saw that it was empty, and pushed it aside. "Dan could never prove the Russians let them know we were coming. The operation was an unauthorized run into another Department's territory, so there were no permissions, no call logs to check. But that didn't matter to him. Your father defended the SPC, told Dan he didn't believe they would let Blacklight men die to make a point. But the director was convinced. He ordered Department 19 to sever all ties with the SPC and drew up a letter asking the prime minister to expel Russian diplomatic staff from London. The letter claimed that the SPC had committed an act of war, and it should be treated as such."

"But if it was an unauthorized mission . . ." protested Jamie.

Frankenstein smiled at him. "You can see the problem, fourteen years later. And your father and I could see it then. We weren't alone, either. At that point, the mission was the biggest disaster in Blacklight history, and losing fourteen men in one day had a terrible impact on the Department. Just about every operator knew one of the men who had died, and there was a lot of anger about what had happened. A lot of it aimed at Dan Morris. So your father took control of the situation."

"What did he do?"

"He and a number of senior operators—Henry Seward, Paul Turner, and myself among them—made a formal motion to the chief of the general staff that Dan Morris be removed as director. We explained the mistake he had made in ordering the mission, and the huge overreaction he was planning in response to its failure, and we asked that he be relieved of duty, for the good of Blacklight. Thankfully, the general agreed with us and did as we asked."

"No wonder you and Tom don't get along," said Jamie, softly. "He must hate you for doing that to his dad."

"He can hate me all he wants," said Frankenstein, sharply. "I don't give a damn what he thinks. We did what we did because it needed doing, because more men would have died needlessly if we hadn't. I don't regret it for a moment."

"What happened to Tom's dad? Did he stay in Blacklight?"

"He could have," said Frankenstein. "He was removed as director, not from the Department. And there were plenty of people who tried to persuade him to do so, including your father. But his pride would not allow it. He left the day after he was removed from office." The monster looked at Jamie. "He put his pistol in his mouth six months later."

"Jesus," whispered Jamie.

They sat in silence for a few minutes, the sad tale of Thomas Morris's father hanging in the air between them.

Eventually Jamie spoke. "So that was when Admiral Seward took charge?" he asked.

Frankenstein nodded. "He was Commander Seward then. But, yes. He steadied the ship, with your father's help. And the Department recovered. Everything was fine for more than a decade. Henry and Julian were a great team, and Blacklight prospered. And then Budapest happened, and nothing was ever really the same again."

Jamie sat forward, his eyes full of dreadful inevitability.

"What happened in Budapest?" he asked.

THE BEGINNING
OF THE END

Molnár estate near Budapest, Hungary
February 12, 2005

Julian Carpenter fired his T-Bone at point-blank range, turning his head away as the vampire exploded in a shower of blood, soaking his Blacklight uniform. He turned to the four men standing behind him.

"Be careful from here on," he said.

Four faces looked back at him. The huge mottled face of Frankenstein gave him a quick grin, and Paul Turner stared at him without expression, his gray eyes cold and calm. The two young operators, Connor and Miller, looked at him with queasy uncertainty, their training just about masking their obvious fear. Carpenter felt for them; neither should have been on a mission with such a high-value target, and all five men knew it. The two young privates had less than a year's experience between them, and it was Connor's first live operation.

There had been no time to examine records; the intelligence

that had drawn them to this exquisite estate on the edge of Budapest had needed acting on immediately, and Carpenter had gathered the first four able-bodied men he could find. He was grateful that two of them had been Frankenstein and Turner, veterans of hundreds of operations, and two of his closest friends in Blacklight. Connor and Miller would just have to do what they had been trained to; eventually, every operator was required to sink or swim.

Carpenter had been overseeing the shift change in the Ops Room when the report had come in. At first he had thought it was a practical joke. It was written by a Blacklight major called John Bryant, who was celebrating his thirtieth wedding anniversary with his wife on a cruise down the Danube. He and his wife had taken a stroll along the river banks of Budapest and had literally walked into Alexandru Rusmanov and his wife, Ilyana.

Ninety minutes later, Carpenter's team were in the air, heading east. They were strapped onto benches inside an EC725 Cougar that had been stripped down and essentially rebuilt. The improvements that most pleased Julian Carpenter had been to the rotors and the engines, which now delivered a cruising speed of just over 300 miles per hour. This was significantly faster than the publicly acknowledged world-record speed for a helicopter, and it meant that the flight to Budapest would take little more than an hour. The *Mina*, the supersonic Blacklight jet that could have covered the distance to Budapest in less than twenty minutes, was in Tokyo, and he could not afford to wait for the Harker brothers to bring her home.

Julian pressed a button in the console next to his seat, and a screen folded down from the ceiling. The most recent photo of Alexandru filled the frame, and he told the four men on the benches to study it carefully.

"This is Alexandru Rusmanov," he said, raising his voice slightly above the steady pulse of the helicopter's engines. "Turner, Frankenstein, I know you don't need reminding of just how dangerous this target is. So Connor, Miller, I say this for your benefit; nothing in your training has prepared you for dealing with a vampire as old and powerful as Alexandru. Nothing." He contemplated the eager, nervous faces of the two privates.

"You're looking at the second oldest vampire in the world. He was turned by Dracula himself, along with his brothers, Valeri and Valentin, more than four hundred years ago. He is powerful in a way that distorts the scales; he can knock down buildings, he can move faster than your eyes can follow, he can fly indefinitely. And more than that, he is clever, and he is vicious. He views humanity as nothing more than a herd of cattle from which to draw his sustenance. If he chooses to, he will kill you without a millisecond's hesitation."

Carpenter pressed the button again, and the image changed to a black and white photo of a stunningly beautiful woman with dark hair and sharp features. "This is Ilyana, Alexandru's wife. She is almost as old as he is; he turned her himself, with Dracula's permission. She has stood at his side for more than four centuries and is every bit as dangerous as her husband. In modern psychological terminology, Ilyana is a pure sociopath, without empathy for others, without feelings for anyone apart from her husband. She is unpredictable—and she is deadly."

A final press of the button sent the screen folding back into the ceiling. Carpenter looked at his team and saw fear in the faces of Connor and Miller.

Good, he thought. *They need to be scared.*

"Both these individuals are high-value targets, rated A1 by every Department in the world. Our orders are to eliminate them both. If that proves impossible, if the opportunity only arrives to make one kill, then Alexandru is the priority. Understood?"

The four men on the benches shouted that they did, and Julian nodded.

I hope you do, he thought. *I really hope you do.*

The helicopter touched down at a Hungarian Air Force Base on the outskirts of Budapest. The aircraft's call sign meant it did not appear on civilian radar, and only a handful of military air traffic controllers in the world would have recognized the unique combination of letters and numbers that signified a Department 19 vehicle.

Working quietly and inconspicuously through the bars and restaurants of Budapest, the team picked up Alexandru's trail. They followed an elderly vampire to his small apartment below the castle, and he told them about a bar called the Ramparts that had been much busier than usual in recent weeks, busy with the kind of creatures the old man stiffly informed them he had no wish to socialize with. When Turner pressed him, he confessed that he felt no kinship with young vampires, found their lust for violence abhorrent and avoided them wherever possible. Carpenter thanked him, and they moved on.

From the Ramparts, they trailed a vampire bartender to

a warehouse rave in Budapest's rundown industrial district. They dragged him out to the parking lot at the rear of the building, the bartender's eyes wide and rolling, his teeth grinding as Bliss pumped through his system, and he told them that a huge man with a child's face had dropped a card as he left the Ramparts four nights ago. The card was for a vampire club near Matthias Church, a place the bartender had only ever heard whispered about. When he claimed not to remember the address, Turner applied a UV torch to the vampire's hand. It burst into flame, jogging his memory.

Outside a beautiful Gothic town house on Balta Köz, the five men sat in a jet-black car, watching. Anderson, the huge child-faced vampire who served as Alexandru's right-hand man, had entered the building two hours earlier, apparently unaware that anyone was watching. A small gold plate by the door of the town house had been engraved with the words TABULA RASA, which Carpenter thought appropriate for a club frequented by vampires.

A blank slate is exactly what it gives them, he thought. *The freedom to leave behind the people they were before they were turned and start again.*

"Colonel," said Paul Turner, in a low voice. Carpenter looked round and saw Anderson emerging from the carved stone doorway. The tall, hunched vampire cast a quick look up and down the quiet street, then stepped casually into the air and disappeared.

Carpenter turned to Private Miller, who was seated in the back of the vehicle, cradling a sleek black laptop that was connected to a spy satellite in geo-synchronous orbit above them.

"Do you have the heat trail?" he asked.

"Yes, sir," responded the young operator. "He's heading north by northwest, sir."

Six minutes after dawn the following morning, Julian ordered their car brought to a halt in front of the Molnár estate. Two ornate metal gates stood open, the first rays of sunlight glimmering on the wrought iron. The five men had strapped and clipped their body armor into place during the drive, and there was a heavy sense of anticipation inside the vehicle. Carpenter looked at his team and decided against saying anything more to them. If they weren't ready, then nothing he could say at this late stage would correct that. And if they were, he didn't want to give them anything extra to think about. They would soon have more than enough to deal with; of that he was quite sure.

The estate's main building, an enormous seventeenth-century country house, squatted on top of a long, shallow rise, its upper floors visible from the gate. The road that led from the open entrance wound left then right, through dense lines of neatly clipped trees, then led straight up the hill toward a wide graveled driveway in front of the house. The trees fell away on both sides, and the five Blacklight operators were confronted with a hundred yards of immaculate, featureless lawn, a vast open space that would have filled Carpenter with dread were it not for the pale yellow sunlight reflecting off the morning dew.

They crossed the lawns quickly, moving in a tight X-shaped formation; Carpenter in the middle, Turner and Frankenstein leading the way, the two privates bringing up the rear. Their boots crunched across the gravel as they approached the home of the Molnár family, and then Turner pushed open the towering front door, and the five men slipped silently into the house.

The smell was the first thing that hit them as they stepped onto the tiled marble floor of the atrium; a stench of rot so thick it felt as though you could have bitten into it. A dark haze of flies looped lazily in an open doorway at the rear of the room, and Carpenter led them toward it. Beyond the door was a large, spotlessly modern kitchen, big enough to have serviced a medium-sized restaurant. The smell intensified as they entered, waving the swarming flies away with their gloved hands. On a counter above one of the ovens, in a steel baking tray, was a leg of roast lamb. It was a virulent purple color and had swollen to almost double its size as the rot set in. The meat was leaking a milky fluid that was collecting in a thick pool in the tray, and maggots were swarming in wide crevices that had split open in the decaying flesh. Flies buzzed in a dense cloud above it, landing and taking off in a swirling pattern of shiny black bodies and translucent wings. Beside the tray stood bowls of black, liquidizing potatoes and vegetables, and a tray of crystal champagne flutes, their contents now long since flat.

Private Miller gagged, as quietly as he could.

"How long?" asked Turner, his voice as calm as ever.

"This time of year?" replied Carpenter. "A week, at least."

The five men stood in silence, regarding the spoiled food. The likely implications for those who had been intending to eat it did not need vocalizing.

"Let's keep moving," said Carpenter.

The team moved into the lobby, a beautiful, cavernous space, with wooden walls and gleaming black-and-white marble tiles. Above them, a domed window let in the morning sun, lending the place a sense of peace and calm that couldn't have been further from what the men were feeling.

In the dining room, they found the bodies.

It was more a hall than a room, a long oak-paneled hall, lined on one side by windows that overlooked the pale green grass of the lawns. A dark wood dining table sat in the middle of the room; stale bowls of bread sat on delicate serving plates in the middle of the surface, and gleaming water glasses and ornate silver cutlery stood expectantly in front of empty chairs.

A cavernous fireplace sat in the middle of the far wall and arranged around it were a number of comfortable-looking armchairs, no doubt the setting for thousands of after-dinner brandies over the years, and it was around these chairs that the Molnár family and their servants had been arranged.

There were six bodies in all. A man in his late fifties or early sixties sat in one of the armchairs, his head thrown back and his throat torn out. On his knee had been placed a girl, no more than seven years old, whose slender, pale neck bore two circular puncture marks. No other torment had been visited upon her, as far as Carpenter could see, and he felt a rush of relief at the quick death she had received, a privilege that had not been afforded the rest of the household.

The men approached slowly, although it was immediately obvious that nothing lived in this room. Their boots crunched softly as they tracked through a huge oval of dried blood, and even Turner winced at the sound. Two servants, a butler and a maid, had been laid end to end on the floor, their heads next to each other, their dead eyes staring up at the ceiling above them. Their throats had been slashed so violently that they almost appeared decapitated. Carpenter forced himself to focus on the last two victims, a boy and a girl in their early twenties. They had died with their arms around each other, huddled into one of the armchairs. The boy's face wore an expression of defiance that brought a savage joy to Carpenter's heart.

Good for you, boy, he thought. *Didn't give them the satisfaction. Good for you.*

The girl, whose arms were wrapped tight around the boy's neck, had clearly possessed no such steel; her face was a mask of terror and utter, hopeless misery. She had been beautiful, her face a perfect narrow oval, her hair the color of barley, her limbs long and slender. She was dressed in a ball gown made of a silver material that shimmered in the morning sunlight.

They had both been bled white. Below the girl's shapely face, a second mouth had been opened on her throat, a savage grin of torn skin. The boy's hands had been removed, the stumps of his arms ragged and chewed by the teeth of God alone knew how many vampires. There was not a drop of blood on either of the bodies, and it turned Carpenter's stomach to think about where such a huge volume of liquid had gone.

"Sir."

It was Private Miller's voice, and Julian looked in his direction.

"What is it, Private?"

"Footprints, sir." The young man gestured, and Carpenter followed the sweep of his arm. Several people had walked through the blood when it was still wet, toward a door set inconspicuously in the corner of the wood paneling, through which they had disappeared.

Carpenter nodded to Turner. The gray-eyed major stepped carefully forward and placed his ear against the wooden door. After a couple of seconds, he stepped back, drew the T-Bone from his belt, and kicked the door open. The frame shattered, and the door flew against a stone wall, cracking almost in two. There was a pregnant moment, then Turner stepped through the opening.

"Clear," he said.

They stood in a narrow stone corridor, lit by an overhanging lightbulb. The walls were bare, and a worn staircase descended in front of them. Turner led them down it, his T-Bone pointing steadily before him. Carpenter drew his own weapon, motioned for the rest of the men to do the same, and followed.

After perhaps twenty steps, the floor leveled off and the passage widened into a large cellar. Shelves of dry goods lined one wall: sacks of rice and flour, barrels of olive oil and bottles of vinegar, sides of cured meat. The opposite wall was covered in a long row of floor-to-ceiling wooden racks, in which stood hundreds of bottles of wine, port and champagne. At the far end of the room, the final rack had been thrown over, smashing tens of bottles on the hard stone floor and filling the air with the strong scent of rotting fruit. They made their way through the cellar, and stopped in front of the downed rack. Behind it was an ancient carved stone arch, leading into utter blackness.

"Light," said Carpenter.

Private Miller unclipped the torch from his belt and shone the beam into the hole. It illuminated the snarling face of a vampire, his teeth bared, his eyes crimson as he rushed toward them.

Julian wiped blood from his beard and flicked it disgustedly onto the floor.

"First guard," said Turner, quietly.

"Agreed," replied Frankenstein. "It's possible they know we're coming."

"I don't think so," said Carpenter. "I think it was expecting police, or one of the family. I don't think it raised an alarm."

"Let's hope you're right," said Frankenstein.

The team advanced into the darkness, the beams of their torches illuminating a round stone passage, moving as quietly as possible. The path led around a corner and began to widen, until they were standing in front of a heavy-looking wooden door. Carpenter motioned Connor forward, and the young private lowered his shoulder and slowly pushed it open. The hinges screamed as he did so, the door opening onto another stretch of passage. Connor stepped through it, and as the order to wait rose in Carpenter's throat, a dark shadow fell from the ceiling, driving him to the ground. The torch beams converged, and the team watched in stunned horror as a vampire girl, who appeared to be no older than eleven or twelve, ripped his helmet from his head and sank her teeth into his neck. Connor screamed and thrashed in her grip. Blood flew in the enclosed space, splattering the walls and the floor, and when she clamped her teeth together and tore into his throat, the scream dissolved into a terrible gurgling sound.

Turner was the first to react, as always. He stepped forward, pulled the stake from his belt, and slammed it into the girl's left eye. She howled in pain, released Connor, and jumped to her feet, blood and yellow jelly pouring from her ruined eye socket. Frankenstein had drawn his T-Bone, and he pulled the trigger. The projectile thumped into her chest, driving her back along the passage, until she exploded in a torrent of gore. The stake whistled back into the barrel, and the four men rushed to where Private Connor lay bleeding.

Carpenter knelt beside him and took his hand. Connor was on the verge of going into shock, his eyes rolling wildly, his pulse irregular and rapid. Blood was gushing out of the hole in his neck, and Turner took a wad of gauze from the medical kit on his belt and thrust it into the wound, pinching the artery shut. Connor screamed, blood frothing from his lips as he did so, but Turner didn't even flinch.

"Easy, son," said Carpenter. "Easy. We're going to get you out of here."

"Oh God," said Miller. He was standing motionless, staring down at the blood-soaked man, his face a mask of utter horror.

"Come on," said Carpenter. "Let's get him up. Turner, call for an evac. We need to get him out of here, right now."

Nobody moved.

"Come on!" roared Carpenter. "Those were direct orders!"

"Julian," said Frankenstein, in a low voice. "You know it's too late for that. We're at least two hours away from the nearest place we can give him the transfusion he needs. If he doesn't die, he'll have turned by then."

"I don't accept that," replied Carpenter, his voice bristling with anger. "And I don't care if you're right—we're going to try anyway. I'm not going to let him die down here."

"Sir . . ." Private Connor's voice was thick, as though it was being spoken underwater. Carpenter looked down at him.

"I know there's . . . nothing you can . . . do," the young operator continued. "Don't . . . let me turn. Please. Don't . . . let me. . . ."

Connor's eyes rolled back white, and his mouth fell open. His chest was still rising and falling but barely, and blood had started running from his neck again, soaking Turner's hand red.

Carpenter stood up and looked at the three men around him. Miller was staring blankly down at Connor, his eyes blank and lifeless. Frankenstein was returning Julian's gaze, an even look on his face, and Turner was looking up at him with his expressionless gray eyes. Carpenter clenched his jaw, reached down, and pulled the Glock from its holster.

At the sight of the gun, Miller cried out. "What are you doing?"

"What needs to be done," said Frankenstein.

"He needs a hospital!" shouted Miller, tears brimming in the corners of his eyes. "He doesn't need putting down like a sick dog!"

"We don't let people turn. Ever. And he doesn't want to. You heard him say so."

"He doesn't know what he's saying!"

"Yes," said Frankenstein, firmly. "He does."

Miller's face contorted into an expression of such terrible misery that Carpenter's heart nearly broke.

"But . . . it's not fair," he said, his voice cracking.

"I know," said Carpenter. "It's not. But letting him turn would be worse than letting him die. You understand that, right?"

Miller nodded, slowly.

Carpenter turned back to Connor, who was still unconscious. He knelt down beside him and placed the muzzle of the Glock against the young private's temple. Turner stayed knelt on his other side, staring levelly at his commanding officer. Julian placed his other hand above the barrel and pulled the trigger.

The remainder of the team were silent as they made their way deeper into the tunnels, passing through a second door and arriving at a large stone arch, topped with a sculpted image of the crucifixion. Turner shoved open the ancient wooden door, and the four operators walked into a wide circular chapel. The walls were covered with statues of saints, and a huge stone crucifix stood behind a plain stone altar at the rear of the room.

The floor was covered in vampires.

There had to be at least twenty of them, sleeping, tightly packed together like bats. As they took in the scene, Private Miller gasped. The vampire nearest to them, an old man with a beard almost to his bare waist, opened his eyes, which instantly boiled red. He let out a piercing scream, and every vampire in the room awoke, and leapt to their feet.

The Blacklight team launched themselves into the chapel, a blur of black uniforms and piercing weapons. Frankenstein lowered his head and barreled into them, sending vampires flying in every direction. He pulled the MP5 from his belt and emptied it into the crowd of stumbling, half-asleep vampires, who were so tightly packed together, they were struggling to move. The bullets tore into them. Miller, whose young face bore the look of a man who had already seen more than he had ever wanted to, attacked the disorientated crowd with a fervor that bordered on mania, staking vampire after vampire, an inarticulate roar emanating from his wide open mouth. Turner sidestepped along the wall and drew his T-Bone. Calmly, without hurrying, he shot six vampires one after the other, letting the stake wind back in each time, then taking new aim and firing again. Carpenter ran to Frankenstein's side, and the two of them pressed the howling, injured vampires back against the stone wall, then staked them in a flurry of sharpened metal.

It was over in less than a minute.

"Alexandru?" asked Carpenter, breathing deeply.

Turner shook his head.

"In there?" suggested Frankenstein, motioning toward the altar.

They walked forward. Behind the altar, beneath the sculpted crucifixion, was the entrance to a short corridor. Carpenter leaned down and looked along it. The stone passage was no more than twenty feet and ended in what looked like a prayer room; he could see a kneeling board against the back wall.

Frankenstein led them into the corridor, bending slightly to fit his large frame through the opening. He had replaced the empty MP5 on his belt and had drawn the silver and black riot shotgun he always carried with him; he loaded it with solid shot, and it could blow a hole through a tree trunk.

They were almost at the door when something emerged from it, moving fast. Frankenstein pulled the trigger on the shotgun, and fire exploded from the barrel as a deafening noise filled the passage. The thing smashed against the wall, slid to the floor, and started to scream.

As the smoke cleared, Carpenter stepped forward and looked at the shape. A beautiful female face, twisted into a grimace of agony, stared back at him.

"Ilyana," he said. "Where is your husband?"

She snarled and then spit a thick wad of blood into his face.

"Too late, valet! He's gone! Too late!" she shrieked.

Julian's boot thumped into her ribs, sending her crashing into the wall. An enormous hole had been blown in her stomach, and blood was gushing out across the stone floor.

"Too late! Too late!" She started crawling again, screeching obscenities as she did so, and Julian walked back to the rest of his team.

"He's not here," Carpenter said.

"What do you mean, he's not here?" asked Turner.

"I mean he's not here," Julian snapped. "He's somewhere else, he's gone, he's not here. Understand?"

Turner didn't reply, but nor did he drop his gaze. "I'll finish her," he said. "She's a valuable target. It means the mission wasn't a failure."

"Tell that to Connor," said Miller.

"No. I'll do it," said Carpenter, pulling the T-Bone from his belt. "You stay here."

He walked down the corridor.

Ilyana had dragged herself into the room at the end, and Julian followed her in. Above the kneeling step, a carving of the Virgin Mary stared down at him as he entered, the door swinging shut behind him.

At the other end of the corridor, the three Blacklight operators waited. From behind the door came a piercing scream, a rush of air, then a wet splashing sound. The door opened and Julian Carpenter emerged, his uniform soaked in blood. Behind him, the walls of the room dripped red, and he left crimson footprints on the stone floor as he returned to his men.

THREE'S A CROWD

Jamie lifted his hands away from his face and looked at Frankenstein. He had covered himself when the monster finished his story; he didn't want to let him see his tears.

"So that's why Alexandru has my mother?" he said, his voice shaking. "Because Dad killed his wife?"

"I don't know," said Frankenstein. "It would appear so."

"Why does it appear so?" said Jamie, anger filling his voice. "It seems pretty clear to me."

"I'm sure it does," replied Frankenstein. His calm tone was maddening.

"Why doesn't it to you then?" he said, fiercely. "What aren't you telling me?"

The monster sighed. "There are a lot of people who, in light of what happened later, don't believe your father killed Ilyana at all. Neither Major Turner or I saw her die. We just heard the shot."

Jamie stared at him. "You think he faked it."

Frankenstein slammed his fist down on the surface of the table. "I was your father's closest friend," he said, his voice like ice. "And I have stood at the side of your family for almost ninety years. And yet you sit there and question where my loyalties lie? I have done things in the protection and service of your ancestors that would make your ears bleed, and you question me?"

"I'll question whatever I want!" yelled Jamie, standing up from the table and sending his chair clattering to the floor. He put his hands onto the surface and leaned toward Frankenstein. "Do you think Ilyana is still alive? That my father let her go? Tell me!"

The monster slowly unfolded himself out of his chair and rose to his full height. His shadow engulfed Jamie. "Listen to me," he said. "I would have died for Julian Carpenter. I never doubted or questioned him, until a swarm of vampires brought the Blacklight jet down in a ball of fire on the runway of this base, killing eight good men in the process. It happened a quarter of a mile beyond the outer fence, on the edge of the most strictly classified and highly protected base in the country. A place that doesn't exist on any map, a place that planes and satellites are not permitted to fly over. A place—"

"A place where hundreds of people work every day," interrupted Jamie. "Any of them could have told Alexandru where we are."

"No," said Frankenstein. "They couldn't. The civilian staff are flown in and out every day on a plane with no windows, from an airport fifty miles away from here. They have no idea where they are. Only senior operators are allowed to come and go."

"And there's how many of them? A hundred? Two hundred? More?"

"About two hundred. And you're right, any of them could have told Alexandru where Blacklight is. But very few of them could have given him a map of the infrared sensors that fill the woods for ten miles beyond the fence. Only about six people in Department 19 have access to that information. And without that information, there would have been time for the passengers to pull their chutes. But she was so low when they hit her, there was no time for anyone to do anything. She exploded, right out there on the runway. The investigation was still ongoing when your father died, ten days after the crash. He left base the night he died without warning or permission, without telling anyone where he was going. But he was still logged into the network when he left, and a duty officer saw something unusual on his screen. When they investigated, they found an e-mail your father had sent to an unknown address. Attached to it were maps of the infrared sensor array."

Jamie walked stiffly away from the table and slid down the wall to the floor. He wrapped his arms around his knees and buried his head against them. When he spoke again, his voice was tiny. "Why would he do it? It doesn't make any sense."

Frankenstein lowered himself back into his chair. "After he died, the data forensics team dug through every key Julian had ever pressed on a Blacklight computer. Buried way down in his personal folders, behind about a dozen passwords and layers of encryption, they found a letter he had written. In it, he claimed to be righting the wrongs that had been done to your family, the injustice you had suffered at the hands of the other founding families. He believed that they still only thought of him as the descendant of a valet, and they would never see or treat him as an equal. He cited the fact that no Carpenter has ever been director as proof of how your family was perceived, and he said that he was not going to tolerate it any longer."

"How would bringing down the jet accomplish that?" asked Jamie, without raising his head.

"The *Mina's* pilots that day were John and George Harker," said Frankenstein. "Two descendants of arguably the most famous name in Blacklight history."

The image of the plaque in the rose garden burst into Jamie's mind.

Oh God. Oh God. Oh, Dad. What did you do? There was only one thing he didn't understand: one final straw to cling to. "Why did Alexandru come for us, if Dad was working with him? Why would he want us dead?"

"I don't know," Frankenstein said, simply. "Maybe Julian did kill Ilyana and made a deal with Alexandru so that he would spare you and your mother. Maybe Alexandru double-crossed him. Or maybe he did let Ilyana live, and Alexandru double-crossed him for the sheer hell of it. It doesn't matter now. He's gone."

Jamie raised his head and looked at Frankenstein with puffy, teary eyes. "Isn't there any part of you that still believes in him?" he asked. "That believes he didn't do it?"

The monster turned his chair toward Jamie, rested his

elbows on his knees, and leaned forward. "I believed in him for as long as I could," he said. "I fought his case for months after he died. I examined every scrap of the evidence against him, reviewed every line of the data forensics report, checked and double-checked every word. I refused to even entertain the idea that Julian could have done such a thing; I threatened to resign a dozen times."

He looked sadly at Jamie, and took a deep breath. "I never found anything that would exonerate him. We buried John and George, and we waited for Alexandru to make his next move. But it never came. And as time passed, I eventually had to accept what everyone else had come to realize; that Julian had done what they said he had done, and I was just going to have to live with it, no matter how much it hurt my heart to do so."

Frankenstein sat patiently, watching Jamie. But Jamie wasn't thinking about his father; he was thinking about his mother and the awful way he had treated her after his dad had died, the terrible things he had said. Hot shame was flooding through him, and he would have given anything to be able to tell her how sorry he was, to tell her he was wrong and ask her to forgive him.

"I was so angry with him for leaving us," he said, eventually. "My mother always told me I was being unfair. But I wasn't. He betrayed everyone."

"Your father was a good man who did an awful thing," said Frankenstein. "He made a terrible mistake, and he paid for it with his life."

"And eight other people's lives," said Jamie, his voice

suddenly fierce. "What did the people on the plane do to deserve what happened to them? Not be nice enough to anyone whose surname was Carpenter? How pathetic is that?"

Frankenstein said nothing.

"I'm ashamed to be his son," spit Jamie. "No wonder everyone in this place looks at me like they do. I would hate me, too. I'm glad he's dead."

"Don't say that," said Frankenstein. "He was still your father. He raised you, and he loved you, and you loved him back. I know you did."

"I don't care!" Jamie cried. "I don't care about any of that! I didn't even know him; the man who raised me wasn't even real! The man who raised me was a case officer at the Ministry of Defense, who went on golf weekends with his friends and complained about the price of gasoline. He didn't exist!" He leapt to his feet and kicked his fallen chair across the room. It skidded across the tiled floor and slammed into the wall. "I won't waste another second thinking about him," he said, his pale blue eyes fixing on Frankenstein's. "He's dead, my mother is still alive, for now at least, and we need to find her. I'm going to talk to Larissa again."

The monster stiffened in his seat. "What good do you think will come of that?" he said.

"I don't know. But I think she wants to help me. I can't explain why."

Frankenstein stared at the teenager. He was about to reply when the radio on Jamie's belt crackled into life.

Jamie pulled it from its loop and looked at the screen. "Channel 7," he said.

"That's the live operation channel," said Frankenstein. "No

one should be using it."

Jamie keyed the CONNECT button on the handset, and then almost dropped it as a terrible scream of agony burst from the plastic speaker. Frankenstein stood bolt upright, staring at the radio in the teenager's hand.

A low voice whispered something inaudible, and then a man's voice, trembling and shaking, spoke through the radio.

". . . Hello? Who i-is this?"

"This is Jamie Carpe—"

There was a tearing noise, horribly wet, and the scream came again, a high-pitched wail of pain and terror.

"Oh God, please!" shrieked the man. "Please, please, don't! Oh God, please don't hurt me anymore!"

Jamie looked helplessly at Frankenstein. The monster's face had turned slate gray, and his misshapen eyes were wide. He was staring at the radio as though it were a direct line to hell.

Something whispered again, and then the voice was back, hitching and rolling as the man who was speaking fought back tears.

"You have to come," the voice said between enormous sobs of pain. "H-he says you h-have to come to him. He s-says if you d-don't then you'll n-never see your m-mother again."

Rage exploded through Jamie. "Alexandru," he growled, his voice unrecognizable. "Where are y—"

The man screamed again, so long and loud that the scream descended to a high-pitched croak. Something laughed quietly in the background, as the man spoke two final, gasping words. "Help me."

Then the line went dead.

Jamie stared at the radio for a long moment, then dropped it on the table, a look of utter revulsion on his face. Frankenstein slowly lowered himself back into his chair and looked at the teenager with wide, horrified eyes.

"How would he have that frequency?" Jamie asked, his voice trembling. "How could he possibly have it?"

"I don't know," replied Frankenstein. "It's changed every forty-eight hours."

"So someone must have given it to him in the last two days?"

Frankenstein's eyes widened as the realization of Jamie's point sank in. He pulled his own radio from his belt, twisted the channel selector switch, then spoke into the receiver.

"Thomas Morris to Level 0, room 24B, immediately," he said, and then Jamie gasped as the monster's voice boomed out of the speakers that stood in the high corners of every room in the base.

"You'll wake the entire Department," he protested. "What are you doing?"

"Getting some answers," replied Frankenstein.

Barely a minute later, Thomas Morris pushed open the door to the office and staggered inside. His face was puffy and his eyes were narrow slits, and he was yawning even as he asked them what the emergency was.

"You're security officer, Tom. So you can search the network access logs, correct?" asked Frankenstein.

Morris rubbed his eyes with the heels of his hands. "I can do that," he replied.

"Good. I need you to search for anyone who has accessed the frequency database in the last forty-eight hours."

Morris groaned. "This couldn't have waited until—"

"I need you to do it now, please," interrupted Frankenstein.

Morris shot the monster a look of mild annoyance, then pulled his portable console from the pouch on his belt. He placed it on the desk, coded in, and ran the search, as Jamie and Frankenstein watched over his shoulder.

Beep.

The three men looked at the words that had appeared on the console's screen.

No results found.

"There you go," said Morris. "No one's accessed the frequency database in the last forty-eight hours. Can I go back to bed now?"

Frankenstein stared at the screen, then looked at Morris. "Yes," he said, his voice low. "Sorry to have disturbed you."

"It's all right," said Morris, a weary smile on his face. "Good night, gentlemen."

"Good night, Tom," said Jamie.

Morris closed the office door behind him, leaving Jamie and Frankenstein alone again.

"So," said Jamie, in a tired voice. "I think you're going to struggle to blame my dad for this, don't you?"

"Jamie—" Frankenstein began, but the teenager cut him off.

"Not now. I can't even think about who gave Alexandru the frequency now. We have to find him, and we have to do it before he hurts anyone else. I'm going to get some sleep, and then I'm going down to the cellblock, and we're going to do whatever she says we should do."

Jamie walked toward the door and was about to turn the handle when the monster called to him.

"Do you really think you can trust her?"

He turned, and looked at Frankenstein with sadness in his eyes. "As much as I can anyone else around here," he replied.

Jamie had lied to the monster.

He was tired, that was certainly true, but he wasn't going straight to the dormitory. Instead he pushed open the door to the infirmary, walked quickly across the white floor and into the room marked THEATER.

"I don't know what to do," he said, flopping gracelessly into the chair beside Matt's bed. The teenage boy was still as pale as a ghost, and the rhythmic beeping of the machines still filled the room.

"I don't know what to believe, or who to believe, or anything. I feel like I'm completely lost."

Jamie looked at the peaceful expression on Matt's face, and found himself envying it. He didn't know what he was doing in the infirmary, but he had been filled with a powerful compulsion to see the injured teenager. He wondered if it was because this boy was the one person in the Loop who would not tell him something new, who didn't know who he was or what his father had done, and who he could talk to without worrying how he sounded.

"Frankenstein was my dad's closest friend, and even he thinks he betrayed the Department. And if he thinks it's true, then it probably is. But then who gave Alexandru the operational frequency so he could call me on it? It's been changed a thousand times since Dad died. Larissa knows more than she's telling me, and the Chemist definitely did, and I'm pretty sure Frankenstein does as well. Why doesn't anyone want me to know the truth about anything? It's like no one cares if I find Mom or not."

His hand went involuntarily to his neck, and he felt the wad of bandages that had been stuck to his skin. "I got hurt today. Not as badly as you, I know, but I got burned. And it made me realize something, you know? It made me realize that this isn't a game, or a film, where the good guys win in the end and the bad guys get what's coming to them. It's real life, and it's messy, and it's complicated, and I'm scared, and I just don't know what to—"

Jamie lowered his head into his hands and wept. The machines beeped steadily, and Matt's eyes remained closed.

Jamie didn't think he would be able to sleep when he lay down on his dormitory bed fifteen minutes later, but he was out as soon as his head touched the pillow. His sleep was long and dreamless, and when he awoke, his body feeling rested but his mind racing with the enormity of the task before him, he saw that it was past three in the afternoon.

He showered, dressed quickly, made his way back down to the detention level, and walked quickly down the long block. When he reached her cell, he looked into the square room, and found Larissa standing in her underwear, pulling on her jeans. She was facing away from him, and he hurried back along the corridor, flushing a fiery red.

"I can hear you," she said conversationally, and he closed his eyes and groaned. "You might as well come out."

He stepped back in front of her cell and looked at her. She was now fully dressed, standing easily in the middle of her cell, looking at him with her head tilted slightly to the left.

"Your heart's pounding," she said. "I can hear it. Is that embarrassment or excitement?"

"Embarrassment," said Jamie. "Definitely embarrassment."

"Pity," she said, and flashed him a wicked smile. He blushed again, his face now feeling as though it must erupt, it was so hot, and then a thought occurred to him.

If she can hear my heartbeat, she must be able to hear my footsteps like an elephant's. Why didn't she hurry up and get dressed when she heard me coming down the block?

"Because it's fun to tease you," she said, and Jamie took a shocked step backward.

"How did you know—"

"You're a smart boy," she said, smiling again.

She floated across the cell and spun elegantly onto her bed. She laced her hands behind her head and looked at him. "Did you talk to the monster?" she asked.

"I did."

"And?"

"I wish I hadn't. But I'm glad I did. Does that make sense?"

She smiled at him, and Jamie's heart leapt in his chest.

"I know exactly what you mean," she said.

Jamie composed himself. "I want to take you up on your offer," he said. "I don't have permission to take you off the base, but I'll do it if you to take me to the person you think can help me."

Larissa untangled her fingers and pushed herself up on her

elbows. "Are you serious?" she asked. "This isn't you getting back at me?"

"I'm serious."

"What brought on the change of heart?"

"I've got no choice," he said. "I don't know what else to do. I get why Alexandru wants to hurt me now. I know about what my father did. You were right; it all started with him."

She looked at him with kindness in her face. "I bet that hurt to say," she said.

"A little bit, yeah."

Larissa flipped up off the bed, soared slowly through the air, and landed silently in front of him, a look of excitement on her face.

"Let's do it," she said, eagerly.

"You'll need to wear an explosive belt."

"Fine."

"You can't leave my sight."

She fluttered her eyelashes at him. "Why would I want to?" she purred.

"I'm serious."

"So am I."

"You take us to this person who can help, we get the information from them, and then you come back here. Quietly and peacefully."

"Of course. Let's go, let's go."

Larissa was hopping gently from one foot to the other, such was her excitement at the prospect at being allowed to leave her cell, to stand under the open sky again, to feel the night air in her hair.

"Not just yet," said Jamie, and smiled at her.

She stopped still and looked at him.

I don't like that smile, she thought. *I don't like it at all.*

"Why?" she asked, cautiously.

"You're going to tell me something first. And you're going to tell me the truth."

ALL THE FUN OF THE FAIR

Reading, England
July 24, 2004

Larissa Kinley knew it was early before she opened her eyes; it was too dark in her bedroom, too quiet. She forced her gummy eyelids open and saw that she was right. The digital alarm clock on her bedside table read 5:06 in glowing green numbers. She sat up in bed and stretched her arms above her head, yawning widely. It was the eighth night in a row that she had found herself awake when she should be asleep, watching the green numbers tick over until she could legitimately get up and go in the shower. She hadn't told her parents about what she was beginning to think qualified as insomnia; she knew that they would nod, halfheartedly sympathize, and then go back to whatever they were doing.

Larissa rolled out of bed and walked over to her bedroom window. She was about to open it, to let some fresh air into the room in the hope that it would tire her out, when she looked down into the small garden at the back of their little semidetached house and clapped her hand over her mouth so she didn't scream.

The old man was standing in her garden, looking up at her with a gentle smile on his face, his gray overcoat wrapped around him, his hands casually in his pockets. His eyes were bright in the soft orange light of the streetlight that stood beyond the garden fence—and horribly, revoltingly friendly.

She took a step backward and tripped over one of the leather boots she had dropped at the end of her bed the night before. Her arms wheeled as she tried to keep her balance, but it was futile. She fell to the floor, hard, her teeth clicking shut on her tongue and sending a dagger of agony through her head. Tasting blood in her mouth, she scrambled to her knees and crawled back to the window. She inched her head above the windowsill and looked down into the garden.

The man was gone.

There was no more sleep for Larissa that night. She lay on her bed, playing the events of the previous two days over and over in her head, looking for a way to put the pieces together. She was still trying when she heard her brother's bedroom door thump open, and she got up and raced across the landing, shoving him out of the way and closing the bathroom door behind her. Liam hammered halfheartedly on the door, but they both knew how this game went, and he quickly gave up and went back to his room.

Standing in front of the mirror, Larissa poked her tongue out and looked at the tiny cut her teeth had made. She sucked the blood away, watched it instantly well up again, then brushed her teeth, carefully, and stepped into the shower. She emerged twenty minutes later with her mind no clearer. Every time she managed to push the old man out of her head and think about something else—her coursework, the fair she and her friends were going to that evening—he would suddenly appear, smiling his soft smile, staring at her with those wide, friendly eyes.

Her parents already sat at the table when she made her way downstairs to breakfast, her wet hair wrapped in a towel and piled on her head. Her dad was reading the business section of *The Times* and slowly demolishing half a grapefruit, while her mother nibbled unconvincingly at a piece of toast and stared into thin air. Neither of them said anything as she sat down and poured herself a bowl of cornflakes and a glass of orange juice. She again considered telling them about the old man but decided against it.

No point in talking to them at all these days.

She knew Liam felt it, too, although he refused to talk about it with her. Their father had stopped going to Liam's soccer matches at the start of the summer, without ever offering an explanation or an apology, as though he had simply forgotten that it was something he used to do. Larissa knew it had hurt her brother more deeply than he would ever admit, particularly to his big sister, but he had never questioned his dad about it. It was obvious that something bigger than football was going on: A thick cloud of disinterest had settled over their parents at the start of the year and showed no signs of lifting. She was sure that telling them about the old man would bring nothing more than tired suggestions that she had had a nightmare, that there was nothing to worry about.

Even if she told them it was the third day in a row she had seen him.

Larissa ate her cereal in silence, said good-bye to her parents as they left for work, then went upstairs. As she passed her brother's room, she saw him sitting at his desk instant messaging with someone, probably one of the large number of seemingly identical adolescent boys who were his friends. They were polite and more than a little shy when she answered their knocks at the door in the evenings, but she nearly always caught their eyes crawling over her chest, and it made her shudder.

"Morning, Liam," she said.

He grunted, which Larissa knew was the best she was likely to get from him.

In her room, Larissa apathetically flipped through *Emma* for the next couple of hours, her mind on anything but Jane Austen. She made herself some lunch, downloaded some music, lay on her bed, paced around her bedroom, and generally killed time until it was time to go to the fair. Her father was getting out of his car when she stepped out of the house, and he waved a halfhearted greeting at her. She returned it with an equal lack of enthusiasm, and he stopped her as she passed him.

"Are you OK?" he asked, peering at her from sleepy, hooded eyes.

"I'm fine, Dad," she snapped. "What about you? Are you OK?"

Her father looked at her, then dropped his gaze.

"That's what I thought," she said, and walked down the driveway and out onto the street, the heels of her boots clicking furiously along the pavement.

The fair was an annual event, beloved by the town's teenagers and children alike. The kids loved the bumper cars, the small roller coaster, the Barrel Roll, and the Chair-O-Planes; the teenagers loved the neon lights, the dark corners where they could kiss, the games and the arcades. It was, in truth, little more than a collection of sideshows with two or three half-decent rides, but the strips of lights mingled with the scents of cotton candy and roasting nuts and the tinny sound track to create something that was slightly magical.

All this was lost on Larissa's friend Amber, who was enthusiastically kissing a boy from their history class, her back pressed against the wall of the coconut-shy booth, her hands holding his firmly at his sides so he didn't get any ideas about putting them anywhere else. The rest of the girls had wandered off to smoke a spliff behind the bumper cars, and Larissa found herself alone. She waited a few minutes for Amber to disentangle herself from the boy, who had greasy hair and acne, but Amber seemed in no hurry to do so, even though he was the third boy she had kissed in the little over an hour they had been at the fair. Eventually Larissa wandered away.

She walked down the fair's main street and out into the darkness of the park, following the fence that separated the fields from the main road. Cars sped past her, their headlights blazing, snatches of music floating from open windows, and she was overcome with a sense of sorrow and loss. Her hands shook as she dragged a pack of Marlboro Lights from her pocket, pulled one from the box, and applied the small yellow flame of her lighter to the tip.

"Those things will kill you."

Larissa jumped, her heart lurching in her chest, at the sound of the old man's voice. She knew it was him even as she was turning toward the source of the words; the voice was extraordinary, unlike any other she had ever heard. It rolled and swooned, as deep as a double bass and as smooth as honey, full of whispered promises and dark secrets. She turned to the fence and saw the old man on the other side of it, standing on the pavement with his hands in his pockets. For the first time since she had seen him two days ago, standing quietly on the corner of her road as she walked home from the library, he was not smiling. Instead he was looking at her with an expression of great sadness.

The fence between them was more than six feet high, green metal topped with wicked spikes, and it emboldened her. She took a step toward the old man.

"Why are you following me?" she asked, her voice sharp. "What the hell were you doing in my garden this morning?"

The old man's smile returned. "I'm sorry," he said. "You look like someone I used to know."

She opened her mouth to ask who, but before she could form the words, the old man moved. He stepped into the air, as casually as most people would climb a staircase, and floated up and over the fence. His coat billowed out behind him, the sleeves riding up, and Larissa caught sight of a narrow black V tattooed on the inside of his left forearm, before he landed gently in front of her. She opened her mouth to scream, but he closed the distance between them impossibly quickly and clamped a hand over her mouth.

"I'm sorry," he whispered, his breath hot in her ear. "I truly am." Then he buried his face in her neck. She felt pain, so sharp it was almost sweet, and then she was gone.

It was still dark when Larissa awoke. She was lying on the grass beneath an oak tree, and she was cold and damp with dew. Her head felt heavy, and she struggled to her feet. She walked through the quiet stalls and rides of the fair, kicking through piles of litter and abandoned food, heading toward the park gates.

She remembered nothing about the previous night, nothing after she left her father standing in their driveway. Where were Amber and the rest of the girls? How could they just leave without her—hadn't any of them bothered to look for her when they left? In the back of her head, a deep, gentle voice told her that everything was going to be all right, but she didn't think it was.

She didn't think that was even close to the truth.

The house was dark as she turned into the driveway, shivering, her arms wrapped tightly around her. She hoped that her parents were worried out of their minds, but she knew they would probably not have even noticed that she hadn't come home.

She crept up the stairs, not because she cared if she woke anyone up, but because she didn't want to be asked questions that she had no answers to. She would get some real sleep in a proper bed, then phone Amber and find out what had happened. Larissa undressed, lay down on her bed, pulling her duvet around her like a cocoon, and was asleep in less than a minute.

An hour later, she awoke and buried her face in her pillow so she didn't scream. Her head was splitting in two, a huge thunderbolt of agony running through her forehead, as though someone had buried an axe in it. She rolled over, the pillow clamped to her face, her eyes wide with pain and terror, and then the hunger hit her, and she doubled up into a fetal ball. It was like nothing she had ever felt before, a pain so huge it felt as though it must have come from somewhere outside the universe, an enormous, howling emptiness that filled her entire body. She screamed into the pillow, her body convulsing, thrashing back and forth as though she was having a seizure. She screamed and screamed, and after what felt like an infinity of time, but was probably no more than a minute, the hunger subsided.

Larissa pushed the pillow away from her face. She felt as weak as an infant, and saliva was running down her cheeks and chin in sticky rivulets. Pushing the duvet away, she rolled over and flopped out of bed and didn't hit her bedroom floor.

She floated a foot above the carpet.

Incomprehension flooded through her, and she was overcome by a terror so profound she felt her eyes begin to roll back in her head, as unconsciousness fought to claim her. She thrust her hands down and felt rough material under her fingers, and her vision cleared. The floor was still there; at least that was something. She twisted in the air, tears of panic springing involuntarily into the corners of her eyes and spilling down her cheeks, and she spun slowly, rotating so she was looking down at the floor. Then suddenly, whatever was holding her in the air was gone, and she thudded face down on to the ground.

Larissa pushed herself to her feet, weeping openly, and stumbled out of her bedroom and into the bathroom. She had barely closed the door behind her when the hunger struck again, driving her to her knees. The vacuum in her stomach and chest reared open, spilling waves of agony through her body, and she shoved her fist into her mouth and screamed around it, a muffled shriek that tore at her throat. She flopped to the bathroom floor and writhed on the cold tiles, her body spasming, her mind emptied by the enormity of the pain. She twitched and convulsed and waited, desperately, pleadingly, for it to pass.

Eventually it did. She gripped the sink and pulled herself up in front of the mirror. It took her a few seconds to recognize the reflection in the mirror as her own; her skin was pale and beaded with sweat, her body was visibly trembling, and when she looked closely at her eyes, she jammed the fist back into her mouth and screamed again.

Dark red was spreading from the corners of her eyes, as though blood was being dripped slowly into them. The crimson was slowly diffusing through the white of her eyeballs and darkening her irises to a shiny black. Her vision was clear, and as she watched her eyes change, she wished it wasn't; the red in her eyes seemed to be almost alive, swirling and spinning like an oil slick, darkening and pulsing in lazy motions that turned her stomach.

The hunger hit again, a sledgehammer of agony and emptiness, and she bit down on the fist in her mouth, involuntarily spilling blood into her mouth. And instantly, the hunger was gone, replaced by a pleasure so enormous it was heavenly. Her blood ran down her throat, and she felt her knees weaken as a feeling beyond anything she had ever felt overwhelmed her; she felt as though she could push down walls, run for a hundred miles, leap, and fly like a bird.

She felt like there was nothing she couldn't do.

Then the feeling was gone, and she slumped back to her knees. She hungrily sucked more blood from her hand, but the pleasure did not return. But although she didn't know what had happened to her, although the part of her that was still recognizably Larissa was frightened beyond measure, she realized she now knew one thing, knew it with great certainty.

Blood had taken the pain away. And if her own no longer worked, she would need some from somebody else.

Larissa staggered to her feet and stumbled out of the bathroom. Then she crossed the landing and turned the handle on the door to her brother's bedroom. He had thrown the covers off during the night, and his skin was pale, bathed in a shaft of moonlight that was creeping in between the curtains above his bed. She could see the veins in his neck pulsing steadily, and the hunger screamed and thrashed in her head, driving rational thought almost entirely out of her, bellowing for her to feed, screeching and cursing in her reeling mind. She took a step toward him without even meaning to, then stopped.

It was Liam lying there; her annoying, infuriating, beautiful, funny little brother, who had never hurt her on purpose, never hurt anyone as far as she knew. She summoned up the last of her dwindling strength and ran from his room, slamming the door shut behind her. She heard him rise from his slumber, grumbling something inarticulate, then she was gone, sprinting down the stairs and through the front door, the street outside still dark, and she was running, away from the people she loved, away from the only home she had ever known.

A CALCULATED RISK

29

"I just want to say again how unhappy I am about this," said Morris.

"Do you really have to?" asked Jamie. "I think you've made it pretty clear already."

Jamie had explained his plan to Morris on their way down through the levels of the Blacklight base; he had listened incredulously before telling Jamie that there was no chance that Admiral Seward would allow it. The two were standing in the corridor outside the cellblock, waiting for Frankenstein. The monster was making his way down and had ordered them to do nothing without him present.

"I just don't understand why you trust this girl so much," said Morris. "She tried to kill you, and she ran with Alexandru. I know she's pretty, but—"

"That's got nothing to do with it," interrupted Jamie, anger flashing in his eyes. "And I don't trust her, not really. But I think someone she knows has information that I need, and I think she'll take us to them if we play along with her. I don't know why, before you ask. I just think she will."

Jamie was lying to Morris about one thing; he was starting to trust Larissa. When he thought about her, which was increasingly often, he was starting to see the teenage girl she had been, whose biggest problems had been her friends and her parents until she had wandered off on her own at the fair, and her life had been thrown into darkness.

"I hope you're right," said Morris.

"No you don't," snapped Jamie.

"Don't what?" rumbled Frankenstein's voice.

The huge man rounded the corner and stood, towering over Jamie and Morris.

"Nothing," said Jamie. "Don't worry about it."

Frankenstein gave the teenager a long look, then turned his attention to Morris. "Why are you carrying that?" he asked, pointing to a belt slung over the man's shoulder.

Morris slipped the belt down into his hands and didn't reply.

"I told him to bring it," said Jamie.

"And why would you have done that?" Frankenstein asked, his voice low and ominous.

"Larissa says she can take us to someone who will know where my mother is."

"And you're actually stupid enough to believe her?"

Jamie flushed a deep red and fingered the bandage on his neck. "I do believe her. And to be honest, I don't see how listening to her could be any worse than listening to you."

Frankenstein went very still, so still he appeared to be

holding his breath. "Excuse me?" he said, in a voice like ice.

"You heard me," said Jamie. "Following you got me nothing, apart from this burn on my neck and a lot of wasted time. I'm pretty sure wherever Larissa takes us can't be any worse."

Morris shuffled his feet and looked desperately from the teenager to the monster and back again. "Why don't we just make her tell—"

"Shut up, Tom," said Frankenstein, not taking his eyes off Jamie. "So. Even if I believed this vampire has any information that might be useful, which I don't, you're asking me to directly disobey Admiral Seward's orders and take her off base? Or were you just planning to try and sneak her out?"

"I need to know what she knows," replied Jamie. "If you won't help me, then I'll do it myself. You can try and stop me if you want."

"This isn't necessary," said Morris, an anguished look on his face. "We can just—"

"Didn't you hear me, Tom?" said Frankenstein. "If I want your opinion, I'll ask for it. Until then, be quiet."

He turned back to the teenager. "This is how it's going to be?" he asked.

Jamie shrugged. "I need to get my mother back," he said. "Nothing else matters. I thought you understood that."

For a long moment, no one said anything. Frankenstein appeared deep in thought, Jamie was standing defiantly, his head upright, his eyes wide open, and Morris was glancing furtively between them. Eventually, Frankenstein spoke again.

"Give me the belt," he said, extending a hand toward Morris, who eagerly placed it in the huge gray palm. Frankenstein tossed it lightly up and down, then looked at Jamie.

"I'm going to help you do this," he said. "On one condition: When she fails to tell you anything that helps us find your mother, you will take your lead from me for the remainder of this mission, without objection. Is that clear?"

"Yes," replied Jamie. His face was twisted, as though the word had tasted bitter as he said it.

The monster nodded. "Let's put this on her then," he said, and strode into the cellblock.

"Let me give it to her," said Jamie quietly, as they approached Larissa's cell.

Frankenstein held on to the belt for a moment, then passed it to him. "You're not trying to save her, are you?" asked the monster, as they walked between the rows of empty cells.

Jamie didn't answer.

They stopped in front of the vampire girl's cell. Larissa was sitting on the floor at the back of the square room, her arms resting across her raised knees. She smiled as they appeared.

"You brought some friends with you," she said, her red lips curled back from her gleaming white teeth. "Don't you trust yourself to be alone with me?"

Morris said something under his breath, and she widened her eyes in mock offence. "Don't be jealous," she said. "It doesn't suit you."

"Jealous?" snorted Morris. "Of a foul creature like you? Please."

Larissa's smile returned, and she fixed her gaze on the belt in Jamie's hand. "Have you brought me a present?" she asked.

"It's a restraining belt," said Jamie, his face slightly red. "You need to put it on before we can take you out of here."

She stared at him, then slid liquidly to her feet and crossed the cell to stand in front of Jamie. The UV field was all that separated them.

"Throw it to me," she said.

Jamie raised his arm to do as she asked, but Frankenstein stepped forward and stopped him.

"Before he gives this to you," he said, "there are some things I need to make clear. If you try to remove the belt, if you even give me the suspicion that you are intending to do so, I'll stake you where you stand. Is that clear?"

"Why, yes," said Larissa. "It's perfectly clear."

"Good. Secondly, if you endanger Jamie, or any of us, in any way, I'll tear you to pieces with my bare hands. Is that also clear?"

"Abundantly so."

Frankenstein released his grip on Jamie's arm. He threw the belt through the field, and Larissa plucked it out of the air. She set it on the floor by her feet, then started lifting her shirt, her eyes never leaving Jamie's.

He turned away, looking down at the floor, as Morris and Frankenstein did the same.

"You can watch if you want," said Larissa. "I don't mind."

Jamie didn't answer. He could feel his face burning as blood flooded into his cheeks.

"You can look," she said, and the three turned back toward the cell. The belt was safely hidden beneath her shirt, two raised areas at the shoulders the only clues she was wearing it at all.

The restraining belt was made of two loops of material that crossed in the front. Where they met, a flat round explosive chamber was attached to the material, positioned so it would rest directly over her heart. A small red light flashed steadily on the top of the chamber, signifying that the explosive was live. The charge was controlled by a small cylindrical detonator that Morris was holding in one slightly trembling hand. If the button on the top of the detonator was pressed, there would be a wide ring of blood and flesh where Larissa had been standing.

"Shall we go?" she asked sweetly, and Frankenstein nodded.

Thomas Morris keyed a nine-digit code into the panel next to the cell, and the UV field disappeared. Larissa moved forward, slowly, as though she was worried that it might reappear at any moment, then stepped quickly out into the corridor. She walked up to Jamie and planted a kiss on his cheek. He blushed again.

They led her through the cellblock, past the guard station, and out into the base. An elevator took them up to the hangar, and Frankenstein asked her where they were going.

"I don't know," she said, smiling.

Frankenstein stopped. "What do you mean, you don't know?" he asked.

"I mean I don't know. You're going to tell me."

The monster rolled his eyes. Jamie caught the look, and frowned at him. Frankenstein shrugged.

This is your deal, he seemed to be saying. *I'll keep my mouth shut. For now.*

"Mr. Morris," Larissa continued. "How high does your access to the Blacklight mainframe go?"

"I'm security officer," he replied, with a hint of smugness. "I have access to everything."

"And aren't you just terribly pleased with yourself?" she asked. "Very well. I need you to search the word Valhalla, if you please?"

Morris pulled a small console from his pocket, tapped a series of keys, and waited for the search to run. There was a beep, and the screen lit up.

"Nothing," he said.

"Where did you look?"

"I searched the entire network," Morris replied, defensively. "There's no mention of that word."

"Did you include the personal servers?"

"No. Why would I have?"

"I don't know, maybe because then I wouldn't have to tell you how to do your job in front of your friends?"

Morris muttered under his breath and ran a new search. When the console beeped a second time, a list of documents filled the screen.

"I don't understand," he said, softly.

"What is it?" asked Frankenstein.

"There are dozens of documents here, all relating to a place called Valhalla. Coordinates, reports, short and long histories. But they're not on the Department network."

"Where are they?"

Morris looked at the monster. "They're on Admiral Seward's private server," he replied.

"Oh, dear," Larissa said with a sigh. "Maybe there are one or two things Mr. Security Officer doesn't know about after all?"

"Shut up!" yelled Morris, his face contorting with anger. "Just shut your mouth!"

Jamie placed a hand on his friend's shoulder, and Morris

turned on him, color high in his cheeks. "Tom," he said, gently, "you said there are coordinates. Where would they take us?"

Morris frowned and looked back down at his console.

"Western Scotland," he said, eventually. "North of Fort William. The middle of bloody nowhere."

Larissa smiled.

"That's the place," she said.

Frankenstein led them through the hangar. Several operators looked curiously at Larissa, but the presence of a Blacklight colonel and captain escorting her appeared to satisfy them. Frankenstein spoke to the duty officer, requisitioned a pilot and a helicopter, and within five minutes, they were making their way out of the hangar and to one of the helipads, where a squat black chopper was waiting, its engine idling. As they stepped through the door, Frankenstein spoke to Larissa in a friendly voice.

"The detonator has a fifteen-mile range, so don't even think about taking off. You're not that fast."

"I wouldn't dream of it," replied Larissa. "Not when I'm having so much fun."

30

VALHALLA

The Blacklight helicopter flew north, carrying its four passengers across the border between England and Scotland. The pilot kept the chopper low and away from built-up areas, the green-black landscape of the Scottish countryside rolling quickly away beneath them. They flew northwest toward Fort William, then turned true north and headed into the wilderness. At Loch Duich, they joined the River Shiel and followed it north along the glen that bore its name. At the northern end of the valley, the chopper slowed, hovered, then touched down with a thump, shaking the passengers in their seats.

Frankenstein unfastened his safety belt. "Let's get this over with," he said, gruffly.

The door of the helicopter slid open, and Frankenstein stepped down onto thick grass. Morris followed, and Jamie and Larissa brought up the rear. As he gripped the door rail, the vampire girl's hand closed over his momentarily, and he felt heat surge through him. Then he was down and making his way over to where Frankenstein was standing waiting for him. Larissa followed behind, her eyes firmly locked on the detonator in Morris's hand.

They were standing in front of what appeared to be a small village; a loose arrangement of wooden buildings that ran from the bank of the river to the rising slope of the woods at the rear of the plain. A wooden wheel had been set into the clear rushing water of the Shiel, and a small generator sat humming next to it; a thick bundle of wires ran across the grass and disappeared into the village. Jamie noticed with bemusement that heather had been twisted into the wires at irregular intervals, like a kind of decorative camouflage. In front of them, a metal arch had been sunk into the grass and wound with vines and flowers. A single word had been placed at the top of the arch, the letters crafted from twigs tied together with green cord.

"*Valhalla*," read Jamie. He looked at Larissa. "What is this place?"

The vampire smiled at him. "This is where we'll find answers," she replied.

"Let's get on with it then," said Frankenstein, and walked toward the sculpted arch. Larissa strode quickly after him, with Jamie and Morris following slightly behind.

They walked under the arch and onto what passed for Valhalla's main street. Wooden houses, two and three deep, ran along both sides of a rutted dirt track, the grass long since worn away by feet, hooves, and tires. There were at least thirty homes, ranging from simple wooden cubes to more lavish dwellings, with raised porches and tiled roofs. The road sloped gently upward, flanked by carefully tended flowerbeds, wild shrubs, and strings of multicolored lightbulbs, toward an open circular area. From this clearing, the track diverged left and right, forming a T shape; more buildings were set into the lower levels of the hillside, among tangles of gorse and wild flurries of heather.

Standing at the back of the clearing, facing down the road, was a wooden house. The largest building in the village had a series of wooden steps leading up to a long porch, on which sat two benches, from where the occupants would be able to look out across Valhalla to the river and across to the rising eastern slope of the glen.

"Why don't we know about this place?" wondered Morris aloud, as they made their way up the track.

"Admiral Seward seemed to know about it," replied Jamie. "I wonder who else did?"

As they walked, the doors of several of the houses opened, and people stepped out to watch them as they passed. Jamie saw instantly that they were vampires: They stood easily in the doorways of their homes, a feeling of calm, almost of welcome, exuding from them. There were men and women, young and old, vampires of every race and color. Some were dressed in worn clothing, T-shirts, and jeans that had borne the brunt of years of outdoor work. Others were dressed in suits and ties, or shirts and trousers. One vampire, a graying man in his forties, was naked; he stood casually outside a house that was covered with colorful murals of flowers and water. Jamie found himself nodding at them as he passed, and they returned his greeting with nods and smiles of their own.

"Someone's coming," said Larissa, and pointed up the track.

A vampire in his late twenties, in a beautiful charcoal-gray suit and a bright scarlet cravat, was walking down the road toward them. Beside him, a small figure was floating through the quiet air, and Jamie heard Larissa gasp.

It was a boy, no more than five or six years old. He was wearing a T-shirt, a pair of shorts that had seen better days, and a wide, welcoming smile that faded as soon as he saw Larissa.

"I knew you would come back to haunt me," he said, softly.

"Hello, John," Larissa replied. "It's good to see you again."

"Again?" asked Jamie. "Do you two know each other?"

"We met once before," said the vampire child. "Several years ago."

"When?" demanded Jamie. "How?"

"The day I was turned," said Larissa, softly. "I didn't know where to go, so I went back to the park and—"

"Please," interrupted the vampire in the suit. "I'm sure your story is fascinating, but we do have rules here. People are not encouraged to just turn up out of the blue, without one of our own to introduce them. I'm afraid I need to ask you who you are and what your business is here."

Frankenstein answered him, his deep voice rumbling around the silent valley.

"I am Victor Frankenstein of Department 19. This is Jamie Carpenter and Thomas Morris, both also of Blacklight. And this is Larissa, who is one of you."

"And your business?"

"We want to ask Grey some questions," said Larissa. "Is he here?"

"He is," replied the vampire. "He's been away, but he came home three days ago."

Larissa bared her teeth.

Only Jamie saw her do it, and he cocked his head to the side. She shook her head at him, quickly.

"It's a pleasure to meet you all," continued the vampire, smiling widely. "My name is Lawrence, and this is John Martin."

Jamie could not restrain himself any longer. He was overwhelmed by this strange, idyllic village. There was a palpable sense of peace and well-being emanating from the buildings and their residents, a feeling of contentment and happiness.

"What *is* this place?" he asked.

Lawrence smiled at him. "In Norse mythology, Valhalla was the place where heroes go when they die. This is the equivalent for vampires who have sworn not to taste human blood: a place where you can live in peace."

He gestured to a fenced-off area at the edge of the village. A herd of cattle, huge Angus cows with shimmering flanks that gleamed white in the moonlight, were grazing idly at the lush grass.

"They provide all the blood the residents need. There are vampires here of every age, gender, nationality. You can come and go as you please, as long as you obey one rule: you must never harm a human being, under any circumstances."

He held out his arm toward them. Tattooed on the inside of his left arm was a thin black V.

"This is the mark of Valhalla. I was brought here in 1967 by Grey, the man who founded this place. I can leave for years on end, but this means I will always be welcome."

Jamie stared at the tattoo, then frowned at Larissa. She met his gaze and shook her head.

"How does all this work?" Morris asked. "Is it some kind of commune?"

Lawrence laughed. "Basically, yes," he replied. "Anyone who agrees to obey our rules is welcome to be here. Some stay for weeks, other for years, decades, even. We generate the power we need, we tend the herd that provides us with blood; all residents are expected to help with whatever needs to be done to keep Valhalla running smoothly. Apart from that, they may do as they wish."

"It sounds great," said Jamie, smiling.

"It's the best place in the world," said Lawrence, simply. "I've seen most of it over the years, and there is nowhere I'd rather be than here."

"It sounds like a bunch of sixties crap to me," muttered Frankenstein.

Lawrence shot him a sharp look. "It's a life of peace," he said. "If that sounds like crap, then I feel sorry for you."

Frankenstein grunted, but he said nothing more.

"Follow me," said Lawrence. "I'll take you to Grey."

The vampire led them up the track toward a clearing. John Martin floated alongside him, casting nervous glances at Larissa.

"This Grey," said Frankenstein, in a low voice, "he is the one you've brought us here to see?"

Larissa nodded.

"Exactly who is he?"

"He's supposed to be the oldest British vampire," she replied.

"He's been around for more than two hundred years; if anyone knows anything that can help us, it should be him. And he hates Alexandru, and all the vampires like him. They're the opposite of everything Valhalla stands for. Apparently."

"Have you been here before?" asked Jamie.

Larissa shook her head.

"Why not? Why didn't you leave Alexandru and come here?"

She laughed. "You heard him. You can't come in unless you're introduced by one of them. Truth is, I wasn't even sure this place existed. I thought it might just be a legend."

She lowered her head, and Jamie stared at her as they entered the clearing at the end of the track.

A wide metal shed with an open front stood in the northwest corner, set into the hillside. A small tractor was parked inside, beside an ancient-looking plough and sacks of fertilizer and grass seed. They walked up the steps of the large house and waited on the porch as Lawrence disappeared inside.

He emerged a minute later and told them that Grey would see them.

They followed him into the house, and Jamie looked around as Lawrence closed the door behind them. They were standing in a large square living room, made entirely of wood. The floorboards were uneven and creaked beneath their feet, and the walls were painted bright white. It was surprisingly domestic; a rug lay over the middle of the floor, red curtains covered the windows, and two large homemade bookcases stood in the corners that faced the door. They were piled high with books: some that looked as though they had to be at least a hundred years old, others that appeared brand new. Two doors led further into the house, and Lawrence walked over and stood beside one of them.

"Only Mr. Carpenter and Mr. Frankenstein are to go through," he said, a hint of apology in his voice. "Grey does not like crowds, and he believes that what he has to say is only of interest to the two of you."

Morris opened his mouth to protest, but Jamie fired a warning look at him, and he closed it again. Larissa nodded.

"Please make yourselves at home while you wait," said Lawrence. "Gentlemen, please come with me."

He opened the door, and Jamie and Frankenstein stepped through it.

The room was a study, dominated by a large window that looked out onto the hill that rose behind Valhalla. A homemade desk stood before it, and in a chair behind the rough wooden surface sat Grey, smiling at them as they entered.

It was immediately obvious how the vampire had got his name; his head was covered in a mane of hair that was almost silver, swept back from his high forehead and temples, descending below the level of his collar and on to his shoulders. His face was that of a man in his late sixties, lined and creased, but the eyes twinkled with life, and his lips were curled into a broad, welcoming smile.

He stood up from the chair and walked around the desk. He was wearing a blue-and-white checked shirt, faded blue jeans, and battered brown boots. He looked like a cowboy on the verge of retirement; all that was missing was a worn ten-gallon hat. He extended a hand toward Jamie.

"Mr. Carpenter," he said, and the teenager gasped. Grey's voice was unearthly, a rolling blast of bass and treble, a sound that was both swaggeringly large and charmingly soft. "It's an absolute pleasure to meet you. My name is Grey."

In the living room, Larissa's heightened ears heard this greeting, and crimson spilled into her eyes. She reached out, grabbed Lawrence by the lapels of his suit jacket, and threw him across the room. He was taken utterly by surprise and didn't react until he crashed into the wooden wall, splintering the planks, shattering the glass in the window above him, and shaking the entire house.

Morris started to say something, but Larissa was already moving. She crossed the room in a flash, threw open the door of the study, and disappeared inside.

ONE RULE FOR EVERYONE

The door to the study crashed open, and Jamie jumped around in time to see Larissa fly across the room, her eyes molten red, and grab for Grey's throat with hands that were curled into claws.

Surprise flashed briefly across the ancient vampire's face, but then centuries of instinct took over. He reached out, gripped Larissa by the neck, flipping her over in midair and slamming her onto the floor on her back. The air rushed out of her, and he knelt across her chest, pinning her shoulders with his knees, looking at Jamie and Frankenstein with dark, gleaming red eyes. Morris rushed into the room and gasped at the scene before of him.

"What is the meaning of this?" Grey said, his voice like midnight ice.

Jamie looked at Larissa, who was squirming and cursing under Grey's weight.

"I don't know," he said, honestly. "Larissa, what the hell are you doing?"

The vampire girl howled, bucking and kicking like a wild colt.

Then, abruptly, she stopped struggling, lifted her head, and spit in Grey's face.

He recoiled, disgusted, and wiped his face with his shirtsleeve.

"Ask him!" she yelled. "Ask him why he didn't just kill me and get it over with!"

"Oh God," said Jamie, realization flooding through him like cold water. *This* was the man with the tattoo from Larissa's story. He reached for his T-Bone without realizing he was doing so, until Frankenstein stepped forward gripped his arm.

Grey's eyes reverted back to dark green. He looked down at Larissa, and Jamie saw recognition leap into his face. Then he looked at Jamie and Frankenstein, remorse contorting his features.

"I didn't recognize her," he said. "I thought she was here to kill me."

"I am," spit Larissa. "I'm going to kill you for what you did to me."

"What's she talking about?" rumbled Frankenstein.

"He's the one who turned me," said Larissa, her voice dripping venom. "He bit me and left me for dead. But I didn't die."

"This is the man you saw in your garden?" asked Jamie. "The one from the fair?"

Morris looked at him, confusion all over his face.

"This is him," said Larissa. She had stopped struggling, but her chest was rising and falling rapidly. "I'll remember his voice forever."

Grey looked down at her, and an expression of such anger crossed his face that Jamie was absolutely sure that he was going to reach down and kill Larissa there and then. But the moment passed; instead Grey stood up slowly and reached a hand down toward Larissa. She slapped it away and pushed herself to her feet. The two vampires stood, eyeing each other warily.

Then suddenly the room was full of vampires, and everyone started shouting at once. Lawrence was first, his eyes a blazing red, his neat suit rumpled and torn. He stared at Larissa with fury in his eyes, then saw the expression on Grey's face, and went to his friend. The residents of Valhalla followed him into the study, drawn by the commotion. Their faces were full of concern for Grey, and suspicion for the outsiders who had punctured their peaceful village.

"What's going on in here?" demanded one of the vampires, a woman in her thirties wearing a pretty yellow sundress. "Grey, are you OK?"

"I'm fine, Jill," he replied, and gave her an unconvincing smile. "Everything's fine."

"Everything is *not* fine," said Larissa, fiercely. "This is the vampire that turned me four years ago. I don't know how you make that fit with your precious *rules*."

Jill clapped a hand to her mouth, her eyes wide.

"What's she talking about, Grey?" asked John Martin.

There was a murmur from the rest of the vampires in the room. Jamie looked around, saw that there were at least fifteen of them in the study, and a chilly thread of fear crept up his spine.

If they turn on us, we're dead.

Grey looked at the men and women crowded in his study. His face wore a shiny veneer of calm, but it faltered under the gazes of his friends. An expression of terrible misery emerged, as if from a great depth.

"She's telling the truth," he said.

There were gasps throughout the room, and a vindicated snarl of triumph from Larissa. "I told you," she said. "He—"

"Shut up," said Lawrence, his eyes almost black. "Not another word from you." He turned to Grey, who was standing alone in the middle of his study.

"What do you mean, she's telling the truth?" Lawrence asked, his voice almost a growl. "How can she be telling the truth?"

"I mean I turned her," said Grey, simply. "She reminded me of my wife, my Helen. So I followed her, and when I found her on her own, I drank from her. Then I came home. I thought she was dead."

Jill, the vampire in the yellow dress, started to cry. A young vampire in a red T-shirt put a hand on her shoulder, and she gripped it, tightly.

"What about our rules?" said Lawrence, his voice like thunder. "What about everything we stand for? Everything you started?"

Grey looked at his friend, his eyes wide and pleading. "I'm weak," he replied, his voice hitching. "I always have been. I know it's wrong, but I can't help it. Do you understand me? *I can't help it.*"

Clarity flooded into Jamie's mind. "This wasn't the first time, was it?" he asked, softly. "Larissa isn't the only one."

Grey looked at the floor, and a chorus of gasps and groans filled the study.

"How many?" asked Lawrence. "How many innocent humans?"

"A lot," replied Grey in a strangled voice, his eyes fixed on the uneven wooden floorboards. "One every few years, since the beginning."

"Every time you told us you were going away to clear your head?" spit Lawrence. "Every time you told us you were going out into the world to remind yourself why Valhalla was so important, you were taking human lives. You were betraying the one thing we stand for above everything else."

Grey said nothing.

"I can't bear to look at you," Lawrence said, his voice shaking. "You're worse than any of them, the vampires out there killing and feeding. At least they don't pretend to be something they're not."

"What do you want me to do?" cried Grey, his face hot and full of shame. "I can't bring any of them back. I wish I could, believe me I wish I could, but I can't. They're gone. If you want me to leave, I'll go. If you want me to destroy myself, I'll do it. Just tell me how I can make this better."

"You can't," said one of the vampires near the back of the room. The crowd parted, and he stepped forward, a heavyset man in his forties, wearing a thick woolen jumper and a pair of dusty black jeans. "You can't undo what you've done. But you can leave and never come back. That's what *I* want you to do."

Several of the vampires around the man shouted in protest, but he didn't even acknowledge them. He stared levelly at

Grey, his face as rigid as stone.

"That's what I want, too," said another, and the crowd hissed and gasped anew. The second voice belonged to a middle-aged woman wearing a long smock covered in garish splatters of paint.

Grey looked at the two vampires who had spoken and then helplessly at Lawrence, who stared back at him without an ounce of pity.

"Is that what you want?" he asked, his voice trembling. "Do you want me to leave?"

Lawrence looked at his old friend. "Yes," he said. "It's what I want. It's all you deserve."

Grey put a hand over his eyes. For a long moment, it seemed as though no one in the room was breathing; the silence and stillness were absolute. Then Grey lowered his hand and looked around at the men and women gathered in his study.

"All right," he said. "I'll go."

There were shouts of protest, but he raised a hand and silenced them.

"I let you all down," he continued. "Worse than that, I let you believe better of me than I deserved. I'll go, and I won't come home until I find a way to atone for the things I did."

He smiled, the wide, genuine smile of a man who has been keeping a secret for too long and is relieved beyond measure to have finally let it out.

"If you would all excuse me," he said. "There are some things I need to say to our visitors. I'll come and say my good-byes before I leave."

Slowly, reluctantly, the vampires of Valhalla began to file out of the room. Lawrence was the last to go, casting a final look at Grey as he closed the door of the study behind him. The expression on his face was one of profound disappointment.

Grey watched them go, then turned his attention to the Blacklight team standing silently in front of him. Larissa was looking at him with open hatred, a look that Jamie was loyally replicating. Frankenstein and Morris were expressionless, staring at Grey as though they didn't quite understand what had just played out in front of them.

"Before the Russian Revolution of 1917," Grey said, "men who were convicted of treason against the czar were offered the choice of death or exile. The majority chose death. It seemed only fair that I allowed my friends to make the decision for me."

He walked back around his desk and flopped into his chair. "I understand why *you* came to see me," he said, looking at Larissa. "But did the rest of you have something you wanted to ask me? Lawrence thought that you might."

Jamie stepped forward. "There is something," he said. "We're looking for Alexandru Rusmanov. We were told you might know where he is."

Grey looked at Jamie, then burst out laughing.

"My dear boy," he said, gently. "Did you look around as you made your way up here? We live where we live for a reason; because it is hundreds of miles from the nearest vampire. We have no desire to associate with any of them, especially not someone as violent and unpredictable as Alexandru. I'm afraid you were misinformed."

Jamie looked at Larissa, who refused to meet his eyes.

"I must confess, I thought you were here about Dracula," said Grey.

Frankenstein flinched. "Why would we want to ask you about a vampire who's been dead for four hundred years?" he asked.

Grey looked at him with surprise on his face. "Because you know as well as I do that Dracula was not destroyed," he said. "His throat was cut, his heart was pierced, and he bled out, but his remains could easily be revived. I thought you were going to ask me how to destroy him permanently."

Jamie's head was spinning with questions. Thankfully, Morris asked the two most important ones first.

"Why would we need to know that?" he said. "And why would we think you would have the answer?"

"Even all the way up here, we hear rumors," said Grey. "From the vampires who return here from the outside world, from the wolves making their way north. Even Blacklight must be aware that Valeri has spent the last century trying to revive his master; it is my understanding that he is close to accomplishing his goal."

Fear shot through Jamie, and he looked at Frankenstein. "That can't be true," he said. "Can it? They can't bring Dracula back, tell me they can't."

The monster looked at Jamie. "It's theoretically possible," he said, slowly. "With his remains and enough blood, it could be done. But you don't need to worry. The remains are lost forever. At least three expeditions in the last century have dug over every inch of the mountain where Castle Dracula stood and haven't found a thing. He's gone."

"If you say so," said Grey, looking at Jamie as he spoke.

He's not lying. Neither of them are. But one of them is wrong. God, I hope it's not Frankenstein. Please let it be Grey.

"In which case," Grey continued. "My information is useless to you. If you're sure there's no chance of his return."

"Stop prevaricating," growled Frankenstein. "If you are going to tell us what you know, then tell us. If not, then we'll bid you farewell. It's up to you. But I am not in the mood for games."

Grey nodded. "Fair enough," he said, his tone conversational. "I'll tell you. In 1971 I spent some time in New York, for reasons that are personal. Over the course of several months, I became friendly with Valentin Rusmanov, the youngest of the three brothers. We frequented some of the same clubs on the Lower East Side, and I attended some of the parties he threw. He was a notoriously generous host; vampires from the length and breadth of the East Coast would come to his building on Central Park West, to take speed and cocaine, and drink from the seemingly endless supply of teenage runaways Valentin was able to supply."

Grey's eyes glazed over at the memory, and a shudder of revulsion ran through Jamie.

"There was a particular party, for which I don't remember the occasion, that became legendary. By the time dawn broke, the inside of Valentin's house looked like an abattoir. There must have been two hundred vampires there, and God only knows how many boys and girls who never saw the sunlight again. Valentin and I ended up on the roof, watching the light creep across Central Park, waiting until the last possible second to go inside and rest. While we waited, he told me about his family."

The old vampire looked around his study and smiled, almost shyly. "I was a little bit in awe of him, I must confess.

He was beautiful beyond comparison, and he was turned by Dracula himself. In the circles I moved in, he and his brothers were like gods. And they knew it, too. So when he started to tell me how Valeri was just a loyal soldier who had no idea how to think for himself, how Alexandru was little more than an immortal psychopath but was the only creature Valentin had ever been afraid of, I felt like I was being given the key to the inner circle. So I asked him about Dracula, and he told me that the stories failed to do him justice: that he was a greater man than history had ever recorded and a more terrible monster than any legend had ever conveyed. And then he told me that he hoped he never came back, because he liked the world the way it was, and he had no wish to watch Dracula burn it down."

Everyone in the study stood motionless, hanging on Grey's every word.

"I reminded him that the accepted wisdom held Dracula to be dead, and he laughed. He told me that there was only one way to kill Dracula, and slitting his throat with an American cowboy's knife was not it. I almost didn't dare ask, but I knew the chance was never going to come again, so I swallowed hard, and I asked him how to kill the first vampire that ever existed. He didn't even flinch; he told me that only Dracula's first victim could destroy him. So I laughed, and said that he was pretty safe, as Valeri would never let himself be used against his master. And Valentin went very still and looked at me in a way that made me think I'd pushed my luck. I remember thinking very clearly that he was going to kill me. I don't think he wanted to, but I thought I'd given him no other choice. But then he laughed and said that Valeri was not as important as

Valeri thought he was. When I asked him what he meant, he shook his head, and refused to say anything more. Then the sun crept onto the roof of the building, and we went inside. I haven't seen him since, although I'm led to believe little has changed in Valentin's world."

"What did he mean when he said that Valeri isn't as important as he likes to think?" asked Jamie. "What did he mean by that?"

Grey looked at the teenager. "I can't pretend to know for certain," he replied. "I've come to believe that the accepted story—that Valeri was the first human turned by Dracula—is just that, a story. I believe that's what Valentin meant."

"If Valeri wasn't Dracula's first victim, who was?" asked Morris.

"I don't know," replied Grey. "I've thought about that night from time to time, but I've never taken it any further. I busied myself with Valhalla, and the outside world became less and less interesting."

"Apart from when it came to the blood of teenage girls," said Larissa, sharply.

"Indeed," said Grey, and had the decency to look embarrassed as he did so.

"Well, that was fascinating," said Frankenstein, sarcasm thick in his voice. "But it amounts to nothing more than half a solution for a problem that isn't going to arise. So forgive me if I fail to see why we should waste any more time here."

"Why are you looking for Alexandru?" Grey asked Jamie, ignoring the monster. "Most men would do everything in their power to avoid him."

"He has my mother," said Jamie.

For a long moment, no one said anything, then Grey spoke again. "I wish I could help you," he said, looking directly at Jamie. "If I could, I would; you may believe that or not. I won't hold it against you, either way. But I will do something that I should have done a long time ago, something that I believe will help you in the long run, no matter what your friend may think. I will go and find the person that I believe Valentin was referring to, the first victim, and I will bring him to you. Consider it penance for past crimes."

"Thank you," said Jamie.

"Let's go," said Frankenstein, abruptly. "There is nothing of value for us here." He headed for the study door, and Morris followed.

Jamie gripped Larissa's shoulder; the vampire girl was staring at Grey, and showed no sign of leaving. "Come on," he said, softly. "Let's go."

She resisted for a second, then the muscles in her shoulders relaxed, and she allowed Jamie to lead her toward the door. They were about to leave when Grey called her name, and she turned back.

"I'm sorry for what I did to you," he said, softly. "I know that doesn't mean anything to you, but it's the truth."

"You're right," Larissa replied. "It doesn't mean anything to me."

WHOSE SIDE ARE YOU ON?

Larissa opened her mouth to say something but never got the chance. Jamie pulled the metal stake from his belt, gripped her by the neck, and slammed her backward into the black metal side of the helicopter. Her head bounced against it, and she was momentarily dazed. Her eyes reddened involuntarily, and a low snarl emerged from her throat.

"Take us to the last place you were with Alexandru," said Jamie. His voice was almost unrecognizable, it was so thick with anger. "You got what you wanted, so take us there. Right now."

Larissa was impressed. Fury radiated from Jamie's pores, rising from him like a dark cloud, but his face was pale and the hand holding the stake was steady. She knew she could kill him without breaking a sweat if she had to, but for a split second when he grabbed her throat, she had been afraid. She hadn't felt fear for a long time, and it was invigorating.

He's exhausted. But he's still determined. Still full of courage. "Put the stake down," she said. "You're not going to hurt me."

He pressed the sharp metal point forward, against the pale skin of her throat. "I don't want to," he said. "That doesn't mean I won't."

Their eyes met, a moment that seemed to last forever; his pale blue, the color of ice, hers the raging, flickering red of a wildfire.

He's close to breaking point, she thought. *He might actually try it.*

"OK," she said. "I'll take you."

Silence reigned in the helicopter as they flew southeast, toward the destination Larissa had given the pilot. They were heading for a farm in Lincolnshire, a remote spot in the flat East Anglian countryside. There, Larissa promised, was the house in which she, Alexandru, and the rest of his followers had spent the days before the attack on Jamie and his mother. Frankenstein's eyes hardly left the vampire during the hour-long flight. He gazed at her with open loathing and open distrust. Jamie stared at the floor, shame filling his mind.

I thought there was something between us. I believed in her. Stupid.

The realization of why Larissa had led them north and the surge of adrenaline that had seen him press the stake against her throat had exhausted him. He felt tired, and useless. He rubbed his eyes with the heels of his palms and caught Thomas Morris looking at him.

"What?" he snapped. "What is it, Tom?"

Morris didn't look away, as Jamie had been expecting him to do. Instead he held the teenager's gaze for a long moment, then shook his head, grunted something inaudible, and averted his eyes.

Tom told me this was a bad idea. Even he could see she was playing me.

"Shut up," Jamie whispered, and Larissa turned to look at him. She cocked her head, but he looked away; he couldn't bear to see her, was struggling to tolerate being anywhere near her. She reached over and touched his arm, and when he looked into her pale, beautiful face, she smiled at him, an expression of placation, of apology. He didn't return it; he just stared into her wide eyes and waited for her to drop her gaze. After a few seconds, she did so, and he returned his eyes to the floor of the helicopter.

"Ninety seconds," said the pilot, his voice crackling over the intercom.

Frankenstein reached above his seat and pulled his helmet down into his lap. He drew the weapons from his belt and checked them quickly, before replacing them in their loops and holsters. Morris did the same, removing the magazine from his MP5, checking it, and clicking it back into place.

"You won't need those," said Larissa. "There won't be anyone here."

"This may be a surprise to you," replied Frankenstein. "But I don't believe a single word that comes out of your mouth."

Larissa laughed. "You think I care whether you believe me?" she asked.

"No," replied Frankenstein. "I'm sure you don't. But I am sure you care what *he* thinks." He gestured toward Jamie, who looked up at him. "Am I wrong?"

Larissa looked away.

"That's what I thought," said the monster, as the helicopter touched down.

The four passengers leapt down into a dark farmyard. A large metal shed rose in front of them, tractors and other farm machinery looming in the darkness, a round grain store standing silently to their left. To their right sat the farmhouse, a squat building of pale stone behind a neatly kept lawn and two long flowerbeds. There were no lights on in the house and no smoke rose from the chimney.

Morris pressed a button at the rear of the helicopter, and a huge door lowered to the ground with a deafening hiss. He walked up into the hold and out of sight. Frankenstein, Jamie, and Larissa waited in the yard, until they heard an engine fire into life, and a black SUV slowly reversed down onto the tarmac.

"What's going on?" asked Larissa.

"The helicopter needs to be back at the Loop," said Frankenstein. "It was checked out for a training flight. It can't be gone any longer without someone asking questions. We'll drive home."

Morris brought the car to a halt and got out. Frankenstein led them forward, his T-Bone outstretched in front of him. He tried the handle on the front door of the farmhouse, and it turned in his hand. He eased it open, reached inside, and flicked a light switch on the wall by the door. The bulb burst into life, bathing a homely, rustic kitchen in warm yellow light. He held the door open, but Jamie paused.

"Give me the detonator, Tom," he said.

Morris gave him a questioning look, but passed him the cylinder. Jamie wrapped his fingers around it and rested his thumb near the button on the top. "All right," he said, and walked into the farmhouse, ignoring the look on Larissa's face as he passed her.

The rest of the team filed silently inside, Morris closing the door behind them.

"Where's the family?" asked Frankenstein.

Larissa stared at him. "Where do you think?" she asked. "They're gone."

"God damn you," muttered the monster. "You and all the rest of your kind."

Jamie walked through the kitchen, around a battered wooden dining table, and led them into the rest of the house.

It was empty, as Larissa had promised it would be.

They stood silently in the kitchen. Jamie's head was lowered, his mind racing with one terrible image of his mother after another. Morris was looking nervously at the door, desire to leave this place and return to the Loop written all over his face. Larissa was watching Jamie, an expression of shame on her face, and Frankenstein was staring at the vampire girl so intently he didn't appear to be blinking.

"Everything about you is a lie, isn't it?" he said eventually, his voice low.

Larissa returned his gaze, and sneered. "You don't know anything about me," she spit. "Nothing."

Frankenstein's gaze didn't so much as flicker. "I think I do," he said, softly. "I think I know a lot about you. Do you want to hear what I think?"

"I really don't care," Larissa snapped. "If you've got something to say, get on with it."

Frankenstein nodded. "I don't think you've ever killed a single thing in your life. I think you're a scared little girl who was pretty enough for Alexandru not to kill her. I think you were terrified of him, and I think you probably spent every second of every day looking for a way to escape from him. But I think you were too scared to try it. Am I warm?"

Larissa looked away, and the monster continued. "I think you probably lied about the men and women you killed until Alexandru believed you, probably until you even started to believe it a little bit yourself. I think you probably survived on the leftovers of others' kills and on animals when you could find them. I think you lied, and lied and lied so much that you made Alexandru believe you were almost as bad as him, although if you'd asked the rest of his followers, I bet none of them would remember ever seeing you take a life. I think that's why you were entrusted with killing Jamie."

The monster's voice was rising now, thick fury spilling into it. "I don't think you spared Jamie; I don't think you could do it, when it came down to it. I don't think you could kill him. And while I'm grateful for your weakness, your lies and your bravado and your criminal selfishness have wasted time that could have been spent looking for Marie Carpenter, time we did not have to spare. And if we're too late to help her because of the time and attention we wasted on you, wasted on a pathetic little vampire girl we would have been better off letting you die in the garden where Alexandru dropped you, then so help me God I will make you pay for it for the rest of your days!"

Frankenstein was visibly shaking, his great shoulders trembling with anger.

"Look at me!" he roared, and Larissa, whose head was turned toward the wall, jumped. "If you can't, then look at him at least! Do him that courtesy, after you've wasted our time and left his mother in the hands of a madman! Look at him!"

Larissa's shoulders hunched, then she slowly turned back to face them. Jamie felt a gasp rise in his throat as he saw her face.

The vampire was crying.

Tears ran down her pale cheeks, leaving narrow lines that glistened under the electric light above the table. Her expression was one of utter misery, and she looked at Jamie with pain etched across her face.

"The night your mother was taken. After you left me in the park," she said, her voice barely audible, "I ran. I got a couple of miles before Anderson caught me and brought me back to him." She spit this last word, her face momentarily curling with disgust. "Alexandru pulled me into the air, smiling, telling me he had to teach me a lesson, talking to me like everything was normal. Then he beat me until I lost consciousness and dropped me out of the sky."

She looked at Frankenstein and hate twitched across her face. "You're right," she continued. "I've never killed anyone. Never hurt anyone, until the soldier and the boy in the garden, and I didn't mean to hurt them. I was in so much pain, I can't even—"

Larissa looked away, composed herself, then looked directly at Jamie.

"I'm sorry," she whispered. "I truly am. I thought you'd kill me if you thought I didn't know anything, and I don't want to die. I haven't had a chance to live, not yet. I don't want to die."

"Why take us to Valhalla?" asked Jamie, quietly. "Why lead us on a wild-goose chase?"

"It was all I could think to do. I know you think I led you there to get even with Grey, but that wasn't it. I just knew I couldn't stall you anymore, and I couldn't think of anywhere else, and I thought that if it was the last time I was going to see the outside world then at least I could see the person who did this to me and—" she broke off, fresh tears pouring down her face.

Jamie watched her cry and fought back the urge to comfort her, to step across the kitchen and put his arm around her. "Do you know anything that can help us?" he asked. Frankenstein started to groan, but Jamie held a hand up, quieting the monster. "It doesn't matter if you don't," he continued. "But we need to know. Anything Alexandru did, or said, before you attacked us, anything unusual? Anything at all?"

"Nothing," said Larissa. "He was just Alexandru, the same monster he always was. The day before the attack I heard him on the phone ordering more Bliss, but that wasn't unusual. He went through tons of the stuff."

Jamie's blood froze in his veins, and he looked over at Frankenstein, who had turned as still as a statue.

"The day before?" the teenager managed. "The day before my mother was taken?"

Larissa nodded, a confused look on her face.

"What is it?" asked Morris, breaking his silence. "What's wrong?"

Frankenstein's head slowly swiveled toward Jamie, the expression on it full of thunder. "The Chemist," he said, slowly.

"He lied to us."

I told you he knew more than he was saying! I told you that right outside his house! Why wouldn't you listen to me?

"Let's go," said Jamie, walking quickly toward the door, the detonator hanging loosely in his hand.

"Go where?" asked Morris, following the teenager out of the house.

"Dartmoor," answered Frankenstein. "And put your damn foot down."

The Blacklight team stood on the edge of the moor, checking their equipment. A hundred yards along the road stood the Chemist's neat, pale stone farmhouse, smoke drifting lazily from the red chimney.

"We do this my way," said Frankenstein, clipping a pair of UV grenades to his belt. "No arguments. The rest of you have had your chance. Is that clear?"

Jamie stared up at the monster but said nothing. Morris nodded, and Larissa looked away, her eyes still ringed pink from crying.

"Good," said the monster. "Follow me."

The giant man led them along the road, the heels of their boots clattering out a steady rhythm on the asphalt. He pushed open the gate, walked quickly along the path, and knocked heavily on the front door.

It opened immediately.

"There's no need to knock," said the Chemist, smiling at them. "I heard you coming from—"

He didn't finish his sentence. Frankenstein pulled the beam gun from his belt, his hand a blur of gray-green in the night air, leveled it, and pulled the trigger. The Chemist took the concentrated UV light square in the face. His skin exploded into flames, and he staggered backward, screaming in pain. Frankenstein looped the hand that was holding the beam gun into the doorway, and the barrel crashed against the Chemist's jaw. Something crunched, and the vampire went to his knees, still screaming, still beating his face with his hands, trying to extinguish the purple flames. Frankenstein kicked the Chemist onto his back and stepped into the house. The rest of the team stared, uncomprehending; the entire assault had taken little more than three seconds, and the suddenness of the violence had frozen them where they stood.

The monster reached down, grabbed the Chemist by his hair, and dragged him along the hallway that stood beyond the front door. "Close the door!" he bellowed. "Get in here and close the door!"

Fear spilled through Jamie as he looked at Frankenstein's face. The monster's features were twisted into a snarl of savage, brutal enjoyment. His eyes were bright and alive, and his mouth curled at the corners into a terrible smile. He wanted to run, away from that face, away from the thick smell of burning meat that was emanating from the Chemist.

But he knew he couldn't.

Instead he grabbed Larissa's arm with his free hand, keeping the detonator out of her reach, and shoved her into the house. She went without protest, her eyes fixed on the smoking figure on the floor. Morris moved on his own, slowly, staring at Frankenstein, and when they were both in the hallway, Jamie reached back and slammed the front door shut behind them.

The monster hauled the Chemist through the first door

on the right and into a large, comfortable sitting room. He knelt down across the vampire's chest, pulled one of the UV grenades from his belt, and gave it a sharp twist. The red light that signified that the grenade was live lit up on the top of the small sphere, then Frankenstein leaned down, prized open the Chemist's jaws, and shoved the grenade into his mouth.

"What are you—" cried Jamie, horrified.

"Shut up!" roared Frankenstein. "Get one of those chairs and put it down next to me! Now!"

Jamie looked around the sitting room, saw a dining table surrounded by six dark wooden chairs standing in the corner, and ran to it. He dragged one of the chairs over to where the monster was kneeling on the helpless, groaning vampire and glanced down at the Chemist's face.

He wished he hadn't. The skin was burned almost completely away from his skull; bright white patches of bone shone out through raw red and charred black. He gulped and turned away.

Frankenstein lifted the Chemist easily from the floor and placed him on the chair. Then he stepped back, lifted the grenade's detonator into his hand, and stopped next to Jamie. Morris and Larissa stood behind them, silent and terrified.

A terrible sound emerged from the Chemist; a rhythmic series of gasps that sounded like a death rattle. Then the vampire lifted his head, trained his burned eyes on the four figures in front of him and grinned savagely around the grenade.

It's laughing. My God, it's laughing.

"Cover him," said Frankenstein. Morris fumbled his T-Bone from his belt and trained it on the Chemist, and Jamie followed suit.

"You will not move, or say anything," said the monster, staring evenly at the Chemist's ruined face. "You will answer my questions by nodding or shaking your head. If you refuse to answer, or I think you're lying, I will press this button, and your head will explode from the inside out. Then I will stake what is left of you. Is that clear?"

The Chemist snarled but nodded his head.

"Good. You lied to us when you told us you knew nothing about Alexandru. Correct?"

Another nod.

"He placed an order with you the day before we arrived. Correct?"

The vampire's red eyes blazed with hate from his scorched face, but he nodded again.

"Did he ask you to deliver it to an address?"

The Chemist shook his head, sending droplets of blood flying in the warm light of the living room.

"Did he send someone to collect it?"

Another shake.

"Did he collect it himself?"

A long pause, and then the faintest of nods.

Jamie gasped.

"He was here?" he asked, his voice trembling. "Was my mother with him?"

The Chemist stared at the teenager, and then nodded sharply. Jamie felt as though he was going to be sick; his stomach lurched, and saliva splashed into his mouth.

"Was she all right?" he asked. "Was she hurt? Has he hurt her?"

The vampire looked at Frankenstein, who appeared to consider for a moment, then stepped forward and crouched at the Chemist's side, being careful not to block the aims of Jamie and Morris.

"You're going to spit the grenade into my hand," he said. "I'm going to put it inside your shirt, and we're going to continue this conversation. If you move even a millimeter, my colleagues are going to destroy you. Is that clear?"

A frantic nod told the monster that it was, and he held his hand up flat before the Chemist's face. The vampire stretched his torn mouth open and pushed the grenade out with a black, burned tongue. It fell into Frankenstein's hand with a thud. The monster shoved the metal sphere down the front of the white shirt the Chemist was wearing and stepped back.

"You'll die for this," spit the Chemist, as soon as the huge man was out of reach. "All of you will die for what you've done here today."

"If you don't be quiet, there will be death in this room," replied Frankenstein. "But it will be yours—and yours alone. Alexandru placed an order with you five days ago, the day before he attacked Jamie and his mother. When did he arrive to collect it?"

"Three days ago," snarled the Chemist, his eyes fixed on the monster. "But the order was huge, more than I had in store. I had to acquire new quantities and make the order from scratch. He was very . . . angry."

"So it wasn't ready when he arrived?"

"Aren't you clever?"

"Did he leave and come back for it?"

"That wouldn't have been very hospitable of me, would it?

Especially not for one of my very best customers."

Realization dawned on Jamie like the first clap of a thunderstorm. "He *stayed* here, didn't he?" he asked, his voice little more than a whisper. "He stayed in this house while you finished the order?"

The Chemist spit a wad of blood onto the living room floor and glared at Jamie. "That's right, you little brat. Alexandru, Anderson, and his prize."

His prize?

"My mother," Jamie said. "He kept my mother here while he waited for you to make your Bliss. And you let him? How could you do that?"

"Alexandru can do whatever he wants, whenever he wants," replied the Chemist. "I'm not going to cross him for some human."

Fury burst through Jamie, and he launched himself at the Chemist. Larissa blurred forward, wrapped him up, and dragged him back, kicking and punching.

"Some human?" Jamie roared. "That human is my mother, you disgusting creature! My mother, who never hurt anyone in her entire life, who has nothing to do with any of this, and you let him keep her here, in your house? I'm going to kill you!"

Frankenstein shot Jamie a look of sympathy, then turned back to the Chemist. "When did you finish your work? When did they leave?"

The vampire shot the monster a look of savage satisfaction. "Yesterday. About two hours before you came to see me."

The words crushed the fight out of Jamie, and he sagged in Larissa's arms.

So close. We were so close. We missed her by a matter of minutes. Too much. It's too much to bear.

He heard Frankenstein ask the Chemist where they were going, but the monster's voice sounded as though it was coming from underwater; it was distant and muffled. He felt Larissa place her cheek against his as she hugged him, felt the warmth of her body surrounding him, but felt nothing. He would fall to the floor if she released him, he knew it; she was the only thing holding him up.

"They went north," answered the Chemist. "Alexandru sent the rest of his followers ahead, to prepare for some kind of party. That's all I know."

Jamie felt Larissa's muscles tense momentarily, and then she spoke from above him. "I know where he means," she said, softly. "I've been there. I know exactly where he means."

"You've been where?" asked Jamie. "Where's he talking about?"

"I'll show you when we get back to base."

"Why don't you just tell me?"

"So you can let your pet monster blow me to pieces after I do? I don't think so."

Frankenstein rolled his eyes, then stepped away from the Chemist, who was glaring malevolently at the people who had invaded his home.

"I should press this," he said, nodding toward the detonator in his hand. "God knows the world would not miss you. But I suspect you might consider it a kindness, and that is not what you deserve." He looked around at the rest of the Blacklight team and motioned to the door.

"Can you stand?" whispered Larissa, and Jamie nodded. She

let go of him, and he swayed unsteadily for a moment before walking toward the door, followed by Larissa and Morris.

Frankenstein walked backward after them, his eyes never leaving the Chemist, who was staring at him with naked murder in his eyes. "Don't move until we're gone," he warned. Then he pulled the living room door shut in front of him and joined the three figures who were waiting for him on the garden path. They hurried through the gate and along the road toward their waiting vehicle.

"What does all this—" began Morris, but Frankenstein cut him off.

"Not now, Tom. We'll debrief in the car. OK?"

Jamie walked along the road, his mind full of misery and hopelessness, his feet made of lead. He looked over at Larissa as they approached the car and gasped.

Her eyes were a deep, liquid crimson.

Then she moved.

She grabbed his wrist—so quickly it had happened before he even realized—unpeeled the fingers that were wrapped around the detonator, took it easily from his grip, and disappeared into the night sky.

ON THE WAY TO THE GALLOWS

There was silence in the SUV.

Thomas Morris was behind the wheel, guiding the car towards the Loop, and a series of questions that no one in the vehicle was looking forward to answering. Frankenstein was in the passenger seat, staring out of the window at the passing countryside; the flat landscape sped past as the powerful engine devoured the distance. Jamie sat in the back, his hands over his face.

Eventually, Morris spoke.

"How bad is this going to be?"

Frankenstein laughed, a deep grunt without humor in it. "How bad do you think?" he replied. "We took a vampire off base without authorization, disobeying the specific orders of the director, then let her escape. We fraudulently commandeered a helicopter and a pilot, and lost the only lead that might have led us to Jamie's mother. I think it might be quite bad. Don't you?"

Morris nodded glumly, his eyes on the dark road.

"It's over, isn't it?" asked Jamie, his voice barely audible. "We're never going to find her."

Frankenstein leaned around his seat's headrest and looked at him. "I promised you I would help you find her," he said. "And I will continue to do so. But you have to be prepared for the fact that after tonight, we are probably going to be doing this on our own. And that's assuming that Admiral Seward doesn't have us both arrested. Which he very well might."

Jamie nodded. He hadn't expected to be told anything different. He had been wrong, so terribly wrong, and now Larissa was gone, and he had jeopardized the careers of two men who had believed in him, two men who had helped him.

"I'll tell Seward it was my idea," he said. "I'll take the blame for everything."

"I appreciate the gesture," replied Frankenstein. "But that isn't going to make a blind bit of difference. We should never have let you take her out of her cell. You couldn't have done it without the code Tom gave you, and Seward knows that. We're in this together."

Morris groaned and turned the SUV off the motorway, sending it speeding past RAF Mildenhall on their left, approaching the final turning that would take them through the woods and into the Loop. A C-130 Hercules roared low over the road, lights flashing on its enormous belly as it rushed toward the long Mildenhall runway. The SUV shook and rattled as the huge aircraft thundered over them, then there was a loud thud on the roof of the car, and Morris spun the wheel to keep it on the asphalt. He slammed his foot on the brake and brought them sliding to a halt at the side of the road.

"What was that?" asked Frankenstein. Then the passenger door on the opposite side of the car to Jamie was pulled open, and Larissa swung easily into the seat next to him.

"Did you miss me?" she asked, sweetly.

Frankenstein hauled the T-Bone from his belt and shoved it against her throat. She pulled it easily out of his hand and threw it out of the open door. The monster fumbled for his stake, but Jamie shouted at him to stop, and turned to Larissa.

"Where have you been?" he shouted, his face bright red with anger. "What the hell did you think you were doing?"

"I'm pleased to see you, too," she said, then handed him the cylindrical detonator. He looked at it dumbly. "I went to make sure the Chemist was telling the truth," she continued. "Something told me you would be unwilling to take me at my word."

Frankenstein laughed. "This is absolutely—"

"I'm not talking to you," interrupted Larissa. "I'm talking to Jamie."

Jamie looked at the angry gray-green face looming at them from the front seat of the car, then at Larissa's calm expression. "And?" he asked. "Was he telling the truth?"

Larissa nodded. "He was. I know exactly where they are."

Morris craned his head around from the driver's seat.

"How can you possibly expect us to believe you?" he asked.

"I don't expect anything," she replied. "Take us back to base and get a satellite over Northumberland. I can show you with your own eyes."

It took them no more than ninety seconds to cross the distance from the authorization tunnel to the wide semicircle of tarmac in front of the hangar, but in that time a welcoming committee had gathered to meet them.

Morris brought the SUV to a halt, and the four passengers stepped out of the car. Admiral Seward was the first to reach them, his face so red it looked as though he might burst.

"I don't know where to start," he said, his voice tight with fury. "In my twenty years in this Department, I've never seen such insubordination, such flagrant recklessness, or such godforsaken outright stupidity!"

"Sir—" began Morris, but Seward shouted him down.

"Don't say anything!" he bellowed. "Not a damn word, do you hear me? Any of you!"

He waved a hand, and two operators appeared alongside him.

"Take her back to her cell, immediately," Seward said. "If she so much as blinks without your permission, destroy her."

One of the operators drew his T-Bone and pointed it at Larissa's chest. The second hauled the detonator roughly out of Jamie's hand, then placed his other hand on her lower back and shoved her toward the hangar.

Jamie threw a desperate look at Frankenstein, who widened his eyes in a clear warning not to say or do anything. Instead he spoke to the director.

"Admiral," he said. "She says she has the location of Alexandru Rusmanov. Let her show us before she goes back to her cell."

"Are you telling me what to do, Colonel?" asked Seward,

his voice cold.

"No, sir," replied Frankenstein. "I'm just saying that you shouldn't let our actions allow a Priority A1 target to get away. Sir."

Seward stepped forward and stared up into the monster's face. "Do you have any idea how serious this is?" he asked. "I can have you court-martialed for what you have done today. I can make sure you spend the rest of your life behind bars."

"Believe me, sir," the monster replied, "I'm well aware of the likely consequences."

They stared at each other, then Seward shouted for the operators who were holding Larissa to stop.

"Five minutes," the director said. "Then she goes back to her cell. Whether she shows us anything or not."

Admiral Seward stood in the middle of the Department 19 Ops Room, looking up at the huge screen that covered one wall. Frankenstein, Jamie, and Morris sat silently at three of the empty desks, waiting. Larissa stood against the far wall, the two operators training their weapons on her. She had described the location to a young communications officer, who was now tapping at a keyboard. Seward was standing silently, his eyes trained on the silver watch on his wrist. After a few seconds, he looked down at Frankenstein, smiled, and held up four fingers in the air.

"Sir, we have a satellite in geosynchronous orbit over Faslane," said the communications officer. "Do I have permission to move her?"

"Granted, Lieutenant," replied Seward. "Proceed."

"Ninety seconds to target, sir."

"Very well."

The screen bloomed into life, showing HMNB Clyde in stunning high-definition detail. The naval base, home to the UK's Trident nuclear submarines, hugged the eastern shore of Gare Loch, twenty-five miles west of Glasgow on the Firth of Clyde. Jamie marveled at the detail of the live pictures, beaming down from a highly classified Skynet 6 satellite six hundred kilometers above the earth's surface.

The picture began to move, slowly at first, then with rapidly accelerating speed as the satellite's engines fired, sending it east-southeast, over Southern Scotland and into Northern England. It flew over the Cheviot Hills and slowed as it approached Alnwick, settling over a grand country estate on the outskirts of the market town. The resolution intensified as the satellite's powerful cameras zoomed in on the collection of buildings filling the screen.

A large house, built in the shape of a wide capital *H*, was surrounded by a number of outbuildings: stables, sheds, garages. Gravel tracks linked them together, winding through thick copses of trees and immaculately manicured lawns. A swing set was clearly visible at the rear of the house, beside a sandbox and a pair of small football goals.

Nothing moved. The image was as still as a photograph.

Seward checked his watch. "One minute," he said.

Jamie flashed an anxious glance at Frankenstein, then looked over at Larissa and was surprised to see that she was not paying any attention at all to the screen. She was looking directly at him. When his eyes met hers, she made no attempt to look away, or to pretend she had been looking elsewhere. She simply returned his gaze, her eyes calm, her face pale, her skin flawless.

I could stare at her forever.

"Contact," shouted the communications officer, and the spell was broken.

All eyes in the Ops Room turned to the screen. Walking slowly between the main house and one of the outbuildings was a large, hunched figure.

"That's Anderson," breathed Frankenstein.

"Confirm identity," said Seward, and the lieutenant took hold of the small joystick that emerged from the middle of his console. He guided the satellite's camera north, in the direction the figure was heading, and tracked it on maximum zoom. The man—it was a man, the slightly balding pate now clearly visible—walked quickly, his head level, his shoulders back, as calmly as if he were taking an evening stroll along one of the long sand beaches that were little more than five miles to the east. He reached the outbuilding, took a brief look to his left and right, then glanced upward, and pushed open the door, disappearing from view.

"Freeze that image!" shouted Frankenstein.

The communications officer wound the satellite feed back and paused it at the millisecond when the man had tipped his head backward, as though he was looking directly at them. The picture sharpened into focus, and a round, childish face with small features emerged into crystal clarity.

"There they are," said Larissa. "Where Alexandru goes, Anderson goes."

"Run it," said Seward.

Frankenstein groaned. "Sir, it's obvious—"

"I said run it," interrupted the director. "I've had more than enough of people playing hunches today."

The lieutenant punched buttons, opening a window and entering the Department 19 mainframe. He dragged the still of the man's face into a box and hit SEARCH. Less than ten seconds later, the computer returned its results.

SUBJECT NAME: ANDERSON, (UNKNOWN)
SPECIES: VAMPIRE
PRIORITY LEVEL: A2
KNOWN ASSOCIATES: RUSMANOV, ALEXANDRU
       RUSMANOV, VALERI
       RUSMANOV, ILYANA
MOST RECENT SIGHTING: 3/24/2007
WHEREABOUTS: UNKNOWN

Jamie breathed out a sigh of relief and looked at Larissa, gratitude all over his tired face. Larissa smiled at him, and mouthed, "Told you."

"Zoom out and switch to infrared," said Seward.

The picture switched from the still of Anderson to a live close-up of the building he had just entered, then drew out and up until it again showed the entire estate. Then, as the infrared kicked in, it changed to a series of colored swirls; waves of dark blue and black where the cold woods and lawns had been, the *H* of the main house a rainbow of yellow and orange, studded with moving blobs of hot, dark red.

"There must be thirty of them in there," said the lieutenant.

Frankenstein turned his chair and looked at the director.

Seward was staring at the screen, his jaw set firm, assessing what he was seeing in front of him. After a long pause, he spoke, and the monster closed his eyes with relief.

"Scramble a strike team," said Seward. "Four squads. Full weapons and tactical. I want wheels up in thirty minutes." He looked down at the men in the seats below him, as if suddenly remembering they were there. "Frankenstein, Morris, you will lead squads two and four. Carpenter, you will be limited to the transport. I would leave you here, but given the events of today, I believe I would rather have you where I can keep an eye on you."

Jamie opened his mouth to protest, but Seward cut him off.

"Do not try my patience any further, young man. I'm giving you a gift by letting you come at all. Don't make me take it back."

Jamie closed his mouth.

"Security," continued the director. "Take her back to her cell, then report to the hangar for briefing."

Suddenly, the whole room was moving. Seward stepped down from the command platform and strode toward the door. The two operators who had been guarding Larissa took her by the shoulders and led her in the same direction, to the elevator that would return her to the cellblock, deep in the bowels of the base.

Jamie jumped to his feet, calling her name. She looked back at him briefly, then turned away, allowing herself to be led out of the room.

"It's not fair," he shouted at Frankenstein and Morris, who had risen from their chairs and were watching him. "She did what she promised."

"She can't go," said Frankenstein. "You know she can't."

Jamie looked at Morris, who stared uncomfortably at the ground.

"Fine," he spat. "Let's go and get my mother. We can deal with Larissa when we get back."

THE HUNTING PARTY

The mobilization of the Department 19 strike team was a sight unlike anything Jamie had ever seen.

The hangar on Level 0 was a hive of activity; Operators in black uniform and purple visors filled the wide floor, clustered into tight circles as officers, Frankenstein and Morris among them, briefed them on the mission ahead. The hum of voices and the click of weapons being checked was deafening in the silent night air, but Jamie barely heard it; his attention was trained on the large structures that loomed in the darkness on the other side of the runway.

The doors of two of the buildings were slowly rolling open, spilling bright white light across the tarmac, illuminating the white markings that led to the runway. Two enormous black shapes were slowly being revealed, and Jamie watched, fascinated.

Inside the hangars stood a pair of black helicopters, their

fuselages hanging bloated and swollen beneath twin sets of rotors. They were so tall and wide that Jamie could not believe they were capable of flight; their cockpits sat tiny above their bellies, which were the size of a suburban house. Behind him, he could hear the voices of Frankenstein and Morris giving orders to their men, but he paid no attention. It had been made clear to him that he was not going to be allowed to be involved in the mission, that his role was to be purely that of an observer, and so he saw no reason to bother with the briefings and the mission priority checklists. Instead he stood alone in the huge arc of the main hangar's open door and watched.

With two earth-rattling explosions of sound, the engines of the helicopters growled into life. Jamie felt the vibrations shudder through him, even though he was the length of a football field away from the towering vehicles. Lights blinked on in the cockpits, and Jamie could see the pilots, impossibly small, running through their pre-flight checks. Then there were two heavy screeches of rubber, and the helicopters began to move toward him, rolling slowly over the tarmac under the power of their diesel engines, toward the strike team that would soon occupy them.

As they crossed the runway and emerged into the bright light of the open main hangar, Jamie gasped. The scale of the vehicles was vast; they towered above him, at least two stories tall and as wide as a 747. They looked as though someone had taken the cockpit, wings, landing gear, and rotor assemblies from a normal-size helicopter and then glued them onto a huge steel box.

They can't fly. Surely they can't. They're too big. Then a new thought occurred to him. *What the hell goes in there? Sixty men won't fill half of one of them.*

Behind him in the main hangar, the Blacklight officers shouted at their men to form up. Jamie turned and watched the squads line up into four neat lines, evenly spaced, facing out toward the waiting helicopters. Light blasted out of the bellies of the helicopters, and his shadow raced away in front of him, reaching the feet of the motionless soldiers.

"Jamie!" shouted Frankenstein. "Get out of the way! Next to me!"

Covering his eyes with his forearm, Jamie squinted up at the huge transports. The near sides of both vehicles had lowered, meeting the tarmac as wide ramps. Inside, beyond the blinding white lights, he could see hulking shapes at the top of each ramp, then he was grabbed by the arm and pulled to the side as the squads of Blacklight operators marched forward and upward, disappearing into the cavernous interiors.

Frankenstein loomed over him.

"Are you going to make this difficult?" he asked, leaning down so his eyes were level with the teenager's. "Or are you going to stay out of the way and let us do our job? Tell me now, so I know."

Jamie stared up at him. Frankenstein was looking at him with no compassion, no pity; he was all business.

OK. Have it your way. If it brings my mom home, have it your way.

"You don't need to worry about me," he answered. "I won't get in the way."

Frankenstein smiled at him. "Thank you," he replied.

They ran out to the nearest helicopter, crouching low beneath the screaming rotors. They climbed the ramp and headed to the right, where two of the Blacklight squads were sitting, in eight rows of heavy-duty flight seats. Frankenstein and Jamie sat down alongside them and strapped themselves in. Jamie looked around the enormous interior of the helicopter, his eyes widening.

In front of him were two jet-black armored vehicles, huge and heavy-looking, with two enormous wheels on each side, the kind of wheels that looked like they belonged on a monster truck. Guns bristled from a turret atop each vehicle, and a purple spotlight sat on a swiveling arm at the front. Beyond the two vehicles were four more lights, three times the size of the ones on the armored cars, lashed safely to the floor and walls alongside racks of beam guns and UV grenades.

The rotors rose to a whining scream, and the seat beneath Jamie shook and rattled as the huge helicopter lumbered into the air. The exhaustion he had been battling all day returned with a vengeance, and he shut his eyes as the strike team headed north.

He was woken by the sound of Frankenstein's voice ordering the operators to carry out their final checks. The men, who looked to the half-asleep Jamie like rows of black robots in their identical uniforms and anonymous helmets, pulled their weapons from their belts, unloaded and reloaded them, and replaced them in their loops and holsters.

"Absolute silence until we reach the go point," said Frankenstein, looking around at the men. "No one moves until the UV cannons are in place and all four squads are in position. Is that clear?"

"Yes, sir," chorused the soldiers.

"I want this to run smooth and simple," Frankenstein

continued. "I don't want any heroics. We go in, we eliminate the targets, we bring the package out. Understood?"

The package? Is he talking about my mother?

"Yes, sir."

The helicopters landed a mile away from the target, sending cut grass spinning into the air and startling a herd of grazing cows. The ramps lowered and the Blacklight team deployed, the four armored cars rolling silently down into the field, their wheels propelled by engines that were surrounded by sound-dampening ceramic plates. The UV spotlights came next, attached to purpose-built housings at the rears of the vehicles. The squads of operators followed them, their purple visors lowered, their T-Bones held loosely across their chests. The men climbed into the vehicles, and Frankenstein called for a readiness report over the closed-circuit radio system that linked them together. The four squads reported back ready, and Frankenstein ordered the driver of his vehicle to proceed. The armored car moved smoothly across the field and out onto a narrow country road. Jamie sat next to Frankenstein, his visor raised, his weapons checked and rechecked, his leg bouncing nervously up and down as they neared their destination.

Light blazed from the windows of the estate's main house, and the sounds of music and voices floated out on the night air.

The Blacklight team brought the vehicles to a halt in the trees at the bottom of the driveway, where they would be invisible from both the road and the house, and the operators disembarked. Frankenstein and Morris directed them into position, giving their orders via a series of complex hand signals that Jamie found utterly impenetrable. The first squad, Morris's squad, took one of the UV spotlights, flanked the house, and took up a position at the rear, covering the back door and the outbuildings that stood in a loose semicircle around it. The second and third squads took a spotlight each and positioned themselves at the sides of the building. Frankenstein waited until he received silent confirmation that each of the teams were in position, then led his own team slowly forward toward the house. He turned to Jamie as his men started to move through the trees.

"Stay here," he whispered. Then he smiled.

Jamie stared, unsure how to respond, and then the monster was gone, just another shadow moving through the black columns of trees. Jamie stared after him for a few seconds, then climbed back into the armored car.

Suddenly, the estate was filled with purple as the UV spotlights burst into life, covering the doors and windows. Jamie heard the bang from a hundred yards away as one of the operators kicked the front door of the house in, then a millisecond later saw it happen on one of the monitors on the vehicle's control console. A moment later, he heard the first shouts and screams as he watched the Blacklight squads pour into the house.

I want to see this for myself.

Jamie leapt down from the vehicle and streaked through the trees toward the house. The noise rose as he ran across the wide lawn in front of the building, and then he was through the front door, directly disobeying the only order Frankenstein had given him. The noise was coming from behind a huge carved wooden door at the rear of the lobby, and he hauled it open, his heart pounding, his mind racing with what he was going to say to his mother when he was reunited with her.

It was a large dining hall, set for a dinner that was never going to be served. A huge open fire roared in a fireplace at the back of the room, sending orange light reflecting off an ornate chandelier that hung above the long table. Standing in front of the fire were maybe twenty men and women in tuxedos and cocktail dresses. The Blacklight strike team surrounded them, their T-Bones set against their shoulders and pointing at the protesting crowd.

Jamie's heart sank.

His mother wasn't there.

Neither was Alexandru.

As he stared into the room, Frankenstein pulled the beam gun from his belt and raked purple UV light across the group. Several of the women shrieked, and most of the men bellowed angrily, but there were no screams of pain, and no smoke rose from the exposed skin. Frankenstein turned away from them, his face as dark as thunder, and Jamie saw him speak into his radio.

"I demand to know the meaning of this outrage!" shouted one of the men by the fire, a large, portly man in a tuxedo that was straining at the seams. His round face was bright red with indignation, a glistening black mustache quivering on his upper lip. "This is private property! I demand an explanation, this instant!"

A Blacklight operator stepped forward and jabbed the tip of his T-Bone into the man's chest, hard. Several of the women cried out; the man backed away in a hurry, shouting as he did so, until a striking woman in a figure-hugging black dress placed a hand on his shoulder, and he was quiet.

Frankenstein strode back through the operators and addressed the small crowd.

"Where is Alexandru Rusmanov?" he growled.

"Never heard of him," snapped a woman at the front of the group.

Frankenstein strode to a table set against one off the long walls of the hall. On it were glasses, plates, and a silver tray containing glass vials of a dark red powder. He picked one of the vials up and held it out toward the woman.

"I suppose you don't know what this is either?" he snarled. "Or do you always keep a supply of Bliss on hand for whenever you throw a party?"

"I've never seen that before in my life," the woman replied, a maddening smile on her face. "I don't know what it is, or why it's here, and I challenge you to prove otherwise. Now, why don't you get the hell out of my house?"

Frankenstein threw the vial to the floor. It smashed, and Bliss flew into the air in a small red cloud. He saw a number of the guests eye the spilled powder with naked desire and felt himself teeter on the edge of control of his temper. He took a half step toward her, but the woman didn't back down an inch. She stared up at the monster, her eyes narrow, her face calm. She was standing steadily, her hands on her narrow hips, wearing a dark red cocktail dress and a white shawl around her shoulders.

"Tell me where Alexandru is, and we'll go," replied Frankenstein, his voice low and dangerous.

They faced each other for a long moment, until a voice

called from the back of the group. "You'll never find him, you filthy monster!"

The crowd parted, revealing the woman who had quieted the blustering man. She was incredibly beautiful, her limbs long and slender, her narrow face framed by jet-black hair that fell across her shoulders. She smiled at Frankenstein as he walked slowly toward her.

He leaned in until his enormous face was only inches from hers. "What did you say?" he asked. His voice sounded like tectonic plates shifting.

"I said you'll never find him, you filthy monster," she replied, calmly. "He floats above the earth like a god, while you crawl on your stomach like a beetle. You could never hope to understand him, or find him, or stop him."

A smile broke slowly across Frankenstein's face, and hers faltered in response. "When I pierce Alexandru's heart, and his warm blood sprays across my face," he said, softly, "I will think of you." He stood up, abruptly, and the woman recoiled, as if anticipating a blow. Instead the monster turned his back on her and strode across the dining hall to the door where Jamie was standing. "Everybody moving," he bellowed. "Let's get the hell out of here."

"Who are they?" whispered Jamie as the monster passed him.

"Vampire lovers," spit Frankenstein. "Acolytes. They follow vampires around like doting children, give them money, places to stay, hoping to be turned. They're the worst kind of scum."

The Blacklight team returned to the helicopters as silently as they had advanced. Admiral Seward had called the four officers into his vehicle, his voice tight and strained, as though he was almost too angry to speak. Jamie was riding in the third of the four armored cars, sandwiched on a bench between two operators he didn't know. As they crawled along the country road toward the drop point, the inquest began.

"Just bloody groupies. Someone tipped Alexandru off," said the operator to Jamie's right.

"You think so?" said another. "What was your first clue? When he wasn't there?"

"Go to hell," said the first operator.

They rode in silence for several minutes, until the same man spoke again.

"The director didn't look happy," he said.

"That," said the operator opposite Jamie, "is the understatement of the year."

They arrived back at the Loop at midnight.

The exhausted men were dismissed and fled for the elevators, while Jamie, Frankenstein, and Morris waited in the Ops Room for Admiral Seward to finish his phone call to the chief of the general staff.

When the director appeared ten minutes later, he was white with anger, the veins standing out on his neck and the backs of his hands like ropes. He walked slowly to the front of the room and took a deep breath, as if to steady himself.

"I'm sure I don't need to tell you," he said, his voice that of a man trying his hardest to keep his temper, "that tonight was nothing less than a catastrophic embarrassment for this Department. Do I need to tell you that?"

"No sir," they said.

"Good. That's good. The only silver lining is that the men and women we apprehended were clearly already aware of our existence, so the PR damage is minimal. The damage to your careers, on the other hand, and to mine, is likely to be significantly more severe." He clenched and unclenched his fists, several times. "I'm going to leave it to you to ascertain exactly how this disaster was perpetrated, although I'm sure we all know the answer. I want a full report on how this came to happen on my desk in the morning, or I will have your resignations. Is that clear?"

They told him it was, and he nodded, stiffly.

"I suggest you start your investigation in the cellblock. Beyond that, I have nothing to say to any of you. Good night, gentlemen."

Seward walked slowly across the room, opened the door, and left without looking back. Jamie, Frankenstein and Morris waited until they were certain he was gone, and then began to talk.

"How did this happen?" asked Morris.

Frankenstein grunted. "As if we all don't know," he said, looking steadily at Jamie.

"What's that supposed to mean?" demanded the teenager.

"It means your girlfriend tipped off Alexandru," Frankenstein replied, his voice maddeningly calm. "It means she went to him when she escaped, then told him to wait two hours after she left so she could come back here and save the day. It means she played you—again."

"You're wrong," said Jamie, and the venom in his own voice shocked even him.

"It makes sense, Jamie," said Morris. "Who else could have done it?"

"I don't know," replied Jamie, fighting hard to control his temper. "But it wasn't her. That I do know."

Frankenstein began to say something, but then the radio on Jamie's belt buzzed, a thick whirring noise that made all three jump. He pulled the handset from his belt, thumbed the RECEIVE button and held the handset to his ear. When he heard the voice on the other end, he nearly dropped it onto the table in front of him.

"Good evening, Jamie," said Alexandru Rusmanov. His voice was slick like castor oil. "How are you?"

The color drained from the teenager's face, and Frankenstein and Morris leaned toward him, concern on their faces.

"Who is it?" asked Morris.

Jamie composed himself. Think of your mother. *Think of your mother.*

Think of your mother.

"I'm fine, Alexandru," he said slowly, causing Morris to gasp and Frankenstein's eyes to open wide. "How are you?"

"I'm a little bit annoyed, to tell you the truth," the vampire replied, his tone friendly and cheerful. "I was in the middle of a party, thrown by some of my most loyal subjects, when all of a sudden I was told I had to leave. And all because some child who should already be dead has decided to take it upon himself to hunt me down. Can you imagine?"

"I think I—"

"No, you can't!" roared Alexandru, his pleasant demeanor gone, replaced by the screeching voice of a madman. "You can't even begin to imagine what you've done this night! Your tiny little human brain is incapable of even attempting to grasp the repercussions of your actions!"

Jamie closed his eyes. He had never been so scared in all his life.

"But you will," continued Alexandru, and now he was friendly again, his voice warm and charming. "You will understand. I'll make you understand, starting now. I've just killed a lot of people, and every single one of them has you to thank for their deaths."

There was a click, and the line went dead.

Jamie was about to tell his friends what Alexandru had said, was about to try and articulate the way the madness in the vampire's voice had made him feel, the basic wrongness of it, the terrible, unspeakable horror he had heard, when an alarm exploded through the base, and the giant wall screen burst into life.

ALERT STATUS 1
IMMEDIATE ASSISTANCE REQUIRED
ALL DEPARTMENTS RESPOND

Morris ran to a console in the middle of the room. He read the screen, then looked up at Jamie and Frankenstein.

"It's coming from Russia," he said.

YOU REAP WHAT YOU SOW

Carpathian Mountains, Transylvania
June 17, 1902

The fine layer of dirt and rock shifted beneath Abraham Van Helsing's feet, and the old man's center of balance hurtled backward. He spun his arms, his silver-topped walking stick clattering to the ground, and he pitched toward the hard ground. Then a hand appeared, as if from nowhere, gripped him around his upper arm, and steadied him. The professor, blooming red with embarrassment, spun around to see the identity of his rescuer and stared directly into the cool, steady face of Henry Carpenter, his valet.

"Thank you, boy," he grunted. "Unnecessary of you, though. I was in no danger."

"Of course not, sir," replied the valet, and released his master's arm.

You stupid old fool, Van Helsing told himself. *You're nothing more than a liability. You should have trusted this to Henry,*

Lord knows he's proven himself more than capable. You proud old fool.

"Everything is fine?" called a voice from down the trail, and master and valet turned to regard the source of the question.

The man who had spoken was standing beside the low wooden cart, looking up at them with concern on his face. He was small and uncannily thin, his proportions rendered comical by the enormous fur ushanka that covered his head. His face was thin and pointed, the eyes dark, the hair of his mustache and triangular beard jet black.

"Yes, Bukharov," snapped Van Helsing. "Everything is fine. Bring your men up to me. We should be able to see the castle once we round this bend."

Ivan Bukharov nodded, then let loose a galloping string of Russian at the three men who sat astride aged horses before the cart. They dug their heels into the flanks of their mounts, and the wheels of the vehicle creaked into life. Bukharov swung himself nimbly up onto his own horse and clattered along the treacherous path to where Van Helsing and the valet were waiting. The two Englishmen mounted their own animals, one with significantly greater difficulty than the other, and the three men trotted slowly around an enormous outcrop of rock that caused the path to make a wickedly sharp turn to the right. They rounded it with great care and then stopped, transfixed by the sight before them.

The Borgo Pass widened and dropped before them, before rising steeply and disappearing out of sight. Above them, more than a thousand feet from the distant valley floor, perched on the very edge of the mountain like a vast bird of prey, stood Castle Dracula.

The turrets and ramparts of the ancient building were black in the cool morning light, spiked and twisted and fearsome. The central spire of the residence of the world's first and most terrible vampire rose boldly toward the heavens, a blasphemous challenge to the authority of God, an unholy blade cutting into the pale blue sky.

Behind them came a flurry of movement and muttered Russian. The valet turned, and saw Bukharov's men crossing themselves frantically, their eyes cast at the ground, unwilling to even look directly at the castle that loomed over them.

"So it real," breathed Bukharov. "I was thinking legend only. But it real."

The man's pidgin English was a source of constant annoyance to Van Helsing, but he barely even noticed it, so lost was he in the memories of the last time he had seen this terrible place.

I was on the other side of this plain, with Mina Harker pressed into a stone crevice behind me. I drew a circle around her, and I waited. There were screams and the thundering of hooves and blood, and a friend of mine was lost.

"It's real," he said, composing himself. "But it is merely a building, stone and mortar. It cannot harm us; whatever malevolence it may have possessed is long gone. Now come—our destination is no more than five minutes' ride from here." The old man kicked his horse into life, and cantered down the shallow slope of the pass, toward the clearing where the course of his life had been forever altered.

The negotiations that had brought Van Helsing back to Transylvania—eleven years after he had sworn he would never set foot on her cursed soil again—had been long and arduous. In London, his hours were full, fuller than those of a man of his advanced years ought to have allowed, as the fledgling Blacklight began to take shape. The days were spent at the premises on Piccadilly, which Arthur Holmwood, the new Lord Godalming, had secured for them, a noble use of the section of his father's estate that had been set aside for charitable works, planning and organizing and writing reports for the prime minister, alongside the friends with whom he had undertaken the protection of the Empire from the supernatural. The nights found him in tombs and graveyards and museums and hospitals, battling the growing number of vampires that were infecting London and its surroundings, sending them one after another to their grisly ends.

He spent precious little time in his laboratory, even though he believed that the vampire problem would ultimately be solved by science, rather than at the point of a stake. There was simply no time; it was taking all of Blacklight's efforts merely to stem the tide of the epidemic that was washing across Europe, an epidemic that had started in the building that was casting its shadow over him as he rode down the pass. It was obvious that the four of them were going to be unable to keep the darkness at bay on their own, and tentative plans had been put in motion to increase their number. The first prospective new member was riding silently alongside the professor now, his eyes keeping a sharp watch on the treacherous terrain around them.

Henry Carpenter will do fine, perhaps even better than fine. He alone will not be enough, as my days on this earth are undoubtedly drawing to a close. But he is a start, and a good one at that.

Despite the endless demands on his attention, Van Helsing had been able to draw two reasonably firm conclusions from his study of the vampire. He was confident that the transmission of the condition occurred when saliva was introduced to the system of the victim, during the act of biting. And he was also sure that a vampire who had been incinerated to nothing more than a pile of ash could, with sufficient quantities of blood, be made whole again. This conclusion had been reached after the professor had conducted a series of experiments in a heavily fortified room beneath the cellar of his town house, experiments he had told no one he was undertaking for fear of rebuke. And it was this conclusion that had led him to the realization that a return trip to Transylvania was imperative—as the count's remains, buried though they were under the heavy Carpathian soil, were too dangerous to leave unattended. The opportunity to bring Quincey Morris home, to give him the burial he deserved, was merely a bonus.

At Van Helsing's request, telegrams had been sent to the heads of Russia and Germany, inviting them to send envoys to London on a matter of grave importance to the entire continent. Men from these nations had duly arrived in the summer of 1900, and, after signing declarations of utmost secrecy, had been admitted to the Blacklight headquarters and briefed on the threat that was facing the civilized world. They had been sent home with much to ponder, and in the two years that had passed, encouraging word had reached Van Helsing's ears of equivalent organizations being birthed in Northern Europe. It had been a gamble and a dangerous political move to show their cards as plainly as they had, but without other nations joining the fight, the battle was sure to be lost.

When Van Helsing informed the prime minister of his intention to return to Transylvania, to secure the remains of Dracula and bring them home to be safely stored, a telegram had been sent to Moscow, inviting the nascent Supernatural Protection Commissariat to send a man to accompany the professor on his journey in the spirit of international cooperation that befitted the new century. And so it was that when the old man and his valet disembarked at the port of Constanța, they were met by Ivan Bukharov, who introduced himself to the professor as special envoy to the State Council of Imperial Russia, under the authority of Czar Nicholas II himself. The six men—Van Helsing, Henry Carpenter, Ivan Bukharov, and the latter's three Russian aides—had spent the night in Constanța before making their way north via carriage, through Brăila and Tecuci, where they spent an agreeable evening and night in one of the town's three inns, through Bacău and Drăgoești, where they again took rest, and on to Vatra Dornei, where they left the carriages and advanced on horseback, pulling with them the low wooden cart that would ferry the remains of the dead back to England.

They rode up onto the Borgo Pass at first light, the mood of the travelers and the urgency of the journey far removed from the previous time Van Helsing had stepped onto the steep ridges of the Carpathian Mountains, when he had been chasing evil with one hand, while trying to protect innocence with the other.

Van Helsing recognized their destination when he was still more than a hundred yards away from it. A natural canopy of rock, not deep enough to be called a cave, that nonetheless offered protection from the elements to the souls sleeping eternally beneath it. He called for Bukharov to follow him, then urged his horse onward, its hooves clattering across the loose rock. He drew the animal to a halt and dismounted. His valet appeared instantly at his side but offered no assistance; the lash of his master's tongue had taught him that it would be requested if it was needed. The old man lurched unsteadily as his feet touched the earth, but he did not fall.

Carpenter and Bukharov followed the old man at a respectful distance as he approached the rock doorway. He paused as he reached the threshold, then sank to his knees so suddenly that his valet ran forward, alarmed.

"Back," hissed Van Helsing, waving an arm at him, and Carpenter did as he was told.

The professor knelt before the opening, his heart pounding, his throat closed by the terrible wave of grief that had driven him to the cold ground.

Beneath the canopy of rock lay the two flat stones that he and Jonathan Harker had placed there in 1891: a lifetime ago, or so it seemed. The one on the right was pale gray, and had carved upon it a simple crucifix, a narrow cross that Harker had chiseled with the end of his kukri knife, tears falling from his eyes as he did so. The one on the left was black, and it, too, bore a carved crucifix, only this one was upside down, the ancient mark of the unholy. Van Helsing had carved it himself, using Quincey Morris's bowie knife, bitter satisfaction filling him as he did so.

"Professor?" It was Bukharov's voice, low and full of worry. "Professor, you are being fine?"

The old man laughed, despite himself, a short bark of mirth.

"Yes, Ivan, I am being fine." He pushed himself back to his feet and turned to face the rest of the men. "It looks undisturbed. Have your men dig up the ground, but tell them to be careful. The coffin is large but it may be fragile, and it contains both sets of remains. I do not want my friend's bones spilling out across this mountainside, is that understood?"

Bukharov nodded, then spoke a short sentence of Russian to his men and waved them forward. They set about their orders manfully, hacking at the hard ground with pickaxes and shovels, and Van Helsing retired to a flat outcropping of rock, where he sat and waited for them to complete their task. After a minute or two, his valet joined him, leaving Bukharov overseeing the excavation.

"All would appear to be going to plan, sir," said Henry Carpenter.

Van Helsing grunted. "So far, Henry. It appears to be going to plan so far. There will no doubt be ample opportunity for the Russian half-wit to jeopardize matters before we have the remains safely on their way to London."

Carpenter looked at Bukharov, who was encouraging his men with a steady stream of Russian.

"Do you believe the special envoy is truly slow-witted, sir? I suspect a sharp mind is at work behind his limited English."

"Nonsense," growled Van Helsing. "The man is a fool and a liability to this undertaking. And I shall be instructing the prime minister to convey my opinion of their man to the Russians as soon as we return."

"I'm sure you are correct, sir."

"As am I, Henry. As am I."

After little more than twenty minutes, there came the heavy thud of metal on wood, and the three Russians dropped to their knees and began clearing the dirt away with their gloved hands. Van Helsing got to his feet and walked over to where Bukharov was standing, observing his men.

"Will remains be good condition still?" he asked Van Helsing, who shrugged.

"How on earth should I be able to tell you that?" the old man replied. "The elevation and the climate are certainly suitable for preservation, but I won't know for certain until I see them."

Under the canopy, two of the Russians inserted metal bars along the front edge of the coffin, and slowly applied their weight to them. With a long, high-pitched creak, the coffin that had carried Dracula across Europe and had become his final resting place lifted slowly into view. The men pulled it forward so its bottom edge lay on the lip of the hole they had dug around it, then joined their comrade at the rear of the canopy. Silently, they gripped the end of the box that still lay in the ground, lifted it, and pushed it forward.

The dark wooden coffin slid out of the enclave of rock like a ship being launched from a dry dock. It rolled across the loose surface with the three Russians at its rear and came to a halt before Van Helsing and Bukharov.

"Henry," said the professor, and the valet stepped forward.

Carpenter inserted a thin metal bar under the lid of the coffin and applied pressure to the lever. There was a moment's resistance, before the lid separated from the box and slid to one side, exposing a narrow sliver of pitch black. The Russians approached and took three corners of the lid, as Henry

Carpenter took the fourth. Then slowly, taking great care as they did so, they lifted it clear of the coffin and placed it gently to the ground on one side.

Van Helsing and Bukharov looked down.

Lying in the coffin, clad in the brown jacket and trousers he had been wearing when he died, was the skeleton of Quincey Morris. His bones were bright white, and the cowboy hat resting above his skull gave the gruesome tableau a comical feel, as though his mortal remains were a stage prop in some macabre play. On his chest lay his bowie knife, where Van Helsing had placed it before they had closed the coffin lid eleven years earlier.

Beside him was a large mound of gray powder, much of it piled against the sides of the coffin and in the corner nearest the two gravedigger's feet. This was all that remained of the first vampire, the cruel, ungodly creature that had tormented Van Helsing and his friends and had sent Lucy Westenra to damnation.

The professor crouched painfully, examining the joins between the sides of the coffin and the base. They appeared solid, as he had expected; this wooden vessel had been built to carry its occupant across much of the European continent, unharmed.

"Joins are good," grunted Van Helsing. "That should be all of him. Put the lid back on and fetch down the canvas."

Henry Carpenter and the Russian aides hoisted the coffin lid back into the air and carried it delicately back toward the box. At the last second, before the lid was re-sealed, Van Helsing darted a hand into the coffin and pulled the bowie knife out. He didn't know why he did so—he just knew that it seemed important. He attached it to his belt and stood back as the Russians hammered fresh nails into the lid, sealing it tight against the elements. One of them went to the cart and came back with a thick square of folded green canvas, which he spread wide on the loose ground. The coffin was lifted and placed in the middle of the green square, which was then folded up and over the wooden box. Nails were driven in to hold it in place, then a long red candle was lit, and hot wax was applied to every open fold, sealing the parcel airtight. Finally it was lifted onto the cart and lashed down with thick lengths of rope.

The men mounted their horses, and Van Helsing walked his alongside Bukharov, who was watching his men make final preparations to leave.

"I understand you wish to accompany us back to London, to observe the examinations. Is that correct?" asked Van Helsing.

"Much correct," replied Bukharov, a look of great excitement on his face. "Very much correct, Professor."

"Very well. Whether I allow that will depend exclusively on the condition the remains are in when they arrive at Constanţa. You would be well advised to communicate that to your men."

Van Helsing spurred his horse onward, and Bukharov and Carpenter followed him. Behind them, the Russians began to haul the cart back toward civilization.

The journey back to Constanţa was significantly quicker and less comfortable than the journey from the port had been. When they arrived back at the port town, shortly before dawn, men and horses alike were exhausted, but Van Helsing paid no attention to their suffering. He drove straight to the docks, left Bukharov and the Russians with his valet, and boarded the ship the British government had chartered for the journey, the *Indomitable*. He ordered the captain to make ready for sail, then descended the gangway to instruct Carpenter to oversee the loading of the remains onto the ship. The valet was standing by the cart with the three Russian aides, but there was no sign of—

Click.

The noise came from beside Van Helsing's head, and he slowly turned in its direction. Six inches in front of his forehead hovered a Colt 45 revolver, the silver gleaming yellow beneath the oil lamps that were suspended above the docks. The gun hung motionless in the air, and holding it at arm's length, smiling gently, was Ivan Bukharov.

"What is the meaning of this?" growled Van Helsing.

"I'm afraid my orders regrettably contravene yours, my dear Professor," said Bukharov, his English suddenly smooth and flawless. "They are to bring the spoils of this journey back to Moscow for inspection by the imperial czar. Which means that I cannot allow you to return the remains to London, an inconvenience for which I sincerely apologize."

You stupid fool. You underestimated this man because his manners were rough and his English was poor. Now you stand without a single card to play. Stupid old man.

Bukharov sidestepped in a tight circle around Van Helsing, the gun never so much as flickering in his grasp. He stopped beside the cart and regarded Henry Carpenter. "Please step back alongside your master," he said, pleasantly.

The valet did so, walking slowly backward until he was beside the old man, revealing to the professor the identical revolvers held in the hands of the three Russian men, guns that had been pointing silently at the valet while Van Helsing descended the gangway.

Bukharov said something quickly in Russian, and one of his men holstered his pistol, before climbing up into the first of the carriages that had brought them to the docks. When he emerged, he was carrying the two Englishmen's suitcases and traveling bags, which he placed on the ground before them. As the man bent to release the bags, Carpenter flashed a glance at his master and twitched his hand toward the pocket of his waistcoat. Van Helsing shook his head, so sharply it was almost invisible; the two-barrel derringer that the valet kept upon his person at all times would not be sufficient to extricate them from this situation.

"I wish you a safe and speedy journey home," said Bukharov, the Colt still pointing squarely at the old man. "I'm afraid we must say our farewells now, as we have a ship of our own to catch and many miles to travel once we reach Odessa. But I would like to say that it has been an absolute priv—"

"You have no idea what you're doing," interrupted Van Helsing. "Those remains are quite likely the most dangerous thing in existence. They need to be studied and stored where there is no risk of their seeing the light of day again. I implore you; let me have them."

Bukharov's genial expression faded and was replaced by a look of cold displeasure.

"Such arrogance to assume that only in Britain can anything be studied or safely hidden. I can assure you, Professor, that once we are finished with our examinations, the remains will be stored where no one will *ever* be able to find them."

THE SECOND INVASION OF LINDISFARNE

Lindisfarne Island, Northumberland
Two hours ago

They came from the mainland, when the island's inhabitants were curled up in front of televisions or asleep in their beds.

There were almost forty of them, emerging from the mist that wreathed the causeway, some walking along the damp road, others floating inches above it. Alexandru led them, his long gray coat flapping gently around his ankles, his crimson eyes blazing with madness.

Behind him strode Anderson, a large object wrapped in a cloth sack over his shoulder. Further back was the ragtag group of vampires that had attached themselves to Alexandru, overlooking or ignoring his sadistic extravagances for the protection his favor afforded.

Two dark, silent men walked behind the rest. They scratched at themselves almost continually, and every few minutes, they cast furtive glances at the moon. It was hours from full and hung large and bright in the night sky.

They approached the island in silence. They could already see the distant lights shining through the windows of the houses and the amber glow of the streetlights, rising up the hill from the harbor that opened on to the North Sea.

Kate Randall woke with a start.

She had been awake since five that morning, helping her father prepare bait and line, washing the small fishing boat on which he spent his days, and she had fallen asleep on her bed as soon as she had finished dinner. She had no doubt she would have slept through until the following morning if something hadn't disturbed her.

Kate sat up on her bed and stared across her bedroom at the open window above her desk. The pale yellow curtains fluttered in the night breeze, and the cold air raised goose bumps on her arms.

It's just the cold, she thought, rubbing her arms with her hands, trying to warm the skin. *Just the cold.*

But she wasn't sure that was true.

She had heard something out there in the darkness.

Something that sounded like a scream.

Kate climbed out of her bed, wincing at the temperature. She was still dressed in a sweatshirt and jeans, but she reached for the dressing gown hanging on the back of her door regardless. As she slid her arms into the sleeves, she felt the air swirl as something moved behind her, near the open window.

She spun round.

The room was empty.

Fear rippled through her like one of the slate-gray waves that pitched her father's boat. But she did not cry out.

Her father would be asleep by now, and if she had learned anything in her sixteen years, it was that she must not wake her father under any circumstances. This rule, this nonnegotiable law, had sunk so deeply into her that she obeyed it even now, as she stood trembling with fear in her own bedroom, no more than fifteen feet away from him.

Instead she walked toward the window.

She could smell the crisp, dry scent of a fire on the beach far below the small house she had shared with her father since her mother had died, could see a thin pillar of pale gray smoke rising above the small island, small clouds of sparks and orange embers floating lazily on the night air.

She could hear music, a classical piano piece, drifting out of the windows of her neighbors' house. Mr. Marsden was away on business in Newcastle, and his wife was making the most of her opportunity to control the stereo. It was normally the heavy bass and driving drums of Metallica and Motörhead that echoed out of their attic sitting room, at a volume that had led to more than one complaint.

Everything seemed to be normal. But Kate could not shake the feeling that something was wrong.

A dark shape, far too large to be a bird or a bat, swooped past her bedroom window, close enough to brush the blonde hair that fell untidily across her forehead, and this time she did scream, long and loud.

Kate staggered back from the window. In the bedroom across the hall, she heard her father swear, and then the thump of his feet on the wooden floorboards. She was so relieved to hear the movement in his room that she didn't even worry that she had woken him.

Half asleep, Pete Randall pulled a T-shirt over his head and staggered to the wooden door of his bedroom.

Damn girl, he thought. *If there's a spider in there, I'm not going to be happy.*

He had no idea that his teenage daughter had just saved his life. Or that he would never get a chance to thank her.

Pete crossed the small landing, his bare feet thudding on the uneven wooden floorboards of the old house, and pushed open the door to his daughter's room. He did not even have time to close it behind him before she flew into his arms, burying her head in his chest. She wasn't crying, but she had her eyes squeezed tightly shut.

Christ, she's shaking like a leaf, he thought. *What's going on in here?*

"There, there," he said softly. "You're safe. Tell me what happened."

Kate felt her father's strong arms around her shoulders and immediately started to feel stupid for having woken him.

It was just a bird, she told herself. *One of the big gulls. Stupid girl, scared of a bird when you live on an island. Now you've woken him up, and you know how hard he works, how difficult it's been for him since—*

There was a soft thump behind her, and she felt her dad's arms tense. She twisted, looked across the room, and bit her lip, hard enough that she tasted blood in her mouth. Otherwise she would have surely screamed again.

Standing in front of her bedroom window was a middle-aged man. He was wearing a pair of tattered blue jeans, so full of holes it seemed that they were holding together through sheer force of will alone. The rest of him was naked, although very little of his skin could be seen. His emaciated body was covered in tattoos, long loops and whorls of blue-black ink that stretched up and down both of his arms, across his narrow chest and concave stomach. Words she didn't recognize mingled with pictures of screaming faces, skeletal wings, and patterns so intricate they made her head swim. Hair hung from his head in black greasy locks that rested on his chest. His face was inhuman, with blazing red eyes that stared at her from sunken sockets.

The man opened his mouth and let out a deafening screech; Kate saw bright white fangs protruding from below his upper lip, and fear flooded into her as a series of answering screeches floated through the window on the cold evening air.

Like animals calling to each other, Pete thought. *My God, what is this?*

He pushed his trembling daughter behind him and faced the creature. "What do you want?" he asked, shocked at how small and weak his voice sounded. "We have no money here."

The thing by the window twisted its head left and right, its mouth curled into a grin of pure delight, as if Pete had told the most delicious joke.

"I want you," it answered. "I want to make you bleed." It smiled again, then walked toward them.

"Kate, go!" shouted Pete, reaching back over his shoulder and yanking the bedroom door open, never taking his eyes off the thing that was slowly approaching, a look of terrible calm on its nightmare face.

"No, Dad," she screamed.

"Now!" he bellowed. "Don't argue with me!"

Kate let out a scream of pure terror and fled through the

door. Pete heard her rattle down the stairs and throw open the front door.

At least she's safe, he thought. The thing was less than a three feet away from him, its arms out before it, a look of inevitability on its face. Pete ducked under the arms, noting as he did so in the slow-motion attention to detail that comes with panic, that the fingernails on the thing's hands were thick yellow talons. He spun around the open door and made for the landing.

One of the thin, ink-covered arms looped through the opening and slammed across his throat, pulling him back against the wood of the door, cutting off his air supply. Pete Randall dipped at the waist, then drove himself backward with all the breath he had left. The door swung in a sharp semicircle on its hinge, and he heard a satisfying crunch as the thing was driven hard into the bedroom wall. The arm around his throat came loose, and he shoved it away.

He stepped forward into the bedroom, one hand on his neck, and kicked the door closed. The thing slid down the wall, leaving a thick smear of blood behind. Pete looked down at it.

The metal doorknob had pierced the thing below its ribcage, and blood was running from the wound in dark rivers. The white fangs had been driven through the thing's bottom lip by the impact, and crimson streamed down its chin and neck. Its eyes were closed.

Pete looked at it, breathing heavy, the pain in his throat worsening by the second. He reached for the door, ready to follow his daughter down the stairs and out of the house, when the thing laughed. It was a terrible noise, full of pain and cruelty. The red eyes opened and regarded Pete calmly.

"Stay and play," it said, the fangs sliding out of its lip. "There's nowhere for you to go. I'll make it quick." It spit a thick wad of blood onto the carpet. "Can't say the same for the girl, mind you," it said, then winked at Pete, who kicked the thing in the face as hard as he could. He heard its nose snap, heard it scream in pain, and then he was moving, out of the bedroom and down the stairs, through the open front door.

Kate was nowhere to be seen.

Nononononono.

Panic rose through his stomach and settled into his chest.

"Kate!" he yelled. "Where are you? Kate!"

He ran down their narrow road toward the Marsdens' house.

She'll have gone for a phone, he told himself. *She'll have gone to the neighbors. Please let her be at the neighbors.*

He kicked open the gate and ran up the short driveway toward the house. He had reached the three wooden steps that led up to the front door when something fell to the ground in front of him with a horrible crunching thud, and something warm sprayed across his face and chest. Pete shrieked, throwing his hands up to his face and wiping the liquid from his skin. He looked down at the ground in front of him, and Mrs. Marsden stared back up at him from wide, lifeless eyes. There were two ragged holes in her throat, and the white dressing gown she was wearing looked like it had been dipped in blood.

He heard a triumphant screech and looked up. Staring down at him from the attic window was a woman's face, the lower half smeared with red, the crimson eyes wide and devoid of humanity. The face jerked back from the window, and he heard footsteps inside the house.

Pete Randall fled. He turned and ran back the way he had come, now hearing for the first time the sounds of violence and pain that were drifting from every part of the island, a terrible cacophony of screeches, breaking glass and screams.

So many screams.

He reached the gate at a flat sprint, and when his daughter stepped out in front of him, he threw himself to his right, crashing hard onto the pavement. He would have run straight over her if he hadn't.

"Dad!" she screamed, and then she was crouched next to him, asking him if he was all right. He sat up, ignoring the grinding pain in his right arm where he had landed on it, and hugged her so tightly she could barely breathe.

"Where did you go?" he sobbed. "I couldn't find you."

"I went to the Coopers," she gasped, crushed against her father's chest. "I went to the Coopers'. There's no one there. There's blood . . . so much blood."

Pete let go of her and stood up, unsteadily. He was about to ask her if she was all right when the door to the Marsdens' house slammed open, and the woman he had seen in the attic window howled at them. There was an answering call, terribly close, and Kate looked around and saw the thing that had come into her bedroom walking down the road toward them, blood covering its face and neck. She scrambled to her feet, then her father took her hand, and they ran down the hill toward the center of the village.

Floating fifty feet above the top of the hill on which the village was built, Alexandru surveyed the carnage beneath him. Maybe half the villagers were already dead, and those who had survived the initial attack were fleeing toward the dock and the boats that would carry them off the island. He supposed a few of them would make it, and that was fine. They would add weight to the message he was sending.

He spun gently in the cold air and looked across the hill that formed the middle of the island, at the ancient stone building standing above the cliffs against which the North Sea crashed in plumes of white spray.

Tonight's work has barely begun, he thought, and permitted himself a small smile. He pulled a silver phone from his pocket, and keyed a number.

"Brother," he said, when the call was answered. "You may proceed."

In the village streets below, panic gripped the surviving islanders. They ran for their lives along the narrow roads, heading for the small dock that served the island's fishing fleet, stumbling in the gathering dark, staring wildly in every direction, screaming the names of husbands and wives, parents and children.

Pete Randall sprinted down the hill toward the concrete dock, hurdling the bodies that were lying in the narrow road, forcing himself not to look at them. Every one of the island's one hundred and sixty inhabitants knew each other, and he knew that he was running around and over the lifeless corpses of his friends and neighbors. Kate ran beside him. Her face was pale, but her eyes were bright, and Pete felt a rush of love for his daughter.

How did she get so strong? he marveled. *I won the bloody lottery with her.*

Men and women were streaming out of the houses, some screaming, others weeping and sobbing, running and stumbling down the hill. Dark shapes moved among them, floating across the cobblestones, lifting them shrieking off their feet as they ran. Blood pattered to the ground in a soft crimson rain.

On the dock John Tremain, the island's biggest fisherman, had reached his boat. The *Lady Diana* occupied the largest berth at the end of the horseshoe-shaped dock, and acrid blue smoke was pluming out of her weather-beaten funnel as the big diesel engines roared into life.

"Hurry!" Tremain yelled from the deck. He was holding the mooring ropes in his gnarled hands, ready to cast off. "I'm not waiting! Move!"

The desperate, panicked group of islanders ran toward him.

Pete and Kate were the first on to the slippery concrete of the dock. On the ground in front of them lay the twisted body of a teenage girl, and Kate slowed as they approached the corpse. Pete grabbed her wrist and hauled her forward.

"Keep moving!" he yelled. "Get to the boat!"

"It's Julie!" Kate cried. "We can't leave her here."

Kate's best friend, realized Pete. *Oh God.*

Kate yanked her hand out of his and skidded to a halt next to the girl's body. Pete swore, turned back to grab his daughter, but was forced backward as the fleeing, terrified survivors cannoned into him, blindly running for the boat. He screamed and punched and kicked as hands gripped him, but the flow of people was relentless, and he was driven back along the dock.

Through the crowd, he saw his daughter kneel down next to the corpse, reach out and gently touch the girl's face. He screamed her name, helplessly, as he was dragged over the boat's rail, but Kate didn't even seem to hear him.

There was a thud, and a dark shape landed on the dock, between Kate and the running crowd. She leapt to her feet, the paralyzing shock of seeing her friend's body broken. She looked for her father and saw him being hauled onto the *Lady Diana*, kicking and screaming her name. In front of her was the terrible thing from her bedroom, its skeletal body drenched in blood. It flashed her a hideous lustful smile, and without hesitation, she turned and ran back toward the village.

Pete saw Kate sprint away up the dock and disappear into the darkness, and he threw his head back and howled, a scream of utter desperation. He fought with renewed strength against the hands that held him, but it was too late.

John Tremain threw the mooring ropes into the water and ran up the steps to the small cabin above the deck. He threw the *Lady Diana* into gear, and the big propellers churned water as the boat slowly, terribly slowly, began to move away from the island.

Pete Randall threw himself at the stern rail as the *Lady Diana* picked up speed and the dock disappeared into the darkness.

"Kate!" he screamed. "Kate!"

But there was no answer.

His daughter was gone.

AT THE ROOF OF THE WORLD

SPC Central Command

Kola Peninsula, Russia

Thirty-five minutes ago

Valeri Rusmanov thanked his brother, then closed his cell phone.

His heavy boots crunched snow beneath his feet as he crested the hill, and paused. The freezing night air was still. There was a gentle lapping from the Murmansk fjord to his left, the black water visible through a spider web of cracks in the thick, dirty-gray ice. An icebreaker slowly ground its way up the middle of the fjord, clearing a dark strip of open water, belching diesel smoke from its funnels.

Directly ahead of him, perhaps five miles away, was the closed city of Polyarny. The gray industrial town was dominated by the tall cranes and sodium arc lights of Russian Shipyard Number 10, the top-secret submarine base. During the Cold War, Soviet Typhoons and Akulas had slipped out from Polyarny and disappeared under the Arctic ice, hidden from the watchful eyes of the American satellites.

In the distance, to the southeast, Valeri could make out the dull yellow glow of Murmansk, the home port of the Russian Northern Fleet. The administrative center of the Kola Peninsula was not officially a closed city, but the FSB station in the city was the third largest in Russia, and the whole region was littered with checkpoints and armed patrols.

This huge, barren swathe of Arctic wilderness was the heartland of the classified Russian military community. But the horseshoe of white buildings that filled the small peninsula below him, and what lay beneath them, were worth the risk.

The SPC base was arranged around a long runway that ran parallel to the ridge of cliffs to the north. The gray tarmac was clear, the snow that had covered it piled in long banks on either side. To the south, a long line of ancient firs hid the base entirely from the narrow road that wound toward Polyarny. A tall electrified fence ran through the trees, a small guard post and heavy metal gate at the center the only clue to passing civilians that anything lay beyond the thick forest. A squat white building sat at the eastern end of the runway. Valeri knew that beneath the frozen ground the base was a single enormous bunker, guarded by the elite SPC soldiers, and home to the scientists, analysts and intelligence officers who served the Supernatural Protection Commissariat.

Snow thudded against his black greatcoat, dampening the wool and settling around his ankles as he watched the silent base. He whispered two words and a large number of dark shapes dropped from the sky behind him, landing softly in the snow. "Do you all know what I require from you?" he asked, without turning round.

There was a general murmur of assent, and then a single

low voice said, "Yes, Master."

Valeri's eyes flickered shut, and a grimace spread across his face.

It was Talia's voice. The beautiful young Ukrainian girl had been with him for a year, since he had turned her in a moment of lonely weakness, a moment that he had come to deeply regret. The girl followed him everywhere, her blank, pretty eyes staring at him with open devotion, her soft, pleading voice asking if there was anything he needed, anything she could do for him.

He supposed she loved him, or believed that she did, but she was wasting her time. Valeri had only ever loved one woman, and she had been gone for more than half a century.

"Very well," he said. "It's time."

He stepped lightly into the night air, his greatcoat billowing out behind him. Below him the base was quiet, the lights casting pale yellow semi-circles on the snow.

Valeri swept down the hill toward it, his army of followers behind him, a wide, silent shadow full of death.

In the SPC control room a heat bloom appeared on the surveillance screen of Private Len Yurov. The signature was like nothing he had seen before, a wide band of dark red flowing across the blue-white topography of the tundra, so he called the Duty Officer, General Yuri Petrov, over to look at his screen. The General, a thick-set man in his early sixties, who had spent the majority of his illustrious career with the Spetsnaz, the elite special forces unit that had been controlled by the KGB, and later the FSB, strode over to Yurov's console and looked at the monitor. His eyes widened, and he called instantly for the general alarm to be sounded.

But it was already too late.

At the perimeter of the SPC base, crunching through the drifts of snow that had gathered at the foot of the electrified fence that ran high above their heads, Sergeant Pavel Luzhny was engaged in a heated discussion with his partner, Private Vladimir Radchenko, about the result of the previous night's basketball game. Luzhny, a die-hard CSKA Moscow supporter, was lamenting the performance of his team's point guard, a young man who the Sergeant had wasted no time in pointing out had Chechen blood on his mother's side. The hapless player had missed three of the final four free throws in the previous night's game, and his team had slumped to a 112–110 loss against Triumph Lyubertsy. Luzhny, a native Muscovite, was not taking the defeat at all well. He had moved on to listing the tactical errors made by the team's coach when the alarm wailed across the freezing night. He instantly grabbed his radio from its loop on his belt, keyed a series of numbers, and held it to his ear, looking down at the base as he did so. An automatic voice in his ear told him that the base had been moved to red alert, so he slid his other hand to his waist and freed the SIG Sauer pistol that hung there.

"Training exercise," he said, turning back to Radchenko. "I'll bet my—"

Radchenko wasn't there.

Luzhny turned in a full circle, looking for his partner. There was no sign of him. Radchenko's footsteps were clearly visible in the deep snow, two lines marching in parallel to Luzhny's own. Then they stopped. There were no tracks in any direction, just a final pair of footprints, then nothing.

"What the hell?" muttered Luzhny.

Then he was airborne, as something grabbed him beneath his armpits and jerked him violently upwards. His trigger finger convulsed, and he fired the pistol empty, the bullets thudding into the rapidly receding ground. Luzhny didn't scream, until he felt fingers crawl across his throat and dig for purchase. Then the fingers, which were tipped with nails that felt like razor blades, pulled his throat out, and he could no longer have screamed, even if he had wanted to.

The external microphones in the control room picked up the pistol shots, and Petrov tapped a series of keys on the console in front of him. The huge wall-screen that dominated the room separated into eight sections, each one showing a silent black and white view from the perimeter cameras. As the men in the control room watched, a black shape flitted across one of the cameras, then its picture disappeared into a hissing mass of white noise. Moments later, a second screen fizzed out, then a third, then a fourth.

"Send the general alert," said Petrov, his eyes never leaving the screen. "Call for immediate assistance."

"But sir—"

"That's a direct order, Private. Do it right now. And summon the guard regiment. There isn't much time."

As he spoke, the final camera screens disappeared into snow. At a console in the middle of the room, a deeply frightened radio operator punched in the emergency frequency that linked the supernatural Departments of the world together, and sent the distress call Petrov had ordered. He had just finished sending the message, which was only six words long, when there was an audible thud on the external microphones, and the communications went dead.

"General," he said, looking up from his screen, fear bright in his eyes.

But Petrov was gone.

The General ran through the bowels of the SPC base.

Sirens shrilled in his ears and the light that flooded the corridors hurt his eyes, but he didn't slow his pace. An elevator stood open at the end of the corridor, and he sprinted toward it, his chest burning.

Been behind a desk too long, he thought. *Run, old man. Run.*

Inside the elevator, Petrov pulled a triangular key from a chain around his neck and inserted it into a slot on the metal panel beside the door, below the numbered buttons. The doors closed immediately and the elevator shot downwards, the sudden motion churning Petrov's stomach. He fought it back, and watched as the buttons that marked the floors lit up and went out, one after the other.

-2...
-3...
-4...
-5...
-6...
-7...

Level -7 was the bottom of the SPC base, seven stories beneath the frozen Arctic ground. It was home to the enormous generators that powered the complex, as well as accommodation for the maintenance crews and support personnel; as a result it was rarely visited by SPC soldiers or scientists, and it was not General Petrov's destination now. There was only one thing in the base worth the risk of a frontal attack, and he was one of the few men on the planet who knew what it was.

The -7 button lit up, and then blinked out, but the elevator continued its descent, into the unmarked depths. When the doors slid open ten seconds later, Petrov ran out into a single corridor of gleaming metal, lined on both sides by huge, heavy-looking metal doors, doors that looked like they belonged on the airlock of a submarine, or a space station. Each was stamped with a single number, in black letters three feet high; there were sixty doors, but Petrov was already running toward the one stamped 31.

In the control room, the men of the night shift looked at each other nervously. Static squealed from eight screens of white noise, and the external microphones were silent. The men, eight of them in all, had broken out the arms locker and were holding Daybreakers, the heavy SPC explosive launchers, as they waited for whatever was out there in the snow.

The door to the main access corridor suddenly flew open, slamming against the concrete wall, and the men jumped in unison. The thirty-two men of the Base Protection Regiment flooded silently into the control room, taking up almost every inch of space. The duty staff did their best to contain cheers of relief; the BPR was made up of the finest SPC officers, the very best of the very best. They took up a wide semi-circular formation, facing the heavy air-locked door that led to the outside world, their gray uniforms bristling with weapons and webbing that was heavy with equipment. They trained their Kalashnikovs and Daybreakers on the door, and the duty staff withdrew, taking up positions behind the soldiers.

Silence.

Then, slowly, a terrible sound of rending, buckling metal filled the room. Private Yurov, who was holding a Daybreaker with two shaking hands, had just enough time to say a silent prayer, before the huge metal door was wrenched from its hinges and hurled out into the black and white Arctic night.

Snow swirled into the room in thick flurries, driving the men of the SPC back. The air was so cold that it closed their throats, trapping the oxygen in their lungs, and the snow was thick and blinding. Dark shapes, impossibly fast, flooded in through the gaping door, and the soldiers began to fire their weapons, almost randomly, hands covering their streaming eyes, their chests burning. Bullets whined off the walls, shattering monitors and punching holes in consoles, and the fiery crunch of Daybreaker rounds rang through their ears. The dark shapes seemed to be everywhere; they slipped through the snow-filled room like shadows, rending flesh and spraying blood as they went. A jet of crimson spurted from within the cloud of snow and hit Yurov in the chest and face. He recoiled, and then suddenly there was a dark figure in front of him, no more than six feet away. He raised the Daybreaker and fired, the recoil jolting up his arms. The figure staggered as the round hit home, and then lurched forward out of the snow.

It was Alex Titov, the young Siberian who shared his desk. He looked at Yurov, his eyes wide, his mouth moving silently.

The projectile had stuck to the front of his chest, over his solar plexus. As Yurov watched, helpless, the pneumatic charge fired, driving the charge through his breastplate. Yurov heard bones break, then Titov's scream cut through the wind that was howling through the control room. Blood spilled from his mouth, and he looked at his friend, a pleading expression on his face. Then the explosive charge fired, and Titov erupted, covering Yurov from head to toe. He stared blankly, his friend's blood dripping down his face. When a vampire slid out of the blizzard, moments later, and tore his throat open, it was almost a kindness.

Thirty-eight men died in the SPC control room in less than three minutes.

The vampires struck with dizzying speed, emerging from the swirling snow, biting and clawing and tearing, and the men of the night watch and the BPR were slaughtered side by side. They never stood a chance; they were blinded by the snow and numbed by the freezing cold, and Valeri's followers butchered them where they stood. Two BPR soldiers ran for the access corridor, and made it into an elevator. They survived, huddling in the mess hall on the second subterranean level, with the scientists and doctors and general staff that kept the SPC running on a daily basis.

When the control room was clear, the ancient vampire stepped out on to the frozen ground and hauled the door back into its frame. It no longer fit properly; it had been bent and twisted when he had pulled it free, but it stopped the worst of the wind. The snow dropped to the floor in drifts, piling up against desks and chairs, covering the bodies of the fallen SPC officers, turning pink where it settled over pools of blood.

The horde of vampires, most of them streaked red, their eyes blazing, gathered quietly behind Valeri, and followed him into the base.

General Petrov set his back against the door to vault 31, raised his Daybreaker, and pointed it at the elevator doors. The radio on his belt periodically buzzed into life, issuing forth screams of pain and snarls of violence. He did his best to ignore the sounds, and concentrate solely on the metal doors that stood closed at the other end of the corridor. Eventually the radio fell silent, and he pulled an encrypted satellite phone from his belt. He typed a message on the glowing screen, nine short words, and sent it. Then he replaced the phone, and waited for them to come.

Even though he was expecting it, the doors slid open so quietly that it took him by surprise. Vital milliseconds passed, and then he pulled the trigger of the Daybreaker, aiming into the confined space of the elevator. A vampire roared out of the open doors and took the charge in the shoulder. A second later it exploded, spraying the walls, floor and ceiling crimson. Two more clambered through the spilt blood of their companion and suffered the same fate, before a fourth shot went wide, clanging off the wall and attaching itself harmlessly to the ceiling. Petrov's fifth shot caught a vampire girl in the forehead, and destroyed her down to her knees. Petrov fought down rising bile, and fired his final shot. For a fleeting second the gray-haired head of Valeri Rusmanov swam into view amidst the smoke of the explosives, but he was gone again before the charge had left the Daybreaker's barrel. Instead it thumped into the chest of a vampire woman, who cast an imploring look into the elevator before the explosive annihilated her. Petrov threw the spent weapon to the floor, pulled his ancient AK47 from his shoulder harness, leveled it at the elevator, and prepared to fire.

There was a moment of calm, as if he had succeeded in discouraging the vampires, but then they swarmed out of the elevator again, and Petrov knew he was lost. There were too many of them, far too many; they crawled up the walls and across the ceiling, and bounded along the floor, their mouths open, excitement and sadistic joy etched on their faces. He pulled the worn trigger of his rifle and the corridor was filled with acrid blue smoke. The heavy rounds blew off limbs, punched holes in heads and torsos, but still they came. He was screaming, although he couldn't hear himself above the rattling din of the gun, and he fired and fired until the hammer clicked down on an empty chamber.

General Yuri Petrov lay on the metal floor.

Something wet was trickling down his back and pooling along the ridge of his belt, and he could see only red through his left eye. He realized with detached curiosity that he couldn't feel either his arms or his legs. There was no pain, which surprised him, because he was dying; of that he had no doubt.

Vampires stood quietly all around him. He tried to raise his head to look at them, and found that he was unable to do so. Valeri stepped away from the door to vault 31, where he had been examining the fifteen-digit keypad set into the wall beside it, crouched down in front of the stricken officer, and smiled at him.

Petrov forced a smile in return, and found that he could still speak.

"It's… no use," he said, his breath whistling as it struggled to form the words. "I will… never give you… the combination."

Valeri's smile widened, and one last clear thought rang through the General's faltering mind.

We are betrayed.

Petrov's smile faded as Valeri stood up. He watched the vampire in the black greatcoat step across the corridor and tap rapidly on the keypad next to the door of vault 31. There was a long beep, and then the locks released with a series of clicks and thuds, and the door hissed slowly open. For a brief moment, Petrov had a clear view into vault 31, and he laid his dying eyes on something that only a handful of human beings had ever seen.

There were only two objects in the vault. In the middle of the metal floor stood a square steel cube, each edge a meter long, and on top of the cube stood a clear plastic tube with thick black metal lids at each end. The container was three-quarters full of a gray powder, and had a label that Petrov couldn't read pasted on to its side. Then Valeri stepped into the vault, blocking the contents of vault 31 from view, waving a hand over his shoulder as he did so.

With a chorus of snarls, the vampires fell on Petrov.

He had enough time to scream, once.

LOVE BURNS

For the second time in less than eight hours the general alert rang through the Loop. Operators who had flopped into their beds on the lower levels less than forty minutes earlier were dragged back to the waking world, swearing and cursing as they pulled their uniforms back on and fastened their weapons into place.

Admiral Seward was in the main hangar, directing the sluggish men and women of Blacklight. Out on the runway two EC725 helicopters sat on the tarmac, light blazing from their open passenger compartments as technicians pulled hoses from trapdoors in the ground and filled them with fuel.

"Where's the jet?" Seward shouted. "Damn it, we'd be there in forty minutes."

"Cal Holmwood took the *Mina II* to Nevada three days ago, sir," replied a passing Operator. "He's running a training exercise with the Yanks, sir."

Seward swore heartily, and turned his attention to the line of Operators forming behind him. He spoke to Paul Turner, who was overseeing the mobilization.

"You, me, and the first eighteen men to report," he ordered. "Comms and weapons check, then load them up. I want to be in the air in five minutes."

"Yes sir," replied Turner. He strode over to the reporting men, and began checking their radios and weapons. When an Operator was equipped to Turner's satisfaction, the Major jerked his thumb toward the waiting helicopters, and the soldier ran out on to the tarmac and climbed up into one of the choppers.

Admiral Seward left him to it and walked quickly through the corridors toward the Ops Room. He was about to open the door when his cell phone buzzed into life. He hauled it out of the pocket of his uniform and checked the screen.

NEW SMS
FROM: PETROV, GEN. Y.
VAULT 31 ABOUT TO BE COMPROMISED. HURRY
OLD FRIEND. YURI

A chill raced up Henry Seward's spine.
How do they know about 31?
He shoved the Ops Room door open and stepped inside. Jamie, Frankenstein, and Morris were gathered around a desk in the middle of the room, the teenager holding his radio in a slightly shaking hand. They looked up when he entered.

"Colonel Frankenstein, Lieutenant Morris, Mr. Carpenter," he said. "You are confined to base until further notice. I'm taking a rescue team to Russia immediately; I'll deal with you when I return. In the meantime, I suggest you focus on the report I asked you for."

Admiral Seward strode out of the room, without a backward glance. After a minute or so, Jamie was first to speak.

"We're totally screwed," he said. "I'm never going to see my mother again."

Frankenstein looked at him, alarmed at the resignation in the teenager's voice. It was as though the fire that usually burned inside him had been extinguished.

Morris spoke nervously. "It's not as bad as—"

"Tom," interrupted Jamie. "Don't try and placate me. I'm not a child."

Morris looked down at the table, and the teenager continued. "I want to know what happened in Northumberland. Don't tell me that Larissa tipped off Alexandru, because I don't believe that. I want to know what really happened."

Frankenstein looked steadily at him. "As far as I'm concerned," he said, "you're asking the wrong people. I'm sorry if that isn't what you want to hear."

"Fine," replied Jamie.

He stood up from the table and walked out of the Ops Room, without a backward glance. In the elevator at the end of the corridor, he gripped the metal rail until his knuckles turned white. Anger squirmed in his stomach, hot and acidic, and he bore down on it with all his strength, pushing it down as far as he was able. Then the elevator door slid open onto the cellblock, and he strode along it toward Larissa.

She was waiting for him.

The vampire girl stood in the middle of her cell, just beyond the UV wall; she smiled at him as he appeared in front of her, a smile that faltered slightly when she saw the thunderous expression on his face.

"What's the matter?" she asked.

"Did you tell Alexandru we were going to come for him?" he asked, his voice straining with the effort it was taking to keep his temper in check. "Did you tell him to run?"

Larissa's eyes widened with realization.

"He wasn't there," she said, "was he?"

"No," replied Jamie. "He wasn't there. Neither was my mother. They were both gone, to God knows where. Only a handful of people in the world knew we'd found him, but by the time we got there, less than ninety minutes later, he was gone. I want to know how that happened."

"Ask me," said Larissa. "Ask me the question again."

"Did you tell him we were coming?"

"No," she replied. "I didn't."

He sagged before her eyes. His shoulders slumped, and his head tipped forward, his eyes squeezed tightly shut.

It's over. Oh God, I'm never going to find her. It's all over.

"I don't know what to do," he said, his voice choked with despair. "I want to believe you, but I don't know if I can."

She took half a step forward and said his name in a low voice.

"Jamie."

He looked at her, his eyes red, pain etched in every line of his face.

"You can trust me," she said, and then she moved.

Her hand shot through the UV field and grabbed him. Her whole arm burst into flames, purple fire erupting from the skin, but she didn't even flinch. She pulled him through the barrier, spinning him to the side, and kissed him, as burning skin crackled in his ears and flooded his nostrils.

He kissed her back, his hands finding her hair. He could feel the heat of her burning arm through his uniform, but it felt as though it was coming from a thousand miles away, felt as though it was coming from another world. He surrendered himself entirely to the kiss, her lips cool and soft against his, her hands on his waist, his entire body trembling.

Then, as suddenly as it had begun, it was over.

She pulled away from him, and he opened his eyes. Her face was barely an inch from his; he could feel the heat of her breath on his mouth, could see the intricate pattern of yellow that traced through the dark brown of her eyes.

They stared at each other as though they were the only two people alive.

Pain finally broke across her face, and she fell to the ground, thumping her arm, putting out the flames that were rising from it, until all that was left was gray smoke drifting toward the roof of the cell. The smell was nauseating, and he knelt beside her. The smoke cleared, and his stomach lurched.

Her arm rested across her knee, burned almost entirely black. The skin had peeled away in sheets, revealing muscles that had been seared into tough dark ropes. Beneath them he could see the gleaming white of bone, and he looked away, afraid he would be sick.

"It's all right," she gasped. "It'll grow back. I just need blood."

Without thinking, Jamie pulled the collar of his uniform down and turned the uninjured side of his exposed neck toward her. She laughed, despite the agony in her arm.

"That's sweet," she said, through a grimace of pain. "But I don't think we're ready for that just yet."

Jamie flushed red, then ran down the block to the guard office.

She could have put her arm through the barrier anytime she wanted if she wanted to hurt me.

Anytime.

"I need blood," he said. The guard started to ask him a question, but Jamie was in no mood for it. "Now," he said. "On Admiral Seward's authority. Check with him if you like, but I don't think he'll appreciate being disturbed."

The operator behind the glass looked at Jamie, his mouth hanging open. After a moment, he sighed, rolled his chair back across the office, and pulled open a stainless-steel fridge set into the wall. Cold air flooded out, and the guard reached in and pulled out two liter pouches of O-negative blood. He pushed the chair back across the tiled floor, the wheels rattling across the shiny surface, and brought himself to a halt in front of Jamie. He shoved the pouches through the slot in the plastic, then rolled back to his desk, without giving Jamie another glance.

The teenager ran back down the block. Larissa had crawled to her bed and was holding her injured arm against her chest. She smiled at him when he reappeared, but her eyes were full of pain.

Jamie walked straight through the UV field and went to her. He handed her the blood and sat on the bed next to her as she tore the first one open with her teeth, holding it in her good left hand.

"Look away," she said.

"No chance," he replied.

She didn't wait to see if he would change his mind; she upended the plastic pouch and squeezed the contents into her mouth. Her eyes turned red as the blood slid down her throat, and she swallowed convulsively, her throat working, her head thrown back. There was a fizzing sound, and Jamie looked down at her arm.

What he saw astonished him. The charred, blackened skin was bubbling, as though it had been soaked in acid. Before his eyes, the flesh lightened to a dark red, then a bright scarlet, then to the same pale pink as the rest of her. Muscle fibers and thin sheets of skin regrew, knitting to the revived flesh and filling the holes the fire had burned.

The fizzing lessened, and Jamie gasped. Larissa's arm looked no worse than if she had been lying in the sun for an afternoon.

She was breathing hard, her lips thin, her eyes crimson.

"Does it hurt?" he asked. "When it grows back?"

She nodded, then opened her trembling mouth. "Not as badly," she said. "But it hurts."

She pulled open the second pouch and drank it hungrily. A thick stream of blood broke from the corner of her mouth and ran down her chin; Jamie fought the absurd urge to lick it off. The fizzing noise came again, and the color of her arm faded until it was impossible to believe any injury had been done to it. He reached out and stroked the new skin; it was warm and smooth.

She took his hand, looked him in the eyes.

"I would never hurt you," she said. "I'm sorry for leading you to Valhalla without telling you why I wanted to go. But you can trust me. I'll never lie to you again."

He leaned over and kissed her. Her lips met his, but this time he pulled away and stood up off the bed. She looked at him, confusion on her face.

"I'll be back," he said, and smiled.

A FORMAL INVITATION

39

Department 19 Northern Outpost
RAF Fylingdales, North Yorkshire Moors
Fifteen minutes ago

Flying Officer John Elliott checked his screens, stepped through the door of the bunker into the cold evening, and breathed out a cloud of warm air. Night watch was the worst. The hours stretched out forever and tiredness pulled constantly at him, no matter how many coffees he drank and cigarettes he smoked.

He checked his watch: one eighteen. Forty-two minutes to go.

Elliott lit a Camel Light, grimaced as the smoke crawled across his dry throat but persevered. Dave Sargent had the next watch, and as soon as he keyed in his access code and swung open the door of the bunker, Elliott could stand down. He could be in his bed within four minutes. He had timed it.

The young flying officer looked out across the base and to the moors beyond. The giant pale blue golf balls that had hidden Fylingdales' Cold War radar dishes were gone now, but the vast three-sided phased array pyramid that replaced them rose up from the top of Snod Hill, silent and still ominous even after a year stationed here.

The Blacklight outpost was at the western edge of the base, away from the roads that carried busloads of tourists to Whitby during the summer months, away from the RAF personnel and their families, a nondescript gray concrete square with a heavy steel door set into it that led down into a small bunker, one square room with two desks set into the walls and a tiny bathroom at the rear. The barracks was a short distance away along the route of the fence, linked to the front of the bunker by a gravel path. The low brick building was dark; the rest of Elliott's unit were asleep in their beds.

Beyond the fence that ran past the bunker were the empty moors, the bracken and long grass undisturbed by ramblers and hikers who knew better than to approach the base. Across the moors, in the hills above Harrogate, was RAF Menwith Hill, the NSA listening post that was sovereign US territory.

Elliott had been there a couple of times, had eaten a burger in the diner and drank Coors Light and lost forty dollars in the bowling alley. The Yanks had made themselves right at home, building an authentic American small town in the shadows of the vast radar fields that scanned the world's airwaves for the words and phrases that threw up red flags on the Echelon database.

Before he joined Blacklight, Elliott had thought the people who believed in things like Echelon were crazy loners who spent all their time wearing tinfoil hats and feverishly posting on the Internet. Now he knew things that would make them weep into their keyboards.

Something crunched the gravel softly behind the bunker.

Instantly, Flying Officer Elliott drew his Glock from its holster and pulled his radio from its loop on his belt. He keyed his ID code into the pad and held it to his ear.

"Code in." Commander Jackson's voice sounded tired and grumpy.

"Elliott, John. NS303-81E."

"What's going on, Elliott?"

"I heard something, sir. Behind the bunker."

"Did you investigate?"

"No, sir."

The commander swore heartily. "Go and check it out. I'll be there in three minutes."

"Sir, the protocol—"

"Three minutes, Flying Officer. Do I make myself clear?"

"Yes, sir."

Elliott placed the radio back in his belt and wrapped his left hand around his right. Treading softly, he stepped along the side of the bunker. Experience told him it would be an animal of some kind, a badger burrowed under the fence from the moors, or a seagull come inland from the coast and too tired to fly back. But the protocols existed for a reason. No one came near the Blacklight bunker without authorization, and any unusual noise was taken very seriously.

He reached the corner of the bunker and steadied his Glock in his hands. He took a deep breath, then stepped around the corner.

Nothing.

The wide space between the wall of the bunker and the fence was empty, the gravel track undisturbed. Elliott lowered his weapon and reached for his radio to let Commander Jackson know it was a false alarm.

Thunk.

Adrenaline splashed through Elliott's nervous system. No animal had made the heavy noise that had come from the front of the bunker. He raised his pistol again and stepped sharply round the corner and against the long wall of the bunker. Before him, RAF Fylingdales glowed brightly with amber yellow light, and Elliott wished for the first time that the flat expanse of grass that separated the Blacklight bunker from the rest of the complex didn't exist.

He checked his watch as he inched along the concrete wall. Forty-five seconds since he had spoken with Commander Jackson. Just over two minutes until backup arrived.

Elliott crept along the wall, the nose of his gun steady in the cool evening air. Then he heard a noise that chilled the blood in his veins, and he saw the muzzle of the pistol start to tremble involuntarily.

It sounded like a laugh.

A high-pitched, almost childlike laugh.

The hairs on the back of his neck stood up, and his whole body began to shake as a second huge dose of adrenaline crashed through his system. He inched forward, took a deep breath, covered the last two feet to the corner of the bunker, and swung himself around the corner.

There was a figure standing in front of the door.

Everything moved in slow motion. Elliott stifled a scream, his eyes bulging in terror, and he began to pull his finger back against the feather-light trigger of the pistol. The figure was wearing a white T-shirt, and it was this detail that sank into

Elliott's brain just quickly enough to halt his finger. He took a second, closer look and then lowered the gun, panting, his breath coming in sharp hitches.

It wasn't a person.

It was just a T-shirt, fastened to the door of the bunker. There was something dark sticking out of the middle of the chest, and there were words printed on the white material. He stepped forward to take a closer look, then a hand fell on his shoulder, and this time he did scream.

"What the hell's wrong with you, Elliott?" barked Commander Jackson, spinning the young flying officer around to face him. "Are you . . ."

He trailed off as he saw the T-shirt flapping gently in the night air.

The two men stepped forward, and Commander Jackson took the heavy torch from his belt and shone it on the bunker door.

The T-shirt was pinned by a heavy metal bolt, at least a foot long, that had been driven through the material and several inches into the steel bunker door.

How much force does it take to do that? Elliott wondered.

Printed on the T-shirt was a line drawing of an island with a single word below it in cheerful yellow type.

LINDISFARNE

Below that, across the stomach, in a dark red liquid that turned Elliott's stomach, five words had been scrawled:

Tell
the Boy
to
Come

"Issue a proximity alert," Commander Jackson said, in a low voice. "And wake the rest of the unit."

Elliott pushed open the heavy door, noticing with slightly numb horror that a small pyramid of metal now emerged from the inside of it.

It almost went right through.

He sat at the communications desk and punched in the command to issue the proximity alert. This signal would be sent to every military base within a fifty-mile radius, ordering them to check their radars for any unexplained aerial phenomenon in the last thirty minutes. The radar operators in the bases would not know what they were looking for, or why, and would delete the record of their search as soon as the results had been transmitted back to the Northern Outpost, as the protocol dictated.

Elliott was about to key in the command to wake the rest of their unit, when something on one of the monitors caught his eye. It was a BBC News 24 feed, and the words *Breaking News* were scrolling along the bottom of the screen.

"Better let the Loop know about the message," Jackson called through the open door.

Elliott didn't take his eyes from the screen as he replied. "I think they already know, sir."

BREAKING POINT

40

Jamie shoved open the door to the Ops Room.

Frankenstein and Thomas Morris were exactly where he had left them; the two men were not looking at each other, and Jamie doubted a word had been said in the time he had been underground. They looked up as he entered, and he sat in a chair in front of them.

"She didn't do it," he said.

Both men opened their mouths to protest, but he didn't give them the chance.

"I don't care whether you believe me or not. I know she didn't do it. Which means you two, me, Admiral Seward, and the operator who moved the satellite are the only other people in the world who knew we had found Alexandru. The rest of the strike team were briefed in the air, and all radio traffic was monitored. So one of those has to be the person who tipped him off."

He ran his hands through his hair, rubbed his eyes with the heels of his palms.

"To be honest," he continued, "I don't care who did it. All I care about is what we do next. As far as I can tell, we have no more leads, and Alexandru has more than likely killed a load of innocent people to punish me just for looking for him. So I want to know what happens now."

With a whirring noise and bright flash of light, the screen that covered one entire wall of the Ops Room burst into life. The Department 19 crest appeared on the screen, six feet in diameter, as automated security protocols were implemented, then a window opened in the center of the Blacklight system desktop, and a BBC news report appeared in front of the three startled men.

"What's happening?" asked Jamie.

"The monitoring system checks all civilian media for potential supernatural incidents," answered Morris, staring up at the screen. "This is happening now, whatever it is."

The words BREAKING NEWS were scrolling along the bottom in thick white text. The screen showed a reporter addressing the camera from a beach, his hair blowing in the wind, the sound crackling as the night air whistled across his microphone. Behind him a pair of portable spotlights were trained on the water's edge, where a fishing boat appeared to have run aground. There were men and women wandering over the sand, dazed looks on their faces and blankets wrapped around their shoulders, while a number of policemen and paramedics moved among them.

The caption at the bottom of the screen informed the viewer that the report was coming live from Fenwick,

Northumberland.

In the bottom-right corner of the screen, a man was standing still, a grimace of pain on his face as a paramedic applied a bandage to his neck. Two policemen were wrestling a screaming woman to the ground, and the reporter was trying desperately to find someone coherent enough to answer his questions.

A lightbulb suddenly blazed on in Jamie's head.

"Tom!" he yelled, and the security officer jumped. "Can you rewind this report?"

Morris looked confused but said that he could.

"I need you to take it back thirty seconds and freeze it. Quickly!"

Morris opened a window and keyed a series of buttons. As he did so, Frankenstein lumbered to his feet and walked over to stand beside Jamie.

"What's going on?" he asked.

"You'll see," replied the teenager, without taking his eyes away from the screen.

As Morris worked the controls, the news report stopped, then began to run backward.

"Freeze it there!" shouted Jamie after a couple of seconds, and Morris did so. "Zoom in on the man in the bottom right of the image."

A grid of thin green lines appeared over the picture, dividing it into sixty-four squares. Morris highlighted the four at the bottom right and clicked on them. They expanded to fill the screen, a blurry image twelve feet high. He clicked a series of keys, and the image sharpened into perfect clarity.

The paramedic was about to place a bandage over the man's

neck. Blood was splattered over the pale skin, almost black in the silver light of the full moon that hung above him, now removed from view. Jamie drew in a deep breath sharply, and held it.

In the center of the matted blood were two round holes of pure black.

Jamie followed the blood down to the man's shoulder, where it had spilled onto his upper arm and across onto his chest. He was wearing a white T-shirt, now stained a dark red.

"Where is this place?" demanded Jamie. "I need a map of the surrounding area. My mother is wherever this boat came from, I know it."

Morris leapt down from his control panel, opened a long narrow cupboard set into one of the metal walls, and hauled out a sheaf of maps. Jamie ran over to him, and they began to spread them across one of the tables.

"Northumberland, Northumberland," said Morris aloud, casting aside map after map. Behind them something beeped, but neither he nor Jamie looked up.

"This is the one," exclaimed Morris, and spread a map of the North Sea coast across the desk. The two men huddled over it, their fingers hovering in the air as they searched for the tiny coastal town of Fenwick.

"Jamie," said Frankenstein, but the teenager didn't even look up, just waved a hand and continued to pore over the map.

"Jamie!" said the monster again, loudly, and this time the urgency in the voice lifted the teenager's head, a scowl creasing his features.

"What is—" Jamie stopped dead, his eyes following

Frankenstein's pointing finger to the giant screen. A new window had opened, containing an e-mail from an address that was an indecipherable combination of letters and numbers. There was no text in the body of the mail, just a single high-quality photograph of the T-shirt that had been hammered into the door of the Department 19 Northern Outpost. The yellow lettering that spelt out the word *LINDISFARNE* was clearly visible, as were the words scrawled below it, the drying blood a sickly black color:

TELL

THE BOY

TO

COME

Jamie took a long, deep breath and looked around at his friends. "That's where she is," he said.

Jamie unloaded his weapons on to the Ops Room desk and checked each one in turn. He didn't look up when Frankenstein and Morris walked back into the room.

"I've spoken to the Northern Outpost," Morris said. "They'll control the press and keep the police off the island until we give them the all clear."

"Good," replied Jamie. "That's good." He retied the laces on his boots, clipped his body armor into place, and replaced the weapons in their holders. "I can feel you looking at me," said Jamie, pulling one of his gloves on and fastening it to the sleeve of his uniform. "Say whatever you've got to say."

"The rescue team will be back in a few hours," said Morris.

"Why don't you wait, and then we can—"

"No waiting, Tom," said Jamie. "I'm going now. Give me the code for Larissa's cell."

"What for?" asked Frankenstein.

"I'm taking her with me," Jamie replied. He saw the look on the monster's face, and he stopped what he was doing and faced him. "She didn't do it, Victor. I know she didn't. If you can't believe me, that's fine, but I trust her, and I'm taking her with me."

"Jamie," said Morris. "If she didn't do it, then who did?"

"I don't know," replied Jamie. "All I know for certain is that it wasn't her."

Morris swallowed hard, then looked at Jamie, his face solemn, his eyes wide. "I think there's something you should know," he said. "But it's not my place to tell you."

Frankenstein stiffened in his chair. "Shut the hell up, Morris," he said, his voice laced with threat.

Jamie looked at his two companions. "What's going on?" he asked.

Morris lowered his eyes. "Ask him," he said, pointing at Frankenstein. "Ask him where he was when your father died."

Jamie stared at the monster, who was looking at Morris with open fury. Then the teenager's head seemed to split open, and the memory of that night flooded into his mind.

Eight policemen wearing black body armor and carrying submachine guns were arranged across the driveway, the barrels of their weapons pointing toward the door that Julian was walking through.

"Put your hands above your head!" one of the policemen

shouted. He was a huge man, wearing a full balaclava and a riot helmet that looked comically small atop his enormous shoulders. Jamie stared at the giant figure, blind terror coursing through him, and saw that the man's tree-trunk arms were different lengths. "Do it now!"

Horror beyond anything Jamie had ever felt ripped through him, dumping ice-cold water down the length of his spine and turning his legs to jelly. He looked at Frankenstein.

Nonononononononononononononononononononononononono nonononononono.

His throat closed, and he gasped for air, bending over and placing his head between his legs, his hands gripping the thick pads on his knees, as he tried not to collapse.

Think of your mother. Don't let her down now. Think of your mother.

He forced himself back upright and looked at Frankenstein. The monster was staring at him with a look of utter anguish on his face, and he had extended his hands across the table, as though he was reaching for Jamie.

The sight of the gray-green hands at the end of the monster's uneven arms broke Jamie's paralysis, and he recoiled, back-pedaling away from the table.

"Jamie—" the monster began, but he was cut off.

"You were there," said Jamie. "I remember now. You were there when they shot my dad."

"Jamie, I—"

"Were you there or not?" screamed Jamie. "Don't lie to me anymore! Were you there?"

Frankenstein shot a look of pure murder at Morris, who

was looking at his hands, then returned his gaze to the teenager in front of him.

"I was there," he said.

Jamie felt numb; as if he might never be able to feel again.

"Don't you ever come near me again," he said, his voice trembling. "I swear to God, I'll kill you if you do."

He turned his attention to Morris, who stared at him with the look of a man who has just committed a crime he knows he can never atone for.

"Tom," Jamie said, "if you were willing to come to Lindisfarne with me and Larissa, I'd be very grateful. If you don't want to, I understand. But I need the code to her cell, either way."

Morris stood slowly up from the table. He avoided the gaze of Frankenstein, who was staring silently at him with hatred burning in his eyes.

"The code is 908141739," he said, in a low voice. "Give me five minutes, and I'll meet you in the hangar."

"Thank you," said Jamie. "Thank you very much."

Then he turned and ran out of the Ops Room, toward the elevator at the end of the corridor.

Larissa was lying on her back in the middle of the floor when he ran down the cellblock. She sat up and smiled at him when he skidded to a halt in front of her cell.

"Back so soon?" she asked.

"I told you I would be," he replied between deep breaths. He composed himself and looked at her.

"I know where my mother is," he said. "I'm going to finish this, one way or the other, and I could use your help."

She stood up slowly and stretched her arms above her head. "There's not much I can do from here," she said.

Jamie reached over and pressed the buttons on the keypad beside her cell. The UV field disappeared.

Larissa walked out of her cell and kissed him quickly on the cheek. "Let's go," she said.

THE EASTERN FRONT

SPC Central Command
Kola Peninsula, Russia

The two Blacklight helicopters descended toward the SPC base, their engines roaring in the freezing air, their rotors churning the falling snow into spinning flurries. Their wheels skidded across the icy surface as they touched down, then the doors were flung open and Admiral Seward led the rescue team toward the SPC control room.

Twenty Blacklight operators ran across the snow, dark shapes moving quickly through a landscape of pure white. The men shivered as the Arctic wind whipped through the mesh of their uniforms; snow slid in torrents down their purple visors, obscuring their view.

They reached the entrance to the base, skidding and sliding to a halt in front of a ragged metal hole where the heavy airlock door should have been.

"Christ," muttered one of the operators.

The door had been ripped out of its frame; it lay to one side, buckled and twisted like an empty drink can. The hinges that had held it in place were eight-inch cylinders of solid steel, more than two inches in diameter, and the vacuum seal that connected it to its housing should have been able to withstand an earthquake almost twice as strong as the Richter scale was able to measure.

"Alert One from here onward," said Seward, and stepped through the hole.

Snow was piled high on every surface in the control room and lay in deep drifts against the sides of the desks and tables that had until very recently been the work stations of the SPC duty staff. In places it had turned a bright pink, as blood soaked up from beneath it.

Admiral Seward almost tripped over the first corpse.

It lay in front of the empty doorway, the body of a man who could have been no more than nineteen or twenty. He was covered in snow, and Seward ordered the men to clear the man's body. They knelt and brushed the snow away with their gloved hands, uncovering the dark gray SPC uniform inch by inch.

There was a gagging sound from one of the men working at the man's waist, and Seward stepped up next to him. The man turned away, his hand over his mouth, and the admiral felt his gorge rise.

The soldier had been pulled in half.

Below his waist there was nothing but an enormous quantity of blood, covering the floor in a thick pool.

Admiral Seward split the rescue team into two groups and addressed the first.

"Clear this room," he told them. "I want these men taken

out of here. The rest of you, come with me."

He left Major Turner overseeing the recovery of the bodies in the control room and led the rest of the men deeper into the base. They walked slowly along a wide gray corridor and into an elevator that stood open at the end of it. Seward pressed the button for the first underground level.

"Search this building floor by floor for survivors," he said. "I don't want anyone left behind."

There was a ringing noise, and the doors slid open. The operators filed out, split into two-man teams, and started checking the doors that ran along both sides of the corridor. Seward watched them until the elevator doors closed in front of him, and he began to descend again.

The director of Blacklight pulled a triangular key identical to the one General Petrov had used little more than two hours earlier from a chain on his belt and inserted it into the slot below the numbered buttons. The elevator swept past the -7 floor and slowed to a halt. The doors opened, and the long rows of heavy vault doors stopped him momentarily in his tracks. Seward had only been here once before, shortly after he was appointed to the position of director. Yuri Petrov, a man he had fought side by side with on several occasions, in some of the darkest corners of the globe, had escorted him down and taken him through the vaults one by one, a personal guided tour of the most secret artifacts the Russian nation had collected over the course of its long history. For a moment, he was overcome by the loss of the SPC men who had died in the control room, the latest casualties in a long, bloody war that the public could never know was being fought. Then he shook his head to clear it and hurried onward.

The corridor was slick with gore and splattered with chunks of scarlet meat, and Seward held his breath as he stepped around the carnage; the air was thick with the scent of blood and the foul stench of the vampires who had spilled it. He forced himself onward until he was at the door marked 31, where he found General Petrov staring at him from the empty table inside the small metal room.

His severed head had been placed upright, his dead eyes pointing toward the door. Blood had run down the metal pillar and pooled at the base, drying black. The face itself was almost unrecognizable; long ridges of purple bruising crisscrossed the skin, the nose and jaw were broken in several places, and the mouth was swollen to huge proportions. But the eyes were clear and full of defiance.

Petrov was Spetsnaz when it meant something. I bet they tired before he did.

Seward walked round the pillar, checking every corner of the vault. He knew it was futile, but he did it anyway; he would not dishonor Petrov's memory by missing something obvious. But there was nothing in the vault apart from the Russian general's head.

He walked back out into the steel corridor, stepping carefully around the remains, and pulled his phone from his pocket. He dialed a number and held it to his ear. "It's gone," he said, when the phone was answered. "Yes, I'm sure. I'm standing in the empty vault right now."

There was a long silence.

"I understand that," he said, eventually. "I need a list of anyone who accessed encrypted SPC content on the Blacklight mainframe in the last forty-eight hours. Yes, I'll wait."

He paced up and down the corridor, waiting for the information he had requested. After almost a minute, the voice told him there were no records of anyone accessing the information he had requested.

"Rerun the search, overriding the security protocols. Use my access code, 69347X. Do it quickly."

Almost instantly a single name was read to him.

Seward swore. "I need an immediate current position," he said. "Run his chip."

Agonizing seconds passed. Seward had stopped in the middle of the corridor and was holding the phone to his ear with knuckles that were gradually turning white.

Not him. Please not him.

The voice on the end of the line reappeared and described a location.

"Any other operators with him?" asked Seward.

The voice answered.

"Thank you," said Seward, and hung up. He swore heavily under his breath, dialed a second number, and waited for Cal Holmwood to answer. The operator picked up after the third ring.

"Cal?" Seward said. "It's Henry. I need you to bring *Mina* to Russia, immediately. To SPC Central Command. Apologize to the Americans and take off, right away. We've got trouble."

Holmwood sounded surprised, but immediately told the director that he would do as he was ordered. Seward thanked him, hung up, and dialed a third number. He was about to punch the CALL button when the phone rang, vibrating in his hand. He looked at the screen and saw the same number he had been dialing. He pressed ANSWER and put the phone to his ear.

"Listen to me," he said, interrupting the voice on the other end. "I need you to tell me where Jamie Carpenter is. His life may be in danger."

There was a pause, and then the voice answered him. The color drained from Seward's face.

"He's walking into a trap," he said. "Call—"

But the person on the other end of the line was gone.

UNHOLY ISLAND

42

The picnic area at the end of the causeway that linked the island of Lindisfarne to the mainland was deserted. The last tourists had packed up their blankets and hampers the previous evening, climbed into their cars and caravans, and left, leaving behind overflowing rubbish bins and drifts of litter, floating lazily in the damp mist that covered the ground like a funereal wreath. The wooden tables and benches were empty, and the children's playground was dark, the swings creaking back and forth, the carousel revolving gently.

A low rumbling noise punctured the silence.

Anyone standing in the picnic area would have felt it before they heard it, a trembling beneath the ground, gathering strength as it approached from the southwest. Then it became audible; a steady thump, regular as clockwork, that grew louder and louder until it would have sounded like they were standing beneath a hurricane. The wind picked up, and the litter sped around the picnic area in rapid circles. One of the bins toppled over, depositing its collection of polystyrene containers, drink cans and empty potato chip bags onto the grass, where it was sucked into the spiraling air, creating a miniature tornado of rubbish.

Two blinding white lights pierced the night sky, illuminating the picnic area. The beams were wide and bright, and they grew as something descended from above, their circular fields spreading until they merged into one, until, with a bone-shuddering roar, an EC725 helicopter emerged from the mist, sending the wet air spinning into columns and tunnels as it was displaced by the aircraft's rotors.

The black helicopter descended quickly, its huge wheels bouncing hard on the worn grass of the picnic area as it touched down. Then a door slid open in the side of the aircraft; five figures jumped down and ran across the grass until they were out of range of the blades.

Jamie Carpenter looked around at his companions, dust and litter thumping against the purple plastic of his visor. Thomas Morris's face was visible beneath his raised visor; he was looking at Jamie with worry creasing his face, but there was a determination in his eyes that Jamie was heartened to see. Two more operators stood in black and purple, their hands hanging loosely at their sides. Their names were Stevenson and McBride; they had been waiting in the Loop's hangar with Morris when Jamie arrived with Larissa, and the boy was glad to have them. The vampire girl was staring steadily at Jamie, encouragement on her face. He smiled at her, and she returned it instantly.

"I don't know what we're going to find on the island," Jamie said, raising his voice above the howl of the rotors. "I'm going to assume that Alexandru knows we're coming, and you should, too. He told me he had killed a lot of people, so you should also expect bodies, lots of them. You've seen the layout of the island; it's one small village rising up a hill, with a dock at the bottom. The rest of the island is wilderness, except for the monastery at the north end. I think that's where we'll find my mother, but I could be wrong. So we're going to go through the village first and look for survivors." Jamie looked around at his team. The faces that looked back at him were calm.

They're looking to me to lead them. How did this happen?

"Any questions?" he asked. It was something he had heard army officers in films say before they led their troops into battle, and it seemed appropriate.

Everyone shook their heads, and he nodded. "Then let's go," he said.

They walked steadily across the causeway that led to Lindisfarne. The mist had closed in, and it was impossible to see more than ten feet in any direction. Jamie heard invisible water lapping on both sides of him, and he shivered.

If they come for us in this mist, we won't even see them until it's too late.

They followed the white line in the middle of the road, walking single file. Jamie was in the lead, followed by Larissa, the two operators, and Morris, who was bringing up the rear, his T-Bone wedged hard against his shoulder. Every few minutes, Larissa reached out and brushed the back of his neck with her cool fingers, and his stomach fluttered.

The mist began to thin, and the island appeared in front

of them, a dark looming shape that rose into the dark night sky. They walked on, the sharp clatter of their boots on the asphalt the only sound, until two tall, thin shapes emerged at the sides of the road, and Jamie stopped, holding a hand out behind him.

"Oh my God," said Stevenson. His voice was low and tight, as though a hand was gripping his throat.

On each side of the road was a flagpole, a white metal tube rising from the sediment at the edge of the water to a height of twenty feet. The flags that had fluttered in the sea breeze were lying on the ground, torn to ribbons; one was a Union Jack, the other the yellow-and-blue flag of the European Union.

In their place, impaled on the sharp points of the flagpoles, were two of the residents of Lindisfarne, their teeth scraping on the flagpoles as they twisted in the air.

"I don't understand," said Jamie, his voice thick with horror. "Why would he do this?"

"Dracula used to do it," said McBride. "When he was still a man. He would impale prisoners of war and stand them where opposing armies could see them. It's a warning not to go any further."

"It's not a warning," said Larissa. "It's a welcome. He knows we aren't going to turn back, so he wants Jamie to see what he's capable of. He wants him to be scared."

Jamie stared up at the impaled bodies.

Were they alive when he did that to them? I hope they were already dead.

"Come on," he said, with more conviction than he felt. "Let's keep moving."

There were three more pairs of flagpoles, all decorated in

the same terrible fashion, but Jamie kept his eyes focused on the island, which was now taking shape in front of him. He could see streetlamps rising up the hill and squares of yellow light that were the windows of houses. At the foot of the hill, to the right of the causeway, he saw waves breaking on the gray concrete of the dock, and a small fleet of fishing boats bobbing up and down on the tide.

The team walked on, and after five minutes or so, the water that surrounded them receded, and they were standing on solid ground. The road wound to the right, and they followed it, their weapons drawn. They reached the bottom of the hill, and Jamie looked around him, up the two narrow roads that led up the hill to his left, along the dock to their right. The team stood still at the dark junction, and he listened for any signs of life.

The island was silent.

Dead. It's dead.

"Check the dock," he said. Morris and Stevenson set off toward the fishing fleet. He looked over at Larissa, who returned his glance with a nauseous expression on her face. "What's wrong?" he asked.

"It's this place," she replied. "It stinks of death. Can't you smell it?"

Jamie sniffed the air. He could smell the salty residue left behind by the seawater, and the oily stench of gutted fish, but that was all. "No," he told her. "I can't smell it."

She looked at him with resignation in her eyes. "Just wait," she said.

They watched Morris and Stevenson make their way back to them, their weapons hanging by their sides, their heads lowered as they examined the ground. They stepped off the dock and walked over to the rest of their team.

"Anything?" asked Jamie.

"A teenage girl," Morris replied. "Dead about three hours, by the look of it. And blood. Lots of blood. No sign of any survivors."

Jamie looked up the hill.

Two roads. Maybe forty houses.

"Let's split up," he said. "McBride, you come with me. We'll take the road to the left. Morris, Stevenson, take the one to the right." He looked at Larissa. "Will you take a look from the air?" he asked. "You can see things we can't."

She nodded.

"OK," he said. "We'll meet at the top in fifteen minutes. Leave the bodies where they are. Survivors are all we're interested in."

The team went their separate ways. Morris and Stevenson jogged quickly across the junction and made their way up the right-hand road. Larissa rose gracefully into the air, smiling at Jamie as she did so and disappeared into the darkness, leaving him and McBride alone.

They found the first bodies immediately.

Blood ran thickly between the uneven cobblestones, pooling in the drain entrances and against the wheels of the cars that were parked outside the large, neat houses. They followed the river of crimson to the second house on the right and found a couple lying facedown in their driveway. The woman's long blonde hair was matted with blood, the man missing the fingers on his left hand and one of his ears. Behind them, electric light blazed out of broken windows, and the front door of their home hung limply from its upper hinges. The wood panels had been splintered, and the lock was lying on the front step.

"There's nothing we can do for them," said McBride, pulling gently on Jamie's arm.

Jamie was standing at the open gate that led into the driveway, staring at the corpses. He was sickened by the casual brutality displayed by Alexandru and his followers, unable to comprehend the violence that had been unleashed for no reason.

Those poor people. Oh God, those poor, unlucky people.

"Come on," urged McBride, hauling on the teenager's arm. "They're dead. There might be someone up there who isn't."

The thought of survivors broke Jamie's paralysis, and he started up the hill again. He took the left-hand side, McBride the right; they checked the bodies that were strewn across the cobblestoned streets, shouted into houses, and listened for any response, followed trails of red that led to atrocity after atrocity. Jamie felt light-headed, as though he might faint, but he persevered; door after door, victim after victim.

Near the top of the hill, he heard music emanating from a house, a classical piano piece he was sure he recognized, and followed it to a house set back from the road. He checked the woman who was lying on the path outside the front door and moved on, past a house that stood open to the night, a rectangle of warm yellow light glowing out onto the street.

At the top of the hill, where the houses curved around to meet the top of the street that Morris and Stevenson were making their way up, he stood with McBride in the middle of the road.

"Nothing?" asked Jamie.

"Nothing," confirmed McBride, pushing his visor up. His face was pale and drawn tightly, as though it had been stretched. "You?"

"Nothing."

Then they heard a high wavering cry behind them, where the road ended and the thick woods that covered the heart of the island began, and Jamie and McBride turned and ran toward it.

They crashed through the undergrowth, snapping twigs beneath their heavy boots as branches whipped against their visors, running between dark trunks and over banks of earth and ridges of shrubs. They got turned around; the trees were dense, and the darkness was thick. The cry came again, but it sounded like it was all around them, like a hundred voices crying in unison. Then suddenly Larissa was next to them, grabbing their hands and lifting them into the air.

She soared between the trees, banking effortlessly left and right, holding Jamie and McBride beneath her as though they were weightless. They came to a clearing, and she swooped down and released them; they hit the ground rolling and came up pointing their T-Bones into the middle of the clearing, where a man in his twenties was squirming in the grip of a vampire woman who could have been no more than twenty herself. She had the man's arms pinned behind his back and was stroking his throat with the long fingernails of her right hand; she either didn't notice the appearance of the two black-clad figures, or didn't care.

Jamie leveled his T-Bone, and shouted, "Hey!" at the same

462

moment as he pulled the trigger. The vampire dropped the man and reared up, snarling to her feet. The projectile took her in the middle of the chest, punching a hole through the white vest she was wearing, sending blood gushing into the air. A second later, she exploded, sending a spiral column of crimson into the sky. It pattered to the ground, coating the grass.

Jamie and McBride stood up and walked over to the man, who was cowering on the ground, soaked with blood. He looked up at the two men as they approached him, his eyes wide with terror, and backed away, pushing himself backward with his hands, his feet digging long furrows in the grass. A thick trail of something dark covered the ground where he had been sitting, and McBride swore loudly.

"He's bleeding," he said. "Grab him, Jamie."

Jamie strode forward and scooped the man up from the damp grass. His hands slid into something wet; the man screamed, and Jamie almost dropped him. He stumbled, threw the man's arm around his shoulders, and ran with him back to where McBride was standing. He lay him down; the operator flipped him gently over, then recoiled.

There was a wide hole high on the man's back, a deep conical wound covered in dirt and flecked with tiny chips of wood.

"Probably a branch," said McBride. "Turn him over."

Jamie did as he was told, rolling the injured man onto his back as carefully as he was able. McBride laid his head on the narrow chest, listened for several seconds, then pushed himself back up to his knees, a helpless look on his face.

"There's blood in his lungs," he said, in a low voice. "There's nothing I can do for him. He needs a hospital, right away."

A terrible sensation of being trapped swept through Jamie.

It's this man or your mother. You know that's the truth. If you take him to the mainland, your mother will be dead by the time you get back here.

The wounded man spared him the decision.

He looked up at the two men with terrified eyes, his chest rattling up and down as he took shallow panic breaths. Then his heart gave out, and he died of shock in Jamie's arms.

"Jesus," whispered McBride, then lowered his head and crossed himself.

Jamie just stared at the man. His last moments on earth had been full of pain and fear, and he had done nothing to deserve it, except be in the wrong place at the wrong time.

You did this. Alexandru did this because you tried to find him.

A great wracking sob escaped from Jamie's mouth. Behind the purple visor, tears spilled down his cheeks and dripped on to his Blacklight uniform.

It's your fault. It's all your fault.

He slumped onto the grass and lowered his head to his chest. It felt heavy, too heavy for him to go on. He was suddenly more tired than he had ever been in his life, and he fell backward into the cool grass.

He didn't get there. Two hands caught him lightly under his shoulders, pulled him up to his feet, and turned him around. Larissa was looking at him with an expression of absolute anguish. Then she reached up, lifted the helmet from his head, and kissed him, tenderly.

Jamie kissed her back, acting on pure instinct. The dead

man lay behind him, McBride was weeping gently on his knees beside him, and Jamie kissed her, sure that he would go mad if he didn't find a way to feel something.

She gently pulled away and looked at him. "You won't give up," she said. "I won't let you."

Jamie looked inside himself and saw that she was right. He would not give up; he would see this nightmare through to its conclusion, even if it meant his death. He owed it to everyone whose lives Alexandru had ended before their time.

He gave her a weak smile, and she returned it. Then he reached down, pulled McBride up by his shoulders, and looked the operator in the eyes. "We go on," he said, as firmly as he was able, then gestured to the man lying on the grass. "We finish this. For him, and for all the others."

McBride looked at him, his eyes red.

"Yes, sir," he said.

Larissa floated back into the air, promising to keep watch. Jamie and McBride were about to make their way back to the road, where Morris and Stevenson would be waiting for them, when McBride suddenly stiffened.

"Someone's watching us," he whispered. "Don't look. Your three o'clock. Behind the tree."

Jamie waited five seconds, then slowly, ever so slowly, turned his head in the direction McBride had indicated. At first he saw nothing, just the black outlines of the trees. Then as his eyes focused on the spot, he saw the pale face of a girl staring at them. He turned back to McBride, just as slowly.

"It's a girl," he whispered.

The operator nodded.

"What do we do?" Jamie asked.

McBride said nothing. Then he shouted across the clearing, in a calm, even voice. "We are not going to hurt you," he said. "Come out. I repeat. We are not going to hurt you."

There was no movement from the edge of the clearing. The girl didn't appear, but nor did they hear the burst of noise that meant she had run.

McBride turned to face the spot where the girl was hiding and motioned for Jamie to do the same. He placed his T-Bone on the ground and held his empty hands out for her to see. Jamie followed his companion's lead, placing his weapon carefully on the ground and reaching toward the darkness at the edge of the clearing. They stood still and waited. Eventually, there was a rustling noise from where she was standing and the snap of a branch. Then the girl emerged from the undergrowth and took a hesitant step toward them.

She was a teenager, roughly Jamie's age. She had blonde hair, cut short and angular so it fell across her forehead, and was wearing jeans and a dark T-shirt. She stared at them with an expression that was not fear; rather it was caution. She took another small step forward, her eyes flicking constantly to her right and left, then there was a blur of movement above her as Larissa dropped from the sky like an eagle and effortlessly lifted the girl into the air.

She screamed as her feet left the ground, then she was moving through the air and into the clearing. Larissa dropped her from a couple of feet up, and she landed in a heap in front of McBride, who leapt forward and pinned her to the ground. The vampire floated down to the ground next to Jamie and watched as the operator wrapped his arms around her waist and held the struggling, squirming teenage girl still.

"Let me go!" she yelled.

She whipped her head backward, and it connected squarely with the bridge of McBride's nose, breaking it. He grunted, pain shooting through his head, and his grip loosened. The girl shoved his arms down and pushed herself loose. She leapt to her feet, looking wildly around for an escape route, and then Larissa stepped forward, pulled her arms behind her back with one hand, and lifted her casually off the ground by the nape of her neck with the other.

"Hold still," she said. "I'm not going to hurt you if you hold still."

McBride got unsteadily to his feet. Blood was streaming from his nose and dripping steadily onto his uniform. He walked over to where the girl hung, suspended in the air by Larissa, and Jamie joined him.

"What's your name?" asked Jamie.

The girl grimaced and didn't answer.

"This will be easier if I know your name," he said, calmly.

"It's Kate," she spat. "Kate Randall."

"I'm Jamie," he said. "Pleased to meet you."

She glared at him, and didn't respond.

"In a few seconds, I'm going to ask my friend to put you down," Jamie said. "Please don't run, or attack any of us. We really do mean you no harm, but we'll protect ourselves if we have to. OK?"

No response.

"I'm going to take that as a yes," he said, and nodded to Larissa. She smiled at him and released her grip on the girl. Kate fell to the floor in a heap, but her head came up immediately, her eyes flashing with anger.

"Who are you?" she asked. "Are you with them?"

"No," said Jamie. "We're not with them. We're here to stop them."

Kate laughed. It was a dry, brittle sound, with no humor in it. "You're a little bit late," she said.

Then she burst into tears.

As McBride knelt down and tried to comfort the crying girl, the sound of footsteps crashed through the undergrowth, and Jamie heard his name called through the darkness. It was Morris's voice, and he shouted in response.

"Over here!"

The crashing and thudding increased, then Morris and Stevenson burst into the clearing, their weapons drawn. They skidded to a halt, taking in the scene before them; Jamie standing next to Larissa, McBride kneeling beside the weeping teenage girl, the pale body of the man lying on the ground.

"What happened?" demanded Morris, striding over to Jamie.

Jamie explained.

"Jesus," said Morris, and shook his head. "What a mess."

Stevenson went to McBride and knelt down beside him. Kate was starting to compose herself, the tears drying up, her weeping diminishing to small gulps of air. She looked at the two men in their black uniforms crouching beside her, then over at Jamie.

"What's happening?" she asked, simply.

Morris strode over and stood in front of her. "Have you read *Dracula*?" he asked.

She nodded.

"It's not a story; it's a history lesson."

Kate looked up at him, then burst out laughing. "Wow," she said, wiping her nose with the back of her hand. "How many times have you practiced that one?"

Morris flushed red and looked over at Jamie for help. A big grin had crept over the teenager's face, and he walked over and hunkered down in front of Kate.

"Vampires are real," he said, softly. "They're what attacked your island tonight. Their leader is one of the oldest vampires in the world, and he's holding my mother captive. This had nothing to do with you, or anyone else who lived here. But you need understand what we're dealing with. OK?"

Kate nodded. Her eyes were clear, and her face was remarkably calm. "Do you know if anyone made it off the island?" she asked. "My father . . ."

She stopped and gazed into the distance, lost for a moment in the memory of what had happened to her sleepy little village.

"There are survivors," Jamie said, and her eyes snapped back into focus. "I don't know how many, and I don't know if your father was among them. But there are definitely survivors; they ran a fishing boat aground on a beach near Fenwick."

Relief spilled through Kate like a warm wave.

I'll see him soon. I'll see him once the sun comes up.

"What happens now?" she asked. "There's no one else alive here. Ben was the last." She motioned to the body lying on the grass. Its wide eyes stared lifelessly up at the night sky.

"We have a job to do," said Morris. "I want you to go down into the village, lock yourself in your house, and wait for morning. When the sun—"

Kate and Jamie interrupted him at the same time.

"You can't leave me here!"

"We're not leaving her here!"

Morris pulled off his helmet and threw it to the ground. It thudded to the wet grass, and the rest of the team jumped.

"For Christ's sake," he shouted. "This is not a youth-club hike or an Outward Bound trip. This is a classified military operation, I am the senior officer here, and you will do as I tell you. Is that understood?"

There was silence in the clearing; five faces were turned toward Morris, who had gone a deep shade of angry red.

"That was very impressive, Tom," said Larissa. "Really. Very forceful."

Kate giggled, and Jamie felt a smirk creep involuntarily across his face. Even McBride and Stevenson smiled, despite themselves, and after a moment, Morris himself broke into a grin.

"Sorry," he said. "Got a bit carried away there for a minute."

Jamie stood up and clapped his friend on the shoulder. "We can't leave her, Tom," he said. "You know we can't."

"I know," replied Morris, then turned his attention to Kate. "Can you take us to the monastery from here?"

Kate stood up.

"What are we waiting for?" she asked.

THE STUFF OF NIGHTMARES

The Blacklight team, now one member larger than it had been when it landed, walked through the woods. In the distance, the ramparts of the ancient monastery could be seen above the trees, lit by orange light flickering off the pale stone.

Kate had guided them onto a rough trail that wound through the woods. Jamie had given her the stake from his belt, and she carried it before her like a divining rod, her fist clenched tightly around the rubber grip. Larissa was floating above them, her eyes peeled for any sign of movement, as the team walked beneath her. They crossed a large clearing, on which a soccer pitch had been marked out in lines of fading paint, and then the trees enveloped them again.

McBride led the way, followed by Jamie and Kate, who were walking side by side, then by Stevenson, and finally by Morris, who had again taken up the rear position.

"So how old are you?" asked Kate, her voice trembling.

Jamie could see she was trying to hold herself together. "I'm sixteen," he replied. "You?"

"Same," she said, and grinned at him. "My birthday was last month."

"What did you do?"

"Nothing," she said. "My dad had to work. But he's going to take me to the mainland next month. We're going shopping." Her face creased with pain at the thought of her father, and Jamie's heart went out to her.

"I'm sure he's fine," he said.

"So am I," she replied.

They walked on in silence for a few minutes, then she spoke again.

"How did you end up here?" she asked, looking over at him.

This time he did laugh. "That's a long story," he replied.

"We've got time."

"No," said Jamie. "We really haven't. Trust me."

They emerged into a round clearing, and McBride held a hand up, bringing them to a halt. Larissa floated down next to Jamie and eyed Kate with a look of mild suspicion as the team fanned out in a tight line.

"What's wrong?" Morris asked.

McBride glared at him, then held a finger to his lips. "Something's not right," he whispered. "I don't—" He didn't finish his sentence. Larissa tipped her head back and sniffed the night air, then gripped Jamie's arm and turned to him, her eyes wide.

Vampires flooded into the clearing.

They emerged from the darkness at the edges, dropped from the overhanging branches. There were twelve of them, male and female; they formed into a loose line in the middle of the clearing, snarling at the Blacklight team.

Crimson spilled into Larissa's eyes, and she bared her fangs at the group of vampires. Jamie grabbed at his belt for a UV grenade and felt only air. There had been no time to visit the armory before they left; the operators were carrying only their basic equipment. They raised their weapons and waited for the vampires to make a move.

They didn't have to wait long.

Alexandru's followers rushed toward them, snarling and hissing, their fangs gleaming in the silver moonlight. Stevenson was the first to fire; his T-Bone shot slammed into the chest of a man in his thirties wearing a stained yellow T-shirt and ripped khakis, obliterating his heart, and he exploded in a fountain of gore.

McBride dropped to one knee and strafed the approaching vampires with his MP5. The bullets tore through them at knee height, sending blood and white shards of bone flying into the air. Three of the vampires fell, and slid across the damp grass, howling in agony.

The rest kept coming.

Jamie fired his T-Bone squarely into the chest of a vampire woman. She threw her head back and howled in pain, blood gushing from the round hole the projectile had made, then she exploded, and the howl died with the rest of her.

Larissa leapt forward and sank her fingers into the eye sockets of two of the onrushing vampires. Blood squirted around her knuckles as she pressed deeper, blinding them with her razor-sharp fingernails. She pulled her hands free, her arms soaked with blood to the elbows, and ducked as Morris and McBride fired in unison. The vampires exploded above her, drenching her in gore. She shook her head, blood flying in thick streaks from her long hair, and then she was moving again, back to her position next to Jamie.

Stevenson ran forward and hand-staked the three vampires lying on the ground. They twisted and rolled on the grass, their faces contorted with pain, until the operator put them out of their misery in three splashes of blood.

The five remaining vampires backed away, hissing. Their numerical advantage was gone, and Jamie saw fear in their red eyes. Adrenaline surged through him, and he charged forward, without any idea of what he was going to do. All he knew was that there were vampires to be killed, and he wanted to be the one who did the killing.

Morris shouted something, but Jamie didn't hear him. He sprinted across the clearing toward the vampire in the middle of the retreating group, a man in his forties who looked like a roadie for a heavy metal band, a black T-shirt and blue denim vest covering bulging arms that were coated in blue ink.

Three projectiles shot past him, metal cables trailing behind them, and thudded into a trio of vampires. They exploded as he dodged between them, splattering him with blood. A dark shape swooped over him, and Larissa hauled a vampire girl up into the trees. She came back down in pieces. Larissa reappeared, a blood-soaked nightmare, her red eyes glowing brightly, her teeth bared, and she tore open the severed torso and crushed the heart that was still beating inside it. The pieces of the girl exploded, and suddenly Jamie was running toward the last vampire in the clearing.

The roadie backed away, buying himself time and distance, then leapt forward. Jamie fired his T-Bone, but the shot went wide, disappearing into the dark trees at the edge of the clearing. He threw the weapon aside, reached for the stake on his belt, and found the loop empty.

I gave it to Kate.

The vampire crashed into him at waist height, knocking the air out of him and driving him to the ground. It straddled him, its knees on his elbows, sending pain screaming up his arms. He kicked his legs, but the huge vampire didn't move an inch. It snarled, a grin on its contorted face, its eyes deep pits of crimson. Behind him he heard his companions winding in their T-Bone projectiles and realization hit him.

I ran too far. By the time they fire again, I'll be dead.

A dark blur flashed to a halt at the vampire's shoulder, and Larissa appeared, her wide eyes streaming red, her teeth bared. She reached for the vampire, but it swung an arm like a tree trunk and caught her square on the jaw, sending her flying into the darkness, where she hit something with a sickening crunch. The vampire leaned slowly toward him, its mouth peeling back to reveal two enormous fangs, at least an inch long, and then there was a wet crunching noise, and the vampire's expression changed. A second later it exploded. Jamie shielded his eyes with one of his arms, and then hands were pulling at him, hauling him to a sitting position. He opened his eyes, and found Kate looking down at him, his stake in her hand, her chest rising and falling rapidly.

"Are you all right?" she asked, breathlessly. "Did it bite you?"

Jamie shook his head, slowly, and clambered to his feet. The three Blacklight operators appeared at his shoulder, and McBride spun him around.

"Did you get bitten?" he demanded. "Tell me the truth."

"He didn't get bitten," said Kate. "I got it."

McBride looked at her with open admiration, and then stepped forward and hugged her. She stood stiffly in his embrace for a few seconds, confusion on her face, then gradually gave in and wrapped her arms around the black-clad man. He broke the hug and held her by her shoulders.

"Well done," he said. "Very well done."

Kate flushed with embarrassment, but she smiled broadly.

A crash of noise came from the edge of the clearing, and Larissa reappeared. She strode toward the others, blood pumping down her face and neck from a wide gash at her temple, her left arm hanging at an unnatural angle at her side, pain and panic on her face.

"Are you—" started Morris, but she brushed past him without a glance and stopped in front of Jamie, grabbing his chin and tilting his head back and up. She inspected his neck carefully, and then released her grip. They stared at each other for a long moment, until Larissa turned sharply on her heels, walked over to Kate and kissed her on the cheek.

Then she sat on the grass, cradling her broken arm in her lap, her crimson eyes glowing in the dark. After a few seconds, Jamie walked over and sat down beside her.

Ten minutes later, they moved on.

Beams of moonlight shone down through the canopy of the woods, long streams of silver light that gleamed and twinkled in the night air. They made their way along the trail in the same order they had entered the clearing. Larissa held her broken arm as still as she was able to, pressing it gently to her side. She was a terrifying vision, soaked from head to toe in blood that was starting to harden and crack, giving it the look of flaking war paint. Jamie was similarly coated; he had wiped most of the roadie's blood from his face, but his uniform was drenched, and the coppery scent of blood hung around him like a cloud, turning his stomach. Kate was pale, as the shock of the things she had seen over the course of this long, bloody night began to settle into her mind, but her face was determined, and she walked steadily. McBride had reset his broken nose, and the blood had stopped flowing. It was badly swollen, and there was a high whistling noise when he breathed, but the operator cared little for a broken nose, and his eyes were clear.

Jamie walked next to Larissa, who was floating six inches above the ground so she didn't jar her broken arm. Neither of them said anything, but every couple of minutes, one cast a sideways glance at the other. Kate followed behind, watching them.

They emerged from the woods at the top of a wide plain, studded with low bushes and tangles of shrubs, that gently sloped downward before them. The monastery stood at the top of the rise on the other side, a crumbling building of pale stone rising above the row of cliffs that marked the edge of the island. Jamie could hear the distant crashing of waves and smelled salt in the air. Light blazed from the uneven windows of the monastery, the flickering yellows and oranges that came from open fires.

They set out across the plain, unaware that one of them had less than three minutes to live.

Larissa smelled it before she saw it.

"Something's coming," she said. "Something bad. I've never smelled anything like it."

Adrenaline splashed into six nervous systems.

Morris, McBride, and Stevenson immediately pulled Larissa and Jamie into a circle around Kate. The five members of the Blacklight team scanned the empty plain, their visors sweeping left and right, their weapons at their shoulders.

For long seconds, they stood motionless, silent apart from the sound of their own breathing. Then Stevenson lowered his weapon and turned to his companions.

"There's nothing here," he said.

A dense tangle of bushes behind the operator exploded in a shower of leaves and splintered wood as something huge leapt across the dark grass. It growled as it moved on four powerful legs, its yellow eyes glowing, thick ropes of saliva trailing from jaws that were filled with gleaming teeth. It clamped its mouth on Stevenson's throat and hauled him forward, barreling into the rest of the team and sending them tumbling across the plain. As he fell, Jamie heard a terrible ripping sound as the creature pulled out a ragged chunk of Stevenson's neck, and heard the operator scream in pain.

He dug his heels into the grass and pushed himself back to his feet. He saw Kate sliding down the slope, heard her shouting for his help, and ignored her. The further she was away from whatever had leapt from the bush, the better. He turned back, ready to run up the slope to Stevenson, but what he saw at the top of the rise froze him to the spot.

The operator was lying on his back, blood gushing from the hole that had been torn in his neck. His face was pale, and his eyes were closed, but Jamie could see the black material of his uniform rising and falling.

He's still alive. You have to help him.

But he couldn't make his petrified limbs move.

Standing over Stevenson was a huge gray wolf, as large as a small car. Its coat was thick and tangled, its snout soaked with the operator's blood, its eyes gleaming. A terrible smell was emanating from it; a thick fog of spoiled meat and sickness. It looked down the slope at him, and Jamie felt his insides turn to water. Then it threw back its head and howled, an awful, deafening noise that sounded like damnation. It lowered its mouth toward Stevenson again, the moonlight gleaming off its enormous teeth.

The crack of gunfire rang across the plain, and the wolf twitched, red blooms of blood appearing along its flank, then howled again. Jamie looked round and saw Morris and McBride making their way up the slope, fire spitting from the barrels of their MP5s.

Where's Larissa?

He looked around wildly and saw her near the bottom of the slope. She was crouching next to Kate, holding the girl's face in her hands, and a surge of affection so hot it was almost something else shot through him. He drew his MP5, then ran back up the slope and fell into step next to McBride, who acknowledged him with the briefest of looks. The three Blacklight men pressed forward, their submachine guns screaming in the night air.

The wolf leapt down from Stevenson's unconscious body and roared at them, a sound so gigantic it physically drove Jamie back a step. His ears rang as he stepped forward again, his finger clamped tightly on the trigger of the MP5. Bullets slammed into the wolf, tearing clumps of fur from its coat, spraying dark blood across the grass. Jamie saw a round take one of its eyes out, leaving a neat black hole where the pale yellow ball had been. But the huge animal seemed to barely notice.

"Take it down!" bellowed Morris. "Take out its legs!"

Jamie's MP5 clicked empty. He hauled a new clip from his belt, slammed it into place, and pulled the trigger again. The three operators concentrated their fire on its left foreleg, and the limb splattered apart, wet chunks of flesh raining to the ground. The wolf howled in pain, and leapt forward, propelling itself across the grass on its three remaining legs, closing the distance in long, shambling strides. They fired at its right foreleg, bullets flying wide as the creature swayed toward them.

Ten feet away, the wolf dipped, the muscles in its powerful back legs tensing, ready to leap. Then with a sickening tearing noise, the right foreleg came apart under the weight of the gunfire, and the leap was a howling, aborted thing. The wolf flopped into the air, screeching in pain, and crashed to the ground before them. They jumped back, out of the reach of the jaws that were snapping blindly at the air, the teeth clamping together over and over with a sound like breaking pottery. The wolf pushed itself forward, its back legs digging into the ground, and they emptied their guns into its exposed underside. Explosions of blood burst from the white fur, and the animal bellowed. Then it lay still, its ruined chest rising and falling, great jets of warm air blasting out of its nose and mouth.

"Jesus," said McBride, breathing hard, staring down at the fallen animal.

Jamie stepped forward slowly and looked at it. The wolf was lying on its side, its shattered forelegs hanging uselessly, its snout soaked red with blood. Its one remaining eye revolved, looking at nothing.

"Check on Stevenson," said Morris, and McBride ran up the slope to the fallen operator. Jamie walked over next to Morris and gestured down at the animal.

"What is it?" he asked.

"It's a werewolf," replied Morris, his eyes never leaving the stricken creature. "An old one. A hundred years, at least."

Jamie stared at him. "A *werewolf*?" he asked.

Morris nodded, without looking at him. He was watching the creature's flickering chest, the white fur moving in waves as the flesh beneath it rose and fell.

"Frankenstein told me they were real," said Jamie in a low voice. "I didn't believe him. Not really."

Morris pulled the Glock pistol from his belt, then darted toward the wounded animal. He placed the muzzle of the pistol beside its one remaining eye and pulled the trigger. There was a dull thud, and the wolf lay still.

Then as Jamie watched, it began to change.

The fur began to thin and seemed to withdraw into the creature's flesh. There was a horrible series of cracking noises, and angular shapes emerged beneath the thick gray skin. The snout shortened, drawing back and flattening, the nostrils narrowing, the teeth pulling up into the gums. The lower legs straightened in a series of crunches, and the color of the animal began to shift from gray to pale pink. Jamie's mouth hung open; less than a minute after the transformation had begun, the wolf was gone. Lying on the grass where it had been was a naked man, his body twisted and broken. His arms were in tatters, his eyes were missing, and his torso was covered in holes, from which blood began to ooze.

"Believe him now?" asked Morris, placing his pistol in its holster.

Jamie nodded, slowly.

"There aren't many of them," said Morris. "Most of them live in isolation in the forests, but a few act as hired muscle. Alexandru must be serious."

Larissa and Kate appeared at Jamie's shoulder, and he jumped. They looked down at the broken body, identical expressions of disgust on their faces. Then McBride shouted that Stevenson was still alive, and they ran over to where he was lying.

The operator was convulsing on the ground when Jamie reached him. McBride was holding the sides of his head, trying to steady him; his arms and legs beat the grass, his body jerked and twisted despite McBride's strong grip.

"What's wrong with him?" cried Kate.

"The change is coming," replied Morris, his face ashen.

A terrible crunching noise emerged from Stevenson's body, and Jamie saw his forearms break. They folded on themselves, until they were almost at right angles. The operator opened his mouth and screamed, a high, terrible wail of agony. Then the noise came again, and his shins snapped. This time the scream was so loud it was like an ice pick through Jamie's head. Stevenson thumped against the ground, his body rocking back and forth, foam frothing from his mouth, blood squirting from his injured neck. Then, as his helpless companions watched, his jaw began to stretch, the bones grinding against each other, and his scream turned into a howl.

Thick black hair began to sprout from Stevenson's skin, bursting through his pores and tearing through his uniform. His eyes turned yellow, and his shaking became so frenzied that McBride was thrown loose.

"Somebody help him!" cried Kate, her voice high and anguished.

Morris pulled the Glock from his belt for a second time and knelt down next to Stevenson's head. The man—if he still was a man—was twitching and shaking on the grass, apparently oblivious to the small crowd gathered around him. Morris cocked the gun, and placed the barrel against Stevenson's temple.

Larissa turned Kate away from the stricken operator and held the teenage girl's face tightly against her shoulder, covering her eyes. Jamie watched, unable to tear himself away, as Morris pulled the trigger.

A spray of blood and brain flew in the dark air, and then Stevenson was still. The change, which was less than half complete, reverted quickly, and within thirty seconds, the operator was lying motionless on the grass, the coarse black hair gone, his limbs straight and human again.

They dragged him under the shelter of a tangled bush and left him. There was nothing else they could do for him; time was becoming short, and they needed to keep moving.

After a few minutes, in which time Kate composed herself and McBride said a silent good-bye to his friend, they walked down the slope toward the monastery.

IN THE HOUSE
OF GOD

Jamie stepped into the monastery's courtyard and stopped dead, his breath caught in his throat. He didn't believe in God and, therefore, didn't believe in hell, but he doubted that even if it were real, it couldn't be any worse than what he was looking at now.

The team had made their way across the plain and approached the monastery silently, spread in a line across the dark grass, crouching as they moved. They had stopped with their backs against the stone wall beside the tall arch that led into the building, three on either side, their weapons drawn. Screams of pain and high shrieks of pleasure floated on the night air, and thick smoke drifted across their nostrils, alive with the acrid scents of burning wood and meat. Morris motioned silently for McBride to lead them in, but Jamie shook his head vigorously. They were so nearly there; so nearly at the place where Alexandru was waiting for them, where his mother was being held, and he would not stand still while other men led the way. He crouched low and swung around the edge of the stone arch into the courtyard.

The cobblestoned yard was small; it was walled on all sides, and an opening stood in the middle of each. The ones to the left and right led into low buildings that Jamie guessed had been stables, and the one at the rear, opposite the arch through which he had just entered, led into the monastery itself. But between it and him was a scene dragged bloodily from the very worst corners of his imagination.

A large bonfire had been built in the middle of the courtyard. Jamie felt the heat of it on his face as soon he rounded the corner; a thick column of gray smoke climbed into the pale silver sky, and explosions of sparks burst into the air.

The bodies of monks were strewn around the cobblestoned ground. Many were naked, others still wrapped in their brown robes. Appalling violence had been visited on them. Blood was everywhere; dripping into pools at the bases of the walls, splashed in crimson swirls on the pale stone, running freely between the cobblestones beneath their feet.

Kate began to weep, quietly. The rest of the team looked slowly around the courtyard, their faces gray, their eyes wide.

"I've never seen anything like this," said McBride.

"Me neither," said Morris, shaking his head.

They walked slowly around the bonfire, their weapons at their shoulders, and faced the open doorway that would take them inside the monastery's main building. The opening was dark and uninviting.

"Follow me," said Jamie, softly, and stepped inside.

In front of Jamie was a solid stone wall on which a single

word had been scrawled in thick streaks of red:

WELCOME

Corridors led away to his right and left, lit by oil lamps that hung in ornate metal holders at head height. The watery-yellow lamps illuminated the passages, and Jamie saw dark shapes lying on the ground in both directions.

Get a hold of yourself. It's only going to get worse.

"Which way?" he asked.

"It doesn't matter," said Kate, her voice trembling. "The monastery is a square, with the chapel hall on the other side. We'll end up in the same place either way."

"All right," said Jamie. "Then we split up."

He looked at Morris and McBride, who were standing together, their black uniforms rendering them almost invisible in the darkness.

"You two, take Kate and check the right corridor. Me and Larissa will take the left."

A look of panic rose in Kate's face, but he ignored it.

Nearly there. You're nearly there.

He was, and he knew it. Somewhere in this building, probably waiting for him to appear, was Alexandru. And if the old vampire was here, then so was his mother.

I'm sure of it.

He grabbed Larissa's hand and pulled her along the corridor that led away to the left. She came without protest, curling her fingers around his, as the two operators led Kate to the right. She cast a nervous look over her shoulder but allowed herself to be led away.

Jamie and Larissa stepped around the bodies of dead monks that littered the floor of the narrow passage. They stared blankly, their eyes wide and uncomprehending, blood pooled around them, their mouths twisted in pain. Jamie ignored them; there was nothing that could be done. They passed wooden door after wooden door. He pushed one open and looked in on a bedroom so austere it was closer to a prison cell. The stone walls and floor were unadorned; the only contents of the room were a wooden chair that stood in front of a small desk on which lay a large Bible, and a wooden bed that looked incredibly uncomfortable. He closed the door, and they rounded a corner at the end of the corridor.

Movement flashed in front of them, and Jamie held his T-Bone out in front of him. He pulled his torch from his belt as Larissa's eyes reddened beside him, and shone it down the passage. Crawling up the wall ten feet in front of them, like an awful overgrown insect, was one of the monks. It turned its head toward them as the light from Jamie's torch passed over it, and the look on its pale, narrow face was purgatory. Its eyes gleamed red, but the mouth was contorted into a wide silent howl, and tears spilled down its cheeks. It clawed at the pale stone of the wall, tearing its fingers to shreds, and then it slammed its forehead into the wall, splitting the skin, sending blood pouring down its face. It did it again and again and again.

"Stop that!" yelled Jamie, and the monk fell awkwardly off the wall, landing in a heap on the floor.

It looked at them with an expression of pure agony, and Jamie thought he had never seem such misery in the face of a living creature. It crawled a few feet toward them, sobbing and weeping, and Jamie took a step backward, leveling the T-Bone at the approaching figure. It shuffled onto its knees and faced them.

"Damned," it said in a choked voice that was almost a whisper. "Damned."

Larissa made a noise in her throat, and Jamie looked at her. She was staring at the vampire, and he realized with horror that she knew exactly what he was going through.

"Tried not to do it," the monk whispered. "Not strong enough. Damned. Damned for all eternity."

Jamie shone the torch past the weeping figure, and the beam picked out the body of a second monk, lying slightly further down the corridor. His neck had been ripped out, but there was very little blood on the floor around him.

The hunger was on him, and he fed on one of his brothers. Oh God.

He raised the T-Bone and pointed it at the monk's chest. The broken, anguished figure in the brown habit didn't so much as flinch. It simply linked its hands in front of its stomach and closed its eyes. Jamie took a deep breath and pulled the trigger.

The explosion of blood brought two more vampire monks shambling along the corridor. They swayed out of the darkness, their red eyes gleaming, but Jamie and Larissa were ready. He tossed her the stake he had reclaimed from Kate, and they strode forward to meet them. Larissa leapt into the air, her broken left arm hanging beneath her, taking the confused, newly turned vampires by surprise, and plunged the stake into the chest of the nearest monk. It grimaced briefly, then burst in a shower of blood. Jamie T-Boned the other, the projectile punching a neat round hole in his brown robe and the skin beneath. It exploded, soaking the pale walls a dark crimson. Larissa stepped forward, leaned toward the dripping blood, then stopped, and turned to Jamie.

"Look away," she said.

"Why?" he replied.

"I don't want you to see this. Please, Jamie."

He nodded and turned his back on her. From behind him came a wet sound, then a stifled grunt of pleasure.

"OK," she said, after a long moment.

He turned back and looked at her. Her lips shone red, and her arm was no longer broken; she was rotating it in its socket, inspecting it, and looking at him with shame on her face.

"Come on," he said. "Let's keep going."

He reached a hand out to her, and she accepted it, gratitude on her beautiful, blood-streaked face.

They were nearly at the end of the corridor when they heard a soft weeping from behind one of the wooden doors. Jamie pushed it carefully open.

The room was identical to the one that he had inspected earlier, but this one wasn't empty. Huddled in the corner was a monk, his knees drawn up to his chest, his arms wrapped around his legs. His head was lowered, and he was shaking and weeping as Jamie crossed the room and knelt on the cold stone floor in front of him. Larissa stayed in the doorway, watching the corridor.

"Are you hurt?" asked Jamie, placing a hand on the man's arm.

The monk raised his head, and Jamie cried out, shoving himself backward across the stone floor.

A crucifix had been carved into the man's face; across the ridge of his forehead and then down from his hairline, along the length of his nose, through his mouth, splitting his lips into flapping chunks, and down to the end of his chin. The wound was wide and deep, and blood was gushing down his ruined face and onto his habit.

"Oh God," said Jamie.

At the mention of his Lord, the monk began to babble, a running stream of prayer.

"YeathoughIwalkthroughthevalleyoftheshadowofdeathIwillfe arnoevilbecausethouartwithme."

Jamie stood up and backed away from the huddled shape, his face twisted with despair.

There's nothing you can do for him. Think about your mother. Focus.

But he couldn't. He could think only about the tortured, violated man curled in the corner in front of him and wonder again what manner of creature he was dealing with, a creature that would inflict such savagery on men who had devoted their lives to peace.

"Come on," said Larissa, softly, and he turned to look at her. "We have to keep moving. You can't help him."

He followed her out into the corridor, and they rounded the final corner together. On the ground in front of them, a large arrow had been painted with blood, pointing the way they were facing. Two words had been written beneath it:

THIS
WAY

Hatred spilled through Jamie, hatred for Alexandru and all his kind, a hatred that burned so hot in his chest he thought he would burst into flames. "Does he think this is a game?" he hissed.

Larissa grabbed his arm.

"It is a game," she said. "To him, that's all this is. Ilyana, your father, your mother, those are just details. It's violence and pain and misery that he loves. Remember that when you face him."

A shout echoed down the corridor, and Jamie shone his torch along it. Morris, McBride, and Kate were walking quickly down it, and Jamie and Larissa went to meet them.

The team was reunited in front of a large wooden door.

"What did you find?" asked Jamie.

"Later," said McBride, his face drawn and pale, and Jamie nodded.

They stood in front of the door, the five of them, with Jamie in the center.

This is it. No matter what lies behind this door, you don't leave this place without her. You make her proud.

"Ready?" asked Morris.

Jamie took a deep breath. "Ready," he said, and pushed the door open.

But he wasn't ready at all.

THE TRUTH HURTS

Alexandru Rusmanov sat in the chapel hall on a wooden chair so ornately carved it looked like a throne.

It stood on a raised stone platform at the back of the large hall. An enormous wooden cross stood behind it, before a tall stained-glass window that faced the gray surface of the North Sea, a hundred feet below. A wooden lectern, from which Jamie guessed the abbot had conducted the monastery's services, had been thrown aside and lay broken on the stone floor.

A long wooden dining table had been treated with similar disdain; it lay smashed along one of the long walls of the hall, surrounded by the plain wooden chairs that had seated generations of the monks of Lindisfarne. Above it, set into alcoves along the high wall, were crude statues of saints. Their carved faces stared down solemnly into the middle of the hall.

Then Jamie saw her.

His mother.

Marie Carpenter stood at Alexandru's left, her face pale and tightly drawn.

"Mom!" he cried. He couldn't help himself.

She's alive. She's still alive. Oh, thank you. Thank you.

His mother's eyes lit up at the sound of his voice, and she looked at him with such love that he thought his heart might burst. She hadn't realized that one of the figures that had entered the hall was her son, but even as relief flooded through her that he was still alive, Jamie was still alive, she was screaming at him not to come any closer, to stay away, to run for his life.

"Listen to your mother, boy," advised Alexandru, his voice warm and friendly, and spread his arms wide.

Jamie had taken a step toward her, without realizing he had done so, and he paused. He looked along the length of the stone platform, beyond Alexandru's outstretched hands, and his heart sank.

Standing silently along the platform were more than thirty vampires in a loose line. At Alexandru's right was Anderson, the huge vampire with the child's face. His shoulders rose like a ridge of mountains, vast and misshapen, a long black coat covering them and reaching almost to the floor. Beyond him, and beyond his mother on the other side, were vampires of every age and gender. A woman in her sixties, dressed in a prim trouser suit, stood alongside a skeletally thin teenage boy, wearing torn jeans and nothing else. His ribs stood out on his narrow torso, and his eyes were sunken into his skull. Beside his mother, looking at her in a way that made Jamie want to tear his eyes out, was a fat man in a shiny gray suit. His face was red and a coating of sweat stood out on his forehead as he stared at Marie. The vampires looked contemptuously down at Jamie and his companions, while their master regarded him calmly.

"So," Alexandru said, leaning forward and rubbing his hands together, as though he were about to start a particularly exciting debate. "Jamie Carpenter. We meet again, if you'll forgive the cliché."

His eyes flickered to Jamie's left, his attention caught by something. Then his face twisted into a scowl, and he stared at Larissa with his blood-red eyes. "*You*," he said, all the warmth gone from his voice. "You dare show your face in front of me again?"

"I dare," replied Larissa.

"Your death will be my masterpiece," Alexandru said, and grinned at her. "No creature on earth has ever suffered like you will suffer."

"I'm not afraid of you anymore," said Larissa, staring up at the ancient vampire.

"You should be," said Thomas Morris. Then he pulled Quincey Morris's bowie knife from his belt and ran it across McBride's throat. The operator fell to his knees, blood jetting from severed arteries, and folded to the floor. McBride was dead before Jamie had time to realize what had happened.

Morris walked slowly across the chapel hall, his head lowered, like a man going to the gallows, and stepped up onto the platform. Anderson moved aside to accommodate him, and Alexandru laughed gently as the Blacklight operator took his place at his side.

Jamie stared at the platform, at Morris standing stiffly

beside Alexandru, and realized he was dead. They all were; Larissa, Kate, his mother, and him.

All dead.

Oh, no. Oh, please, no.

"Tom," he said. "Tom, what are you doing?"

Behind him he heard a small noise emerge from Kate's throat, and a snarl emanate from Larissa.

Morris was looking down at Jamie with pure hatred; it twisted his features into a face he didn't recognize. "I'm doing what needs to be done," he said. "What should have been done a long time ago."

Jamie felt tears welling up within him and shoved them back down. He had never felt so utterly alone.

"But *why*?" he asked in a broken child's voice. "We're friends. You said we were the same."

Anger flashed across Morris's face. "We are nothing alike," he spit. "My family has been betrayed and held back by Blacklight for more than a century. Yours was given every advantage, even though you never deserved them." He smiled cruelly at Jamie. "You want to know why I did it, is that it? You want an explanation? Fine, I'll tell you why. Your father killed my father."

Morris sighed deeply, as though he had wanted to get this off his chest for a very long time. "He didn't pull the trigger," he continued. "But he might as well have. Him and Seward and Frankenstein, and the rest. He gave his life to Blacklight, and they turned on him at the first sign of trouble. They betrayed him and sold him down the river, and they did it with smiles on their faces."

"But we checked the logs," said Jamie, desperately. "You

haven't accessed the operational frequency in weeks. How did you give it to Alexandru? How did you tell him we were coming to Northumberland?"

Morris smiled at Jamie, a wicked grin that turned the teenager's stomach. "You should read your Juvenal, boy. '*Quis custodiet ipsos custodes*'? I'm the security officer. I can access the entire Blacklight network, including the security protocols; I can add, amend, and delete anything I want, as I did the log of my accessing the frequency database. When your father, your arrogant, superior father, destroyed Ilyana, I reached out to Alexandru, and we came to an understanding. He would give me two things I wanted, and I would hand him Department 19; your family in particular. I sent him the maps that let him bring down the *Mina*, just like I hacked the personnel files and found him your address. You should have died the same night as your father. But someone interfered and warned your father they were coming. So when he ran home to protect you, I faked the e-mail from your father to Alexandru and framed him as the traitor. Alexandru could have you and your mother, and I would get him access to Julian later. But your father died, and you were hidden away. So I wrote the document that implicated Julian, making sure no one would suspect anyone else was involved, and spent years tracking down your whereabouts. Once I had it, I passed it on, and we moved against you and your mother."

He glared at Larissa. "But she failed to kill you, and the goddamn monster rescued you. I've been working to get you into the open, away from him, ever since. And now here we are. Blacklight are in Russia on a rescue mission that is far, far too late to do any good. There's no one to help you this time."

Jamie stared at Morris, his whole body numb. His mother was looking at him with panic in her eyes, Larissa was snarling beside him, but he felt nothing. It was too much for him to bear, one last betrayal too many, and he was on the very edge of collapse.

"What did you get?" he asked. "What did you get for helping to kill my family?"

"Eternal life," replied Morris, simply. "And the righting of the greatest wrong in Blacklight history: the death of my great-great-grandfather Quincey Morris. He died on a mountainside in the middle of nowhere, while lesser men survived. But the Russians found his remains in 1902, when they recovered Dracula's ashes. Alexandru is going to bring him back to me."

"You're wrong," said Jamie. "Dracula's remains were never found."

"You really shouldn't believe everything the Department tells you," replied Morris. "It's a shame Seward isn't here; if he were, you could ask him about vault thirty-one. But he isn't, so you're just going to have to trust me. Dracula's remains were recovered, along with my great-great-grandfather's. And soon they will both walk the earth again."

Grey was right, thought Jamie. *We should have listened to him.*

Then he looked at Morris, saw the desperation lurking an inch beneath the surface of his face, and felt savage satisfaction flood through him.

"You *idiot*," he said. "Quincey Morris wasn't turned. He just died. They can't bring him back. They're just using you to get to Dracula's ashes."

Morris's smile remained in place, but the light in his

eyes faded. He looked at Alexandru, who was watching the exchange with obvious relish. "That isn't true," he said. "You promised."

Alexandru grinned; an expression of pure malice, of utter sadism. "It seems that even the valet's great-grandson is cleverer than you," he said.

Far, far too late, Thomas Morris saw how simply and completely used he had been. His face fell, as the realization of what he had done sank into him, and he staggered on the raised platform.

You fool, thought Jamie. *You poor, desperate fool. You've given away everything for nothing. For absolutely nothing.*

Morris let out a strangled cry and fumbled the bowie knife from his belt. He lunged at Alexandru, who laughed delightedly, and slid liquidly to his feet. He reached out a hand and snapped Morris's wrist, the sharp crack echoing around the chapel hall. Morris screamed, until Alexandru plucked the bowie knife from his fingers and slid it easily into his throat, silencing him.

Marie Carpenter screamed as blood sprayed across the pale stone platform. Morris took a single halting step and then pitched forward, crashing to the floor of the hall. He lay there, blood pumping from the hole in his throat, his mouth working silently, his wide eyes fixed on Jamie.

"Oh God," whispered Kate. "Oh God, this is too much. That poor man."

Larissa flashed her a look of anger, but Jamie reached out and touched her arm. She looked at him, and he shook his head slowly. Her expression softened, and she returned her gaze to the platform, her red eyes gleaming.

"That was fun," said Alexandru, settling back on his seat.

"Now. Mr. Carpenter. Why don't you come up here with your mother and me? There are things we need to talk about, just the three of us."

Larissa reached out and gripped Jamie's hand so tightly he felt the bones grind together. With considerable effort, he stopped the pain showing in his face.

"Let my friends go, and I will," he replied.

"Jamie—" started Larissa, but he cut her off.

"Be quiet, Larissa," he said. "It's all right."

"They're free to go," said Alexandru. "You have my word. I couldn't be less interested in the girl, and Larissa will keep for another day."

Jamie nodded and started forward. Larissa held on to his hand, pulling him back. He turned to her, a tender expression on his face.

"Let me go," he said.

She looked at him for a long moment, then released her grip.

Jamie walked toward Alexandru. The ancient vampire was sitting forward, clearly excited by the sight of the approaching teenager. His mother was staring down at him, her eyes full of terror. Behind him he heard Kate start to cry, and Larissa breathing heavily, in and out, in and out.

He was halfway across the chapel hall when the huge wooden door behind him exploded.

STAND, AND BE TRUE

Frankenstein strode through the jagged hole where the door had been, followed by two Blacklight operators, their visors down and their weapons drawn. The monster towered over them; he had drawn himself up to his full height, and he stared at Alexandru across the blood-soaked room. He was holding a T-Bone in one of his gray-green hands, an enormous silver shotgun in the other, and he was very, very angry.

"Where is Thomas Morris?" he bellowed, his voice reverberating around the stone walls.

Everybody in the room stopped dead.

Jamie pointed to the floor in font of the stage, his heart overwhelmed by the sight of his friend, his head spinning with gratitude and guilt and anger. Frankenstein saw Morris, his body twisted awkwardly, blood pumping steadily from the wide hole in his throat, the last of his life ebbing away. His eyes widened as the monster slowly approached and knelt down on one knee ten feet away from him.

"Thomas," said Frankenstein, his voice low.

The dying man moved his eyes, slowly, and looked at him.

"Your great-great-grandfather would be ashamed of you," the monster said.

Morris stared at him, his face a pale mask of fear and pain. Then he died.

Sitting on the platform, Alexandru applauded, slowly. The claps echoed around the room, and Frankenstein looked up at him. Then he walked quickly over to Jamie's side and led the teenager back to Kate and Larissa.

"Such theater," said Alexandru, a wide smile on his face. "Wonderful. Just wonderful. Now, come up here, boy. Your friends may still leave, even the rather large one, but I ask you not to try my patience further."

Frankenstein looked at the old vampire, his face curled in a grimace of disgust. "There's no way that's going to happen," he said, firmly.

Alexandru sighed, a look of seemingly genuine disappointment on his face. "Have it your way, monster." He motioned to the vampires lined up beside him. "Kill them all, apart from the boy. Bring him to me."

The vampires leapt down from the stone platform and rushed headlong toward the remnants of the Blacklight team. Kate cried out as they sped across the stone, their eyes flashing, their fangs bared, their faces twisted with venom, and Frankenstein pushed her firmly back against the wall beside the door, behind Larissa and the operators. He pressed a stake into her hand, and she held it out before her in a trembling fist.

One of the men who had arrived with Frankenstein fired his T-Bone into the snarling line of vampires. The projectile flew high, tearing off the upper half of the head of a vampire man in its twenties. He went down, twitching, his eyes rolled back in his head. But as Jamie stared, the shattered, open skull began to repair itself before his eyes. He circled back against the wall, next to Kate. Larissa fell in next to him, and they pressed their backs to the cold stone as Frankenstein and the operators faced the onrushing vampires.

Frankenstein took half a step back, then hurled himself forward, careening into the vampires, his huge, uneven arms whirling around him like tree trunks in a tornado. Vampires flew through the air, trailing blood behind them, and crashed into the walls. The second operator emptied his MP5 into a cluster of vampires that were trying to surround him, driving them back, before a snarling vampire appeared behind him, and wrenched the helmet from his head. Frankenstein swung a long arm, placed the enormous barrel of the shotgun against the side of the vampire's head, and pulled the trigger. The report was deafening in the stone hall, and the vampire's head disappeared in a cloud of blood.

Larissa snarled and leapt into the fray, a crimson nightmare of biting teeth and clawing fingernails. She tore the throat out of the vampire woman in the trouser suit, who fell to the floor, clawing at her open jugular; she crawled for a few feet, then slumped to the stone.

Jamie raised his T-Bone and destroyed a vampire girl who was approaching Frankenstein from the rear; the shot thudding into her armpit and tearing through her chest. She exploded, showering the monster with blood, but he didn't even turn. Jamie waited for the projectile to wind back into the barrel of his weapon, and he hurled himself bellowing into the battle.

They fought for their lives.

They fired T-Bones and guns, they swung stakes and knives, and they punched and kicked at the horde of vampires that spun and circled around them. Blood flew in the air and pooled on the ground. Vampires exploded in fountains of crimson, limbs were blown from snarling bodies, and screams of pain and bellows of fury filled the chapel hall.

But it wasn't enough.

Two vampires leapt onto the shoulders of one of the operators and dragged him to the ground. He pulled the trigger on his MP5 as he was overwhelmed; the bullets raked across the ceiling of the hall, sending flurries of dust down onto the heads of the humans and vampires below. The operator screamed once as the helmet was pulled from his head and the vampires buried their fangs in his face. Blood gushed from beneath their gnawing mouths, and the operator lay still.

Then a high-pitched scream cut through the noise of the battle, ringing sweetly off the stone walls. Jamie spun toward the source and saw the skeletal male vampire holding Kate, his left hand around her waist. With the forefinger of his other hand, he lightly drew a razor-sharp fingernail across her throat. He smiled at Jamie, a look of revolting excitement on his face as he stroked the teenage girl's skin.

Something crashed into the back of Jamie's neck, and he sank to his knees, seeing stars. Gray spilled across his vision, and nausea swirled in his stomach. He pitched forward, and his forehead cracked sharply against the stone floor. He rolled over onto his side and saw the vampires take the rest of his team.

Three of them launched themselves at Frankenstein, who had stopped to look at Kate. They hung from his enormous frame like leeches, clubbing at his face and neck with their fists, and he was driven slowly to his knees. A vampire woman in a black T-shirt and glistening black PVC jeans pulled a short serrated knife from her boot and held it to the monster's neck. He stiffened, but the vampire didn't kill him. She held the knife to his neck, and he was still.

The surviving operator was sent spinning by a haymaker punch that he never saw. He was backing away from a pair of snarling vampires, a man and a woman who were almost naked, their clothes hanging from them in ribbons, and he was almost decapitated from behind by the blow. It was thrown by Anderson, who put every last drop of his unnatural strength into it. The operator flew into the stone wall, his helmet shattering under the impact, and he slid to the floor. Anderson walked slowly over to the fallen man and put one of his huge feet on the man's throat. He increased the pressure, pinning the man against the wall, and looked happily at Alexandru.

Larissa was herded against the wall, snarling and spraying blood from her face and hair with every quick dart of her head. Four of the vampires surrounded her, and she stood still, hissing and twitching, knowing she could not take them all.

Jamie pushed himself dizzily to his feet and saw that he was standing alone in the middle of the chapel hall; the vampires had backed away to the walls, taking his companions with them. His head was ringing, and his gorge had risen. He swayed unsteadily on his feet and turned to face Alexandru.

The ancient vampire was standing on the edge of the platform, staring down at him with delight in his eyes. Behind him stood Marie Carpenter, her arms dangling at her sides, her eyes wide with concern for her son.

"Move an inch, and I'll gut you," said Alexandru, in a voice that was little more than a whisper. Marie moaned, but she stood still.

I'm going to kill you, thought Jamie. *Even if it costs me my life, I'm going to kill you for what you've done to my mother.*

"So," said Alexandru. "It appears we have reached an impasse. I no longer feel inclined to let your friends go, but I will make their deaths quick if you come up here to me now. If you don't, you will have the privilege of watching them die, one after the other. It's entirely up to you."

Jamie stared up at the vampire, looking for something, anything that might help him. His eyes flicked to the huge window behind the ancient vampire, and then suddenly he saw it.

He put his hands to the belt on his waist. He brought his T-Bone and his MP5 up, and pointed them at Alexandru, his hands shaking.

The ancient vampire laughed.

"Oh, good Lord," he said, bemusement in his voice. "Take your best shots, Mr. Carpenter. If it will make you feel that you did everything you could, then by all means take them."

Jamie looked around the room at his friends.

Frankenstein was staring levelly at him, a look of confidence on his face, and it heartened Jamie to see it.

This needs to work. I'm only going to get one chance at this.

Larissa looked at him, her eyes shining red, her chest rising and falling. There was pride on her face and something else, and Jamie felt heat rise in his face. He didn't care; he let it flood through him and looked at Kate.

Her face was full of fear, but there was a determination there, as well as revolted anger at the touch of the skeletal vampire.

Finally, Jamie Carpenter looked at his mother.

She returned his gaze, favoring him with an expression of unadulterated love. He smiled at her, and she smiled back at her son.

He lifted the MP5, twisted its selector to full auto, aimed it, and pulled the trigger. The bullets streamed past Alexandru's head, who didn't even flinch, and thudded into the huge cross that stood behind him. The wood splintered and shattered under the impact, and the great crucifix creaked on its suddenly unstable base.

Alexandru didn't notice. He looked down at Jamie and opened his palms toward the teenager, as if to say, "What now?"

Jamie threw the gun aside; it clattered to the floor, and slid to a halt in the middle of the room. He raised the T-Bone against his shoulder.

One shot. Just one shot.

He fired, and the projectile screamed across the chapel hall. It sailed over Alexandru's head, and crashed into the center of the cross with a heavy thud, digging deeply into the dense, ancient wood.

"Oh, dear," said Alexandru, softly. "You missed."

Jamie set his feet against the uneven stone floor, and held the T-Bone against his chest. The motor whirred as it tried to wind the metal stake back in, and he felt his feet slide momentarily toward the old vampire, who was looking at him with an expression that was close to pity.

Then the bullet-weakened base of the cross creaked, and gave way.

Alexandru Rusmanov, who could move so fast he was a blur to human eyes, who had walked the earth, killing and torturing, for more than five hundred years, never saw it coming. At the last second, a shadow fell across him from behind, and his forehead creased into a frown before the huge cross, which had overlooked forty generations of the faithful, annihilated him.

It landed on his shoulders, shattering his spine and crushing the back of his skull to powder, driving him from the platform and onto the ground. His legs broke, and he crumpled to the stone floor, his pelvis cracking in two and filling instantly with blood. He rolled as he fell, and the right arm of the cross ripped his left arm out at the shoulder, sending it sliding wetly across the floor. The vampire hit the ground, a limp sack of flesh and blood. The cross settled on top of him, tearing his chest open as it slid to a creaking halt.

For a second, there was silence in the chapel hall, as the vampires stared blankly at their fallen leader.

Then the Blacklight team moved.

Frankenstein reached out and crushed the PVC-clad vampire's hand. Her fingers broke, and she dropped the knife, shrieking in pain, until the monster staked her and she exploded in a pillar of blood. He rose from the floor like an erupting volcano, firing his shotgun and his T-Bone, scattering vampires across the hall.

The operator grabbed Anderson's ankle and twisted it, sharply. There was a loud crack as the bone broke, and Anderson howled, the high wavering cry of a child. He reeled backward, his infant face clouded with pain and confusion, his eyes flicking from Alexandru's fallen form to the operator in front of him, who was pushing himself up the wall. Anderson backed away, then turned and leapt into the air. He flew across the hall like a swollen, misshapen bird, smashed through the stained-glass window, and disappeared into the night sky.

Larissa lunged forward and sank her hand into the chest of the vampire nearest her, who was staring with a look of incomprehension at the fallen cross. The woman screamed as fingernails tore through her skin and found her heart. Then Larissa clenched her fist, and the organ exploded. A moment later, the rest of the woman erupted, and Larissa moved forward, a snarling, blood-soaked angel of death. The other three vampires who had backed her against the wall turned and fled, leaping across the room and disappearing through the broken window.

The rest of Alexandru's followers went after them. Frankenstein and the operator each T-Boned one of the fleeing vampires, smashing them out of midair with the screeching projectiles. They were hauled back to the ground and exploded on impact, sending fresh blood running across the stone floor.

Kate saw her chance and sank her teeth into the skeletal vampire's arm. She shook her head like a terrier, then pulled hard. A chunk of meat tore out of the vampire's arm, and he screamed in pain. His fingernail left her neck, and she ducked out of his grip, spit out the chunk of meat, and turned to face him. The vampire looked up at her with red eyes, and she plunged the stake into his chest, driving him back against the wall. He burst in a great explosion of blood, soaking her from head to toe, but Kate didn't flinch. Instead she turned back to the center of the hall, saw the blood-soaked remnants of the Blacklight team walking toward each other, and ran to join them.

As his friends routed the remainder of Alexandru's followers, Jamie walked slowly across the room to the fallen vampire. His mother took a tentative step toward him, but he held up a hand.

"Stay where you are, Mom," he called. "It's not over yet." He crossed the stone floor of the hall and knelt down next to Alexandru.

The vampire's face was destroyed; one of his eyes was missing, his mouth opened and closed silently, and blood was pumping steadily from the back of his head, running freely across the ground. The severed arm lay beside Jamie, and he pushed it away, disgusted. Then he looked at Alexandru's chest and smiled at what he saw.

The skin had been torn away, and the ribcage had been shattered to pieces. Alexandru's insides lay open to the cold air of the monastery, and Jamie could see the slowly beating red bulb of the ancient vampire's heart. He reached down to his belt and pulled his stake from its loop.

"Too . . . late."

Jamie looked round, and saw Alexandru's remaining

eye looking at him. The vampire's mouth was twisted into a ghoulish approximation of a smile, and he was trying to speak again. Jamie leaned down next to the swollen, broken mouth and listened.

"Too . . . late," Alexandru said again and laughed, a tiny grunt that was full of pain. "*He rises*. And everyone you love . . . will die."

Jamie looked down at the old vampire, then yawned, extravagantly, throwing his head back and squeezing his eyes shut. When he had finished, he smiled down at Alexandru, who was looking at Jamie with dying outrage on his face.

Then Jamie raised the stake above his head, held it for a long moment, and hammered it into the vampire's beating heart.

A column of blue fire shot out of the organ as Jamie's stake pierced it. The chapel hall shook as a tremor thudded through it, then what was left of Alexandru exploded in a series of deafening thunderclaps, blood thudding into the air in great bursts that splashed across Jamie and onto the stone floor around him.

Jamie stared for a long moment, then closed his eyes and slumped to his knees. Frankenstein, Larissa, and the rest of the Blacklight team ran toward him, but before they were even halfway there, Marie Carpenter leapt down from the platform, slid to the blood-soaked floor, and wrapped her arms around her son.

THE HUMAN HEART IS A FRAGILE THING

Six figures made their way slowly out of the Lindisfarne monastery, as the first glow of the imminent dawn began to creep over the horizon to the east. Jamie and Frankenstein had each placed an arm under Marie Carpenter's shoulders and were helping her across the thick grass that covered the cliff tops. Kate and Larissa walked side by side, a comfortable silence between them. The Blacklight operator brought up the rear, his weapon still set against his shoulder, his visor sweeping slowly from left to right.

On the headland above the monastery stood a Blacklight helicopter, its angular shape a dark silhouette against the coming dawn. The pilot who had delivered Frankenstein and the two operators to Lindisfarne was standing at the cockpit door, his MP5 drawn. He lowered it as they approached, and a smile broke across his face.

Frankenstein went to the man, and they embraced, laughter

echoing in the predawn air, the simple laughter of men who are glad to be alive. Jamie let go of his mother, reluctantly, and shrugged his weapons and body armor to the grass. He stood up and stretched his arms above his head; he felt lighter than he had at any point since his father had died. Then Larissa pressed herself against him and kissed him. He hesitated for a moment, knowing his mother and his friends were watching, but then he gave in, and kissed her back. They broke the embrace, and Jamie flushed a deep red, looking around at the grinning faces of the survivors.

The operator lifted his helmet and rotated his head, his neck creaking as the muscles relaxed. His face was pale, but his eyes were alive with adrenaline, and he smiled at Jamie. The teenager's heart leapt as he found himself looking into a familiar face.

"Terry?" he said, a smile creeping over his face.

The Blacklight instructor grinned, then stepped forward and wrapped Jamie up in a crushing hug. "You did it," he whispered into the teenager's ear. "You really did it."

He released his grip, and Jamie stared at him, overcome. "What are you doing here?" he asked. "I don't understand."

"Frankenstein told me you were in trouble," Terry replied. "And I don't get many chances to put on the old uniform."

He smiled warmly at Jamie, but the teenager's mind was already elsewhere.

Frankenstein.

Jamie looked over at the monster and was about to ask him for a word in private when a voice shouted his name. It was Kate who called out, and when he turned toward her, panic spilled through him like ice. She was kneeling on the ground beside his mother, who was convulsing.

He ran to her, sliding to the ground next to Kate. He grabbed his mother's shoulders and tried to slow her thrashing. Her head was whipping from side to side, her long hair fanning out around her, her arms and legs drumming the grass.

"What happened?" yelled Jamie.

Kate looked at him, a frightened expression on her face.

"I don't know," she replied. "She just fell down. I was holding her arm, and she just fell down."

Frankenstein, Larissa, Terry, and the pilot were suddenly next to him, helping him hold his mother, demanding to know what had happened. Then Marie's head suddenly jerked up, and she looked round at them with crimson eyes.

Jamie's heart stopped, as Kate screamed and Larissa gasped in shock.

Oh, no. Oh, please no. Not this. Not after I've got her back. Please, not this.

"I'm sorry!" screamed Marie. "I'm so sorry, Jamie! I'm sorry!"

There was movement as the pilot fumbled the stake from his belt. Without thinking, Jamie pulled his Glock pistol from its holster and leveled it at the man's head. For a second, no one moved, until Jamie found his voice.

"Get some blood from the medical pack in the helicopter," he said. "Do it now."

The pilot backed away, his eyes locked on the barrel of Jamie's gun, and then turned and ran to the helicopter. He returned less than a minute later, holding a plastic pouch of O-negative blood.

Jamie snatched it out of his hands, tore it open, and pressed the opening to his mother's mouth, as if he was feeding a baby. Her head was twisting slowly from side to side, her eyes were closed, and she was moaning gently, but her mouth latched on to the plastic nozzle.

He turned away as his mother drank the blood.

He couldn't watch her do it, couldn't bear to see her reduced to this. When the pouch was empty, he cast it aside and looked down at her. She was staring up at him with the pale green eyes he recognized, a look of terrible, painful shame on her face. He reached toward her, but she scrambled away from him, pushing the restraining hands from her body, and jumped to her feet. He tried to go to her again, his arms outstretched, ready to hug her, ready to let her know that he didn't care what had happened to her, she was still his mother and he still loved her. But she turned her back on him.

"I don't want you to see me like this," she whispered. "I'm revolting."

"You're my mom," said Jamie.

He saw her shoulders heave as she began to cry, and he stood there helplessly, without the slightest idea of what to do. He looked around at Frankenstein, who was watching Marie with a solemn expression on his face. The monster caught his eyes, but he said nothing. Larissa stood with her hand over her mouth, her eyes wide and wet. In the end, it was Kate who moved.

The teenage girl stepped slowly over to Jamie's mother and placed an arm carefully around her waist. She crouched and leaned around so she could see her tear-stained face and spoke to her in a low voice.

"Mrs. Carpenter?" she said. "My name's Kate. I lived here on

Lindisfarne until Alexandru and the others came. I'd probably be dead if your son hadn't rescued me."

Jamie felt his heart swell with gratitude as he heard a small laugh of pride escape from his mother's mouth.

"He's a good boy," Marie said, softly. "And you're a kind girl."

"Do you want to go and wait in the helicopter?" asked Kate.

She nodded, and let herself be led slowly to the chopper. She kept herself turned away from Jamie and the other survivors as she moved, then stepped carefully into the black vehicle. Larissa watched them go, a flicker of jealousy pulling at her heart, and she chastised herself for it.

Jamie stared after his mother, his exhausted mind unable to comprehend what he had seen.

A vampire. She's been turned into a vampire. What does this mean? What's going to happen to her?

"We can look after her," said Frankenstein, as though he could read minds. "At the Loop. We can keep her safe, keep her fed."

"Like we did Larissa?" asked Jamie.

Frankenstein nodded, and the teenager looked at the ground.

"Why?" he asked. The word came out like a sob. "Why would Alexandru do this?"

"It's just one more way to hurt you," said Frankenstein. "Even though it would never have occurred to him that you might defeat him. I'm sure he intended to tell you before you died."

"But she never . . . she didn't do anything."

"It doesn't matter," replied Frankenstein. "To Alexandru that would have only made it sweeter. But he won't get to do it to anyone else. Because you killed him."

A savage smile flickered briefly across Jamie's face.

"I did, didn't I?" he said, quietly. "I killed him."

Then he started to cry, and Frankenstein put an arm around him and led him away from the rest of the survivors, who were looking at each other as though no one knew what they were supposed to do next.

Jamie and the monster stood near the edge of the cliff, the waves roaring and crashing far beneath them. Frankenstein held Jamie until his tears came to a heaving halt.

"I didn't shoot," said Frankenstein, softly. "That night, with your father . . . I didn't fire. You have to believe me."

"I do," said Jamie. "I should have believed in you all along, like my father and my grandfather did. Instead I doubted you, and it almost cost me and my mother our lives."

"I was there that night," said Frankenstein. "But I went there to try and bring him in alive. I didn't want what happened to happen."

"I believe you," said Jamie.

Then there was a snarl from a clump of bushes, and the second of Alexandru's werewolves launched itself at Jamie from the undergrowth.

Frankenstein didn't even hesitate.

He shoved Jamie to the ground and caught the snarling, snapping wolf out of the air, holding it at arm's length, keeping the razor-sharp teeth away from his throat. Jamie yelled for help and heard the thud of footsteps as the survivors grabbed their weapons and ran toward them.

But it was too late.

The two huge creatures staggered back and forth along the lip of the cliffs, the wolf on its curved hind legs, its yellow eyes gleaming in the pink light of the horizon, the monster straining to stay upright, forcing the wolf's head back and up. Then blood flew in the air as the wolf's teeth closed over Frankenstein's fingers, severing one completely and sending blood running down the monster's arm. He didn't make a sound; he just gritted his teeth, and bore down on the squirming creature in his grip, forcing it backward, toward the edge. They teetered there, seemingly defying gravity, then the wolf lunged and snapped its frothing jaws shut on the monster's neck. This time Frankenstein did make a sound, a deep rumbling bellow that shook the ground beneath Jamie's feet. The werewolf roared through its teeth, a sound of wicked triumph, then slowly, agonizingly slowly, the two creatures fell backward over the lip of the cliff, and disappeared from view.

"No!" screamed Jamie. He ran to the edge and looked down at the crashing white foam that sprayed into the air a hundred feet below him.

There was no sign of either the wolf or the monster.

Frankenstein was gone.

He craned his head forward, stretching his neck muscles, his arms reaching out behind him for balance, trying to get a better view, hoping to see his friend, to see some sign of the man who had saved his life—again.

The slick grass at the cliff's edge moved beneath his feet, and he felt his center of balance pitch forward. He looked out at the horizon, at the pink light blooming above it, and realized he was going to fall. The ground slid away beneath him, sods of earth and clumps of grass tumbling down the sheer rock wall, and he felt himself tumble forward. Then a hand grabbed the back of his collar, lifted him into the air, and pulled him back onto solid ground.

Jamie fell to his knees, and looked up into Larissa's pale, beautiful face. She knelt down in front of him and put her arms around him. He embraced her and laid his head on her shoulder, overcome with more grief than any one person should ever have to bear.

They stayed that way for a long time.

Sometime later, Jamie could not have guessed how long, a gentle rumble began to vibrate through the ground beneath him. He raised his head from Larissa's shoulder and looked out across the sea. A speck of black was approaching on the horizon; as he watched, it grew larger and larger, the rumbling increasing. Less than a minute later, Jamie got his first look at the dark shape that he had seen beneath the hangar on the day he arrived at the Department 19 Base.

The *Mina II* blasted above the surface of the North Sea, raising two columns of white water a hundred feet high in its wake. It decelerated as it approached the wall of cliffs, Cal Holmwood firing its vertical thrusters and pulling the control stick backward, guiding the supersonic jet up and over the lip. The thrust from the powerful engines swirled dust into the air and sent the survivors running for the cover of the helicopter, with the exception of Jamie and Larissa, who held each other at the edge of the cliff and watched the plane slow to a halt, then begin to descend.

The *Mina II* was a huge black triangle that seemed to hang

in the sky in front of them. Its rear edge was longer than its sides, making the wings curved as they reached their tips, and its underside was absolutely flat, painted a bright, featureless white. As the jet lowered itself toward the ground, Jamie saw the small bubble of the cockpit appear above the sharp nose, followed by the thick, angular fuselage. Then three sets of landing gear slid smoothly out of the plane's belly, and the *Mina II* was on the ground. A wide ramp descended, and then Admiral Seward was running down it, followed by a small group of black-clad operators.

"B Unit, secure the monastery," yelled the director.

Four of the operators split away from the group, their weapons drawn, and ran toward the ancient stone building. Seward scanned the group of survivors, until his eyes rested on Jamie, and he ran to him.

Over the shoulder of the oncoming admiral, Jamie saw one of the operators lift his helmet to reveal Paul Turner's glacial face. Then he saw something that qualified as one of the most unexpected sights of this strangest of days; he saw the major smile at him.

"Morris," said Seward, slowing to a halt in front of Jamie and Larissa, and looking at the teenager with an expression of immense regret on his face. "It was Morris who betrayed us. I knew it as soon as I discovered he had accessed the codes for the Russian vaults. It was Morris. Not your father. I'm so sorry."

Jamie looked at him, his expression unreadable.

"Where's Alexandru?" asked Seward. "Did he escape?"

The teenager shook his head. "I killed him."

Seward paused and looked carefully at Jamie, admiration

blooming on his face. "You killed him?"

Jamie nodded.

"Where's your mother?" asked Seward, looking around. "And Colonel Frankenstein? I don't see them."

Jamie looked at him, his face streaked with tears, and didn't answer.

THE END OF THE TUNNEL

"You're not putting my mother in a cell," said Jamie.

They were standing in the Ops Room—Jamie, Marie, Admiral Seward, Larissa, Kate, Paul Turner, and Terry.

Jamie's heart was being pulled in what felt like a hundred directions. The euphoria of destroying Alexandru and rescuing his mother was tempered by the loss of Frankenstein and the discovery of his mother's fate; Alexandru's last cruel, spiteful attack on the Carpenter family. Pride and guilt and terrible, empty loss fought for control of his exhausted mind and body, and then Admiral Seward had pulled his radio from his belt and asked the person on the other end to prepare a cell for an immediate occupant.

"You're not putting my mother in a cell," he repeated. "She hasn't done anything wrong."

Marie Carpenter looked at her son, and felt her chest swell with pride.

He can barely stand up, he's so tired. But he's still fighting for me.

They had sat next to each other on the flight back to base. Paul Turner, Admiral Seward, and the survivors of Lindisfarne had flown home on the *Mina II,* the supersonic jet covering the distance in less than twenty minutes. The rest of the operators, the men dispatched to clean up the blood-soaked monastery, would return home in the helicopters that were waiting on the headland and at the mainland end of the causeway.

Mother and son had said very little during the flight. As they had blasted off from the small island, the jet shuddering beneath their feet as it hauled itself into the air, Marie had stayed turned away from Jamie; her shame at what had been done to her, and what he had seen her do, still too great for her to bear. He hadn't pushed her, or hurried her; he just sat next to her, his head back against his seat, his eyes open, looking at his mother with a smile on his face. Larissa and Kate watched him from across the cabin, as did Admiral Seward and Terry, expressions of sadness on their faces. Paul Turner appeared to be asleep, his cold eyes closed, his head tipped back. Jamie barely noticed them; he just looked at the back of his mother's head, his face alight with love, and relief.

Eventually, she spoke. "Stop it, Jamie," she said. "I can feel you staring at me."

He didn't reply, nor did he stop looking at his mother.

She spun around and stared at him. "I told you to stop it, Jamie," she said, fiercely. Then she saw the look on her son's face, and the fight went out of her. Her face softened, and she reached over and put her arms around him.

Jamie returned her embrace, wrapping his arms around her and burying his face against her shoulder. "I thought I'd lost you, Mom," he whispered. "I thought I'd lost you."

She shushed him and held him close. Across the cabin, a smile crept across Kate's face, and she looked at Larissa. The vampire girl was crying, tears running down her pale face, but she made no attempt to wipe them away.

When the *Mina II* rolled to a halt at the end of the long runway, the exhausted group of men and women stumbled down the aircraft's ramp and onto the warm tarmac. Marie was walking steadily on her own, having refused all offers of assistance, Larissa was floating a few inches above the ground, and Jamie had fallen in beside Admiral Seward, who kept glancing at him with a look of mild astonishment on his face, as if he needed to keep checking that the teenager had really stood face-to-face with Alexandru Rusmanov and emerged victorious.

They were walking silently toward the hangar when suddenly the great double doors began to slide open, spilling light across the taxiway, illuminating the tired faces of the approaching figures. Then noise filled the air, as tens of Blacklight operators burst from the hangar and ran to them. Jamie cast a nervous look in Admiral Seward's direction, but the director merely smiled.

The tide of black-clad men and women stopped in front of Jamie and Seward, and for a moment, there was silence. Then a lone pair of hands began to clap, then another, and another, until the applause was deafening, punctuated with yells and cheers. Jamie took half a step backward and found Admiral Seward's hand on the small of his back. He looked up at the director, confusion on his face.

"That's not for me," said Seward, softly, then began to clap as well, stepping away from Jamie so the teenager stood alone, surrounded by cheering operators and the beaming faces of his family and his new friends. A smile crept across his face, and he walked slowly into the throng, which quickly swallowed him up in a tornado of hugs and handshakes and thumps on the back that nearly knocked the tired teenager off his feet.

"It's fine, Jamie," said Marie Carpenter. "It's the sensible thing to do. I'll be fine in the cell while we work out what to do."

Jamie looked at her. Her face was open and honest, her eyes wide, a slight flicker of fear at the corners of her mouth.

"Are you sure?" he asked her.

"Of course I'm sure," she replied. "Will you come and see me after you get some sleep?"

"Of course," he said. "I promise."

"I'll escort you down," said Terry, and stepped gently to Marie's side.

"Thank you," she said, then looked at her son. "Thank you," she said again, and he smiled as the instructor led his mother out of the Ops Room.

Tiredness crashed through Jamie.

He looked around the room; Larissa and Kate were chatting amiably, and Admiral Seward was deep in conversation with Major Turner. He walked over and interrupted them.

"I'm sorry, sir," he said, his voice cracking. "Do you think someone can find out if the boy in the infirmary is still in a coma? His name's Matt. I think I'm going to go and lie down, but I'd like to visit him in the morning."

Seward looked surprised at the request but said he would see to it personally. Jamie thanked him, turned, and walked unsteadily out of the room.

He bumped into the wall twice as he made his way to the elevator at the end of the corridor, the low hum of the base all around him. He pressed the button for the second underground level and closed his eyes. When the doors slid open less than fifteen seconds later, they jolted him from sleep that had dragged him down the second his eyelids met. Jamie shoved himself out of the elevator and pushed open the door to the dormitory. He stumbled through the long room and was about to use the last of his energy to hurl himself onto his bed, when a white object caught his eye.

It was an envelope, standing on the small table beside his bed. Two words were written on it in beautiful, elegant script:

Jamie Carpenter

He lifted it from the table, tiredness pulling relentlessly at him, and tore it open. A single sheet of paper fluttered out onto his green bed, covered in more of the same careful handwriting.

Read it tomorrow. Lie down. It's probably not important. Lie down.

Jamie shook his head, and the fog of tiredness lifted temporarily. He lifted the sheet of paper and began to read.

Dear Jamie,

If you are reading this, it means I didn't make it back from Lindisfarne. If that is the case, I don't want you to mourn me—I lived a life full of wonders, alongside some of the finest men and women ever to walk this small planet. I would not have changed a moment of it.

I am now certain that Thomas Morris is working against you—I have suspected it for some time, and I became sure when he brought up the night your father was lost. I believe he has been trying to separate us, as he knew that I would not allow any harm to come to you. And now he has achieved his aim. So I am going to follow you to Lindisfarne—I pray I will not be too late.

You deserve to know the truth, Jamie. I am sorry that I could not tell you the nature of things before now, but until the true betrayer of Blacklight revealed himself, it was too dangerous. I now believe that person has made themselves known, and the truth can come out.

Look after yourself, Jamie. Your ancestors would be proud of what you have done so far, but I believe you have the potential to do extraordinary things in the years to *come. My only regret is that I will not be there to see them.*

Your friend,
Victor Frankenstein

Tears spilled from Jamie's eyes and splashed onto the letter, causing the black ink to run, obscuring Frankenstein's words. His heart felt as though someone had squeezed it; it hung heavily and painfully in his chest, as hot as a furnace, as hard as coal.

You let him down. He tried to protect you, he only ever tried to protect you, and you let him down. He died saving you, died because you didn't believe him, because you turned your back on him and walked straight into Thomas Morris's trap.

Jamie rocked back and forth on the edge of his bed, holding his stomach, sobbing as though the world was ending. He would have given everything he had, everything he would ever have, to be able to bring Frankenstein back, even if it was only for long enough to tell him how sorry he truly was. The monster had honored his oath to the Carpenter family to the very last, and Jamie knew he was never going to be able to forgive himself for creating the situation that had put his friend in harm's way.

For the first time in a long time, Julian Carpenter's voice popped into Jamie's head.

He's gone, son. There's nothing you can do, except prove him right for believing in you. That's the best way you can remember him.

Something in his father's voice calmed Jamie, and a deep resolve settled into his stomach, a resolve to do as his dad suggested, to make the lost monster proud of him; he would never doubt him again.

A knock on the dormitory door roused him from his thoughts.

"Come in," he shouted, his voice unsteady.

The door swung open, and Admiral Seward stepped into the room. The director of Department 19 looked tired, but there was the ghost of a smile on his lined face as he walked down the long dormitory to Jamie's bunk. He was carrying something in his hand, but he was keeping it hidden behind his back as he walked, and Jamie could not make it out.

"How are you feeling?" asked Seward, as he stopped in front of the bunk.

Jamie handed him Frankenstein's letter and watched the director's eyes widen as he read the words the monster had written. He lowered the paper and looked at Jamie with incredible sadness on his face.

"It wasn't your—" he began, but Jamie interrupted him.

"Yes, it was, sir. We both know it was. But thanks for saying it."

Seward looked at him for a long moment, then brought the hand from behind his back. Jamie gasped; in the old man's hand were a small purple box, and the Bowie knife that had once belonged to Quincey Morris.

"May I sit down?" asked Seward.

Jamie nodded, his eyes never leaving the knife. The blade that had pierced Dracula's heart, that had been passed down through the Morris family, that had been used only hours ago to perform Thomas Morris's ultimate betrayal.

The director eased himself down onto the bunk beside

Jamie and passed him the knife. Jamie held it lightly in his hands, a feeling of revulsion spreading up his spine.

"It was handed to me by the men who brought Tom's body out of the monastery," said Seward, gently. "They wanted to know what to do with it. What do you think I should tell them?"

Jamie turned the knife over in his hands. The blade was stained brown with blood and dirt, and the leather of its sheath was worn and battered.

"It belongs with the dead," said Jamie. "It should go back there."

A flicker of a smile flashed across Seward's face, then he gently lifted the knife from Jamie's hands.

"Very well," he said. "I'll have it returned to the Fallen Gallery, where it belongs." The director placed the knife down and handed Jamie the purple box. "The contents of this box, however, I believe belong right here, with you. Open it."

Jamie lifted the purple lid, and for a moment, his heart stopped.

Inside the box was a circular medal, cast in gold, and engraved with the Department 19 crest. Beneath the crest, where the three Latin words of the Blacklight motto usually stood, were two simple words of English:

FOR GALLANTRY

In the lid lay a square plate of gold on which was inscribed the following:

THE MEDAL OF GALLANTRY, FIRST CLASS
PRESENTED TO
JULIAN CARPENTER
THIS DAY OF OUR LORD
FEBRUARY 19, 2005

"It was found in his quarters after he died," said Admiral Seward, his voice little more than a whisper. "When an operator dies, there is rarely anyone to pass such things on to. But I held on to it, in case you followed in his footsteps."

Jamie was still staring at the medal, his throat filled by a lump so large he couldn't breathe, his face hot, his hands shaking.

"He would have wanted you to have it," continued Seward. "But more than that, you deserve it for what you did tonight."

Jamie managed a deep, rattling breath, and felt his composure begin to return. He looked at the director and was shocked to see tears rolling down the old man's face.

"Your father would have been very proud of you, Jamie," said Seward. Then he was on his feet, and striding across the dormitory without a backward glance.

Jamie watched him go, watched the door swing shut after him, and lowered himself slowly onto his bunk. He stared at the ceiling above him, his father's medal gripped tightly in his hands, his mind full of the faces of the lost and the found, and slipped gently into darkness.

FIRST EPILOGUE

Doctor Alan McCall pushed open the door of the Department 19 infirmary, clutching a polystyrene cup of coffee in his hand, and stepped inside. He had been sound asleep in his quarters when the message from the director had beeped across the screen of his handheld console, rousing him.

NEED IMMEDIATE REPORT ON INJURED CIVILIAN MINOR.

McCall had groaned and sat slowly up on the edge of his bed. Matt Browning was still in the coma that he and his staff had induced, a coma from which they were not planning to attempt to wake him from for at least another forty-eight hours. A report would be completely redundant, but the request was from Admiral Seward, and the doctor would do as he was told.

The doctor crossed the infirmary quickly. The beds were all

empty; the operator who had been injured in the same recovery that had brought Matt to the Loop had been discharged. They had transfused every drop of blood in his body, flushing out the infected cells before the turn had been able to take hold of his system. It had been touch and go, but the man would make a full recovery; he had been sent to one of the dormitories on the lower levels to rest.

The only patient in the infirmary was the teenage boy. McCall could see the motionless outline of his body behind the frosted glass of the door marked THEATER. He eased open the door and froze, his heart leaping into his throat.

Matt Browning's eyes were open.

At the sound of the opening door, the teenager slowly turned his pale, waxy face toward the doctor and spoke three words: "Where am I?"

McCall rushed across the room and took Matt's face gently in his hands. He shone a light into the unprotesting teenager's eyes, then placed his fingers against the boy's neck. He felt the steady, rhythmic pulse beneath the skin, and paged the duty nurse to come to the infirmary at once.

"Where am I?" repeated Matt, his voice little more than a whisper.

"You're safe," replied McCall, his eyes scanning the screens on the bank of machines that were attached to his patient. "You're in a safe place."

The duty nurse hustled into the infirmary, calling Doctor McCall's name.

"In here," he shouted, and a moment later, the nurse, a young woman called Cathy who had only been working at the Loop for three months, appeared in the room.

"My God," she exclaimed, her hand going to her mouth.

"I want blood tests run immediately," said McCall. "I want you to take it down to the lab yourself and wait there for the results. Understood?"

The nurse was still staring at Matt's pale, confused face, but her training kicked in.

"Yes doctor," she replied, and set about her task, pulling a syringe from one of the drawers in the room's central console, and bending over Matt's arm.

The boy winced as the needle slid through his skin, but he didn't shift his gaze from Doctor McCall, who was making rapid notes on his console, his fingers flying across the keys.

"Doctor?" he said, softly, and McCall looked up.

"Yes, Matt?"

"I don't know why I'm here. I don't know what's happening." The teenager's face crumpled, and tears brimmed at the corners of his eyes. McCall shoved the console into his pocket and crouched down beside the teenager's bed.

"It's okay," he said, gently. "You were hurt, badly hurt, and we had to put you to sleep for a little while. But you're going to be fine."

"I want to go home. I want my mom."

"I know you do. One of my colleagues will need to talk to you first, but we'll get you home as soon as we possibly can."

The duty nurse withdrew the syringe from Matt's arm and almost ran out of the room, heading for one of the lifts that would take her down to the laboratory, deep into the bowels of the Loop.

McCall watched her go, then turned back to Matt.

"Do you remember what happened to you? Anything at

all?" he asked.

Matt shook his head. "I remember coming home from school. That's all. I don't even know what day that was." Pain and confusion flickered across his face, and McCall's heart went out to the teenager.

He must be terrified. He's doing a good job of not showing it, but he must be.

"I need to go and talk to someone," the doctor said. "I'll be back in five minutes. I promise. All right?"

Matt nodded.

"Okay. Five minutes." Doctor McCall pushed himself up to his feet and headed through the door and out into the infirmary.

Matt Browning watched him go, then let his head roll back onto his pillow, so he was staring up at the white ceiling. His hands were shaking.

He believes you. It's all right, he believes you.

Matt had been awake for almost an hour. His eyes had drifted open onto this unfamiliar place, and fear and disorientation had flooded through him. Then the memory of what had happened to him had burst into his mind, and he had cried out in the silent room. He could see the broken shape of the girl in the flowerbed, hear the deafening thunder of the helicopter as it lowered itself onto their quiet street, and feel the rising fear that had gripped him as the black-clad men with guns had shoved their way past him and his dad and into his home.

He had lied to the doctor; he remembered everything. But he knew, instinctively, that he couldn't tell the doctor that, couldn't tell him that he remembered the girl's red eyes and the white fangs that had stood out in the bloody ruin of her face. Matt trusted his own mind, and he was sure that pretending to remember nothing was the only way he was ever going to be allowed to leave this place.

But he knew what he had seen.

"Vampire," he whispered, and felt goose bumps break out across his skin.

SECOND
EPILOGUE

Eighteen hours later
The Black Sea Coast, Romania

The chapel stood on a barren headland on the eastern tip of the Rusmanov estate, overlooking the distant port of Constanța. A long, gently sloping path led down to it from the sprawling dacha that had housed more than a hundred generations of Valeri's family. Inside the small stone building, two narrow rows of wooden benches faced a plain stone altar. The entire sea-facing wall was a crude stained-glass window, a bloody representation of a crucifixion now weathered and beaten dull by centuries of salt spray.

Behind the altar, a stone staircase spiraled downward into earthy darkness. Flickering orange light drifted up into the chapel, illuminating a building designed for blasphemy; a house of death, decorated with bones and consecrated with blood.

In the chamber beneath the chapel, Valeri tied the final rope into place. He had forced himself to take his time with the preparations, to make sure that every detail was correct, even though his heart was pounding with anticipation at the culmination of a search that had taken more than a century.

The plastic container marked *31* had been placed carefully by the bottom step of the staircase. Its contents, a thick gray powder, had been poured into a round stone pit in the center of the room, Valeri taking care not to spill a single molecule as he emptied the container.

Above the pit, suspended upside down by thick rope from a series of heavy iron hooks, were five naked women.

Their hands and feet were bound, their mouths wrapped in strips of muslin which muffled their screams. The women had been hung with their backs to the cold, smooth walls of the chamber and their gazes met helplessly, tears flooding down their upturned foreheads, their hair hanging almost to the floor, their pale torsos thrashing and squirming in the still subterranean air.

Valeri walked quietly around the chamber, lighting a series of candles that had been darkened almost black with something unspeakable. He appeared not to even notice the women swinging around his head until the final candle was lit and issued a stream of thick, repugnant smoke. Then he drew a curved filleting knife from his belt and slit the throat of the nearest woman from ear to ear.

Around the chamber the thrashing and muffled screaming intensified. The woman's eyes snapped open wide, her pale green irises disappearing almost completely beneath the rapidly spreading black of her pupils. Blood sprayed from her neck in a pressurized jet, splattering her face and hair, and pouring in a crimson torrent into the pit below her.

Valeri dropped to a crouch and stared down into the pit. The blood splashed onto the gray powder like winter rain, and for a second, there was movement, a hint of solidity where the blood was pooling fastest. He stood up sharply and stepped toward the second woman, who arched her back away from him in a futile attempt to avoid her fate.

The old vampire slid his knife smoothly across the white flesh of the girl's neck, then stepped neatly behind her, moving toward the third of his victims, avoiding the arterial blood that gushed down into the pit.

In less than a minute, it was over.

The struggles of the five girls were slowing, their lower legs rapidly turning a pale, mottled blue, as the blood ran from their bodies. Five rivers of blood splashed into the stone pit, soaking the gray powder and mixing with it to form a thick, dark red sludge.

Valeri stepped to the end of the pit and knelt on the cold flagstones of the chamber floor. Below him, the foul liquid began to shift, slow currents starting to move in loose concentric circles. In the center, the blood began to rise in a steep bubble, as if it were being pulled upward by one of the steel hooks set into the walls of the chamber. Valeri looked at the quivering, rising mass of blood, and lowered his forehead to the stone floor of the chamber. The air, already thick with the mingled scents of the sulfuric candles and the coppery, metallic blood, was filled with a terrible sucking noise, like the sound of liquid thickening into clay.

The oldest vampire in the world closed his eyes and smiled. Above him, something wet took the gurgling, rattling breath of a newborn, and Valeri Rusmanov uttered a single word:

"Master."

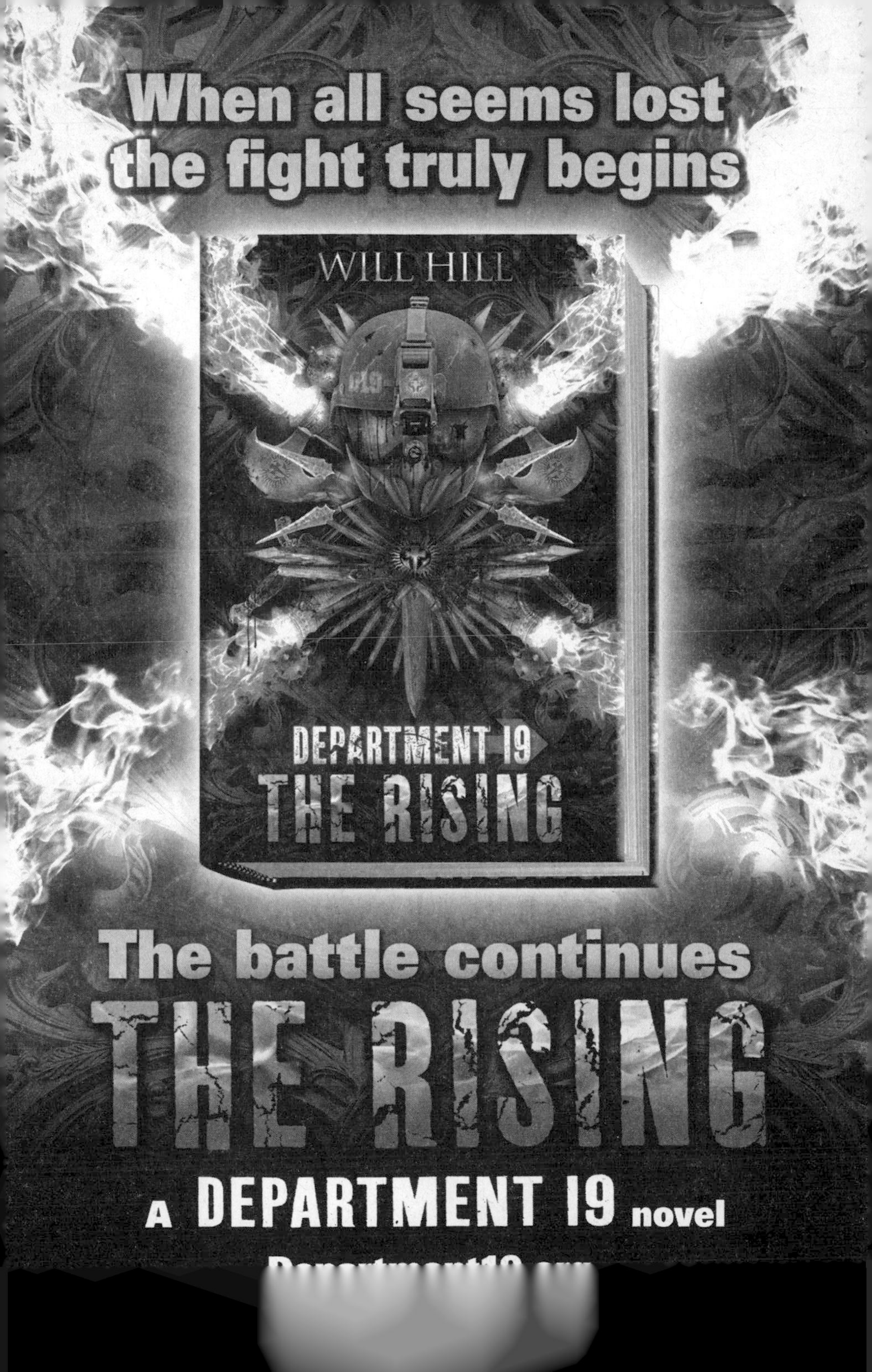
When all seems lost
the fight truly begins
WILL HILL
DEPARTMENT 19
THE RISING
The battle continues
THE RISING
A DEPARTMENT 19 novel